Lily of
Love Lane

By the same author

Lizzie of Langley Street
Rose of Ruby Street
Connie of Kettle Street
Bella of Bow Street

About the author

Carol Rivers, whose family comes from the
Isle of Dogs, East London, now lives in Dorset.
Lily of Love Lane is her fifth novel.

Visit www.carolrivers.com

Carol Rivers

Lily of Love Lane

POCKET
BOOKS

LONDON • NEW YORK • TORONTO • SYDNEY

First published in Great Britain by Simon & Schuster, 2008
The edition first published by Pocket Books, 2008
An imprint of Simon & Schuster UK
A CBS COMPANY

5 7 9 10 8 6 4

Simon & Schuster UK Ltd
1st Floor
222 Gray's Inn Road
London WC1X 8HB

www.simonandschuster.co.uk

Simon & Schuster Australia
Sydney

A CIP catalogue record for this book is available from the British Library

ISBN: 978-1-84739-360-9

Typeset by Rowland Phototypesetting Ltd, Bury St Edmunds, Suffolk
Printed and bound in Great Britain by
CPI Cox and Wyman, Reading, Berkshire RG1 8EX

Readers, this is my chance to dedicate a book
to *you*.

And thanks to libraries everywhere, especially
to Vickie Goldie and the girls of Southbourne
and Kinson branches Dorset and to Eve Hostettler,
co-ordinator of the Island History Trust,
East London.

Special thanks go to Dorothy, a wonderful agent –
the best! Also to the fabulous Kate and Libby and
Joe and all the sales, production and design teams
at Simon & Schuster who have worked so hard
on this series of East End sagas.

Please visit my website for more information
on the books.

www.carolrivers.com

Chapter One

January 1930
Isle of Dogs, East London

Lily Bright watched in concern as her mother pushed back a strand of thin, greying hair from her careworn face. For the last ten minutes she had been searching all the cups on the dresser and was now turning out her purse.

'What's the matter, Mum? Lost something?'

'I thought I'd put a bit more by for the rent but I must have spent it.'

Lily lifted the flap of her bag and searched inside. She gave her mother the two shillings she found. 'Reube pays me tomorrow so I'll be able to give you me wages then.'

'Money seems like water these days,' sighed Josie Bright as she counted the change on the kitchen table. 'It just runs away. But with what you've given me I've got ten bob to give to the landlord.'

'What about the arrears?'

'I'll ask him to call again on Monday.'

Lily silently said goodbye to the pair of boots she desperately needed. She knew the debts were piling up.

Josie sighed once more. 'Your father's gone down the docks again this morning, but I don't hold out much hope. Not when there's so many out of work and he's only a casual.'

'I can work Saturday afternoons, p'raps.' Lily met her mother's anxious blue gaze with an encouraging smile. Lily's own eyes were the same shade of blue but had the shimmering clarity of youth. The cloud of short, wavy fair hair around her face that stubbornly refused to be shaped into a modern cut, made her look much younger than she was. Despite her youthful appearance, at twenty, Lily had had more than her fair share of worry. It was nothing new for her to shoulder her family's financial burdens, as for the past six years, since she'd left school, her dad had been in and out of employment. Bob Bright, a docker by trade, had accepted any kind of work he could get hold of since the general strike of 1926. Now, there were so many men wanting jobs in the dockyards that poverty and unemployment on the Isle of Dogs, East London, was a fact of life.

Sometimes, like this morning, Lily wished her job on a market stall paid better, but she loved working in the open air. The stallholders were a happy bunch and made a joke of hard times. Unlike in the factories, where the pay was better, but everyone was cooped up, doing monotonous work, which could make life miserable.

She loved the market so much she was willing to work long days to make up her wages. And she knew her boss, Reube James who lived opposite, would be happy to give her more hours.

'You're up at the crack of dawn as it is, Lily, love,' her mother replied with a deep frown. 'Saturday afternoons is your only time off with Hattie.'

'We can always go out on Sundays,' Lily shrugged. She didn't want her mother to get any more upset. It was bad enough that her dad couldn't find work. At least one of the family was in employment and Lily was grateful for this. And anyway, Hattie would understand. They had been through bad times before, and always gave one another support. Hattie had been Lily's best friend since school. Wandering around the markets and strolling the streets of the island on a Saturday afternoon was the highlight of the girls' week. But in times of crisis, their outings had to be put on the back burner.

'Your dad said he might be lucky.' Josie Bright's quiet voice held a note of hope. 'There's a skin boat in.'

'Oh, I hope he don't get one of those.' Lily knew all too well that working in the holds of skin ships, the men could catch Anthrax. It was a dangerous task, removing the infected carcasses. Someone had to do it and it was usually the most desperate of the men, like her father, who did. They needed to feed their families. Any job would do, if it achieved a wage. But Lily always hoped that someone else would be given the skin boats. She didn't want her dad put at risk.

'I told him to tie a scarf round his mouth and wash his hands after touching them dead things. And when he comes home, he can have a good scrub in the Naptha.'

Before Lily could reply that the strong smelling disinfectant was no real answer to the deadly disease, a loud banging started up outside. Josie Bright jumped up. 'That'll be your uncle, locked in the closet again. I warned him not to use the latch, it sticks. But does the silly old duffer ever listen? No, I'm just wasting me breath.'

Lily went to the kitchen window and looked out. It was so cold a film of white frost covered the roofs and backyards. Her uncle's bootprints led to the closet halfway down the path. There was no inside toilet in the house; everyone had to go outside, come rain or shine.

'I'm going to scream if your uncle plays me up again today. If I hear just one more daft syllable drop from his lips.'

Lily smiled at this. Her uncle tended to be absent-minded. It was funny if you took it as a joke but it could also be very wearing. At sixty-five, her mother's brother was a confirmed bachelor and ten years older than her mum. Josie had complained to Lily that she rued the day when she'd let him come to live with them after closing up his rag and bone yard. But Lily knew they were really very fond of one another.

'I'll go out and get him,' Lily already had her coat on

as she had dressed to leave the house at half past six. The market started very early but it was now ten past seven, and Reube would be wondering where she was.

Lily hurried into the yard, leaving the warmth behind her. The big kitchen adjacent to the scullery was her favourite room in the dilapidated three-storey house she had grown up in. All the houses of Love Lane were terraced, each one built along the same lines. Most kitchens contained freshly washed clothes aired above people's heads on a wooden pulley. Every corner beneath was usually crammed with cooking utensils. Her mum's pride and joy was a large scrubbed wooden table where she did a lot of mixing and preparing of food next to the black leaded range. Four wooden chairs were stowed under it, so that the cosy space was used more frequently than the parlour for social gatherings.

'Uncle Noah, you shouldn't have dropped the latch.' Lily put her ear against the wooden door.

'I didn't,' came the indignant reply. 'It fell down of its own accord.'

'Stand back then, and I'll push hard. Are you decent?'

'I got me pants up if that's what you mean.'

Lily put her small shoulder to the door. She was only slight at five foot five but was quite strong, even though she didn't look it.

The door groaned loudly and finally gave way. Her uncle stood in his combinations and big black boots. The laces, as usual, were undone. He clutched the newspaper pieces that Lily had cut into squares and dangled them in front of her. 'A lot of use this is!' he exclaimed. 'Must have froze overnight. Good job I didn't need to evacuate me bowels.' Replacing the newspaper on the nail, he crossed his matchstick arms across his skinny chest. 'What you doing out here, gel?'

'I've come to get you.' Lily's teeth began to chatter. She admired her mum a lot, as she had to look after Uncle Noah all day and every day. And he wasn't getting any easier.

'Why's that?'

'Because you're likely to freeze.'

'It's not that cold.'

'Then why are your lips turning blue?' Lily shivered, her feet already growing numb in her leather lace-up boots. For such a small man, with a birdlike chest, bow legs and arms the size of pipe cleaners, Lily knew her uncle was more resilient than he looked. By rights, every bone in his body should be frozen by now, but experience had taught her that just like her mother the same seamless energies ran through the Kelly bloodline.

He stared at her from behind a pair of ancient pince-nez spectacles. 'Is me breakfast ready?'

'No, Mum ain't too good this morning.' Lily knew that if she asked him to hurry, as likely or not he would do the opposite.

'What's up?'

'Dad might have to work on a skin ship.'

'Poor bugger.'

'Why don't you cook breakfast for her this morning,

6

Uncle?' Lily suggested gently. 'It might cheer her up.'

'She won't let me do that.'

'Let's go inside and see.'

'All right, I'm a-coming.' To Lily's relief he sped past her like a two-year-old. 'Lovely fresh morning, ain't it? Let's get the troops sorted.'

Lily smiled as she watched him advance on the back door. A wave of nostalgia filled her as she heard his booming voice call out to her mother. As a child she had travelled beside him on the rag and bone cart. His cry of 'Any old iron?' had caused doors and windows to be flung open. By the time she was five, he had taught her how to use the reins, commanding Samson the horse to 'walk on!' or 'stand!' She still recalled the wonderful feeling of the old animal's response and the strength of his big grey body. But the sentimental moment was soon over as Lily entered the kitchen.

'I warned you not to use the latch, Noah,' her mother was shouting, 'when will you remember it sticks?'

'I never touched it.'

'And look at you, standing there in your underwear. You'll catch your death.'

'Uncle Noah's going to cook breakfast,' Lily interrupted quickly before the quarrel developed.

Josie Bright looked horrified. 'Why should he want to do that?'

'To help, that's all.'

'There'd be a fire before you knew it!'

Her uncle pursed his lips and raked his arthritic fingers

through the thin grey strands sticking up from his bald pate. The cast in his left eye gave him the appearance of one large eye, magnified by the pair of gold-framed pince-nez balanced on his bony nose. 'Told you she wouldn't,' he muttered to Lily.

'A nice piece of fried bread will do you both good,' Lily said, taking her mother's arm and nodding at her uncle. 'He's only got to put the bread in the pan and fry it.'

'I don't know about that—'

Lily gave her mother another little push. 'Now, I've lit the fire in the parlour and it needs a bit of encouragement.'

'Yes, leave it all to me!' her uncle called after them, lifting the big saucepan down from its hook. 'Canteen's open in ten minutes.'

'He thinks he's still in the army,' sighed her mother as they went into the front room. 'He'll be having me out on parade soon.'

'He's only trying to help.'

'He might burn the bread.'

'I doubt it.'

'Men are useless in the kitchen.'

'Only because they aren't given the chance to do something.'

Her mother sighed tiredly. Her once fair hair was scraped back in a bun, revealing fresh worry lines around her eyes. 'You young women just don't understand never having been married.'

'Well, I hope to have the chance one day.' Lily didn't add that looking after her family, and her work at the market, wouldn't leave much time for a husband.

'It would be lovely to have some grandchildren,' Josie nodded thoughtfully. 'A grandson especially. Your dad would have liked a boy.' She sat by the fire and sighed again. 'But the Good Lord never sent us any more children.'

Lily knew her mum didn't mean she was dissatisfied with her one daughter, but as a little girl she had had heard this phrase so often she'd tried to be a boy to please her parents. She was always climbing lampposts and playing football in the street. In spite of this, her tiny frame and long plaits had always made her appear delicate. Eventually Lily had given up struggling to prove she could do anything a boy could and begun to enjoy being a girl.

'I'll put your coat round you till the fire gets going.' Lily made her mother comfortable in the big armchair. 'You can give the fire a touch with the poker when I'm gone.'

'I wish you was staying home, love.'

'You've got Uncle.'

Her mother smiled ruefully. 'Indeed I have.' Josie's eyes had a twinkle in them as she murmured, 'Your uncle is a bit of a mischief, ain't he?'

'Yes, and we wouldn't be without him, would we?'

Josie took hold of Lily's wrist. 'You're the only one who can do anything with him, Lily. You could twist him round your finger as a little girl and still can. Remember when—'

'Mum, I wish I could stop to talk, but I have to go to work now,' Lily interrupted. Reube would think she wasn't going to turn up for work at all.

'I know. I know.' Josie reluctantly released her daughter's arm. 'Someone in this house has to earn a few pennies and I'm sorry to say it's always you, love. You're a good girl, our Lily. A real good girl.'

'I'll see you tonight, Mum.'

'If I survive.' But this was said with a smile.

Lily knew the minute she left the house, her mother and uncle would soon be finding ingenious ways to argue. It was an irony, but the two people she loved most in the world other than her dad, lived to annoy one another. Her dad had always told her it was what kept them going.

Lily pulled her hat and scarf from her pocket. Carefully sliding the blue cloche over her hair, she glanced in the mirror. The cloche was old and she had steamed it back into shape more times than she could remember, but the colour matched her eyes.

'Bye, ducks.'

'Bye, Mum.'

'Who are you dolling up for, our Lil?' Uncle Noah caught Lily at the front door. 'Not some young terrier you've got hidden away?'

'No, Uncle Noah. Just work.'

'A prince wouldn't be good enough for our girl. Not unless he had a nice 'orse and cart.'

Lily grinned as she stepped outside. 'Not many princes own rag and bone carts.'

'Then theirs is the loss, I say. Now take care of yerself.'

'Don't forget to fry Mum some bread.'

'I'll give her an egg as well.'

'We ain't got none, at least till I'm paid.'

'I told you we should keep chickens. Had 'em at barracks. Could do the same here.'

Torn between laughter and tears, Lily kissed him goodbye. Her dad had kept chickens in the yard until last year when her uncle had forgotten to lock them away one night. In the morning they were gone and no one ever found out who took them, or more to the point, who ate them.

'I'm going now. Goodbye, Uncle.'

Lily didn't breathe a sigh of relief until she turned into Manchester Road.

Lily arrived at market out of breath. She had run most of the way and being Friday, it was very busy already. All the stalls were surrounded by shoppers. Cox Street Market was the last port of call before Poplar, the tiny hamlet next to the Isle of Dogs. People were out and about after being confined to home over Christmas. The kids still hadn't returned to school and were playing

11

amongst the stalls or gathered under the railway arches nearby. Since the end of the war in 1918, the market community at Cox Street had thrived.

But it wasn't Reube James who Lily saw behind the stall this morning, it was Ben, his brother. His tall, slim figure, quite the opposite to Reube's short and stocky build, was busy putting out the items for sale. A large iron bedstead stood as a backdrop, in front of which were two brass candlesticks, half a dozen rolls of brightly coloured cloth, a battered brass coal scuttle and fender and a dozen other objects piled beside it. The smaller items were placed on top of the stall: saucepans, tarnished silver cutlery, bone-handled carving knives, old leather boots, a multitude of umbrellas, walking sticks and chinaware.

As Lily approached a young girl passed by, smiling at Ben. He was very quick to smile back, calling out, 'Can I interest you in anything this morning, Miss? Got a lovely bargain here – a quarter of the price to you.' He held out a large feather duster, and the girl went away laughing.

'A married man like you with six starving kids to feed should be ashamed of yourself,' Lily teased as she walked up. He wasn't married or even attached, but Lily enjoyed the fun. They had known each other so many years, he was like her older brother.

Ben removed a carnation from his buttonhole and slid it under the ribbon of her hat. 'I was just getting into me patter an' all.' He was over six foot tall and lean as a beanpole. When he smiled, he showed lovely white teeth and employed his quick, cockney wit to charm the females. At twenty-six, two years younger than Reube, he drove a big, dirty lorry, delivering to all corners of the country.

'Get your beauty sleep, did you?' he asked with a chuckle.

'Sorry I'm late. Uncle Noah got stuck in the closet again. Dad hasn't had time to fix it.' This was half a truth as her father wasn't very quick at repairs.

'I'll pop across with me tools. Won't take long and it gives me a chance to see you.' He winked flirtatiously, his grey eyes sparkling with humour as he took out a comb and ran it threw his thick brown hair. As the James' lived across the road, Ben often helped her dad out with repairs.

She touched the flower in her hat. 'Don't try your patter on me, it's wasted.'

'Why's that?'

'Your head is big enough. I can see it growing by the minute.'

'Me?' he spluttered. 'I'm the modest type, I am.' He elbowed Lily gently. 'In fact I'm fading away from being ignored.'

'You? Ignored? Don't make me laugh.'

'You're lovely when you laugh.'

Lily rolled her eyes. 'Why isn't your brother here?' Ben sometimes stood in for his brother if he wasn't busy with his lorry.

'He's gone to buy stock. Hattie got the day off and went with him.'

Lily removed her hat and tucked it under the stall, shaking her hair loose. 'She didn't tell me she had a day off.'

Ben tapped the side of his nose. 'She's got a tooth-ache. The sort that needs urgent attention.'

'Oh!' Lily smiled as the penny dropped. 'That sort of toothache.'

Lily knew it was unlikely that Madame Nerys, Hattie's boss, would be so generous as to give her a day off right after Christmas. Hattie worked in a prestigious dressmakers at Aldgate and had a responsible job, cutting the patterns. Hattie was very good at this and Madame Nerys paid her well, but she made sure that Hattie worked hard for the money.

'Anyway,' said Ben, giving another wink to Lily, 'Reube and Hat seem to be rubbing along all right, don't they?'

Lily nodded as she reflected over the Christmas holiday. Apart from Christmas morning when the Parks and the Brights had walked to church together, she hadn't seen much of Hattie. Reube and Hattie had spent a lot of time going to the cinema to watch the new talkies. Living in the same road, she and Hattie and Ben and Reube had known each other all their lives. The James boys were older by six and eight years, but not a lot wiser, her mum always joked. Reube and Hattie shared a mutual interest in the cinema whilst Lily occasionally accompanied Ben to a dance, but he was too much of a flirt to take seriously. Now Lily wondered whether the reason Hattie was saving up so hard was to get married.

'Here, take a gander at this,' Ben lifted a large white chamber pot from under the stall.

Lily giggled. 'Watch what you're doing with that. You don't know where it's been.'

'Matter of fact I do. I've just bought it from an old girl up Manilla Street. It was her dear departed hubbie's. She said she wanted to get rid of it quick.'

'Why's that?'

'It's haunted. In the middle of the night she still hears him using it.'

'You're joking!'

'Cross me heart, that's no word of a lie. Said her hubbie had a bladder like an elephant.'

The two friends burst into laughter again. 'Anyway, I ain't heard a tinkle in the last ten minutes.' Ben placed the pot at the front of the stall.

'Where's the handle gone?'

'It's broken off.'

'What use is a chamber pot without a handle?' Lily queried. 'How much did you give her?'

'Two bob.'

'Daylight robbery.'

'She was down on her uppers. I hadn't the heart to say no.'

Lily frowned as she studied the broken article. 'Let's

put this in it.' She took a neglected looking aspidistra from a metal vase and lowered it into the chamber pot, arranging the broad green leaves over the edges, she stood back. 'What do you think?'

'I think if what that old girl says is true, that aspidistra is going to grow into a tree.'

Laughing, Lily placed it in the middle of the stall. The next few hours passed very quickly as the customers seemed determined to start the New Year buying bargains.

Halfway through the afternoon a man came up and stared at the chamber pot for some while.

'Can I help you?' Lily asked eventually, noticing how good looking he was. He had very dark hair and wore a good quality overcoat. He smiled at her. 'I need something for my house, a touch of greenery to cheer it up after Christmas. The plant would do nicely, but that's not a vase is it?'

Lily blushed. She wasn't sure why, normally she would make a joke but for some reason she felt tongue-tied. 'No, it's a chamber pot but the plant goes very well inside it.'

'How much is it?'

'Three and six.' Lily calculated quickly. They would make one and six profit on the original two bob.

'That's reasonable.' He smiled again and Lily felt his dark eyes rove over her.

'You won't be sorry, if you buy that,' said Ben coming up behind her and placing his hands on her shoulders. 'Nice piece of pottery that. Unique I'd call it.'

Lily blushed again. She felt quite strange as she stood between the two men and they looked one another up and down.

'I'll take it, though I would like it to be delivered. I'll pay for the trouble, of course.'

Ben was quick to agree.

'Sunday will be a good time. My name is Charles Grey and I live in Poplar.' He gave his address to Lily who jotted it down on a pad of paper.

Ben nodded. 'There's no market on Sundays, so I'll drop it round.'

The man glanced at Lily, 'Will you be coming too?'

This time Lily's pale cheeks went very red. 'I don't think so.'

'A pity, as a woman's touch would be quite helpful.'

'Haven't you got a—' Lily stopped, feeling as though she was being too forward in asking if he had a wife.

'That'll be three and six, thank you,' said Ben loudly.

Their customer handed over the money. Gazing into Lily's eyes once more, he wished them good day.

Lily watched him go, wondering who he was and what he did for a living. He was tall and upright, not as tall as Ben, but distinguished looking and much older. He had something about him that was very mysterious. She would have liked to talk more and usually she would have, but Ben had been looming over her and she hadn't felt quite at ease.

'That was a good deal,' she said to Ben, who was dropping the change in the cash box under the stall.

'Not bad at all. Specially as it was broken.'

'What time are you going on Sunday?'

'I don't know. Before dinner I expect. Why?'

'Oh, I thought I might come with you after all.'

Ben frowned. 'What would you do that for?'

'Because I'm curious.'

He shook his head slowly. 'I'll never understand women.'

Lily laughed. 'What makes you say that?'

'It's obvious he's a bit of a charmer,' Ben dismissed, 'trying it on with that smile of his and long looks.'

Lily giggled even more, 'Well, you should know, Ben James, as it takes one to know one.'

He didn't deny it, which left Lily even more curious to know more about the mysterious stranger.

Chapter Two

The light was fading when Lily and Ben began to pack away. It promised to be a typical foggy London night. Beyond the lights of the market, every alley and by-way was threaded with mist. Lily knew that it would be treacherous around the murky waters of the docks. In these conditions, the edge of the wharves were invisible; only the river lapping at their mossy walls hinted at the lethal drop. The air was thick with salt and the sickly sweet odour of a ship's hemp cargo as Lily counted the day's takings. Business had been good. After they had sold to Charles Grey, a dealer from the West End had bought the marble clock. Although labelled at six shillings, they had settled on five. The dealer knew it was a bargain, as the clock would treble in value when sold in the City. But as long as the stall turned over a profit, Reube would be happy.

Ben threw on his heavy coat as he packed away the stock. 'Don't reckon Reube and Hattie will be coming back.'

'I wonder where they went?'

He smiled. 'Somewhere nice and quiet.'

'I wouldn't mind going home now.' Most of the shops along Cox Street were shut, the lights of their windows extinguished. The only life came from the fish and chip shop and Mr Mole's pie and pease pudding shop, both of which were counting on cold weather to increase the appetite. In all conditions, people ventured out to buy their mouth-watering fish and chips or boiled beef and faggots. The steam on their windows was already announcing the start of trade.

'All right,' agreed Ben, rubbing his hands together for warmth, 'let's finish packing this lot up.'

Lily helped him dismantle the stall and stow the un-sold stock in the lock-up behind the bolted and barred confectionery shop. When all was done, they left for home.

'Don't you two lovers stay out late,' yelled Ted Shiner from the fruit and veg stall.

'Chance would be a fine thing,' returned Ben, linking his arm through Lily's. 'If I was only taken seriously, Ted, but the girls just play with my affections.'

There were more insinuations from Ted as he chucked the damaged apples, pears and oranges to the street urchins.

Next to Shiner's pitch stood the jewellery and curio stall. 'Oiy my friends, how is it that you are knocking off so early?' joked Elfie Goldblum, wrinkling his weathered face.

'I'm late for me champagne and caviar!' returned Ben.

'The taxi arrives at seven to take me and me girl here up to the Savoy.'

'I wish it was,' Lily sighed as she pulled up her collar, hugging herself to keep warm. 'Just imagine a taxi arriving outside our house, and me wearing this lovely dress, all long and flowing, and there I am ready to dance the night away . . .'

'With me beside you in me top hat and tails—'

'Now you've spoilt it,' Lily laughed.

'See what I mean? You never take me seriously.'

'I've just remembered,' Lily said suddenly, 'there's something I have to ask Reube. But I s'pose it can wait.'

'What's that?'

'I was wondering if he'd let me work Saturday afternoons for a while.'

'You're an eager beaver.'

'Dad's out of work again. He went to try a skin ship this morning, but I hope he doesn't get it.'

'Do you want me to ask for you?'

'Would you?'

'And I'll come over and mend that latch on Sunday.'

Lily smiled. 'Don't forget you've got a delivery on Sunday.'

'Yes, to lover boy.'

Lily laughed again. 'You sound as if you're jealous.'

'Why would I be jealous of him?'

'Can I come with you? It would be a nice ride out.'

'I don't want you heading for a broken heart.'

'Why do you say that?'

Ben frowned as he took her arm and they hurried through the foggy street. 'Because it's types like him that break hearts. Anyway, I'll be there to see he minds his manners.'

'I don't need looking after.'

He looked down at her and grinned. 'That's true. You're only little but you pack a punch, as I found out when you gave me a dirty great black eye once.'

'When was that?'

'A long time ago.'

'You mean when I was a kid?'

He grinned. 'You was always bashing that football around. One day I was walking along the street and you nearly knocked me head off.'

'I don't play football any more, in case you hadn't noticed,' Lily giggled.

'I'm pleased to hear it.'

Beginning to hum a tune Ben slid his hand around her waist and waltzed her over the cobbles. Following in the wake of a horse and cart, he twirled her onto the pavement, narrowly missing a bicycle. He was humming ''S Wonderful' and Lily joined in, knowing the words off by heart as he'd sung them to her so many times.

'You're not a bad dancer, I'll give you that,' she teased, as he straightened his jacket and they fell into step again.

'Thanks for the compliment. S'pose it's the only one I'll get tonight.'

When they turned into Love Lane, the rows of terraced houses were covered in a yellow-grey mist. From out of the James' house, came her friend, Hattie Parks.

Lily noted how smartly she was dressed in a tailored grey coat and scarf. Her dark brown Eton Crop was the height of fashion.

'Did the dentist pull out a tooth?' Ben asked.

'No, it's not me in the wars, it's your brother.'

'What's he done now?'

'He thought he'd broken his ankle, but it's only sprained.'

'How did he do that?'

'You'd better go and ask him.'

He rushed off and as Hattie watched him go, she began to laugh. 'Oh, Lil, you should have seen Reube today. It was so funny.'

'What, spraining his ankle?'

'It was the way he did it. We went to this big, posh house where this woman showed us round. She's going abroad and needs to sell her stuff. Reube would have liked to have had a butchers at what was downstairs, but she asked him go up in the roof first where the good bits were.'

'Funny they was in the roof and not on show,' Lily commented.

Hattie nodded. 'They was packed away, she said. Anyway, Reube was up above and we could hear him moving around when all of a sudden a foot comes through the ceiling. Finally, he lands at me feet with the biggest thump you ever heard. Half the blooming ceiling came down with him!'

'Was he hurt?'

'Only his ankle but with all the moaning he was doing you'd think he'd broken it.'

'What did the woman say?'

'She was really annoyed. Called him a clumsy oaf. He was in pain but she didn't care. She was yelling at him saying he'd have to pay for the damage and he was yelling at her, saying she'd have to cough up for the operation on his broken foot.' Hattie trapped her bottom lip with her little white teeth in an effort not to laugh. 'He had to slide down the stairs on his bum and she never stopped with the insults. For a rich woman she had a mouth like a sewer.'

'That doesn't sound very ladylike.'

Hattie's brown eyes twinkled. 'We managed to get on a bus and Reube was huffing and puffing. He claimed to all the passengers he'd probably broken his leg. The conductor said he'd have to charge him for two as he had his foot up on another seat! It was like one of them Laurel and Hardy films. But I daren't say so as he ain't seen the funny side of it yet.'

'And there was us thinking you were having a romantic interlude.'

Hattie looked scornful. 'My Reube romantic? You must be joking. It's all figures of the wrong sort with Reube. Drives me barmy with his mental arithmetic, how he's going to make a fortune on that stall of his. Talking of which, did you sell much?'

'Yes, quite a few things. Amongst them a valuable clock and an aspidistra standing in a broken chamber pot.' Lily began to tell Hattie the story of Charles Grey, how he had smiled at her charmingly and given her a long, mysterious look.

'What's he like?' Hattie asked curiously.

'Tall and dark, with nice clothes.'

'Will you be seeing him again?'

'Only if I go with Ben to deliver the pot on Sunday.' Lily hesitated. She didn't want to sound too eager. 'He said he would value a woman's opinion on where to put the plant.'

'Hasn't he got a wife then?'

'Didn't like to ask.'

'How old is he?'

'Quite a bit older – about thirty?'

'You want to watch it. The old blokes think they are the cat's whiskers sometimes.'

Lily didn't say how she had felt when he looked at her. 'It would be nice to ride out in the lorry.'

Hattie shrugged. 'Well, I can't stand out here all night. Me feet are freezing. And Mum will wonder what's happened to me. Do you want to come in for a cuppa?'

As Hattie lived right next door, they were always in each other's houses. Lily hesitated. 'I'd like to but I'd better go in to my own disaster.'

'Pistols at dawn, is it?' Hattie giggled, knowing that Lily often went home to a drama.

'No blood has been drawn, thank goodness.'

'See you tomorrow, then.'

Lily caught her arm. 'Talking of tomorrow, it might be our last Saturday for a while.'

'Why's that?'

'I might have to work Saturday afternoons. Dad's out of work again.'

'When will we meet then?' Hattie's father had a regular job as a clerk. She only gave half of her wage to her mum, whereas Lily gave nearly all of hers.

'We've still got Sunday.'

'I have to help Mum with the dinner then. And if they go out for a walk I have to sit with Sylvester.' Sylvester was Hattie's older brother. He'd been gassed in France during the war and suffered violent fits. Although he was older than Hattie by eleven years, Mrs Parks didn't like to leave him on his own for very long.

'Well, I can sit with you, can't I?'

'It's not like going out though, is it?' Hattie looked despondent.

'Cheer up, it's not the end of the world.'

Hattie began to walk away, then turned quickly and called out loudly, 'Sweet dreams of Charles Grey!'

The two girls parted laughing. Lily was relieved that Hattie wasn't upset about Saturdays. She was inclined to be a little spoilt, as she'd come along late in life to her parents. They had had another baby boy after Sylvester,

26

but he had died at birth. The doctor told Mrs Parks her chances of having more children were slim so they had been overjoyed when Hattie had arrived.

Inside Lily's house, all was quiet. She walked slowly down the hall waiting for an eruption, but was relieved to hear laughter. As she took off her hat and coat and hung it on the stand, her thoughts returned to Charles Grey. It was the first time that a man had ever made her feel like this, excited and nervous at the same time. He was much older than her, it was true, but there was something in his gaze that had captured her. As though they had been the only two people in the whole of the market place.

This was something she couldn't really tell Hattie. Not until she knew Charles Grey a little better. *If* she ever got to know him better! And that depended on Ben.

Ben James was standing at his bedroom window looking down on the two figures below. The mist had cleared a little and he could just identify Lily and Hattie. Ben lifted the sash, on the point of calling out. He intended to crack a joke, as usual. But then he heard Hattie shouting something and it was about Charles Grey.

He stepped back quickly. What had Lily been telling Hattie about that smarmy bloke who bought the aspidistra? He was the proverbial wolf in sheep's clothing, no doubt about it. Ben had met a few like him in his time, gents that put on the style, but it wasn't an honest style. Gut instinct told Ben that Lily had swallowed the bait with those long looks and posh accent. But what could he do? He'd only acted like the jealous lover himself.

The two figures disappeared. All he could see now was the beginnings of a good old pea-souper, masking even the lamplight. He pulled the window down, replaced the lace and drew the faded chintz curtains. As he turned back into the room he caught his brother's gaze.

Reube was stretched out on the bed, his back propped by pillows. His right trouser leg was rolled up and a cold compress covered his swollen ankle. A minute or two ago, Ben had helped him up the stairs. They'd had a good laugh about Reube's accident, despite his complaints and grumblings.

'What am I missing?' Reube lowered the newspaper he had been reading.

'Nothing much,' Ben shrugged. The two brothers had shared the large, airy bedroom since childhood. In recent years either one could have moved upstairs to the top of the house, where years of unwanted or outgrown household effects were stored, but the attic room was so small that a person could only stand upright in the middle. Even squashing in a single bed, took up most of the space. But even if the room had been large, neither Ben nor his brother would have wanted it. They enjoyed one another's company, traded insults regularly and did a good deal of business talk before going to sleep.

'You was having a good look for seeing nothing,' Reube observed dryly.

Ben sat down on the single bed next to his brother's. He removed the studs from his collar and the cufflinks from his shirtsleeves. It was his golden rule to look smart at all times, irrespective of whether he drove his lorry or helped on the stall. Reube favoured a working jacket, durable trousers and cap, their differing styles giving rise to a good deal of harmless banter.

'It was Lily and Hattie,' Ben said casually. 'They were gassing as usual.'

Reube smiled. 'About me accident no doubt.'

'No, not about that.'

'What then?'

'I heard Hattie call something about this la-de-dah fella who bought the pot today. Remember? The one I told you about with the broken handle that I bought from the old girl up Manilla Street.'

'What was she saying?'

'I only heard his name.'

'So Lil was a bit taken with him, was she?'

'I didn't say that,' Ben frowned up as he wrestled with his collar.

'You said she wanted to go to his house with you. That's the same thing, ain't it?'

'I wish I hadn't mentioned it now.'

Reube sighed loudly. 'Do you realize you get the hump when anyone tries to get off with her.'

'I never do!' Ben slipped off his suit jacket and cast it aside.

'See? You've got the hump now.'

'No, I haven't.'

'You never chuck your stuff about like that. You always put your jacket straight on a hanger and hang it in the wardrobe. Drive me nuts you do, being so fussy.'

After dragging a woollen jumper over his head, Ben threw a pillow at his brother. 'Don't think you can insult me just because you're at a disadvantage.'

'Only me body is, me mind is firing on more cylinders than a number fifty-six bus. Can't help it if I'm the brains of this outfit.'

'You'd better shut up or I'll twist your toes,' Ben was quick to respond, attempting to deflect the interrogation about Lily. He did his best to act the local Romeo and this fooled most people who thought of him as the island's likely lad. But Reube knew him well and it was difficult to keep his intimate thoughts and feelings private. He had always told himself he believed in safety in numbers and if he wanted to build up his transport business, as a single man he was free of responsibility. Lily was his friend and she could take a joke; insulting one another was a way of life. It was how East Enders managed the ups and downs of everyday life. And there had been plenty of those whilst growing up on the island. Their six-year age gap meant he had spent most of his teenage years kicking a ball around with her. She was like his kid sister, his partner in grime as they used to say. He felt protective of her, but no more than he did for Hattie. They always teased him about being a Romeo. They knew he had no intention of settling down, not until he'd made his fortune. Which was coming by way of a classy looking charabanc he had seen for sale up Aldgate. He could fit thirty passengers in at a time. The perfect vehicle for club outings, weddings and the occasional funeral if they didn't mind the colour beige.

'It's a wonder there ain't a string of blokes outside her door,' his brother was saying.

Ben frowned, tuning back into the present. 'Whose door?'

'Lily's, of course.'

'She's only a kid.'

'In case you ain't noticed, Valentino, she's all grown up now.'

'What are you talking about, you daft prune?'

'I'm talking about the girl who is right under your nose, yet you don't seem to see her. There's all manner of women out there that you flirt with and right old boilers some of them. But Lily is in a class of her own. She's got manners and good taste, which is probably why she can't see you, either.'

'Here, watch it, matey! I've got taste and I know me p's and q's. Anyway, I don't think of Lil like that. She's like me little skin and blister, sort of.'

Reube smiled knowingly. 'You take my advice and put a ring on her finger.'

'Aw, shut that big gob of yours and concentrate on your paper. Ignorant blokes like you need to learn a bit about what's going on in the world.'

'I know enough,' Reube sniffed. 'More than you think.'

'What's that supposed to mean?'

'You can't fool me, Ben James. You're—' Reube went to sit up and yelled in pain. 'Bloody Norah, me foot!'

'I thought it was your ankle.'

'I tell you what, wring that rag out, bruv, and shove another wet one on it, would you? In fact, better go down and bring up a bowl of cold water.'

'Yes, m'lord, anything else, your highness,' Ben muttered, whipping off the cloth and making his brother yell out again.

'That hurt!'

'All right, all right. I'll be back in a minute. Lay back and think of England.'

Ben went downstairs where his widowed mother Betty and her old friend, Pedro Williams, had just finished a game of backgammon and were now playing gin rummy. Pedro was so called because of his little black moustache that curled up at the ends.

In the scullery, Ben rinsed the rag under the tap. He liked Pedro who had run their dad's stall when Ben and Reube had lost their dad in 1916 until Reube was old enough to take over.

The water was freezing as it filled the bowl. Ben was deep in thought once more, wondering about Charles Grey and why he disliked him. He didn't even know the man. But the more Ben thought about him, the less he found to like.

On his way back upstairs, his mother shouted, 'How's the patient?'

'Still clinging to life,' Ben replied.

'I heard voices outside, you know.'

'The Angel Gabriel calling from heaven, I 'spect.'

His mother appeared at the parlour door, her dark brown hair was hidden under a furry type of hat that resembled a deceased animal. She wore the hat winter and summer alike, pleating her two heavy eyebrows underneath it. 'I pulled back the curtain,' she told him, 'and saw Lil and Hattie. Strikes me they was having a good old laugh about something.'

'Well, even if it's the Aga Khan come to pay her a call with five hundred of his camels and a wagonload of dates, that ain't our business anyway.'

His mother blinked at him through the spindles of the banister. 'What's up with you, son?'

'Nothing.'

'I was only saying, ducks. You don't have to bite me head off.'

Ben was immediately contrite. 'Sorry, I'm just a bit done in, that's all.'

'Have an early night, dear. Your brother needs one too if he's to rest that ankle.'

He muttered something inaudible and went on his way. Now he was certain to get another quizzing from Reube who must have overheard all that. You couldn't bloody well take a leak in this neighbourhood without someone knowing.

33

As he entered the bedroom, he shouted at his brother, 'And don't you start or you'll get this lot over you.'

'I never breathed a word,' Reube said innocently.

But Ben knew what his brother was thinking, it was written all over his face.

'And by the way,' Ben said quickly, 'Lily asked me to ask you if she could work Saturday afternoons.'

'Why?'

'Her dad's out of work again.'

'Charming, ain't it? The bloke is only trying to do an honest day's toil for an honest day's pay.'

'Like hundreds of others on the island,' Ben nodded. 'He's even considering a skin boat.'

Reube shuddered vigorously. 'He's gotta be desperate then.'

'So what shall I tell her?'

'If she wants the hours she can have them,' Reube shrugged. 'Pedro offered to come and give me a hand whilst I got me limp, but he don't need the money like Lil.'

'I'll tell her yes then, when I see her on Sunday. *If* I see her on Sunday.'

'Ain't you gonna take her then?'

'Don't know, do I?'

Reube smiled as he shook out the newspaper and raised it. 'Don't worry, bruv, Charlie boy will be a five-minute wonder.'

But Ben wasn't so sure. Lily seemed to have taken a shine to the man or she wouldn't have asked to go with

34

him. And he couldn't think of any way he'd be able to stop her.

Lily was up early on Sunday morning. She wanted to look nice today. Ben had arrived to mend the latch and was now sharing a pot of tea with her mum and dad. Lily had put on her best beige tweed coat with a dropped waistline and exchanged her blue cloche hat for a brown one with a black petersham band above the small brim. Did she look smart enough, or had she overdressed? Then she remembered how nice Hattie had looked. Every once in a while it was good to dress up. She always had to wear warm clothes for the market and her boots. Now she could put on her bar strap shoes, ones she'd had for years, and the only other pair she possessed.

Ten minutes later, Ben was helping Lily into the lorry. He had put a sack over the seat to keep her clothes clean.

Lily smiled as she made herself comfortable. 'I feel like Lady Muck sitting up here.'

He grinned. 'You wait till you see me new motor.'

'What sort is it? Another lorry?'

'Not on your Nellie. It's a charabanc.'

'One of those things that are a cross between a car and a bus?'

'That's right.'

'A lot of people sit in it, don't they?'

'Yeah, this one's got thirty seats. I'm going to take out

groups: women's institutes, the girl guides, the football and billiards clubs, anyone who wants to hire me,' he told her as he drove.

She had to shout as the engine was noisy. 'Will you wear a uniform?'

He nodded. 'A proper chauffeur's outfit with leather boots and a flat cap.'

'Where are you going to park such a big thing?'

'Ernie Roper, the landlord of the Quarry says I can use his yard. He can get me a bit of business from the customers too.'

'Well, don't let them Blackshirts see it. I heard they bashed someone's windscreen out up Hyde Park.'

'Just let 'em try,' said Ben, squeezing the horn as a horse and cart blocked the way. The cart stopped and Ben drove round it, yelling out a thank you from the open window.

'Well, I wish you luck, you deserve it.' Lily suddenly remembered that Ben was going to ask about Saturdays. 'How is Reube's ankle?'

'Oh, on the mend.'

'Did you ask him about me working on Saturday afternoons?'

'Course I did and he said you're welcome.'

Lily sighed softly. 'That's a relief. I'll start next week if that's all right.'

'Do you need any money till then?'

Lily blushed. Ben and Reube were always generous, but she didn't want to have to ask for help, as she had done so before Christmas. She'd paid back the small loan, but it had left her short even though she had got her wages yesterday, most of which she'd given to her mum. 'No, that's all right, thanks.' She peered through the dirty windscreen and changed the subject. 'Do you know where to go?'

'Course I do. Dewar Street.'

'Is the plant in the back?'

'Yes, in the pot.'

'It won't slide about and break, will it?'

'No, I've wedged it in with some bricks.'

'I hope he likes it.' Lily felt quite nervous. She wondered what advice he would want from her. And could she give it?

'Sit back and relax,' Ben told her. 'It's only a broken po!'

But to Lily it was more than that. She had butterflies in her tummy and she was very apprehensive, now that she'd come here, wondering what she'd say to Charles Grey. And what if he didn't even remember her?

Chapter Three

Four Dewar Street had a tall front door and long, Georgian windows. It was the second house of a terrace that stretched behind the High Street.

'I'll knock, shall I?' Lily hesitated as they stood outside on the white steps.

'He won't know we're here by guesswork,' Ben grinned.

Lily stepped up to the big lion's head knocker and rapped. Very soon a young girl appeared. She was dressed in a long black skirt and white apron. 'Oh, it's the delivery,' she said, frowning at the plant.

Ben nodded. 'You're not going to tell us to go to the tradesman's entrance, I hope.'

'No, 'cos we ain't got one. Anyway, you're expected. Come in.'

Lily stepped inside with Ben. To her surprise, the house was much larger than it looked from the road. Past the big, dark hall was a staircase winding up to the next floor. A rather worn carpet led to all the rooms. There was no furniture in the hall except a large umbrella stand.

'Follow me,' said the girl, leading the way through a set of large wooden double doors. As they entered the room, Lily saw a very grand fireplace, the mantelpiece of which was the same height as her, deep green drapes hung either side of it. Sadly there was no fire alight in the big hearth, instead there stood a large oriental fan, opened to its fullest extent. Scattered around the room were upholstered armchairs. Lily recognised the material as watered silk. They had sold some last year from the stall, though they were not nearly as nice as these. Either side of the four long windows were heavy brocade curtains, complete with silk tassels.

'Crikey,' muttered Ben beside her, 'this is a sight for sore eyes, ain't it?'

'Beautiful,' Lily agreed, her eyes wide as she gazed around.

'Mr Grey will be with you in a minute. He said make yerselves comfortable.'

When the girl had gone, Lily looked round again. 'I didn't know there was places like this around here.' She walked to the window and looked out through the dirty panes of glass. She could see the road beneath and over the wall on the other side of the road, the backs of other houses. Some of the yards had small gardens and squares of grass, unheard of on the island.

'Not a bad lookout, is it?' Ben said as he came to stand beside her. 'But they need their windows cleaning.'

'You can still see the top of the Queen's.'

As a child, Lily had come up to Poplar with Uncle

Noah on the rag and bone cart. They had often passed the theatre in the High Street. On Friday night, anyone could do a turn, enjoy the audience applause and become famous for five minutes. The Queen's always held an air of excitement about it. On her fourteenth birthday, she had been treated to a night out at a musical revue. Her mum and dad and Uncle Noah had bought threepenny tickets for the 'gods'. That night she had fallen in love with the main act, a man called Teddy Stream. He could sing and dance and made everyone laugh and cry. She had never forgotten it.

'Is that the laundry over there?' Lily indicated a tall chimney.

'Dunno, why?'

'Uncle Noah and me used to stop in Sophia Street. He collected the unwanted linen from the back doors. I used to look in and see all these poor women covered in sweat.'

Ben nodded. 'It's a back-breaking job.'

'Uncle Noah said the drying ovens can clog up your lungs and kill you off early.'

'Well, someone's got to do it, I suppose.'

'Like me dad on the skin ships.' It didn't seem right that the poor were always given the worst jobs.

Ben nudged her. 'Right, where shall I put this? Here?'

Lily turned round. The small and expensive-looking table had a shiny surface.

'No, if the pot leaks, the table will be ruined.'

Ben picked it up again. A large round circle had

formed in the film of dust, showing the walnut grain beneath.

They were staring at it when the doors opened again. Charles Grey stood there. Lily felt the colour rush to her cheeks. He was even more handsome than she remembered.

'Good morning. How nice to see you both again.' He walked towards them. 'I'm sorry, but I don't know your names.'

Before Lily could speak, Ben answered. 'The name's Benjamin James and this is Miss Lily Bright.'

Lily cast Ben a quick look. He was sounding very formal.

Charles Grey held out his hand but as Ben was carrying the pot still, he turned to Lily. 'I didn't think you were coming.'

'I wasn't, but—' she stopped, blushing under his dark gaze as for a moment he took her hand and held it. 'I changed me mind.'

'I'm very glad you did.' He was still holding on to her hand, gazing deeply into her eyes.

Ben coughed loudly. 'Where do we put this?'

'Ah yes, the aspidistra.' Slowly, without looking at Ben, he let Lily's hand go.

Lily quickly remembered why she had come. 'You said you'd like some advice on where to stand it.'

'I would indeed.' His smile was making her feel just as strange as it had when she first met him. He had very full lips, which made her want to look at them and their lovely curve. And when she lifted her gaze to his eyes, her heart turned over. They were inky dark, lustrous and so intense that it was hard to look away. She was glad when he spoke again.

'Let me show you the house. Ben, would you like to give the plant to my maid?' He pulled a cord by the mantelpiece and the young girl entered. 'Take this to the scullery, Annie, whilst we find a suitable place for it to stand.'

'Yes, Mr Grey.' The girl quickly removed it and Charles Grey led them into the hall again. 'I'll show you upstairs first.'

Lily and Ben followed up the red carpeted stairs. Lily's fingers slid over the solid wooden stair rail as the gaslights flickered on the walls. Magically they spilled light into all the dark corners of the landing. There were many rooms on the first floor and Lily forgot after a while which order they came in. Each bedroom was very cold, as though it hadn't been used for a long time, and each was equipped with a big brass iron bedstead and heavy, sombre covers over the thick mattresses. The curtains were like those downstairs and kept apart by big silk tassels.

'I was wondering about in here?' Charles said to Lily as he opened the final door. It led to the bathroom.

Lily's eyes nearly popped out. There was a deep, white bath with brass feet shaped into an animal's claws. Beside this was a marble-topped washstand fitted with a gilt-edged mirror.

Lily shook her head in wonder. 'I've never seen such a big bathroom, or bath.'

'You could put the pot there.' Ben pointed to a piece of furniture in one corner.

'The chiffonier,' nodded Lily. 'It's beautiful.'

'Do you like it?' asked their host.

'Yes, but should it be in the bathroom? It would look much better in the drawing room or even the back parlour. That is, if you have one.'

He smiled, looking into her eyes once more. 'I can see that you know quite a lot about such things. That must be from working at the market?'

She nodded. 'We have a lot of furniture go through our hands. The West End dealers come down especially to buy.'

'And do you sell them a bargain?'

Lily smiled shyly. 'Of course. But Reube – that's my boss – he's not greedy. He likes to turn a profit and change the stock.'

Charles Grey seemed unable to take his eyes from Lily. 'How fascinating. What an interesting life you must lead.'

Lily didn't know what to say to that. She was a little embarrassed under his scrutiny.

'What do you think of the bath?' Charles asked Lily quickly. 'It's rather a nice piece, isn't it?'

'Does it have hot water?' Lily asked, admiring the shiny brass taps. What would it be like to sit in that bath and be covered up to the chin by lovely warm water?

'It's fed by the range downstairs.'

'We haven't even got a bath,' she sighed, 'at least not a proper one like that. We have to bring the tin one in by the fire.'

'That must be tiresome.'

'Mum says her dream is to have a proper bath.'

'Do you live with your parents?'

Lily nodded. 'Yes, and my Uncle Noah. He used to own a rag and bone yard. We'd come up to Poplar each month when I was young.'

Charles Grey gave her a dazzling smile. 'Is he still in business?'

'No, the horse died and he retired.'

'And you, young man, what do you do for a living?'

Ben said a little stiffly, 'I drive a lorry.' Then he looked at Lily. 'Which reminds me, I've still got a couple of deliveries left today. We'd better be going.'

Lily was fascinated with the house and wanted to see more. She knew for a fact that Ben had nothing else to do today.

'I mustn't take up any more of your time.' Charles Grey closed the bathroom door. 'So, any ideas, Lily, for the position of the plant?'

She walked to the banister and looked over. By the first stair was a small shelf and above it a lovely, ornate barometer. It was the perfect place for the plant. 'Perhaps it would suit nicely just there?'

'Yes, though there's not a lot of natural light,' said Charles hesitantly. 'I've always intended to fill that spot, but thought it wasn't right for such a delicate thing.'

Lily turned to her companion and met his dark gaze. She had butterflies in her tummy as he smiled at her. His dark good looks, grey suit and silk tie made him look so distinguished in the soft glow of the gaslights. 'You don't need to worry about aspidistras being delicate,' she told him. 'They don't mind gas fumes or draughts or even the dark. And all your visitors will have the pleasure of seeing it as they come in.'

Charles Grey's smile faded. 'I don't have many visitors these days. Not since my wife died.'

'Oh, I'm sorry.'

'It was two years ago now.'

Lily saw how upset he was and as Ben failed to comment there was a big gap in the conversation.

'Before you go I must pay you for the delivery,' Charles Grey said suddenly.

'No, it's on the house.' Ben shrugged.

Both men looked at each other. 'In that case I'll show you out.'

It was a swift goodbye as he shook their hands at the front door and thanked them. Lily wanted to know so much more. And she was certain he would have told them had they stayed.

Out in the cold air, Lily pulled her collar up. 'You was in a big rush to leave,' she said to Ben who had his hands deep in his pockets as they walked to the lorry. 'Why did you say you had more deliveries?'

'Because I thought we was gonna be there all day.'

'I was only curious.'

'So was he. About you.'

Lily looked at her friend. 'Do you think so?'

'Yes, I do.'

Lily felt hot colour sweep into her face. She could see Charles Grey now; he had something about him that unnerved her and excited her at the same time.

What had his wife died of? Was that why the house had looked neglected? She wondered if he would put the aspidistra where she had suggested.

Once seated in the lorry, Ben looked thoughtfully up at the house. 'He didn't say what he did.'

'You didn't give him much chance.'

'There was something about him I couldn't put me finger on.'

'It was nice of you to let him off the delivery charge.' Lily had been impressed by that.

But Ben spoilt it by adding, 'I didn't like the way he looked down his nose at us.'

'He did no such thing. He was the perfect gentleman.'

'Maybe it was me, then.'

'Yes, it was.'

Lily was annoyed with her friend. She had enjoyed the morning so much looking round that lovely house. Why had he ruined it?

They drove in silence until Ben narrowed his eyes and said slowly, 'I know what it was. The house didn't look lived in. Didn't see no shoes or clothes about in them bedrooms. Not even a fire in the grate and no umbrellas in the stand. Did you notice there wasn't a jug and basin in the bathroom? No razor or cupboard to put personals in. How does he wash and shave?'

'In the bath?'

'A bit luxurious that, ain't it?'

'Well, he's a man on his own.'

'So he says,' Ben muttered darkly.

Lily decided enough had been said about Charles Grey. Ben was determined to pick holes in an otherwise enjoyable outing. Perhaps he was jealous of him? Though it wasn't usually in Ben's character to find fault.

She couldn't help wondering whether she would ever see Charles Grey again. She felt downhearted at the thought she might not. If Ben hadn't hurried her off like that, she would have found out more about him. Was his wife beautiful? There had been no photographs on the wall that she had noticed. Perhaps he had taken them down in his grief.

'What did you say his name was?' Uncle Noah asked for the third time that evening.

'Charles Grey, Uncle Noah.'

They were sitting in the parlour in front of a roaring fire. Her parents and uncle were listening to her account of that morning's visit to Dewar Place.

'Don't ring a bell to me. What does he do?'

'I don't know. I didn't ask.'

'Must be a professional fella,' said her father as he

placed his tobacco tin on the arm of the big fireside chair. Lily knew he wanted to smoke, but would have to go out in the yard. Her mother didn't like him or her uncle to smoke indoors, although if she was out, they always did.

'He's a well-dressed gent. He could work in the city,' Lily suggested.

'You say he's a widower?' Josie glanced up from her crocheting.

'His wife died two years ago.'

'Poor man.'

'Yes, it must have been very hard.'

'She was young, then?'

'He didn't mention her age.'

'What did young Ben think of him?' Bob Bright changed the position of the tobacco tin yet again.

'He put a bit of a damper on it, actually.'

'Why's that?'

'I don't think he liked him.'

'Did he say why?'

Lily wasn't going to go over that. 'Not really.'

'So where did you suggest the plant went?' Josie began to crochet again.

'In the hall under the barometer, where it could be seen by visitors.'

'He'll have to make sure he hides the broken handle.' Her mother lifted one eyebrow.

'As long as the man that owned it doesn't return to use it,' Lily laughed.

Uncle Noah chuckled. 'Charlie boy will get his money's worth if he does.'

Lily's father stood up. She knew he couldn't go a moment longer without a smoke. He pressed down his waistcoat and rocked on his heels. The one day of the week when he dressed in a suit was on Sunday. Her mother insisted on him looking respectable even though they didn't often go to church. 'Sunday best' was a tradition on the island, no matter how poor or religious you were or weren't.

'Just going out the back,' he said, coughing and banging his chest with his knuckles.

Her father, at fifty-six years of age, rarely got angry or impatient with his family, but his financial worries had turned his thick dark hair iron grey. Lily noticed that, like her mother, the worry lines around the corners of his eyes had increased recently.

'You coming too, Noah?'

'Don't mind if I do.'

'It's parky out there. Better put our coats on.'

Lily saw her mother glance after them. She said nothing as the two men went out, closing the door behind them.

'His cough is worse this winter.'

'Does he rub in the wintergreen the doctor gave him?'

'He says he does, but it doesn't seem to help much.' Josie laid down her crocheting again. 'Good job your father has Uncle Noah to talk to.'

'He's got you as well.'

'I know, but men see things differently. A woman tends to nag or worry or both.'

'Are you worried about him, Mum?'

'I am a bit.' Josie sank back on the chair. 'He got a job yesterday. Was waiting on the stones for hours before one came up.'

Lily realized that this was not good news. 'You mean it was a skin ship?'

'Yes, I'm afraid so.'

'Oh, Mum, I wish he wouldn't take it.'

'So do I, but what choice do we have?'

'I told you I would work Saturday afternoons. Reube said I can.'

Josie's pale blue eyes looked sad. 'Lily, ducks, with all the goodwill in the world, it's not enough.'

'But couldn't we manage?'

'We have been managing, putting things on the slate. Last week I went up to Mr Gane's. He said he was very sorry, but he couldn't let me have any more groceries till I paid the arrears.'

'I thought his bill was settled.'

Josie sighed and shook her head. 'I was going to, but we had no coal. The coalman wants his money the minute he delivers. So the grocery money went to him.'

'You should have told me.' Lily saw the strain on her mother's face and her heart ached for her family.

'What good would it have done, Lily? I was hoping not to tell you. But it all just got worse.'

'I would have asked Reube for a loan.'

'You did before Christmas.' Josie shook her head. 'As good as Reube is, we ain't a charity case. Your father's got his pride too. I don't tell him about going to the pawnshop, mind. That's a secret only you and me share, ducks.'

Lily had been entrusted many times with a journey to the pawnshop. It was always done in strict secrecy. She had to make sure no one saw her go there, which was not difficult in the dark evenings, but very awkward in the lighter ones. It was becoming harder to raise a good price on the sheets, linens and personal effects as the pawnbroker had so many families on his books who were desperate. But as time had gone on and hopes of regular employment for her father had faded, it was the only alternative left. Lily knew her mother was borrowing from Peter to pay Paul, and they were still getting deeper and deeper into debt.

Lily thought of the lovely house she had visited this morning. It wasn't very far from her home, but it seemed as though it was on another planet. She could imagine what it would be like if Charles Grey's house was really loved and cared for. She was now certain that when Mrs Grey had died, her husband had just given up! He'd taken down the photographs so he wouldn't be reminded of his beautiful wife. And he didn't bother about lighting fires or making the place cosy. His heart simply wasn't in it.

Life was strange. There was Mr Grey with an

abundance of money and a desirable home, but he wasn't happy. Lily had seen the sadness in his eyes. Grief was the clue there, she was sure of it now. Then there was her own family who were as poor as church mice but were happy because they had each other. It seemed you had either one or the other, not both.

What would she do if she was wealthy? She could think of a thousand things, the list would be endless. The first and most important action she would take, would be to settle the family's debts. Then she would buy a bath like the one she had seen today, but then she would have to have a bathroom to put it in. And a large range to heat the hot water. In fact, one thing led to another. She would have to move to a bigger house altogether. Was that what she wanted?

Lily's imagination was working overtime as usual. It was as though she had a cinema in her head, showing all the films, with her family and herself taking the leading roles. She could put the characters anywhere she wanted, give them anything they wanted. Often at market she found herself daydreaming. Sometimes it was a shock to come back to earth and find herself still here.

'Lily?'

'What? Oh, sorry, Mum.'

'You were miles away again. Did you hear what I said?'

'About the pawnshop?'

Josie shook her head sharply. 'The winkleman is

outside; I heard him calling. I'd like a couple of penneth for tea.'

'I'll go and get some.' Lily jumped up, found her coat and bag and just in time stopped the man as he wheeled his barrow to the end of the street. The moist winkle shells glistened as he turned them over with a spoon and shovelled them onto newspaper.

As Lily paid him, she imagined she was returning to a large house full of beautiful furniture with a grand and opulent bathroom upstairs. The good feeling inside her was so strong that she could almost believe she was there. She walked home seeing lines of long Georgian windows and white steps that sparkled in the sunlight.

Chapter Four

Rain seemed to blight trading all the next week. There was a wind too, which meant that Lily had to place the heavier objects on top of the lighter ones to keep them from blowing away. All the old magazines and papers became soaked. There were leaks and drips and the customers complained continually. The haberdashery stall which stood outside of the butchers, had all its cottons and laces blown away. Lily helped Florrie Mills retrieve her stock from the fur of the dead rabbits that hung outside the butchers. The Old Girl's Stall, run by Vera Froud, was a pile of wet, soaked garments. Each one had to be taken away and mangled before they could be sold again.

The stallholders were all disheartened. Colds and coughs abounded. It was at times like this that Lily was tempted to change her job as she stood in the miserable conditions, with no let up to the rain that soaked through the holes in her boots and distorted the shape of her hat. If she took a factory job she could earn more money and help her mum. She could also have Saturday afternoons off with Hattie. But as the week wore on, and a bright sky appeared once or twice, the thought of leaving the market dismayed her. Then, at the end of the week, when a sparkle of sunshine dotted the puddles, a trader from the West End appeared. In one fell swoop he bought all the silver and crockery, two old boxes of cutlery, and the fire fender and companion set. Lily achieved almost full price and Reube was delighted.

'Good on you, girl,' said Reube, counting out the pound notes. 'Tell you what, here's a five bob bonus.'

Lily stared at him. 'Are you sure?'

Reube grinned. 'Go on, take it.'

Lily smiled. 'Mum will be pleased with that.'

'You should spend it on yourself. Them boots is as old as the hills.'

Lily glanced down and noticed that the stitching by the soles had come apart. There had been a small hole there before, but now it showed her toe. Her feet had been too wet and numb to notice.

'I'll buy some soon.'

'You do that.' Reube began to put the money in the tin box. Lily dropped her bonus in her bag, her mind doing a quick reckoning. With working tomorrow afternoon, her wage would go up from the usual fifteen shillings to twenty. Today's bonus would give her a total of twenty-five shillings altogether. Perhaps her dad wouldn't have to take the skin job for too long?

The following day Lily missed seeing Hattie, but as the rain had stopped completely, the general public came out to celebrate. It was another good business day for the traders.

'What's all this?' Josie exclaimed when, that night, Lily turned her purse out on the kitchen table.

'Reube gave me a five bob bonus for selling a lot of stuff. And with working Saturday afternoon I got twenty five shillings altogether.'

'You should have some for yourself.'

'No, I'll manage.'

Josie quickly slipped the money in her apron pocket. 'Well, ducks, I'll be able to go to the corner shop and hold my head up high again.'

'And clear the arrears on the rent.'

'Of course. Are you going to see Hattie tomorrow?'

Lily nodded. 'If she hasn't got to sit with Sylvester.' She looked through the kitchen window to the tin tub hanging on the side of the shed. 'Is Dad using the bath tonight?'

'Yes, after what he's been doing on them ships, he'll need a good scrub.'

'Could I have the first bath, then?' Lily hated the smell of the disinfectant he had to use, that clung to the sides of the bath.

'Course you can. It'll be filthy when he's finished with it, anyway. I'll get the water warmed in the copper first.'

Lily hoped she could have a long soak. She wanted to lay in the water and think of herself in a big white bath with lion's claw feet. She had imagined doing this all week through the rain and wind. She had been disappointed not to see Charles Grey again. But what would a man like him want to return to Cox Street for?

On Sunday afternoon, Lily called for Hattie. 'Can you come out?' She stood muffled up to the ears with a scarf and her hat pulled hard down around her ears. It was threatening to rain again.

'I'll ask Mum and Dad. Come in a minute.'

Lily stepped inside. Hattie hurried off and was soon back. 'They ain't going for a walk as Sylvester's poorly,' she said in whisper as she put on her coat.

'What's happened?'

'He had one of his nightmares. Is it gonna rain?'

'It might.'

'I'll take the umbrella then.'

Lily knew that Sylvester had such bad dreams of the war that they made him very ill. As she waited for her friend to put on a hat and tuck her bob gently inside she felt very sorry for the Parks family. Their life was dominated by Sylvester's illness. Despite this, Hattie always managed a smile and to take a pride in her looks.

Hattie glanced in the hallstand mirror. She turned this way and that, pouting her lips, then she drew her middle finger under her eyebrows as if she was urging them up. 'How do I look?'

'Beautiful as always.'

'Don't be funny. I've had a rough night.'

'I mean it. It don't matter what sort of night you've had you always look the same.'

'That's Madame's training for you. She's a stickler for looking your best. She says her girls are representatives of her work. So we all have to remember that outside of work.'

'She expects a lot, don't she?' Lily asked as they stepped out into the gloomy afternoon.

'Yes, but she pays me well, don't she? And in the end it's the money that counts.'

'You're right about that,' Lily agreed, thinking that nearly all her thoughts were taken up with how she was going to pay this or that, or which bill she should help her mother to settle first. It was a relief to know now that at least the rent was up to date.

They walked arm in arm, discussing the events of the past week as they took the foot tunnel from Island Gardens to Greenwich. The tunnel wound under the River Thames to the South Bank, and by the time they saw daylight at the other end, they had begun to discuss Lily's birthday in March.

'I'm going to make a cake for me twenty-first, with twenty-one candles,' Lily said.

Hattie laughed. 'You'll need a lot of puff to blow that lot out. You're getting old, girl.'

'You're only six months younger than me.'

'Are you gonna have a party?' Hattie wanted to know.

'I'd like to. But I haven't asked Mum yet.'

'Can she afford it?'

Lily shrugged. 'I'm trying to save up a bit.' She didn't want to tell her friend just how difficult things were at home. Hattie's Dad brought home a regular wage and with Hattie's contribution they never seemed to struggle.

'Have you seen Ben?'

'No, why?'

'Reube says he's going to buy this bloody great motor vehicle. It's as big as a bus.'

'The charabanc you mean?'

'You know about that?' Hattie asked in surprise.

'Ben said he was hoping to go into weddings and funerals.'

Hattie giggled. 'Trouble is, it's beige, not black. Reube says Ben'll have to tell people he only does happy funerals.'

The two girls looked at one another and laughed.

Lily wiped the tear from her eye. 'Well, it's got to be better than the lorry. The day we went out in it to deliver that aspidistra, I had to shout as the engine was so noisy.'

Hattie put a hand to her mouth. 'Oh, I'd forgotten about that! What happened?'

After describing the lovely house in Dewar Street, in particular the bathroom, Hattie's expression was shocked.

'A real bath you mean?'

'Yes, a huge white one, in a big room all to itself.'

Hattie sighed enviously. 'Me mum and dad would love a bathroom. It would make looking after Sylvester a lot easier.'

Lily was thinking the same. She had managed to have a bath last night, but the Naptha from previous uses had become ingrained in the tin. She could even smell it on her today.

'Where did you decide the plant should go?' Hattie asked.

Lily told her friend the rest of the story, adding that Ben had rushed her off and she was unable to discover more.

'What's he do that for?'

'I don't know.'

'Are you going to see this Charles again?'

'Of course not,' Lily said a little too quickly. 'What would he want with someone like me? I was just curious that's all.'

'You say he's a widower, do you know anything about his wife?'

'I didn't have time to ask, did I?'

'That's a pity.'

Lily nodded, encouraged by this spark of interest. 'I've worked it out though. He must have been heart–broken and just let the house go a bit as the windows were dirty and there wasn't much furniture downstairs. That sort of thing.'

'But you say he had a maid?'

'Well, a hired help anyway. She hadn't cleaned or

looked after the house though. There was a lot of dust around. He just seemed to have lost interest in the place.'

Hattie glanced at Lily. 'I hope you don't feel sorry for him. You're always a soft touch. Don't forget he's not from round here and you haven't known him five minutes.'

Lily didn't like being thought of as a soft touch. She felt she was quite the opposite, with a sensible, level head and wasn't taken in easily.

'Come on,' said Hattie, pulling her along, 'let's go to the park café. I know you're broke, so it's my treat.'

As they made their way to Greenwich Park, Lily wondered what Hattie would think of Charles Grey? But then realized she was allowing her imagination to run away with her again. There wasn't much hope of that. Charles Grey only lived in her dreams!

It was on the last day of January, a Friday, when a group of Blackshirts arrived at market. They stood on boxes and were noisy and disruptive. No one wanted to hear their propaganda.

'Bloody fascists!' Vera Froud exclaimed, coming over to Reube and Lily. 'That's what they are. They'd like to overthrow the monarchy given the chance and have us all under a dictator. Why don't they go back to where they come from!'

'Italy, ain't it?' Florrie Mills suggested as she frowned at the noisy group.

'This is Mosley's lot,' Reube put in. 'Trying to find a way to stir up trouble amongst decent people. Cause unrest, so they can get in with Joe Bloggs under false pretences.'

'They got big gobs on 'em that's for sure.' Vera crossed her arms and frowned. She had squashed her black hat down on her head and the strands of her faded red hair sprang out like snakes. 'My Bert would like to take them down a peg or two. Trouble is, that's what they want.'

'Yer, the buggers,' nodded Ted Shiner, coming up and sticking out his big chest. At over six foot he was well muscled and took after his grandmother, Fat Freda. For years they had run the fruit and veg pitch, and Lily knew Ted had cause to dislike the Blackshirts as he'd got in an argument down the Quarry with them once. He'd come off worst, as they'd made him look daft with their clever words and knowledge of politics. It was an occasion that he'd never forgotten.

'Why don't the rozzers move 'em off, that's what I'd like to know,' said Reube standing beside Ted and throwing black looks at the noisy bunch.

''Cos they'd prefer to pick on an easy touch,' replied Vera angrily. 'Like some poor sod who's got a bit merry and can't find his way home.'

'You're not wrong there,' agreed Florrie.

Lily hadn't seen these men before, and she found them frightening. They shook their clenched fists and shouted ferociously. They were telling everyone that the

Great Depression was a result of the country's manage-
ment and the people should rise up against the restraints
of the government.

Not content with keeping to their group, several of
the dark-clothed men began to infiltrate the market.
They approached the stalls and pushed their way through
the crowd, handing out pamphlets. People took them
because they were too scared not to. When one of
them came over, he made his way towards Lily. Smiling
unpleasantly at her, he waved a paper in her face.

'Read this and learn how to throw off the shackles of
your imprisonment,' he yelled at her.

Lily shook her head. 'I ain't in prison and I'm trying
to get on with me work.'

'You are ignorant of the way you're being used,' he
boomed back. 'Join us sister, and we'll show you the
way to freedom.'

'I ain't your sister,' Lily replied, recoiling.

'Leave her alone!' Reube was beside her, poking the
man in the shoulder. 'Get orf, you bloody troublemaker.
Can't you see you're losing us business?'

The Blackshirt began to shout at Reube and Ted
came running up.

'What do yer want round here?' he demanded,
waving his big fist. 'Clear orf, the lot of you!'

But soon Mosley's men had descended on them.
One man pushed Reube who fell back on the stall. All
the articles went flying. The china cups and saucers
broke on the cobbles. There was shouting and yelling

and Lily's wrist was grabbed by one of the Blackshirts. She tried to wriggle free but he wouldn't let go.

She was so afraid she felt faint. She knew she should take the paper just to satisfy him. Then she saw Reube on the ground, with a man punching him. Ted was trying to drag him off whilst Florrie and Vera were screaming.

Suddenly a figure appeared at her side. She looked up to see Charles Grey. Staring at the man who held her, he said quietly but threateningly, 'You and your friends should leave before the police arrive.' He snatched the paper from the man's hand and tore it in half. 'Your leader won't be too impressed to know that your antics here will cause him a great deal of embarrassment. I believe he is conjuring hopes for a New Party?' At these words, the man froze. 'Go back to Mosley and tell him he has not yet penetrated the East End. Nor ever will whilst you act like ignorant thugs.'

The man glared at him, joined by his companion who had disengaged himself from the fight. One by one they slunk off, casting disgruntled frowns over their shoulders. The market people began to jeer them. As Reube rubbed his jaw, Charles Grey helped him to his feet.

'The buggers,' Reube growled, raising his own fist to the departing group. 'Don't you show yer ugly mugs round here again.'

'I'm afraid they might,' said Charles Grey.

'Well, they'll find us waiting next time,' said Reube

angrily. 'Look what they done to me china.' He bent down and began to pick up the pieces.

As the other stallholders came over to help Reube, Charles Grey took Lily's arm. 'Are you hurt, Lily?'

She smiled shakily. 'No, I don't think so.'

'You're still trembling.'

She didn't know whether she was trembling because of the Blackshirts or because she was looking into the face that she had thought she would never see again. His dark eyes were concerned for her.

'What are you doing here?' she asked.

'I came to find you.'

Lily gasped. 'Has the aspidistra died?'

'No, in fact, it's flourishing.' The smile he gave her made her feel weak at the knees.

'Oh, that's a relief.'

He laughed softly and Lily's heart went off at a tangent again. Why had he come to find her?

'Lily . . .' He moved her across the pavement to the shelter of the café which was now empty because of the disruption. 'I wonder if you have the time one day to join me on a trip to the city? I would like to buy some more pieces for the house. And would value your advice – and of course, your company.'

Lily stared up at him. The noise from the stallholders and shoppers was growing as the excitement of what had happened created a stir. Reube was busy telling the story of how he had sent them off with a flea in their ear.

'I . . . well—' she stammered.

'I shan't be offended if you say no, of course.'

'It's not that.'

'What is it, then?'

How could she explain that she didn't have any spare time? How would a gentleman like him be able to understand that she was the breadwinner of the family?

'I only have Sundays free,' she said at last.

'Oh dear. I was hoping to buy in the city and on Sundays the shops are closed.' He glanced across at Reube. 'Is this young man your employer?'

Lily nodded.

'Would it be possible to ask him for a Saturday off?'

Lily felt disappointed. He was making it plain that their outing wouldn't be a social one. 'I could ask. Pedro might be able to take my place.'

'And who is Pedro?'

'Just a friend who helps out.'

'I shall certainly recompense both you and he for your time.'

Charles Grey looked at her for a long while, then replaced his hat over his smooth black hair. 'This Saturday would be most convenient.'

Lily wanted to accept. Would Reube agree? And even if he did, what would she wear?

But before she could decide on what to do, Charles Grey settled the matter for her. 'It's obviously not the right time to ask him,' he smiled, looking once more at the noisy group of stallholders talking about the Blackshirts. 'But if you find yourself free next Saturday, at say twelve o'clock, I would be most pleased to meet you.'

'Would you go up to the city anyway?' Lily asked.

'Yes, indeed I would. I'm very happy to collect you in my car – that is, if you can come?'

Lily didn't want everyone peering out of the windows. She knew that a motor car of any description would draw attention, let alone someone of Charles Grey's appearance climbing out of it.

'If Reube gives me the time off, I'll walk up to the top of Westferry Road. You'd be going that way to the city, wouldn't you?'

'Yes, I would.'

'I'll wait on the corner.'

He frowned, then gave a slow smile. 'As you wish.'

Lily could do nothing but nod, as he stared into her eyes, causing her to feel faint again. Giving her the briefest of bows, he turned and slipped quietly away.

Lily stood there, bewildered and excited. She could hardly believe Charles Grey wanted to see her again even if it was only in a business capacity! She just hoped Reube would allow her a whole day off.

Lily turned back to the stall, Reube was still in full flow about how he had fought off the gang and given one a black eye. No one it seemed had heard what Charles Grey had quietly said to the thugs.

The next day they replenished the stall with new stock, a few vases, a set of brass candlesticks and some small china ornaments. Reube had been talking non-stop about the fight and had found a large stick to hide under the stall.

'This'll scare them off,' he told her. 'Just let them try threatening me again. If I knew where to send the bill I'd charge them for the damage.' Reube smiled at a woman who was looking at the candlesticks. 'They'd look nice on your joanna, missus,' he said, 'a bit of class those are.'

'I ain't got a piana,' the woman replied.

'You've got a shelf, I'm sure.'

'And it's filled, ducks, I was only looking.' She saw the box of broken china that Lily had managed to salvage.

'You can have that lot for a bob.'

'Sixpence and throw in that teapot.'

'You drive a hard bargain, madam.'

The woman laughed, throwing a sixpenny piece on the stall.

Reube placed the teapot in the box with the china and handed it over. 'You got a bargain there, as it was once bone china before them bloody Blackshirts broke it.'

'I heard about that,' his customer replied. 'How yer fought 'em off after having badly damaged your ankle a week or two back. You're an 'ero mate, you are.'

'Word gets round, don't it?' Reube said to Lily when she had gone. He looked very pleased with himself.

Lily smiled. 'I suppose it's no use me saying we should let the police know.'

Reube almost fell backwards. 'Hey now, Lil, what you on about? The rozzers are worse than the gangs. We'll handle things our own way.'

'I hope they don't come back again.'

'Don't worry, gel, I'll be here to protect you.'

Lily wondered if Reube was beginning to enjoy his new status as a hero as he'd been round every other stall on the market and told his story, gaining new respect from the men.

Lily served an elderly gent with a set of tarnished teaspoons while Reube saw to another customer. Then, still smiling and with his usual light step, he went over to the café, bringing back two chipped enamel mugs, filled with coffee.

'Wet your whistle, Lil.'

They sat down on two small wooden stools. Lily had decided to ask Reube about next Saturday. Last night she had gone through all her clothes, which weren't very many. All she had was her best beige tweed coat and bar strap shoes which she had worn the day she had gone to Dewar Street. But she had found a small black fur on the stall and taken it home to sew on the collar.

Reube suddenly lent forward. 'Here, who was that gent you was talking to yesterday?'

Lily knew this was the right time. 'His name is Charles Grey. He's the man who bought the aspidistra the day you sprained your ankle.'

'Oh, that was him, was it? What did he want?'

'He was looking for things for his house,' she said, hoping this would satisfy Reube.

'Did he see anything he fancied?'

'No. Those Blackshirts didn't help.' She wanted to say that it was Charles Grey's words that had scared them off. But now everyone thought Reube was the hero, she couldn't.

He considered this as he gulped his coffee. 'You never know, he might come back. Got a few bob, so Ben said.'

'He said he's going up to the city next Saturday.'

'What, to buy stuff?'

Lily nodded. 'He asked me to go with him and help him choose.'

Reube lowered his mug and stared at her. 'Why's that?'

'Because he liked what we sold him and where I said to put it.'

'But you ain't exactly an authority, gel,' Reube smirked, shaking his head.

'I know. But it's a woman's touch he wants I suppose. He's a widower, ain't he?'

'Course! I'd forgotten.'

'So I can go then?'

'You'd be losing money not working. And you only just started Saturday afternoons.'

'He said he'd pay us for the trouble.'

A glint suddenly appeared in Reube's eyes. 'He'd pay, eh?' He tilted back the peak of his cap with his mug. 'I dunno if I'll manage on me own. Ben's all taken up with this new motor of his.'

'Pedro would help out.'

'Yer, I 'spose. How much did he say he'd pay?'

'He didn't, but he's not the sort to skimp.'

Reube knitted his brow. 'Well, it might be beneficial to us, seeing as he's got this house to fill. I 'spect it was only the Blackshirts that put him off. You could tell him we're getting in a lot of new stock, even bring him back here to have a look.'

Lily nodded. She was beginning to feel a small thrill inside her that was making her quite light-headed.

'All right then, I'll fix next Saturday up with Pedro.'

'Thanks, Reube.'

'Just as long as he pays for your time and my loss, mind,' Reube warned her, but as the customers began to take his attention, the subject of Charles Grey was forgotten.

As she worked, Lily's thoughts turned to next Saturday, wondering where they would go and what they would buy. Would she be able to choose the most tasteful things for the house? She could recall every inch of it; if she were to live there she knew exactly what she would put in it!

As she sat on the stool beside Reube, with the winter sunshine falling on their heads, she thought about Hattie. Should she tell her friend about this tomorrow?

Only last night the doctor had to give Sylvester an injection of morphine. Hattie said he'd been very poorly and she didn't think she could get out for a walk tomorrow.

Lily felt sorry for Hattie, but she was selfishly excited about her own good fortune. She went to sleep thinking of the tall, dark and unsung hero at the market.

'Why didn't you ask him to fetch you?' her mother enquired a week later. Saturday morning had arrived and Lily was dressed and ready to go out. 'He could have come in and had a nice cup of tea.'

'I thought it better to meet him on his way to the city. After all, if Reube didn't have Pedro to help him, I wouldn't go.'

'Well, you're in luck with the weather, love,' Lily's father glanced over his newspaper. 'It's nice and sunny.'

'But there's a wind,' chipped in her uncle.

'I'll enjoy a brisk walk.'

'Do you want me to stroll up with you?' her dad asked.

'No, it's all right, Dad.' Being escorted by her father was the last thing Lily wanted to happen. She loved her family dearly but wished she could have gone out without so much fuss.

'Where do you think you'll pick up these pieces?' her mother asked as she sat down in the armchair and began to crochet.

'I don't know, Mum. I'll leave that to him.'

'Funny he should ask you,' commented Uncle Noah as he took his place by the fire. 'And not Reube.'

'I do know a little about furniture.'

'Yes, course you do,' agreed Bob Bright frowning at his brother-in-law. 'You're a bright lass.'

'And you look very nice, dear.' Her mother's eyes went over her critically. 'Where did you get that bit of fur round your neck?'

'From the stall. It was left over from something or other. Reube didn't want it.'

'Well, you've made a nice job of doing up that old coat.'

Lily smiled uncertainly at the backhanded compliment, did her coat look old? She hoped that the beige tweed wouldn't be recognizable to Charles Grey with the fur collar she had attached to it. And on an inspired idea, she had removed the petersham trim on her hat, replacing it with the blue band from her old cloche.

'I'd better go now.' She was eager to leave, but apprehensive that Charles Grey might not remember their appointment. Was meeting her just something he had said on the spur of the moment? Would she be waiting for hours on a chilly corner?

'Have you got a clean hanky?'

'Yes, Mum.'

'Well, have a lovely time.'

'I'll see you later.' Lily opened the parlour door and smiled at the three faces looking up at her. They were all a little baffled as well as curious. 'I won't be late.'

As she walked down Westferry Road she wondered if Hattie had seen her walk past.

Lily quickened her steps. Her heart told her that what-ever price she paid to meet Charles Grey, it was worth it. Her head was instructing her not to forget her friends or family, Charles Grey had only said he needed her advice. But he had also added that he would like her company too!

Chapter Five

A large ruby red car with a black shiny roof pulled into the curb. Charles Grey climbed out of it and came towards her. Lily's breath caught. He was so handsome! Although an older man, he dressed with such style. Today he wore a double-breasted navy blue blazer, despite the cold, his grey flannels were perfectly creased and his shiny leather brogue shoes matched his driving gloves. His very dark hair looked shorter, was perfectly groomed and swept back from his head. As usual, the smile he gave her made her go weak at the knees.

She smiled shyly, placing her hand on the rim of her hat to keep the breeze from taking it. Her blue eyes were wide with anticipation and her pulse was racing as he took her arm and escorted her to the passenger door. 'I hope I'm not late.'

'No, not at all.'

'You were given the time off?'

'Yes.'

'May I say how lovely you look, Lily?' His eyes roved

over her with undisguised admiration and Lily blushed deeply. She sat inside, inhaling the wonderful leathery smell; all the seats were covered in real leather. The panel in front of her was a shiny walnut effect with two round dials inset by the big steering wheel. The windscreen was so clean that you could see everything perfectly through it. Unlike Ben's lorry where the dirt and dust had become a permanent feature.

'Are you comfortable?' he enquired as he began to drive.

'Yes. Very, thank you.'

'I have a rug and overcoats in the back should you want one.'

'No, I'm quite warm. This is a beautiful motor car.'

'I'm glad you like it. It's not top of the range, but a good workhorse.'

'You should see Ben's lorry,' she smiled. 'I'd call that a workhorse, not this.'

'Ah, the young man who escorted you to my house?'

'Yes.'

'I didn't see him at the market on Friday.'

'No, he was working. You remember, he delivers all over the country.'

'Are the James brothers in business together?'

Lily nodded. 'I suppose you could say that. Reube runs the stall and Ben's going to buy one of them great big charabancs.'

'Really?' Charles Grey turned to glance at her. 'What

an enterprising pair they are. How long have you known them?'

'All me life. They live opposite in Love Lane.'

'So, you live in Love Lane – I'm afraid I don't know it.'

Lily smiled. 'It's just an ordinary road on the island. But we all grew up together there. My best friend, Hattie Parks, lives next door. She sees a lot of Reube.' She paused. 'I wouldn't be surprised if they get married.'

He nodded thoughtfully. 'And what about young Ben? He seems to think a great deal of you.'

Lily shook her head. 'He's like me big brother. Sometimes we go dancing. He's a very good dancer, actually.'

'A man of many talents.'

Lily frowned. 'Don't tell him that. You'd never hear the end of it.'

After a while, she began to relax. She was amazed at the way Charles Grey drove. The car was smooth and didn't have any clunks and bangs like the lorry. It made conversation much easier. Lily couldn't take her eyes from the scenery. She had gone up West by bus many times. But today was different. Or was it just that she felt different, she wondered? As she glanced at her good-looking companion, she was more than curious to know his plans.

As he drove, Charles told her more about himself. He described how he had once lived up north and married, then brought his wife to London, where she had sadly died. He had been alone for two years, and for a living, dealt in fine quality furniture.

'Is that why you came to the market?' Lily asked.

'Yes, I keep an eye out for interesting pieces.'

'We don't have much that's of great value,' Lily confessed, 'as it's often broken or chipped, like the chamber pot.'

He smiled. 'Yes, but often I can have a piece restored if it's not badly damaged.'

'Like the dealers that come from up West. They think we don't know how valuable some things are. I often tell Reube we're selling too cheaply but he likes to turn a profit.'

'Sensible man,' he agreed.

'I could always put a piece by for you. I mean ...' Lily felt she was presumptuous to suggest it, but added hesitantly, 'that is, if you come our way again.'

He looked into her eyes. 'I'm sure I will.'

He didn't refer any more to his dead wife although Lily was hoping he might. She was even more certain now that he must have loved her very much.

When they arrived in Oxford Street, the traffic almost came to a standstill. From Shoe Lane to Ludgate Circus, taxis, buses and motorized vehicles had jammed the way. But Lily was content. There was time to look out of the window at the busy shops. Marshall & Snelgrove's in particular displayed eye-catching new fashions above which the advertising slogans were waving in the breeze. 'A full shingled head for twenty five shillings.'

'Look!' Lily gasped. 'I've always wanted to sit in one of those places and have my hair waved!'

'But that would be a sin,' Charles replied as he gazed at her, his dark eyes intense. 'I haven't ever seen a more beautiful head of hair than yours, Lily.'

She laughed in embarrassment. 'You haven't seen what's under my hat.'

'I've seen enough.'

She blushed as she looked back through the window. Did he really think she had beautiful hair? She was always trying to straighten it, but it was easier to let it fall in its own way.

'Shall we look around the stores first?'

Lily hadn't expected to be taken to the big shops. But before she knew it, he had parked the car in the Brompton Road and escorted her to the grand terracotta building that was Harrods. Lily was shocked to see the hundreds of items on sale there. Everything from pens and paper to jewellery to household goods, perfumes and fashions. She was so excited as they passed through the glass and marble halls that she could hardly speak. All the women were fashionably dressed and the men all seemed to have handlebar moustaches. She would have been very self-conscious in her old coat and hat, but she remembered how Charles' eyes had gone over her when he had first seen her. He hadn't been able to disguise his approval. Every so often she straightened her back and copied the posture of the other young women who seemed to glide through the store.

After Harrods they went into the arcades. Here there were small salons with fashions from Paris and Italy. Lily couldn't take her eyes off the beautiful designs and colours and every jeweller seemed to have a more varied and sparkling display than its neighbour.

'Before we look round the furniture shops, I suggest we go somewhere to eat,' Charles said as Lily was trying to absorb every single detail. She had come up to the city before but only with Hattie, Reube and Ben. They'd usually gone to one of the parks where they listened to the bands playing. The shops were for the wealthy and to visit them meant you had to spend money.

'Where would you like to go?' he asked her.

Lily was shocked to be given a choice. 'I'm not sure. But I've always wanted to go back to Lyons. Uncle Noah took me once when I was little.'

'Then Lyons it shall be.'

Lily thought she must be dreaming as she was escorted into the gold fronted teashop, J. Lyons. The fascia was embellished with Victorian decoration and Lily noticed a discreet sign on the wall announcing the first Lyons teashop had been opened in 1894.

Inside, Lily closed her eyes and inhaled the mouth-watering aroma of the bakery. 'I'd like to tidy up first,' Lily said, noting a sign on the wall indicating the cloak-rooms. She wanted to make sure she looked presentable before going in to the restaurant.

'Certainly,' he said quietly, smiling down at her. 'But I assure you, that you look quite lovely.'

Lily blushed and hurried off. Charles had paid her so much attention, but she wasn't used to compliments and wondered if he really meant what he said.

The cloakroom was a mixture of pretty colours, feminine and delicate. The ornate mirrors were decorated with bowls of small white roses. There were luxurious towels for customers to use and little round bars of soap that smelt of flowers.

She waited for a space at one of the basins. How could her imagination have ever created a scene like this? It seemed she wasn't expected to pay a penny for their food as Charles had told her it was entirely his treat.

Lily gazed in the mirror. Tucking her hair tidily under her hat, she pinched her cheeks to bring out the colour. The other women were talking in high voices. Some of them balanced their cigarette holders between their manicured fingers. She didn't have their expensive clothes, nor did she smoke, although she almost wished she did. But the fur trim she had added to her collar was just the right touch.

Lily smiled at the girl next to her. She was dark-haired and wore the most gorgeous black astrakhan coat. Although tall and slim, she was bereft of a smile and looked away.

This dented Lily's confidence a little. If Hattie had been here she would have whispered in her ear 'snobby cow' and they would have had a giggle. It was always fun to be with Hattie. Thanks to Madame Nerys' training, Hattie could outshine anyone here.

But now Lily was on her own. Could she remember which knives and forks to use? Was it milk in the cup before the tea or the other way round?

Lily finished her repairs and made her way out. Charles had found them a table and proved the perfect host. He poured the tea and offered her the silver sugar bowl.

'No, thank you. The tea is perfect.'

'Like the lovely young woman sitting opposite me,' he looked into her eyes.

Lily knew she was going scarlet. 'I . . . I didn't expect to find myself here,' she stammered.

'You deserve it. You are giving up your time to spend with me. And don't think I've forgotten this is a business arrangement. I shall make certain you are compensated.'

Lily was disappointed, she wanted him to say she was here because he liked her. One moment he made her feel special, the next he was reminding her that she would be paid.

'What would you like to eat?'

Lily read from the menu. Speciality pastries, House Swiss Roll, fruit scones and sandwiches to order. Hams, cheeses, pickles and home-baked bread. The list went on and on.

Lily looked bewildered. 'I like everything.'

He laughed. 'You're very easy to please.'

She hesitated. 'But the pastries look lovely.' They took sly glances at the cake stand on the next table. It was overflowing with delicious concoctions.

'I'll order a selection, shall I?'

'That would be lovely.'

Whilst he was ordering, Lily looked around. Each table was covered with a pure white linen tablecloth, the cutlery and china were sparkling, and every napkin was folded into a cone.

As her gaze returned to Charles, she felt her heart race again. He was one of the most attractive men in the room. There were other well-dressed men, but he was exceptional with his dark looks and beautiful dark eyes. She could see the other women looking in his direction.

The pastries and sandwiches arrived. She had never seen such a collection. Crustless white bread with dainty fillings and a creamy sauce. Pastries oozing cream, marzipan, currants, sultanas and icing. Lily didn't think they could eat them all, but they did.

'Would you like something else?' the waitress asked when she returned.

Lily shook her head. 'I couldn't eat a crumb more.'

'Just the bill then, thank you,' said Charles with a friendly grin.

The waitress went off. Lily remembered Uncle Noah telling her they were called Nippies. Each girl wore a black dress decorated with red buttons and trimmed with white collars, cuffs and aprons.

'It must be very tiring being on your feet all day,' Lily remarked when the girl brought the bill folded on a small saucer.

'Yes, it is.'

'I hope they pay you well,' said Charles.

'Not terribly, and we have to work in shifts,' the Nippy explained. 'Our salaries don't amount to much, but there's a chance to earn commission of sixpence in every pound at weekends and tuppence the rest of the week.'

'Well, we can't have that,' said Charles, pressing a half crown in her hand. 'At least, not this week.'

'Oh – sir!'

'Think nothing of it,' he said, giving her another smile that had her blushing to the roots of her blonde hair.

'That was very generous of you,' Lily said when they were on their own. 'She was very pleased.'

He looked into Lily's eyes. 'I'm lucky enough to be enjoying myself so much. Why shouldn't I be generous?'

Lily blushed once more. She was keenly aware of the female interest around them. Charles began to tell her what kind of things he wanted to buy and seemed unconcerned by the attention. Lily felt as though she was the only woman in the room. It proved very difficult, in fact almost impossible, to keep her mind on the conversation.

After leaving Lyons, Charles drove them to Shepherd Market in Mayfair. The tiny shops were a stark contrast to the grandeur of Piccadilly and Park Lane close by, but had exactly what they were looking for. Even though the buildings were old and shabby, they possessed an old world charm and plenty of curios, foods, furniture and jewellery to choose from.

'All this was built in the eighteenth century by a builder called Edward Shepherd,' Charles told Lily as he guided her around the small lanes. 'To me, this place has a timeless quality. And as you'll see, I'm sure we'll find one or two bargains.'

As they scoured the tiny shops, they found brass pieces and silverware, pottery and ornaments and dozens of things that Lily had never even seen before. But when she came upon a pair of Georgian figurines, she recognized their beauty immediately.

Charles purchased them at once and arranged for them to be delivered. In the next shop Lily chose larger furniture, a chair in watered pink silk for one of the bedrooms, a bookcase for the back parlour and a thick, Indian rug for the drawing room.

With their task accomplished, they found the car again and Charles drove them to the Embankment. After parking they strolled slowly along, past manicured lawns and secret little gardens. Near Hungerford Bridge, they paused to admire Cleopatra's Needle and its guardian sphinx. Although of a different culture and brought many years before from Alexandria, Lily thought how the monument didn't look out of place. The pathways around it seemed to glow in its honour under the leafless trees. A smell of smoke and salty water rose in the air.

She bent to read the small commemoration. 'A ship was designed to carry it to England,' she murmured in wonder. 'Then it nearly capsized in the Bay of Biscay. It's amazing it ever got here at all.'

'Yes, they are treacherous seas off the coast of Spain,' said Charles, nodding as he bent beside her. 'I've crossed them myself when I was at sea.'

Lily turned, wide-eyed. 'You were in the Navy?'

'Yes, in 1917. I enlisted, eager to serve my country. The sea held many romantic notions for a young man of twenty but the war soon changed all that.'

'My dad don't talk about it much. He was in France and said he was lucky to come home.'

'He was indeed. Many good men died there.'

'Half of our street lost a loved one. Mr James died, that's Ben and Reube's dad. And Sylvester, Hattie's brother, got gassed. He's still very ill because of it.'

'My sympathies are with his family. I saw men suffer and die, but to live and continue to suffer . . .' His voice tailed off and Lily looked at her companion, admiring all she saw. This was a man who was brave as well as handsome and kind; he understood what the men had gone through in the war.

'Let's sit here for a while and rest,' he gestured to a bench nearby.

The river breeze blew her hair from her face as they made themselves comfortable. The exercise had kept the chill at bay. Lily's cheeks were flushed with excitement.

'Have you enjoyed today, Lily?' he asked suddenly.

'Oh, yes, I have.'

He smiled. 'I hope I haven't exhausted you.'

'No. I enjoyed going in those shops and choosing lovely things, especially as I didn't have to pay for them.' She glanced up at him. He was so good looking she had quite forgotten that they must have walked for miles. She didn't care; every minute in his company had been enthralling.

'You have very good taste.'

She blushed again. 'I don't know if I have. But I know what's good and what isn't from working on the stall.'

'Invaluable experience,' he nodded.

'I'm lucky to have a job I like. I'd hate to work in a factory.'

'Surely you wouldn't do that?' he asked, looking shocked.

'It's much better pay.'

'But the repetitive work would be intolerable, wouldn't it?'

She shrugged. 'I'd have to do it if there was nothing else.'

A frown deepened across his brow. 'So what is it you want to do with your life, Lily?'

She paused, looking under her lashes. 'Well, like every girl, I suppose. To marry and have a family of my own.'

'But you have tremendous business acumen. You have taste and style. And for a young woman, a great deal of confidence. You could do a lot with your skills, Lily.'

She laughed. 'Such as?'

'Have you considered working for a bigger concern than a market stall? Perhaps a specialist in furniture?'

Lily had never thought of such a thing. She just did her job and was happy to do it. The experience of selling old but interesting things had taught her a lot. She knew she would never be happy in a factory, but as for working for a big concern . . .? Before she could give her reply Charles spoke again.

'Or perhaps there's someone special in your life and you already know your path? For instance, that young man of yours – Ben James.'

'I've told you, he's not my young man,' Lily said adamantly. 'Just a good friend.'

He looked at her intently. 'I see.'

Why should he be concerned about Ben? she wondered. Or whether there was anyone special in her life? Her pulse began to race as she tried to work out why he was asking these questions.

He turned and slid an arm along the top of the bench. 'Lily, would you agree to help me again?' Sensing her hesitation, he added, 'Those figurines you chose today would have escaped my attention. A man's point of view is so limited.'

Lily could hardly contain her excitement, just thinking about being with him again made her tremble. There might be things about him that she didn't understand but the mystery made him all the more exciting.

'Sunday mornings are the only time I have free.'

'Well then, perhaps our next trip should be to

Petticoat Lane. I have bought many bargains there in the past.'

Lily's eyes lit up. 'I love it there. Uncle Noah used to take me.'

'Well then, shall we say in a week's time?' She nodded and he gave her one of his wonderful smiles. 'Thank you, Lily.'

As they sat in the silence, dusk fell around them, Lily thought this was the nearest to heaven she had ever come.

Then a small group of Salvation Army officers appeared. The women's bonnets were tied with bows and the men wore flat caps, their red and blue uniforms were clearly distinguishable under the lamplight. They sang 'Onward Christian Soldiers' and it brought a lump to Lily's throat; she would always remember this night.

When it was over, Charles turned to her. He sighed deeply, his warm breath curling up in the cold air. 'Lily, as much as I don't want this evening to end, I must drive you home.'

She looked into his gaze and, like him, was reluctant to end their time together. His eyes were dark and shimmered in the lamplight. Their unswerving intensity made Lily's heart race. For as long as she lived she would never forget this day.

It was Sunday night and Ben was standing at the bar of the Quarry. He and Reube were making their ales last as Reube enjoyed another rendition of the fight with the

Blackshirts. Ben noticed his tale had become taller and longer and smiled as he listened to this version, growing like Pinocchio's nose. It was accepted on the island that everyone supported each other when it came to outside disputes. And after a few ales, the loyalties were fierce and passionate.

'If I'd been there I would have knocked his block off,' remarked Solly Maine, a warehouseman from Cubitt Town. He was small in stature and past his prime but he pulled back his shoulders and showed off a bull chest.

Ben grinned. 'You might get your chance,' he said, nodding at Reube. 'They could come back for seconds, by the sound of it.'

'Ain't nothing to what we had just after the war,' Solly shrugged. 'Remember the siege of Sidney Street?'

'They wasn't Blackshirts though, they were villains,' pointed out Harry Ward. 'Now if you're talking skulduggery, them Sabinis have got to take the biscuit.'

Ben listened, as the group of men began to rekindle the heroic and not so heroic past. People's ordinary everyday lives were normally unaffected by the realities of gangs and murderers, but tonight his brother's little 'episode' had caught the imagination and made for a lively discussion.

'Them Sabinis are still operating locally I hear,' nodded Solly Maine as he wiped the froth from his top lip, and the men all nodded.

'They're into the tracks more, though,' Harry Ward

spoke from under his cap. 'Clocked a few of their men round the Newbury and Epsom pitches.' When everyone frowned at him, realizing that he'd had money in his pocket for such ventures, he added quickly, 'As you know I like the occasional punt but only when I'm flush.'

'If it's the dogs and gee-gees they're concentrating on,' Ben, drew back their attention, 'then good luck to them. The heat is off everyone else.'

'The coppers should do something about them Blackshirts though,' nodded Ernie from across the bar. ''Stead of letting them get away with blue murder.'

'There was a time when the Italians would have sorted them out,' Don Harrison remarked. He hadn't found work in a month and was enjoying a free pint on Ben's behalf. 'The Cortesi brothers for instance, they was a real rough lot.'

Reube shook his head. 'The Cortesis have folded, old son, I know that for a fact. No, I have to say it meself, but me and Ted were the ones to teach them Blackshirts a lesson they won't forget.'

'A hundred and twenty boxes of fags went missing from Chalk Wharf the other day,' said Izzy Ware, a foreman at the East India Dock Company. 'Almost as much booze disappeared from the *Gloria*'s hold overnight.'

Ben took a gulp of his drink. He'd heard there had been a lot of pilfering lately, in fact he'd turned down a couple of deals himself. They smelt fishy. Not that he wasn't averse to a little stretching of the law, but nicking and transporting in big numbers was a mug's game. If you had a load of swag and got stopped at one of the bridgers, you might as well give yourself up there and then. There was no way off the island if the bridges were up and the boats going under.

'Is the *Gloria* still in dock?' asked Reube, obviously thinking along the same lines.

'They let her sail yesterday.'

'Where was she out of?'

'Copenhagen.'

'No wonder then,' said Reube, his eyebrows raised. 'I've heard them ships come down from Russia and serve tobacco and booze up to the English like bread and butter.'

Ben didn't doubt this. He'd often seen lorries running at dead of night after he'd parked the lorry up. It was a dangerous game and someone was on a generous back-hander. He knew he could make a good whack if he offered his services, but sooner or later the law swooped. When they did it was curtains for the lorry driver and all his load. Once upon a time he might have been tempted. In the early days when other drivers made five and six times as much as him in a week. He'd heard them boasting often enough, after a few jars. But, thank God, he'd had enough savvy to resist temptation.

'You all right, bruv?' Reube nudged his arm, bringing him back to the present.

'Yeah, was just thinking about me motor.' Ben finished his drink but decided not to have another. He needed a clear head for the following morning. He was off to Bermondsey with a load of bricks. It was supposed to be Monday's job, but he was going to collect his new toy. He couldn't wait to drive the Chariot.

'You'll need a lift up to Aldgate for your flashy new motor I 'spose,' Reube said, grinning.

'You offering?'

'Course.'

'What about the stall?'

'I'll get Lil set up and come back for you about ten, all right?'

'Have you got Pedro to help?'

'Yeah, he needs a drink for yesterday as well.'

Ben frowned as he heard this. 'Saturday?'

'Yeah, there was only me and him.'

'Where was Lil? Thought she was working all day now?'

Reube frowned, knitting his brow reflectively. 'Didn't I say? That bloke you sold the po to, he took her up West.'

For a moment Ben was mystified. 'What, this what's-his-name, Charles Grey?'

Reube put down his ale. 'That's him. Came to the stall to buy more stuff, but those bloody Blackshirts put him off. We didn't have nothing anyway. Told Lil he'd pay me for her time. Wanted her to help him choose more stuff. So I come out all right really. Just got to give Pedro a couple of bob and whatever's left over goes in the kitty.' Reube smiled broadly and turned to raise his

95

empty glass. 'One more, Ernie, for the road, ta mate.'

Ben stared at his brother, an unpleasant feeling settling in his stomach. That Charles Grey had looked up Lily again. But why? Because he wanted her advice again?

Ben straightened his back and twisted his neck in his collar. He felt constricted and uncomfortable. Why the dickens hadn't Reube mentioned this before? He was too busy with his sums!

As Ben's face darkened, he caught his reflection in the mirror. Was he any different to his brother? Nearly every penny he'd earned lately, had been saved for the Chariot. The thought of the motor had obsessed him. All he'd been able to think about was how the first thing he would do was to put his hands on the steering wheel and look over his shoulder at those thirty seats and imagine them all as ten bob notes!

Turning his back on the mirror, he took a deep breath. Clearing his throat, he pulled down his waistcoat. 'Snap out of it, you daft 'aporth,' he instructed himself sharply.

'What's that?' frowned Reube as he turned back to the bar.

'Nothing – nothing at all.'

'When are you going to drive that old bucket of yours into the river and do some real work?' Ted Shiner said as he came over to the bar and dropped his empty glass in front of Ernie.

'As soon as you start eating those rotten apples of yours,' returned Ben with a forced laugh.

'Ah, you're both in the wrong line,' said Reube

good-naturedly. 'Antiques and valuables – now there's money to be made in those.'

'What, your load of old junk?' Ted scowled, his heavy jaws wobbling. 'Bet you ain't even seen a genuine antique, let alone sold one.'

'Had a French clock the other day that Lily sold.'

'Those Frenchies are all con artists,' Ted pointed out. 'And anyway I'd buy a clock off Lily any day, just to see that girl's smile. Now she's your real asset, chum, not your fancy clocks.'

Reube aimed a playful punch at Ted's shoulder and as Ted bought himself ale, the group of men resumed their conversation. But Ben's mind had wandered again. What did Charles Grey want with Lily? He had to find out. Though he wasn't quite sure how.

Chapter Six

It was Thursday and Lily was in a hurry to get home and call on Hattie. They hadn't met up on Sunday as Sylvester had had a fit and the doctor was called. When Lily knocked, Hattie opened the door. She was still wearing her coat and hat. 'Come in.'

'How is Sylvester?' Lily stepped inside.

'He's in the parlour with Mum and Dad. The new pills the doctor gave him seem to be working. I've just got home from work.'

Lily followed Hattie into the kitchen. 'Something smells nice.'

'Mum's baking a pie for tea.'

Lily sat down by the stove. She took off her hat and scarf and Hattie did the same. 'Seems ages since we had a chat.'

'I've got a lot to tell you.'

'Is it about this Charles Grey?'

Lily looked up. 'What makes you say that?'

'Reube came round last night. Dad was giving Sylvester a wash down by the fire and he was starkers in the tub. He's been in bed so he niffed a bit but it was too cold to wash him outside. Anyway, Reube and me sat out here and he said ...' Hattie suddenly stopped mid sentence and looked round. 'I've got to have a fag, Lil. I haven't had one all day and I'm gasping.'

'Look, there's a roll-up on the draining board.' Lily knew that the Parks were all smokers. Any half-smoked cigarette was always kept in a saucer should anyone want a quick puff. Unlike her own mum, Mrs Parks agreed to smoking in the house.

'Oh yeah, Dad always keeps one or two there in case he runs short.'

Hattie lifted the papery thin cigarette from the saucer. She found a match and lit up, breathing in deeply. 'Oh, that's better.' She sat down beside Lily with a sigh. 'Madame Nerys didn't half get on me wick today. Do this, do that, and make it twice as fast as last time I did it. Which I can tell you, don't make sewing diamante onto a satin gown very pleasurable.'

'Who is it for?'

'A Mrs Bennet. One of the country set with more money than she knows what to do with. Madame Nerys wants every stitch doing to perfection. Anyway, I did it, but me fingers are like pincushions.' She spread out her hands and Lily saw the tiny red blisters on the tips of them.

'Oh, Hat, ain't you got a thimble?'

'Course I have, but for that sort of job you'd need ten. It'd be like wearing gloves.'

'Did you finish sewing them on?'

'Got the dress finished tonight.'

'I think you're clever.'

Hattie laughed. 'If I was clever I'd have me own workrooms by now. Not be slaving for someone else.'

'Is that what you'd like? To be in business for yourself?'

Hattie nodded slowly as she chewed on a piece of tobacco and picked it from her lips. 'Yeah, I 'spose.'

'You haven't said that before.'

Hattie looked down in her lap. 'Well, it's all pie in the sky, ain't it? Someone like me owning me own place . . .'

Lily realized they'd never talked like this before. She had known her friend all her life and yet she'd never heard her express these sentiments. 'You might get your wish one day.'

Hattie looked up sharply, her neat brown hair was shining and twisted into kiss-curls, her make-up looked flawless even at the end of the day. Lily thought if anyone deserved to get on in life, it was Hattie. 'Anyway,' said Hattie, waving aside Lily's comment, 'what were we talking about? Oh yes, that bloke from Poplar. Reube told me he came to the market and asked you to go up to town with him.'

Lily nodded, thinking Hattie looked bored. 'Yes, to buy things for his house.'

'What sort of things?'

'A lovely pair of figurines. They were perfect, without any cracks. And a chair and a nice big rug.'

'Did you choose them?'

'Of course. That's what I was there for.' Lily was beginning to think that no one gave her much credit for knowing about such things.

'So what else did you do?'

'We went into Lyons for a bite to eat.' Lily was pleased as this seemed to make an impression.

'Lyons!' Hattie exclaimed. 'Reube didn't mention *Lyons*!'

'I don't think I told him.' Reube hadn't asked much about her day. He'd only really been interested in the three pounds that Charles had given her to pay him.

'Did you go Dutch?'

'No, he paid. The cakes were delicious, Hattie, and all served up so nicely.'

'It seems he has money to burn!'

Lily shrugged. 'I wouldn't say that.'

'Are you seeing him again?'

Lily was reluctant to say she was as Hattie was scowling suspiciously. But as Charles was coming to call for her this time, she had no choice as his car would be parked in the road.

'Yes, on Sunday.'

'But there ain't no shops open on Sundays.'

'We're going to Petticoat Lane.' Lily felt her cheeks going crimson.

Hattie blew out a stream of smoke and allowed the

silence to lengthen. Eventually she knitted her brow again. 'Well, you won't have time to see me, then.'

'Course I will. I told him I always saw my friend in the afternoon.'

'Don't bother on my account. Why don't you take all day?'

'One day you might like to meet him,' Lily suggested.

Her friend fiercely stubbed out the cigarette. 'Why's that then?'

'Because you're my best mate.'

'He don't even know me.'

'I've told him all about you.'

Hattie looked at her with her dark brown gaze and said nothing. Lily glanced at the clock above the mantel. 'Well, I'd better go, then.' She pushed back her chair ready to get up.

'What about them Blackshirts?' said Hattie suddenly, the sparkle returning to her eyes. 'My Reube certainly gave them what for! I'll say that about him, he ain't no coward. It takes a lot to light his fuse, but if anyone touches his property or threatens him . . .' Hattie let her words linger before she raised her eyebrows and giggled. 'It was a good job his ankle was better to kick with.'

Lily smiled. 'His ankle certainly didn't hold him back.'

'Did you see the fight?'

'Yes.'

'It must have been exciting.'

'Not really. I felt quite frightened.'

'What's there to be scared of?' Hattie said dismissively. 'Reube told me he's not going to let thugs like them worry him. He's put a whopping great stick under the stall in case they come back. So you never have to worry, Lil. You've always got Reube to protect you.'

Lily wanted to say that it was Charles Grey who had protected her, but she could imagine Hattie's response if she did. No, she would just have to let Reube take the credit. It was too late now to tell anyone what had really happened.

'For once I had something to boast about at work,' continued Hattie, oblivious to Lily's thoughts. 'I get fed up listening to Ada Hacket, one of our machinists who comes from Stepney. She's as old as the hills, but good at her job. Anyway, her dad was a member of the Green Gate gang, if you please.'

'Who were they?'

'They used to come across the water with the Lambeth Boys looking for fights this side of the river. They all wore belts with these sharp buckles on 'em. Their trick was to whip them off and slash their victims, the poor buggers. Course when the law tackled them after they didn't find no knives, did they? And so they got off scott free.'

Lily shivered. 'I'm glad they ain't around now.'

Hattie was into her stride now. 'Then there was the Blind Beggar gang, from the pub of the same name, who were mostly pickpockets, but were known for driving a man's eye out with an umbrella ferrule!'

'Hattie, you're putting the wind up me.'

'Oh, I'm just having a laugh.'

Just then, Mrs Parks came into the kitchen. 'Hello, Lily dear. I didn't know you was here.'

'Hello, Mrs Parks. How is Sylvester?'

'Much better. We've got some new pills.'

'Oh, that's good.'

'Would you like to stay for supper?'

Lily smiled. 'Thanks, Mrs Parks, but I'd better get home to help Mum with ours. I just popped in to see Hattie.'

'Well, give me love to your mother. I saw her at the doctors last week. Is she better?'

Lily frowned. She didn't know her mother had been to the doctors. 'Er, yes, yes she is.'

As Lily left the Parks' she was thinking about her mum going to the doctors and not telling her. What was wrong? Was she ill? Why had she kept it a secret?

Lily slid her hand through the letterbox to draw up the key string. Suddenly a hand grabbed her arm.

She jumped. 'Oh, Ben! You gave me a scare.'

'Sorry.'

'Where are you off to?'

'I'm on me way home.'

She waited for him to speak. But he just stood there.

'Is there something wrong?' she asked eventually.

'No, why should there be?'

Lily pulled up her collar. The breeze was whistling

around her ears. She shivered. She needed to see her mum. 'Well, I'd better go in now.'

He took her arm. 'Lily, I—'

The door suddenly opened and Uncle Noah peered out. 'Blimey, gel, you're not courting at this time of the day, are you?'

'No, course not, Uncle Noah, it's only Ben.'

'Oh, blimey, so it is.'

'Good evening, Mr Kelly. Keepin' all right are you?'

'Not so bad, son, thanks.' He turned to Lily. 'Your supper's waiting, love.'

'I'm coming. What was you going to say?' she asked Ben quickly.

'Nothing, not really.' He moved awkwardly away. 'Night then all.'

'Night, Ben.'

'You're late tonight,' her uncle said as he shut the door behind them.

Lily hung up her hat and coat. 'I went in to see Hattie. Where's Mum?' she asked anxiously.

'In the kitchen. And before you go along, I'll warn you. It's been a ruddy awful day.'

Lily's heart sank.

'But I thought you were ill!' exclaimed Lily as she sat at the table in front of her unfinished meal.

'Me? I'm all right. What made you think that?'

'Mrs Parks. She said she saw you at the doctors.'

'Oh,' sighed her mother wearily. 'I thought Flo Parks

might be a bit more discreet than that, seeing as how she has Sylvester to contend with and don't want every nosy parker knowing their business.'

'She only asked me how you were.'

'What did you say?'

Lily clattered down her knife and fork. 'What could I say? I would have looked a right chump if I'd said I didn't know you was ill.'

'You needn't use that tone with me, young lady.'

'I was worried you had something and didn't tell me,' Lily protested.

'Well, it was for your father I went to the doctor. For his cough. But, as I've just explained, the medicine didn't do any good. And . . . well, he was taken poorly at work today and had to come home.'

'Why didn't you tell me what was going on?'

'Because, like Flo, I didn't want it spread all over the neighbourhood.'

'But I'm your daughter!'

Josie nodded impatiently. 'I know, I know. But you might have said something at the market by accident. I didn't want to run that risk.'

'I wouldn't have said anything if you'd told me not too,' Lily said, feeling hurt that her mother thought she couldn't be trusted. 'And what's wrong anyway with people knowing?'

Josie sighed again. 'Don't you see, ducks? Healthy men can't even get jobs. Ill ones are discounted completely.'

'But Dad shouldn't be working on a skin ship with a cough like that. He shouldn't—'

Josie jumped up, clutching the towel against her. Her eyes filled with tears. 'I don't need you to tell me what's bad for your dad, Lily,' she cried in a strangled voice. 'I was hoping for a bit of support not criticism.' She turned and bumped into the chair then hurried out of the room.

Lily looked at her uncle. 'What did I say?'

'A bit too much, love. Your mum's very worried. I did warn you.'

'What happened at the docks?'

'They had to carry him out of the hold he was working in. Collapsed, poor bloke, and couldn't stop coughing. One of the foremen brought him home in his van.'

'Has the doctor been?'

'Not yet.'

'But why?'

'He might get up tomorra.' Her uncle stared through his pince-nez. 'A good day's rest will see him better.'

Lily knew it was the money. It was *always* the money. Even a shilling for a doctor's visit was thought of as extravagant.

'I'll go up and see him.'

'I should speak to your mother first. And don't go saying as we should have the doc as she knows that herself. It was your dad that forbade her to call him.'

Lily looked down. She felt ashamed of herself for getting into a panic. 'I just wish I'd been told.'

'There was nothing you could do. Your mum didn't want to heap more worry on your shoulders. Now, calm down and go and make your peace.'

'Sorry I upset you, Mum,' Lily apologised when she found her mother upstairs.

'And I'm sorry you had to hear what you did from Flo Parks,' Josie whispered as she stood on the landing. She held a dark blue medicine bottle in her hand. 'Your dad has had a spoonful of this and he's resting easier.'

'Will he be all right?'

'Course he will. He just needs rest.'

'Can I go in?'

'Yes, he'd like to see you.' Josie gave her daughter a smile. 'But he might drop off. He's very tired.'

Lily went into the bedroom. Her dad was propped up by pillows and looked pale and old. His hair was almost grey now, as though it had happened overnight. He looked much smaller, lost under the sheets and covers. His eyes were closed and he was gently snoring. She sat on the chair beside the bed and waited.

All day Friday Lily wondered how she could get a message to Charles Grey to tell him she couldn't go out on Sunday. With her dad ill, she was needed at home. But by the evening she still hadn't come up with an idea. Dewar Street had been half an hour's drive in Ben's lorry and the bus would take even longer. She was out at work all day tomorrow. Would Reube let her have time off?

That night when she got home, her dad was sitting up in his chair by the fire. He wore his dressing gown and slippers and gave her a big smile.

'Hello, love.'

'Should you be up, Dad?'

'I feel better on me feet.' He laughed and coughed at the same time. 'Well, on me backside.'

'And he don't cough so much,' agreed her mother.

'I'll be as right as rain next week.'

Lily sat beside him. 'Please, Dad, don't go back on the skin boats.'

He coughed again and hit his chest with his fist. 'What's all this about?'

'Mum and me worry when you're on that job.'

'It's the only one I'm likely to get. The dockyards are laying off men by the score.'

'I know, but we'll manage.'

He took her hand. 'You're a lovely daughter, Lily. I don't tell you enough. You're the apple of me and your mother's eye.'

'In that case, will you do as we ask?'

He gave a weak chuckle. 'I let meself in for that, didn't I?'

'At least take next week off. Get your strength back.'

'Your mother said that.'

'So will you do it?'

He rested his head back on the chair. 'I'll give it some thought.'

Lily knew that would mean only one thing; by hook

or by crook he would get back to work. He just wanted to keep her and her mother happy for now.

Lily sat back in the chair as the fire crackled and the smoke curled up the chimney. How much coal was there left in the bunker? She hadn't thought to check this week. And food. What did they have in the larder? Had her mother managed to clear the arrears of the rent? Thank goodness it was pay day tomorrow.

The warmth of the fire radiated on her cold cheeks. As she gazed into the deep red glow of the fire, her dad coughed every now and then, but he seemed comfortable. They could hear Uncle Noah and her mother in the kitchen. They were behaving themselves for once. Lily felt her eye lids flutter; it was the end of a long week. Tomorrow she would think of a way to cancel her arrangement with Charles Grey.

Suddenly there was a tap at the front door. Lily jumped up. Was it Hattie? But when she got to the door, she couldn't believe her eyes. It was Charles Grey.

'Good evening, Lily,' he said, politely removing his hat. Just beyond him she saw the ruby red car parked in the street.

'Oh, Mr – er, Charles,' she corrected herself, blushing.

'I'm extremely sorry for intruding on your evening.'

'Is something the matter?'

'No, but—'

'Lily, who is it?' Her mother's footsteps came down the hall. Lily heard a gasp.

'Goodness gracious – is it your gentleman?'

Lily blushed to the roots of her hair. She daren't look at Charles. She knew that her mother had made a good guess from the description she had given. Before she could make introductions, Charles Grey had stretched out his hand.

'I'm so pleased to meet you, Mrs Bright. And equally apologetic for disturbing your family at this time of night.'

'You aren't,' said her mother, taking the outstretched hand. 'We can't have you standing on the doorstep. Come in.'

'But you must be busy.'

'Not too busy to forget me manners,' Josie cast her daughter a reproachful glance. 'Let me take your coat and come along into the warm.'

Before Lily had chance to speak, Charles Grey had stepped inside. Her uncle was charging towards them and her mother was taking their visitor's heavy overcoat and hat.

Lily watched, breathless and shocked, her heart beginning to pound in the way it always did whenever she saw this man. If she was dreaming, she had better pinch herself and wake up soon.

In the kitchen Lily watched her mother put aside the big pot of stew.

'We'll have it later, ducks.'

'I didn't know he was coming,' Lily was flustered.

'He's more than welcome.'

'I don't know what he wants,' Lily was all fingers and thumbs as she made the tea. She hadn't told her family she was seeing Charles on Sunday. What if he told them?

'Best china, Lily.'

'Oh yes.'

'Now, whilst you're doing that, I'll go and put on my other cardigan.'

Lily watched her mother hurry off. Then she looked down at her own clothes. She hadn't changed from her working skirt and blouse and well worn navy blue jumper. She was even wearing her old boots! The bootmender had stitched round the soles at least. Lily looked in the half mirror over the draining board in which her father and uncle shaved. It had been broken for years but no one had bothered to replace it. She tidied her hair, running her fingers through the waves. She looked very pale. It was probably the shock of finding Charles Grey on the doorstep!

When she took in the tea Charles Grey had made himself comfortable on the couch. One long, tailored leg was crossed over the other and he smiled up at her.

'You shouldn't have gone to the trouble, Lily.'

She gave him the white, bone china cup taken from the best set. Then handed a cup and saucer each to her father and uncle.

'Thanks, ducks.'

'Lovely, Lil.'

Her mother came in the door. 'Has everyone got a drink?'

'Yes, Mum.' Lily smiled. Her mother had taken off her turban and put on a neat cardigan.

'We was just discussing the docks,' said her uncle as they all made themselves comfortable. 'And those ruddy skin ships.'

Lily glanced slyly at Charles Grey. He hadn't batted an eyelid at her uncle's language. In fact he seemed as much at home in their front room as he had at Dewar Street.

'These dreadful conditions should not be allowed to exist,' he said as he gazed at her father. 'Certainly they must explain this bout of ill health, Mr Bright.'

'Without the skin boats I would be out of pocket,' said her father weakly. 'Me and other casuals who don't have a permanent ticket.'

'To be forced into such a diabolical situation is unthinkable.'

'It's been that way for years,' dismissed Uncle Noah. 'It's all the island knows. The docks is like a living being; it thrives and it ails and I'm sorry to say in the Great Depression it ails more than it thrives.'

'But surely the employers must take into consideration the health of their workforce?' posed their guest.

Bob Bright shook his head slowly. 'They couldn't give a monkey's uncle, sir. In fact, our distress suits them. There's always competition for the jobs and those that drop out ain't missed. After the war, for those that came home, we'd lost our positions. We was termed as casuals, and that's where we've been ever since.'

'And your union? What help do you receive from them?'

'Bugger all,' said Uncle Noah angrily. 'They're as bad as the PLA and the politicians. Them bosses line their own pockets first, always have done.'

'It's true,' Bob Bright nodded, hitting his chest as his voice weakened, 'in 'twenty-six we had the first general strike in history. The TUC was all promises to back the miners, and any of us that suffered repercussions from trade stopping,' he paused, getting his breath. 'We'll give you food and see you through, said the union mouthpiece. We'll see to it your families don't starve and you don't go cold. When the country seizes up, we'll make sure you're looked after. But what happened? The men, the workers, was hung out to dry.' He rested back in his chair, breathing heavily. 'Over six thousand of us went begging to the city wallahs, blokes I know who would've carved off an arm or a leg there and then to end the fiasco. But what happened? We lost our jobs after that, was thrown crumbs as we were so desperate and all because of promises broken. The unions, Baldwin, MacDonald, they're all the same, don't even breathe the same air as us. And you know what gets me, Mr Grey? We fought a war, was given exactly the same promises then. And what's happened? We're still starving. My daughter has to go out and work all hours to support a family that a man can't. She's twenty, a kid . . .' Her father's voice broke with emotion and he began to cough.

'Shush now, Bob,' her mother said, jumping up to help her husband drink water from a glass. 'Mr Grey don't want to know about our problems.'

'On the contrary, Mrs Bright,' Charles said gently, 'your husband has enlightened me.'

Lily looked at their guest. What would he think of them? Of her? He came from a different world.

'So what's your line of trade?' Uncle Noah said in a suspicious tone, as he regarded Charles Grey.

'I buy and sell furniture and interesting curios,' Charles replied. 'Some of which I export.'

'You're onto a good thing there.'

'Yes, the profession can be lucrative.'

'I was in the rag and bone business. Had a few nice pieces meself.'

'Indeed, Lily has spoken of it.'

Uncle Noah grinned. 'She's a Jill of all trades, our girl. Is a cracker on an 'orse too.'

Once more Lily blushed. How could she expect someone like Charles Grey to be interested in her life?

'She rode old Samson round the yard without a saddle, light as any jockey,' her uncle continued to her embarrassment. 'And could drive that cart as good as me by the time she was six.'

Charles Grey looked into her eyes, 'A young woman of many talents.' He allowed his gaze to linger on her and then suddenly rose to his feet. 'I've taken up enough of your time,' he apologized in a sharp voice. 'I do hope I haven't worn out my welcome.'

'You come in any time you're round this way,' Josie replied. 'We shall always be pleased to see you.'

'Don't mind if I don't stand up,' said her father.

Charles bent and took his hand. 'It's been a privilege to meet you, sir.'

Lily watched as he did the same with Uncle Noah. 'I'll see you out,' she said quickly, averting her eyes from his.

At the front door, Lily helped him on with his coat. 'It's been a splendid half hour, Lily.'

'All you've heard is our complaints.'

'This is the real world and I am ashamed I have been ignorant of such hardship.'

Lily opened the door and he stepped out.

'Oh, I'd forgotten entirely what I came for!' Charles exclaimed as his breath rose up in the cold air. His eyes were so dark and beautiful that Lily felt breathless. 'I'm afraid on Sunday I've been called away on business.'

Even though Lily was about to tell him that she, too, couldn't keep their appointment, she felt disappointed. Had he decided that what he had seen of their home and her family was not good enough for him?

'I'm so sorry.'

'It doesn't matter.' She didn't want him to see how much this hurt, and she wondered what he really thought of them.

'Could we possibly meet the following Sunday?'

Lily's heart almost stopped. He wasn't making an excuse; he did want to see her after all! 'That is, of course, if your father is improved.' His face was full of concern. He smiled and it was one of his wonderful smiles that seemed to light up even the road.

She nodded, but even as she did so, she was not sure whether he really meant what he said.

Chapter Seven

On Sunday, Bob Bright got dressed. He shaved his growth of beard and sat downstairs in his chair, reading the newspaper.

'I'll be as right as rain tomorrow,' he told Lily, who, with her mother, made him promise to rest for a few more days.

'So when are we going to see Mr Grey again?' asked Lily's mother at the end of the day. The men had gone to bed and the two women were sitting in the parlour by the dying fire. They hadn't spoken again of Charles Grey's visit and Lily was surprised at the question. Had her mother been biding her time till now?

'He wants me to go to Petticoat Lane next Sunday.'

'What does he hope to find there?'

'A bargain, I expect.'

Josie was wearing her dressing gown and had her hair in pins. She raised her eyebrows as she picked up her knitting. 'A lot's been going on in your life, young lady.'

Lily smiled. 'Just work as usual.'

'You know what I mean. What does this gent want with you? Why does he need you to buy things?'

'Because I'm quite good at it.'

'Don't get too big for your boots now.'

No one seemed to give her much credit for her knowledge, Lily thought despondently. Even her parents took for granted what she did for a living.

Her mother sighed. 'Like your dad says, it don't do much for your pride when your daughter has to bring in the money.'

'Pride's expensive, Mum. It's a home to live in that counts.'

'You've got an old head on young shoulders, love.'

Lily laughed. 'I hope it don't look that old.'

Her mother looked up, her faded blue eyes on her daughter. 'If you did, Mr Grey wouldn't be asking you to work for him.'

Lily frowned. 'What do you mean?'

'If you were old and grey I don't suppose he'd want you.'

'If I was old and grey I wouldn't want his job.'

Josie smiled. 'You ain't going to answer my question are you?'

Lily smiled back. 'Which one?'

'What if he wants more?'

Lily felt a flush flow up her neck and into her cheeks. 'Mum, he ain't from our world. If you saw his house, you'd know.'

'Lily, he's a single older man and you are a beautiful

young woman. And he's lonely . . .' Her mother looked deep into her eyes. 'Just a small word of advice, ducks. If he's a true gent, he'll make things proper. He won't—' she paused as she chose her words, but ended with, 'try it on.'

Lily laughed. 'Course he won't, Mum!'

'Men are the same the world over no matter who they are.'

'Mum, he's a gentleman!'

'As long as he remembers he is.'

'He wouldn't "try anything on".'

Josie folded her arms. 'I'm just saying, as you've never really had a boy, only Ben.'

Lily laughed even more. 'Ben is like me brother.'

'Well, if you say so. To my mind – and your father's – we'd always hoped that marriage might be on the cards for you two.'

Lily didn't laugh this time. Her mum was serious. 'Ben ain't ever been romantic, Mum. I've always pitied the girl he'd end up with as he's such a flirt.'

Josie's eyebrows went up again. 'He may only be a flirt in front of you. What does he think of your Mr Grey?'

Lily shrugged. 'It's not his business.'

Josie sat back in the chair and sighed. 'Just make sure that you always remember you're a lady. And that's with a capital "L".'

As Lily lay in bed that night, she recalled the praise that Charles had given her in a business sense. It was nice to be told you had a talent. She wondered if he really would call for her next Sunday. Lily shivered as she thought of how she was beginning to feel about him. The notion of seeing him again made her feel alive and joyful.

Her thoughts drifted to Ben. Was her mother right? That he pretended to be a flirt to hide his feelings for her? But Lily couldn't believe that; they had known each other too long to feel anything more than brother and sisterly love.

She drew the covers over her as she imagined Charles Grey and his lovely dark eyes. It was a long while before she fell asleep.

It was Wednesday when Ben called round. He showed her four tickets he had bought for a dance on Saturday.

'I know it's a bit short notice, but I've just managed to get hold of them. Nudge, nudge, wink, wink, if you know what I mean.'

'Who from?'

'A mate of mine. They were two and six each to him, but I got him down to a bob. Anyway, the evening's on me and Reube, you girls are in for a treat.'

Lily looked away. 'I wish you'd asked me first, Ben.'

He frowned as they stood in the hallway. 'Why's that?'

'Well ...' She was trying to think of an excuse. On Sunday morning she was going to Petticoat Lane with Charles and had planned to wash her hair on

Saturday night and iron out her clothes. But instead she murmured, 'Dad's not gone back to work yet.'

'Is he still ill, then?'

'No, he's a lot better, but I think I should stay in.'

Her mum came out of the kitchen. 'Hello, son. It's nice to see you. How are you doing?'

'Fine thanks, Mrs Bright.' He shifted from foot to foot. 'Er, I was just asking Lil if she'd come to a dance on Saturday at the town hall but she's worried about her dad.'

Josie Bright smiled at her daughter. 'You go and enjoy yourself, love, you've not been out at all lately.'

'But Mum—'

'Your dad would be upset if he thought you refused because of him.'

'I'll give you a ride in me new motor,' said Ben, sticking out his chest proudly.

'Have you bought it yet?' asked Josie.

'You bet!'

'Well, we'll all want a go in that. Do we have to book seats?'

Ben laughed. 'Course not. You and Mr Bright are welcome to come for a spin any day of the week.'

Josie chuckled. 'I'll keep you to that as soon as my other half is better.' She went back into the kitchen.

'So that's settled then!' Ben exclaimed. 'We'll pick you up at half six. Doors open at seven.' He went to rush off then stopped, raising his hand to his head. 'I've just had a thought! Tell your dad I heard of a timber yard job going this morning. I'll make enquiries to see what it's about and let him know later.'

'Oh, all right. Thanks.'

He gave her a wink as he left.

Lily closed the door and leaned heavily against it. How could she have refused going to the dance without offending him? And why had her feelings changed? Dances were always enjoyable with her friends, but now, after what her mum had said, it seemed different.

'Who was that?' her dad asked when she went in the parlour and sat down.

'Just Ben.'

'Nice youngster that,' said Bob Bright.

'He said he's going to ask after a job for you with the timber people.'

Bob Bright lowered his newspaper, looking suddenly like his old self. 'A timber job, you say?'

'Yes.'

'They don't come up very often. That's good of the lad.'

'What would you have to do?'

'Stack all the timbers, I expect.'

'That's a heavy job, Dad.'

Bob Bright laughed and patted his daughter's hand. 'You women are never satisfied. What would you like me to do? Work in a stuffy old office all day?'

Lily wanted to say that was exactly what she wanted, somewhere nice and warm and far away from the infected carcasses of the skin ships.

'That boy's a good 'un,' remarked Bob Bright, giving her a knowing look. 'The type of lad I could look on as a son.'

Lily looked into her dad's hopeful eyes. How could she tell him that she wasn't interested in Ben that way?

It was Saturday night and Lily was pleased with her appearance. She had been reluctant to go to the dance, but now, as she looked in the mirror, some of the old excitement had returned. They had left market early as Reube wanted to wash and change too. Now Lily was dressed in a deep pink georgette dress, with a twenties style dropped waist. She had bought it second-hand years ago, but after adding three strands of beads, all in different shades of grey, and a deep grey chiffon scarf, it looked quite attractive. Although she had no matching footwear, her bar strap shoes went well enough. Having washed her hair the night before, Lily had tried to straighten it overnight. Carefully dampening it and tying on a scarf, it had been much straighter this morning. But later, in a brief shower of rain, it had sprung back into its bouncy waves. Borrowing a thin strand of pink silk from an under bodice, she looped it across her forehead and tied it at the back of her head. The idea had been fashionable in the twenties, but was it now? What would Hattie wear? The last time the four of them had been out together was late summer. The dance had been held at the Dockland Settlement, a club for the young people of the island. It had been a wonderful evening.

She'd last worn this dress then, but had teamed it with a blue overblouse. Would anyone recognize it tonight?

Her mother put her head round the door. 'You nearly ready, ducks?' she called. Then when she saw Lily she came in. 'You look lovely, Lily.'

'Do I?'

'That pink suits you. It makes your eyes bluer.'

'As long as it don't make me eyes look pink!' Lily laughed.

'That's better. It's nice to see you smile. It worries me that you don't get the chance to go out and dress up like young girls should.'

'I'm happy, Mum. You shouldn't worry over me. I'd get meself a job in a factory, you know, if I thought it would keep Dad off the skin boats.'

Josie smiled radiantly. 'You won't have to do that, love. You'll be pleased to know he won't be going on them any more.'

Lily gasped. 'I thought he wasn't going to take any notice of what we said?'

'You thought right, he wasn't.'

'What's made him change his mind?'

'Young Ben James.'

'Ben?' Lily frowned. '*He* persuaded Dad not to go?'

'He got your dad the timber job.'

Lily walked slowly towards her mother. 'He did? How?'

'The Good Lord only knows. But Ben called by this

morning and took your father up to the yard and he was taken on.'

'You mean Dad's got the job?'

Her mother nodded. 'The wage mind, ain't so good, just fifteen bob a week, but we'll be fifteen bob better off with your dad breathing fresh air and not skins.'

Lily grabbed her mother's arm. Tears sprang to her eyes. 'Oh, Mum, that's wonderful.'

'I hope you'll remember to say that to Ben.' Her mother smiled anxiously at her.

'Of course I will. I'm very grateful.'

'We all are.' Her mother's eyes were conveying a message. But Lily didn't want to acknowledge it. She knew that her parents felt grateful to Ben for his good deed. They were hoping that tonight would make a difference to what she had said about her feelings for him.

Lily turned away and picked up her purse. The tears of relief for her father had quickly evaporated as she began to think what this would mean to her personally.

It was hot and stuffy on the town hall dance floor. Crowded with couples with their arms wound round each other, it was hard to breathe. So now they had come to sit down at the table and drink their lemonades.

Lily had danced every dance, either with Reube or Ben. Once, when the boys had gone to buy drinks, she and Hattie had danced with strangers, two young men who were good at the waltz. They'd both giggled a lot afterwards as they sat in their seats.

'Mine trod on me corn,' said Hattie, rubbing her toe, trying to stifle her laughter as Lily nodded.

'Mine had a grip like a vice. I thought he was glued to me hand,' laughed Lily.

When Reube and Ben returned, they pretended to get annoyed they'd been abandoned. Lily and Hattie said what good dancers the other two had been but couldn't keep up the pretence as Reube and Ben had looked forlorn.

It was now half past nine and the band had paused for refreshment. They had played a selection of boogie woogie and swing jazz tunes. Bodies had flown all over the place. Some couples had done the Lindy Hop from America and everyone had stood clear. Legs and arms went everywhere as the girls were thrown skywards and under their partner's legs.

The lights were up and the gleaming boards of the wooden floor were being cleared of any unwanted debris. As Lily and her friends laughed and joked, she thought of the good times they had always had together. She was lucky to have such a good dancing partner in Ben, he made every dance effortless, unlike the tailor's dummy who had stuck to her like glue in the waltz. Reube wasn't as smooth or talented with his steps, but he partnered Hattie perfectly who was very dramatic with her head, shoulders and facial expressions.

The evening so far had been a success. They had travelled up in the charabanc, waving to the pedestrians as they passed. But parking had been a problem as Ben hadn't quite got the hang of reversing. Ignoring the rude comments he'd drawn from his passengers, he had finally found a small stretch of wasteland close by.

Now, as Lily gazed at Hattie and Reube they looked in love. As the lights began to dim, they held hands, with eyes only for each other. Hattie had worn a beautiful calf length chiffon dress and matching silk shoes. Her dark brown hair had been cut carefully into her preferred Eton Crop. Reube was wearing a dark suit and dickie-bow tie. Lily always noted that when Hattie wore shoes with a good heel, as she did tonight, Reube pulled himself up straight to partner her. Ben, on the other hand, was so lean and lanky he towered above Lily. Tonight he looked dashing in light grey. His brown hair was combed back and Lily thought she could smell a certain pomade, an exotic lotion, as she danced with him. These were her friends, and she loved them. But she was not *in* love with Ben, as Hattie was with Reube.

'Hey, Funny Face! What are you thinking?' Ben was staring at her, his arm around the back of her chair. His light grey eyes were bright and sparkling.

'I was thinking about what you've done for me dad.'

'You mean the job at the timber yard?'

'Course I do. We don't know how to thank you.'

'I didn't do it for thanks.'

As there was no music there was no need to shout for the first time in the evening. Lily knew she had to make him see how grateful she was. 'I know you didn't, but it means he won't have to go back to the docks.'

'No one should have to do what he did there.'

'That's what Mum and me said to him, but he wouldn't listen.'

'Well, he has now.'

'You must have done something, Ben, as there had to be others after that job.'

He smiled slowly. 'I shouted "Fire" and the others ran away.'

'Now you're kidding me.'

He laughed and leaned forward. 'No, honest, it was just that we struck lucky. And bear in mind, the wage ain't a fortune.' He lay his hand on her shoulder and gently pressed it. 'Now p'raps you can have a bit of time off yourself.'

'I'll think about it.' Lily could feel the warmth of his fingers and the gentle, intimate pressure that was different from ever before.

'You're only young, Lil. I don't like to see you working so hard. Now that your dad is fixed up, you could drop the Saturday afternoons at market and come out with me.'

Lily sat back a little. Had that been his intention when finding the job for her dad? Had he said anything about this to her parents?

'Would you come out tomorrow morning for a drive?' he asked when she didn't speak.

Lily didn't want to hurt his feelings, but she knew she must tell him about Charles. 'I'm sorry, Ben, but I can't.'

'Why not?'

'I'm going out—'

'On a Sunday morning?' he interrupted, his hand dropping away. 'Where to?'

Lily swallowed and mustered her courage. 'Charles Grey has asked me to help him buy more things at Petticoat Lane.'

Lily saw the change in his expression. She wanted to dispel the coldness that suddenly came into his eyes, but as she was trying to think of something, the band began to play again.

Hattie jumped up beside her. 'Come on, you two lovebirds, this is a good one,' she called as 'I Can't Give You Anything But Love Baby' resounded out.

Lily blushed as she looked back at Ben. He was still sitting down, his eyes staring up at her.

As everyone crowded on the floor, Lily waited. Slowly he got up and took her into his arms. But she knew as they danced in silence that she had hurt him deeply.

'Have a good night, Lil?' Uncle Noah stood in his dressing gown and slippers as Lily hung up her coat.

'Yes, thanks. I'm not too late, am I? It didn't end till eleven and then we had to walk to the bit of wasteland that Ben parked on.'

'What's the new motor like?'

Lily followed him into the kitchen. 'It's not meant for around the town really. It's so big. With thirty seats to fill you need a lot of space to turn it round.'

'It'll take a bit of practice no doubt.'

'That's what Ben said.'

He picked up the kettle that had already boiled and half filled the teapot. 'Here you are. It's a bit stewed from before your dad and mum went to bed. I said I'd wait till you got in to bolt the door.'

'Thanks, Uncle Noah.'

'Well, I'm off to get me z's. Dare say you need your beauty sleep too. Is it in the morning you're seeing your gent again?'

Lily looked up at her uncle and smiled. 'We're off to Petticoat Lane to look for a bargain.'

'Remember when I used to take you up on the cart? How we'd drive past and I'd stop to see my old mate from the china stall? Don't 'spect he'll be there any more, but give the Lane a "hello" from me.' He bent and kissed the top of her head. 'Night, love.'

Lily heard him climb the stairs. She sipped the warm, stewed tea and thought over the evening. Ben had said very little on the way home. Hattie and Reube had chosen to sit in seats at the rear. They hadn't been aware of anyone but each other. When Ben had delivered them all safely, she and Hattie had watched Ben and Reube drive off to the Quarry. It was then that Hattie had landed her bombshell.

'Lily,' Hattie had said breathlessly, holding her arm very tightly. 'I've got something to tell you.'

The stars twinkled above them as Lily held her breath in anticipation. 'What, Hat?'

'Reube says he wants us to get engaged.'

Lily could see her friend could hardly contain her excitement. 'What did you say?'

'I said yes, of course.'

Lily had hugged her close. 'Congratulations, Hat. You make a lovely couple.'

Hattie wouldn't let her go as they stood in the silent, dark street. 'I wish we could make it a double engagement. Wouldn't it be lovely if we could do it together? After all, Ben is crackers about you.'

'Hattie, I don't want to get married.'

'Oh, Lil, it's not that bloke again, is it?'

'If you mean Charles, no, it's not him. I just ain't in love with Ben, that's all.'

Hattie had stepped back and sighed. Then shrugging her shoulders she had said goodnight and gone indoors. Lily had felt desperate. Why was everyone trying to pair them up? She didn't want to lose her friends. But neither did she want to lose Charles.

As Lily thought this over, she washed up her cup and saucer and made her way to bed. No matter what had happened at the dance, she wouldn't trade being with Charles tomorrow for all the tea in China.

It was, as Charles had promised, an early start. She heard his car arrive at eight o'clock and wondered, as she tiptoed down the stairs and opened the front door, if anyone was looking out from their windows.

Charles opened the passenger door and helped her in. She soon forgot all her doubts and worries. His immaculate appearance was almost too much to absorb, from the way his dark hair was hidden under a smart brown felt hat and his overcoat in dark brown wool clung to his broad shoulders.

Soon Love Lane was behind them and they were driving along the Westferry Road. The docks were still and only the seagulls screeched above them. The engine was a comforting purr and although it was cold, once again he provided a warm blanket.

Lily had worn her one and only best coat that he had seen before and couldn't be disguised, but she hadn't worn a hat this time. At the crack of dawn this morning, she had washed her hair. The water had been freezing, but she had lit the fire in the front room and her hair had soon dried. No amount of trying to straighten it overnight had worked before and so she hadn't even tried. After all, he had commented on its appearance on their trip up West. Whilst drying it she had placed her index and middle fingers in the waves, encouraging rather than trying to disguise its natural curl.

Lily looked out on the morning, her heart beating fast. A streak of blue sky between the houses slowly filled with a blush. Like a lovely pink rose opening up, the day was beginning and she was eager to share it with her companion.

There were so many clothes, Lily thought she was in heaven. No wonder Petticoat Lane was called what it was, and not Hog Lane as it had been called in the early 1800s! Stall upon stall of clothing, sold at knock-down prices, so that she wanted to stop at every one. The Old Girl's Stall at Cox Street was nothing compared to this. Though she had come up to Petticoat Lane with Uncle Noah as a child, then with Hattie in later years, she had forgotten how busy it was. The last time they had ventured up it was raining and Hattie had bought an old umbrella. But it had blown inside out before they had got home and the spokes had poked through the cloth. They had had a laugh about it, but Lily reminded herself that today, she was searching for something of real value, not a frivolous amusement.

Now, as she strolled beside Charles, the market was full of tantalizing colour and the sound of voices – some tongues were foreign and some were cockney. The air was filled with scents of perfumes and fragrances of food. Every conceivable article was on display. The stalls and boxes spilled with coats, dresses, underwear, stockings, shoes, trousers and jumpers, all of which were examined in detail by the throng of women who jostled and fought each other. A big man smoking a pipe pushed his way in to restore calm as a fight broke out over owner-ship of a pair of old riding breeches. Neither woman was prepared to let go, and Lily felt Charles laugh beside her. He steered her gently away, as the cursing and oaths became louder.

'Let's hope our bargain doesn't have to be fought over,' he said as they approached a long bench piled high with all sorts of curios. Lamps, crockery, ironmongery, toys, pots, pans, furniture, food, delicacies and, of course, dozens of umbrellas. Beyond were flower sellers, a pie and mash stall, a fish stall and hot baked bread vendor, competing for business with the pastries, sweets and toffee apples. As far as the eye could see, there were articles of every shape and kind. They stopped next at a shelf piled high with Eastern jewels and mystic stones. Little trinkets hung from above against the gaudy silks. Beads, necklaces, bracelets and scarves were entwined as a thick, sultry smell filled the air.

A dark-eyed, brown-skinned woman called out to Lily. 'Come along, dear, and try one of these on your pretty finger.' From a plump purple cushion she lifted a large ring. 'A real ruby this one, just what you've always wanted.'

Lily paused to admire the glistening stone. The woman pounced on her lifting her hand to slide on the ring.

'A ruby indeed,' said Charles smilingly as they gazed at its false brightness.

'To you sir, just three bob. Now what do you say to that?'

Charles cupped Lily's elbow with his hand. 'It's my young friend's decision,' he said quietly. 'Though to my mind a stone of this poor quality does nothing to justify the beauty of the hand it adorns.'

Lily looked up at her companion. In the hustle and bustle around them, the world seemed to stop still. Her blush was almost as deep as the colour of the ring.

'Your gentleman has a way with words,' said the woman, giving Lily a narrowed glance.

'It's a lovely ring,' Lily said politely, slipping it off and handing it back. 'But not for me, thank you.'

'It would have brought you luck,' the woman cried after them. 'Come back and I'll halve the price.'

Charles slid his arm around her waist to guide her from the path of a man carrying a tray of hot bread on his head. 'A bargain of sorts?' he said wryly and they laughed.

'If she had been a true traveller and the ring had been a sprig of heather, I would have accepted as it's considered unlucky to refuse a gypsy,' Lily said.

'Do you really believe that sort of thing?'

'I don't know if it's true. But yes, in a way I do believe.'

Charles nodded slowly. 'Then the next heather sprig I see, I shall buy it for you. I should like us both to have good luck, Lily. In fact, I should like our friendship to prosper in every way.'

Lily looked up at him. Her tummy turned a summer-sault as his dark eyes looked intensely at her. She felt bewildered. What was he saying? That he wanted their business arrangement to prosper? Or was it – dare she even think it? – something of a more personal nature?

The painting was leaning against the wall, hidden by a heap of clothes and women's boots. To the side of it was a large stand of many types of nuts that was looked after by a boy of no more than about nine. He was spooning the nuts into the open bags of the women who paid him and patted him on the head. The walnuts and Brazil nuts and furry-coated coconuts were hidden in a cloud of dust each time he shook the sacks in which they were stored. Lily saw he was a street urchin, dressed in rags, but with the bright, shrewd eyes of a dealer set close together under a shock of black hair. His smile was instant as they approached.

'Here y'a missy, open yer bag for a penneth o' nuts.'

Lily smiled politely. 'No thank you, but I am interested in that picture behind you.'

'It ain't mine,' the boy shrugged. 'You sure you ain't wanting some o' these?'

'I'm sure.' Lily squeezed past him and bent down to the picture. It was in a terrible condition but there was something about it that she liked.

'Who does it belong to?' she asked as she rubbed away the dirt with her handkerchief.

'What's telling worth, then?'

Lily smiled. 'Sixpence, if you can run and find the owner.'

The boy closed the sack with his filthy fingers, looping the string into a light knot. 'Give us the sixpence first,' he demanded, holding out his black palm.

Charles immediately provided the coin. When the boy ran off through the crowd, they examined the painting.

'It's beautiful,' Lily said as Charles held it up.

'Do you think so?'

'Yes, but the canvas is torn. And the frame's broken.'

'No matter, they will mend easily.' Charles nodded as they stared at the dirty oils depicting a young peasant woman feeding a large black bull. 'Tell me, what do you think of the subjects, Lily?'

She gazed at the unlikely coupling. 'I like them because the bull looks strong and powerful, whilst the girl is delicate and yet she's not afraid to feed it.'

'How very perceptive.'

'All I know is, I'd hang it up on me wall, if I had a big house like yours.'

He smiled. 'Well then Lily, let your intuition be our guide. I think this is what we have been looking for. Our morning's search has certainly not been in vain.'

A small man came rushing towards them. He wore a suit that didn't fit properly over his big arms and was too short in the sleeve. His face was ruddy and coarse under a filthy cap. The boy was pointing and the man slipped his thumbs into his waistcoat pocket when he saw them. A crafty smile came over his face as he noted the picture already in Charles' hand.

'How much do you want for this?' asked Charles.

'It ain't for sale.'

'Then why bring it to market?'

'It's me own. For me good lady. I bought it today.'

Charles nodded slowly, replacing the painting by the wall. 'A pity since I was prepared to take it on.'

'I saw a much nicer one along the Lane,' said Lily,

turning to slide her hand confidently through Charles' arm. 'This is torn and tattered and by comparison, quite dull.'

'Yes, indeed,' replied Charles, a smile of complicity playing on his lips. 'It was just a whim, anyway.'

Pleased with their charade, Lily smiled mischievously back. As they walked away, the dealer jumped in their path.

'I could be persuaded to sell, I s'pose,' he muttered, rubbing his filthy hand over the stubble on his jaw. 'If I was offered a fair price.'

'It's broken,' Lily said haughtily.

'And filthy,' agreed Charles.

'Yer, but it would come nice with a clean-up,' pointed out the man.

The boy ran to Lily. 'Tell yer what miss, me gaffer might sell it for what he bought it at.'

'Why would he do that?'

''Cos yer a pretty lady.'

Charles laughed and placed his hand on the boy's shoulder. 'What an excellent young man you are. Why don't you go and make deliberations on our behalf?'

The young boy nodded and ran off. Lily smiled at Charles knowingly as they watched the older man shaking his head fiercely.

'What a clever pair they make,' said Charles softly in her ear.

She nodded. 'But we are cleverer.'

'Do you think we shall win?'

'No doubt about it,' Lily nodded. 'Whatever he asks for, we'll halve.'

Charles looked amused. 'What a clever girl you are.'

When the boy returned, he stood with his thumbs in his ragged pockets. 'It's a gift to you, mister, at five bob.'

Charles glanced at Lily. She shook her head.

'I would consider two and six,' said Charles dismissively. And a little more quietly added, 'Bear in mind, young man, you have already earned a commission.'

Lily tried to hide her amusement as the boy went off again. When he returned, he held out his hand. 'The deal's done.'

Two minutes later, Charles and Lily were returning the way they had come. They drew many glances from the passers-by as Charles carried the picture under his arm.

'We make a good partnership, don't you think?' Charles said as he placed the picture in the back seat of the car and helped her up.

Lily nodded. She had enjoyed every moment.

'Now, here is your pay, Lily.' He pressed a ten shilling note in her hand. She felt embarrassed. She would have willingly accompanied him for nothing.

'This is too much.'

'Not at all. I would have paid full price for that picture. Your knowledge of the trade was invaluable.'

Lily looked at the large note. Somehow it didn't make her happy. Although she knew it would bring a big smile to her mother's face. 'Thank you,' she said quietly.

'The pleasure has been all mine, Lily. Now, I must take you home.'

Lily folded the note into her purse. She looked at all the familiar sights as they passed: the tall, smoke covered houses; the taverns and shops; the dirty gutters and cobbles; the mounds of horse dung being scooped up by the street children that would later be sold for a half-penny a bag. She wanted to sit beside Charles and savour it, let the day go on forever. But she knew it had to end.

She wondered if he would ask her to help him again. But he merely tipped his hat and thanked her for her help as he helped her out from the car.

Lily watched him drive off and was rewarded by the sight of his gloved hand raised in salute from the window. As the car turned out of sight, her happiness faded. Did he now have everything he wanted for his house? Had she only been useful to him for a short while?

Chapter Eight

When, that afternoon, she told Hattie about Petticoat Lane and the picture, Hattie didn't say much. Instead, as they walked through the foot tunnel to Greenwich, Hattie couldn't wait to relay her own news.

'Reube told me last night at the dance that he wants us to go up West for the ring,' she said excitedly.

'Oh, that'll be nice.'

'Did he say anything about the ring to you? Like how much he plans to spend?'

'He wouldn't, would he?' replied Lily as they walked briskly along. It was a cold March day with a stiff breeze. 'We're best friends you and me. He knows I'd tell you straight away.'

Hattie giggled as she laid a restraining hand on her soft brown hat. Lily's blue hat, after so much steaming, was a tight fit and remained in place. 'I'm hoping for a diamond ring,' said Hattie. 'Nothing too extravagant, mind. A single stone, perhaps. It means a lot to a girl, does a ring.'

Lily thought of the wonderful moment when the

dark-skinned woman had thrust the so-called ruby ring on her finger. It had felt so special though the design was far too opulent. She would never wear a thing like that. And it couldn't have been a ruby, as it would have cost the earth. But just feeling it on her finger had been exciting. And when Charles had given her that compliment about it not doing her justice . . .

'Lil, are you listening to me?'

'Yes, course I am.'

'Well, what do you think?'

'Of what?'

Hattie stopped to frown at her. 'You haven't been listening, have you?'

'Course I have.' Lily was grateful for the gust of wind that blew them on.

'You see, my Reube's all right,' went on Hattie regardless. 'But he does tend to be a bit careful.'

Lily smiled as they walked into the shelter of the park. 'Careful' was an understatement where Reube was concerned. Lily hoped that when they got married, Hattie didn't have a shock, as she liked to spend her own money freely.

'I'm sure where you're concerned he's very generous,' Lily said tactfully.

'Yes, he is,' agreed Hattie, looking pleased. 'Matter of fact I've seen a very nice ring in Aldgate High Street near Madame's. In this little silversmiths and watchmakers. It's a sapphire and diamond cluster ring.'

'I thought you wanted a single stone.'

'Well, if I had a choice, I'd have this one.'

'Are you asking me to hint to Reube about it?'

'Well, it's worth a try.'

The two girls burst out laughing. Hattie walked carelessly along, swinging her hips.

They were still laughing as they went in the café and sat down. Lily felt very well off as she had a few pennies left in her purse.

'Did you and Ben enjoy the dance?' Hattie asked as they drank their coffee.

'Yes, the band was very good.'

'What did he say to you on the way home?'

'Not much.'

'That charabanc is going to earn him a good few bob. Reube says it's a thing of the future.'

'I'm sure it is.'

Hattie sighed. 'Well, you ain't got much to say for yourself today.'

Lily didn't want to talk about Ben. She would rather discuss Charles. She wanted to share her feelings with Hattie, especially as she was confused about them. If only she could talk through her innermost thoughts, but she knew this wasn't the time or the place. Hattie was only interested in her forthcoming engagement. She had even forgotten that it was her birthday on the fifteenth.

When Lily returned home, it was time for tea. Her mother and father and Uncle Noah listened to her account of that morning.

'Yer got a bargain there,' her uncle commented as they ate their meal of beef pie and mash. 'Didn't get many pictures like that on the cart.'

'It was a pretty one too,' Lily said enthusiastically. 'A young girl feeding a great big bull.'

'Who painted it?' asked her mother.

'I don't know.'

'It might be worth something if it's by a famous artist.'

'With a little repair it will come up nice,' nodded her uncle.

'Did he say if he wants you again?' asked her father.

'No.' She looked disappointed.

'You did yer best gel.'

Lily nodded. 'Here you are, Mum. Ten shillings.' She placed the note on the table.

Her mother picked it up. 'Ten shillings for just one morning?'

'I told you it was business.'

'Yes, but all you did was walk round the market.'

Lily wanted to tell them of the little act they had played out. But it seemed as though she was boasting.

'It's very good pay,' agreed her mother, tucking the note in the pocket of her apron. 'And all above board.'

Lily didn't know what her mother meant by that. It had been such a wonderful experience to accompany Charles, the pleasure she had derived from their purchase of the painting was payment enough. But now as she saw the light in her mother's eye, she was glad she hadn't refused.

'I got me pay coming next week,' said her father, also looking more cheerful. 'We'll be on the up and up soon.'

'Yes, Bob,' smiled her mother. 'But I don't want you taking any chances at that yard.'

'Thanks to Ben I'll only be stacking wood in the fresh air.'

'He's done us a real good turn.'

Everyone turned to look at Lily. 'Did you have a good dance last night?'

Lily nodded. 'Yes, thanks.'

'Did you say anything to Ben about the job?' asked her father.

'I told him how grateful we are.'

'Good girl. I'll take him out for a drink soon.'

'Or you could ask him round to tea, Lil.' Her mother looked expectantly at her.

Lily knew they were waiting for her to agree. But how could she? She didn't want to give Ben any ideas yet she knew that her family were relying on her to show gratitude. Her dad had been out of work for so long, and after having to work on the skin ships, getting the timber job had been a big turning point in their lives.

'We'll see,' said Lily quietly and, changing the subject, said to her father, 'and don't forget, Dad, you'll need your big coat and coms tomorrow. It'll be chilly in that yard.'

'How could I forget?' chuckled Bob Bright glancing

up at the wooden pulley above their heads. His combinations dangled down, the two legs ironed and aired to perfection.

Everyone laughed. Lily looked at their happy faces. Her father was now in a job he liked and her mother had enough money to pay the rent. There was a fresh delivery of coal in the bunker and the larder was full. Life had suddenly become very good. If only she could make them understand she wasn't attracted to Ben. But she knew they were living in hope that eventually she would change her mind.

All the next week, Lily looked out for Charles. As she spoke to the customers, her mind drifted. She would catch herself thinking about Sunday and the wonderful morning they'd spent together or the day they had gone up West. The week seemed longer than ever with no sight of him.

Late on Friday afternoon, the Blackshirts appeared. 'They're back again, the bloody hooligans,' cried Reube, searching for the stick he'd hidden under the stall.

'They ain't doing anything wrong yet,' Lily didn't want him to get into a fight. She knew if they were ignored the group might go away. But Reube was joined by Ted Shiner and the two men stood throwing angry looks at the gathering.

Vera Froud and Florrie Mills came over. 'Just who do they think they are, shouting and waving their arms like that, on our patch.'

'They'll put off all the custom,' muttered Vera, poking Reube in the side. 'We should send for the coppers.'

'You're having a laugh, aren't you?' scoffed Florrie. 'They don't nick the criminals, it's too dangerous.'

'They're fascists, ain't that enough?'

'No one knows what they really are,' replied Ted sourly. 'But with friends like that two-faced pansy, Boothby, my guess is that Mosley will be kicked out of Labour before he blots all their copybooks.'

At that moment a figure came strolling down the street. Ben had his hands in his pockets and was whistling, until he heard the commotion.

'What you doing here?' asked Reube as his brother stopped to stare.

'I knocked off early. Thought I'd nip round to see if you wanted a beer after you shut shop. What's going on?'

'They're at it again,' Reube complained bitterly. 'I'd like to go over and tell 'em to vamoose.'

'Hark at 'em,' said Florrie, 'spouting off about us claiming our rights. I know what right I'd like to claim and that's to knock their blocks off.'

'I reckon we should go over and tell 'em to sod off somewhere else,' said Ted, squaring his big shoulders.

'What if they won't?' posed Samuel Goldblum who was listening intently. 'I don't want them wrecking my stall. I've seen them up West on their soap boxes. Oiy, they are trouble, dears.'

'I'll go over and ask politely,' said Reube leading the way forward, stick in hand.

The pint-sized jeweller shook his head. 'You ladies should cover your stalls. I am off to protect mine.'

'Mine's only clothes,' said Vera hesitantly.

'They can be torn,' pointed out Samuel.

'Mine's only cottons and silks,' said Florrie, 'but they could throw 'em everywhere I s'pose.'

Florrie and Vera left in a hurry. Lily knew that panic had set in. She also knew that Reube's hot temper would snap if he was insulted. In view of what had happened last time, he was still the hero. She prayed no one would get angry enough to fight.

But her prayer was in vain as one of the Blackshirts, a head and shoulders above Reube, suddenly pushed Ted Shiner. The next thing was, Reube had lifted his stick and brought it down hard on the Blackshirt.

Lily closed her eyes. The fight had begun.

A fist came straight at Ben. For a moment he felt sick as it landed on his chin, but shaking his head, he managed to dodge the next one. The Blackshirt tumbled forward into Ted's stall and all the apples and pears went flying. Ted came running towards them, but two of them grabbed him and brought him down.

Before Ben could reach them, he was punched again. Rallying swiftly he retaliated and the outrush of breath from his enemy told him he'd found his mark. Then something heavy cracked on his back and once more

Ben saw stars. His legs buckled and he fell, as the air was sucked painfully from his lungs. All he could see was a pair of coarse black boots, blurring in and out of focus. He knew that within seconds he could expect another blow. Sinking a little lower and blinking the pain from his eyes he gathered his strength. Opening his arms, he tackled the man and brought him down hard.

'Good for you, ducks,' cried Florrie Mills on the sidelines.

'Give the bugger another one!' encouraged Samuel from a long way off.

Ben struggled to his feet. He was grabbed by the arm and thrown back. Another fist found his nose and the blood spurted out like a fountain. Pain flared into his eyes and across his cheeks. He felt the agony drive down his spine, but anger sent him forward. In a clumsy tackle, he brought down another, winding himself in the process.

From the corner of his eye he saw Reube, kicking and wielding the stick. Beside him Ted Shiner was claiming vengeance, punching the man who had tried to throttle him.

A cheer went up from the crowd. Ben drew breath and wiped the blood from his nose on his sleeve. The Blackshirt at his feet began to crawl away like a wounded animal.

'Ben! Ben!'

He looked round as Lily ran up. She wiped his face gently with a rag. 'Why did you have to fight?'

He looked into her eyes and laughed. 'That wasn't no fight, just a bit of a scrap.'

'Ben James, you and your brother are too old to fight. When will you learn?'

He suddenly wished he could turn back the clock. He'd been a right chump at the dance last week. If only he'd kept his emotions in check and not pulled a long face. But he'd been jealous of the fact she was seeing another bloke and he'd let it show. If he'd had any sense, he would have pretended he didn't care.

Pushing the cloth over his nose, he grinned. 'If Florence Nightingale was as pretty as you, no wonder she cured all them blokes.'

Lily took his arm. 'You ain't so pretty yourself at the moment.'

'Have they spoiled me dashing good looks?'

'You'd better wash all that blood off.' She looked into his eyes and smiled.

'You all right?' asked his brother as they stood at the pump.

'Never been better. And you?'

Reube laughed. 'You turned up at just the right time.'

'Didn't want to miss all the excitement.'

'You're gonna have a shiner in the morning,' laughed Reube.

Ted looked up from splashing his face with water. 'Blimey, look at yer boat race, kid.'

'Next time, I'll move a bit quicker.'

'I hope there ain't going to be a next time,' said Lily, frowning up at him.

Florrie and Vera came over. 'You done all right, boys.'

Ben revelled in everyone's praise as Lily reached up to dab gently over his face. Did she really care about him? And if she did, did she care enough?

'Don't worry, I'm as good as new,' Ben assured Lily after he had washed his face at the pump. The look of concern on her face was enough to make him feel happy. Something he hadn't been since last Sunday when he'd looked from the window and watched her go off with that charmer, Charles Grey.

'They should be prosecuted,' said her mother that night. 'Upsetting hard working, decent people like that. Where were the coppers when they were needed! And poor Ben with a bleeding nose.'

'He's all right now,' said Lily as she warmed herself by the fire. She was still shaking. The fight had upset her. Last time Charles had averted trouble, but left up to the traders, it had been a free for all.

'A man has to stand up for his rights,' her father commented. 'He's got guts that lad. And so has his brother.'

'It was Reube who started it,' Lily tried to explain. 'I'm sure they would have gone away if they were ignored.'

'That's the trouble,' her uncle argued, 'we let these

madmen off by ignoring them, thinking it's better than arguing. But in this case it ain't, as they multiply like flies and cause more trouble.'

'I haven't seen them round here,' said Lily quickly.

'I have,' replied her uncle. 'When I went out for the paper last Saturday, they was on the corner of Manchester Road, yelling and shouting.'

'I don't know why they come round,' said her father. 'They know we don't want them. The blokes at the yard shut the gates if they come by.'

'I think that's best,' said Lily. 'Mum and me wouldn't want to see you in a fight.'

He laughed. 'Gone are those days, gel. Anyway, the blokes at the yard don't hold no high faluting opinions like some of them at the docks. It's only a small concern, see, so the union ain't involved and the boss pays us fair money.' Lily was pleased to hear about her father's new job. Each night he had come home to tell them about it. Though it was hard labour being outside, he enjoyed it.

'You won't ever have to touch one of them dreadful skins again,' said her mother happily.

'Thanks to young Ben,' nodded her father, 'I won't be waiting on the stones any more to pick up what's left over.'

Lily hoped the conversation wasn't going to return to Ben and was relieved when her mother spoke about something everyone else seemed to have forgotten. 'Now, love, in a couple of weeks it's your birthday.

We want to buy you something nice. After all, it's your twenty-first. What about them boots you was after. I can buy a nice pair from the tally man. Get them on tick.'

'No, Mum, I don't need any,' Lily said at once. She didn't want her mother to go in debt again. Then the troubles would begin, as once the tally man called, he didn't stop. 'These will do for another year.'

'You deserve a good present, gel,' her father said quietly. 'We want to show you we appreciate all your hard work.'

'You don't have to do that.'

'But we want to,' insisted her mother.

'All right then,' Lily nodded. 'Can we have a small party?'

'What a good idea!' exclaimed her mother at once. 'This house needs a bit of livening up. I don't know when the piano was last played. It could do with an airing.'

'And I'll get out me records,' said her uncle eagerly. 'Bring the Talking Machine down from the bedroom and we can roll back the carpet and have a bit of a knees up.'

Lily smiled. 'That will be lovely.'

'We'll ask all the neighbours,' said Josie, warming to the theme, 'like the Flocks and their kids, and of course the Parks and the Jameses.' She clutched her husband's wrist. 'Bob, we'll celebrate our daughter's twenty-first in style.'

Lily looked at their happy faces. She was blessed to have a loving family and friends to share her twenty-first birthday, even though she couldn't have what she wanted most, and that was to see Charles Grey again.

On March the fifteenth, Lily woke with a start. She knew something exciting was going to happen, and then she remembered it was her twenty-first.

'Wake up, ducks,' said her mother, entering her bedroom. 'I've made you a nice cup of tea.'

Still sleepy, Lily sat up. 'What time is it?'

'Half past seven.'

She never slept past six, but then today was special.

'Your uncle is downstairs making breakfast. I stayed out of the way because you know what he's like. He'll leave it all in a dreadful state,' said her mother, lowering the cup into Lily's grasp.

'Well, it's nice to be cooked for.'

Her mother was wearing her dressing gown and slippers and as the pins were sticking out of her hair, it was a sure sign that she was far from ready to meet the world.

'Happy birthday, love.' Josie pulled back the curtains. 'It's a lovely Saturday morning. Cold and bright. You've got all day off and don't you deserve it!' She kissed Lily on the top of her head and turned to the dressing table mirror, where their eyes met. 'Twenty-one today my girl is! Whoever would have thought your father and me could have produced such a beautiful child!'

She sniffed emotionally. 'I'd better go and do my hair before someone knocks at the door.'

Lily smiled as her mother left. She drank her tea and thought how strange it was to be lying in bed on a Saturday morning. She had never had a Saturday off before. But Reube had insisted it was his present to her, which had been very generous. After all, he would have to pay Pedro to work in her place and Reube had given her a full week's wage.

Lily sighed happily as she lay there. It was a life of luxury today. What would she wear for her party? Would everyone turn up? Her mother had asked the neighbours and the Jameses and Parks were coming, even Sylvester. Since the fight with the Blackshirts, Ben had been back to his old humorous self. She hoped that tonight they could be good friends again.

At one o'clock, Hattie called. She was out of breath from hurrying from the bus stop. 'Madame Nerys let me off in time to catch the early bus,' she told Lily excitedly.

'Have you been home?' Lily was in the kitchen, preparing the food. She was wearing her mother's pinny and turban, whilst Josie went round with a duster.

'No, I told Mum this morning before I left, I was coming straight here to help you.'

'Have something to eat first.'

'No, I ate me sandwiches on the bus.' Hattie took off her coat and hung it up in the hall.

'You'd better wear this.' Lily pulled the spare apron

from the drawer. 'And here's a scarf for your hair.'

Hattie went to the mirror and tidied her kiss-curls. Turning sideways, she smiled at her profile. 'I look a bit of a wreck.'

Lily giggled as she handed Hattie a paisley scarf to wind round her head. 'I've never *ever* seen you looking a wreck.'

'You wanna clock me first thing in the morning before I've got me make-up on.'

'I don't know where you get the patience.'

'It's all right for you. You've got lovely skin, the proverbial English rose.'

'I'd wear make-up if it was cheap.'

Hattie grinned, making a turban of the scarf. 'I don't care what it costs. As long as I've got me face on I'm ready to deal with what Madame throws me. And lately it's been a lot.' As they began to make the cakes, Hattie told Lily about Madame Nerys' new clients.

'It's a big affair, with a big church wedding.'

'Is the bride pretty?' Lily asked.

'In a horsey sort of way,' Hattie hesitated. 'You see, they're aristocrats, a family with a title and no matter what you look like, if you're rich you have this sort of glow about you.'

'What's the family's name?'

'I ain't allowed to say,' Hattie replied mysteriously as she handed an egg to Lily.

'Why not?' Lily beat the egg into the flour as she listened intently.

''Cos it's a special case – very special.'

'But won't someone at work let it out who they are?'

Hattie rolled her big brown eyes. 'Goodness no, as we've been threatened with the sack if we so much as pronounce the first syllable.'

'So they must be very important?'

Hattie's smile almost twinkled. 'Yes, and there's something else.'

Lily stopped what she was doing. 'Go on, I know you're dying to tell me.'

'The wedding dress has to be made two sizes bigger than the girl's measurements!' She looked under her long eyelashes. 'Get it now?'

Lily shook her head.

'All right, clue number two. The wedding at the church can't be arranged till the bridegroom's parents come back from abroad. Which will be about May.'

'But she won't grow two sizes by then!'

'Oh yes she will.' Hattie nodded.

It took a while before the penny dropped. 'You mean—'

Hattie lifted her finger across her mouth. 'That's why we have to keep it quiet.'

'You mean no one is supposed to know that she's—'

Hattie nodded, her eyes very wide.

'But what about when she has the baby?' Lily blurted.

'Shh!' Again Hattie put a finger to her lips. 'I've said too much already.'

'But someone is sure to work it out,' whispered Lily, not knowing why she was whispering.

'They won't, because money solves every problem imaginable. They'll send her to some posh clinic so she can have the kid and it won't be disclosed till they want it to be. When you've got that kind of wealth, you can do anything.'

Lily began to stir the mixture again thinking about what Hattie said. They were even going to have a church wedding with all the trimmings and a lovely white bridal gown made by Madame Nerys. How much money did aristocrats have? Did it mean the same to them if there was an accident in the family? It must do, otherwise they wouldn't take the trouble to hide it. What would happen if someone she knew – or even herself, got into the family way?

Before meeting Charles, she had never felt such desire. She would have been sympathetic to someone who had got pregnant out of wedlock, but she wouldn't have understood how it could happen; you only had to say no. But Charles had stirred emotions inside her that made her feel like a real woman.

She had wanted to discover more about these feelings, these wonderful highs and lows that touched inside, right to the heart. But she hadn't seen him again since that Sunday. Had her usefulness come to an end?

'You'll take the pattern off that bowl if you keep stirring so fast,' said Hattie, nudging her arm.

Lily smiled, feeling the heat still in her cheeks.

'You won't say anything, will you?'

'About your secret customer? No, course not. I don't know who they are anyway, do I?'

'You know,' said Hattie after a while, 'me and Reube might not have their money, but I've got me fingers and I can buy some really nice oyster satin to make my own wedding dress. In fact, I was thinking about copying the pattern. It's cut on the bias with these beautiful fan-shaped sleeves. And the lace veil has scalloped edges, with a heart-shaped head-dress of wax flowers and pearls.'

Now it was Lily's turn to nudge her friend. 'You'll look a thousand times nicer than her.'

Hattie turned sharply. 'You haven't seen her, so you can't say that.'

'Yes, I can. You said she was horsey so the only thing missing will be the horse.'

They burst into laughter until tears filled their eyes.

At four o'clock a bowl of rice pudding was brought in by Mrs James. Hattie and Lily were trying to decide where it should stand. There was a space left by the tray of fruit scones and the neatly cut sandwiches of cheese and ham. All these were covered by cloths and moving them aside, Hattie carefully squeezed in the bowl.

'There. What do you think?'

'It all looks lovely, Hat. I could eat everything now.'

'I'm saving me appetite for later.'

'So where's everyone disappeared to?' Hattie asked as they put the finishing touches to the food.

'Dad and Uncle Noah have gone down the park to get out of the way. Mum's still dusting.'

Hattie giggled. 'Do you think we'll be like that one day? Our mum's are houseproud, ain't they?'

'I hope not. It only gets dirty again.'

'I'd like a maid.'

Lily turned to her friend. 'I don't know what Reube would say about that.'

'He'd say I've got desires above me station. Or that Madame Nerys is turning me head.'

'Dreams don't cost anything.'

'No, but maids do.'

Once again they were laughing, but then Lily said thoughtfully, 'There was a maid at Charles Grey's house. Though she didn't exactly have a uniform.'

The laughter went from Hattie's face and she gave a little shrug. 'Perhaps she wasn't a maid.'

'What could she have been then?'

'I don't know.' Hattie turned away. 'Someone he knew. A friend. A neighbour. After all, he is a bit – well, different.'

'What do you mean?'

'Dunno. He's just not like us.'

'He's not that different. It's just where he lives and how he speaks.'

'My point exactly.'

Lily looked at her friend who now seemed to be bored again. 'You don't like him, do you, Hat?'

'I don't know him, that's all.' She gazed at Lily. 'Have you seen him lately?'

'No.'

'Ain't he coming to the party?' Hattie said, frowning.

'Of course not.'

'Didn't you invite him?'

'I said, I haven't seen him.'

Hattie wiped a trickle of jam from her chin as she sprinkled the roly-poly with sugar. 'Do you want to though?'

Lily played with the ends of her apron. 'Yes, I suppose I do.'

Hattie was silent. Then softly she said, 'I don't want you to get hurt, Lil.'

'Why should I get hurt?'

'Because he's not one of us.'

'That doesn't mean he'll hurt me.'

Hattie touched her arm as she looked into her eyes. 'He's hurt you already by not coming round.'

Lily felt a hard knot tying in her stomach. 'It was only business anyway.'

'Well then, cheer up. It's your birthday.'

Lily wished she could confide in Hattie as they had done all their lives. She was sure if Charles was someone Hattie knew then she would approve. But islanders were a close community and if Charles had pursued their friendship then Lily knew she would have encountered stiff opposition. But that was irrelevant now, as Charles had lost interest.

'I wish we could go up West together,' Hattie said suddenly. 'A day out shopping would be a nice break. Now your dad's working, you could take a Saturday afternoon off. Reube could get Pedro to help him.'

Lily frowned thoughtfully. The expression on Hattie's face reminded her of when they were kids. Hattie's chin pushed out when she wanted something.

'That would be nice. I'll ask.'

'Have you said anything about the ring?'

Lily shook her head. 'No, all everyone wants to talk about is the Blackshirts.'

'Oh, well, I can point the shop out from the bus when we go up West.'

Lily smiled ruefully. 'So that's all you want me with you for?'

'No, course not. It would be nice, just the two of us for once, like old times.' A genuine smile was back on Hattie's face. She took off the turban and shook out her hair. 'What are you wearing tonight? Did you decide?'

'The blue frock, with the white ruffled collar,' replied Lily, turning her thoughts to the evening.

'I'm wearing me green dress. You know, the one with the short sleeves,' said Hattie, now in a world of high fashion. 'Or should I wear the pink dress I made last year. The one with the ruched sleeves?'

'I like the green,' said Lily.

Hattie smiled contentedly. 'By the way, I've got your

present and card in my bag. I was going to keep them till tonight, but would you like to open them now?'

Lily wiped her hands on the towel. 'Oh, yes please.'

Hattie ran out to the passage returning immediately with her bag. She drew out a small parcel wrapped in brown paper and a white envelope. 'I hope you like them.'

Lily opened the card. There was an illustration of a large red rose on the front and Happy Birthday underneath. Inside, Hattie had written: 'To my best friend on her twenty-first birthday. Mates for ever, all my love, Hattie.'

'Oh, Hattie, thank you.'

'Don't thank me till you see what it is.'

Lily carefully undid the parcel, then gasped. 'It's a fur brooch!'

'A rabbit's foot.'

'A real one?' Lily hoped a claw wasn't going to appear.

'No, silly. It's fur that's cut off from the foot and glued into a shape to look like one. The point is, it's supposed to be lucky.'

'Oh, Hat, you are thoughtful. I'll wear it tonight.'

'Do you really like it?'

'Course I do.' Lily opened the brass pin on which the tiny decoration was attached. She threaded it on her apron. 'How does it look? I'll pin it on the collar of my dress tonight.'

'It's very eye-catching,' said Hattie thoughtfully.

'It will always remind me of you, me best mate.'

'Just so long as it don't remind you of Mrs James's fur hat,' Hattie said, controlling her laughter, 'and if one of the boys dares to say I've cut a bit out of it, I'll strangle them!'

Chapter Nine

The party was in full swing. Lily had opened her presents and placed them on top of the piano for her guests to see. A scarf and leather gloves from Josie, a musical box that played Debussy from Uncle Noah. Handkerchiefs, a bottle of eau-de-cologne and a jar of sweets from her friends and neighbours.

Uncle Noah was hand-cranking the phonograph and Enrico Caruso's voice rang out on the heavy seventy-eight revs per minute recording. As Lily walked in the parlour, a dispute began. Her mother had requested a Marie Lloyd number, but her uncle was guarding the phonograph, refusing all requests in favour of his own.

Lily slipped away, threading a path through her guests. Mollie and Hector Flock and their children had commandeered the couch. There was bald-headed baby Isaac, eight-year-old Suzie and her ten-year-old brother, Freddie, all yelling as loud as each other.

Elsie Barker, the Flocks' neighbour, grabbed a sandwich from the plate Lily offered. 'Lovely party, Lily. And don't you look the dog's dinner in that dress. What's that on your collar?'

'A lucky rabbit's foot. It's from Hattie.'

'Yer, well you need all the luck you can get in this life, ducks.'

Lily glanced at herself in the big bevelled-edge mirror above the mantel. The tiny brooch peeped out from under the white ruffled neckline of her blue frock, which, like the rest of her wardrobe, had been discovered at market. But this time the previous owner had been Lily's size and height and no alterations had been required other than a thorough wash. The pale blue of the bodice matched the blue of her eyes and the calf length swirling skirt made it the perfect party dress.

'When's the knees-up starting?' Mollie Flock shouted above the din in the room.

'As soon as we roll back the carpet.' Although Lily enjoyed Caruso she hoped Uncle Noah would soon change the record. People were eager to dance and let their hair down.

'Can't understand a word that bloke is singing,' complained Mollie, whacking one screaming child over the head with a cushion to quieten them.

'It's Caruso,' Lily tried to explain, 'a famous Italian opera singer.'

'Italian?' roared Hector Flock whose big paw landed on the last sandwich. 'Mollie ain't even learned to speak English, yet.'

Once more Mollie's hand stretched out whizzing past her husband's ear.

'Can I have another slice of roly-poly?' Dark-haired Suzie Flock wiped her nose on her sleeve. 'Me brother pinched mine.'

'The roly-poly's all gone, love.'

'It ain't fair. I didn't have any.'

'Well, I'm lighting the candles on the cake in a minute,' Lily said, giving her a cuddle. 'I'll see you're the first to have a slice of birthday cake.'

'Fanks, Lil.'

Someone tapped Lily on the shoulder. It was Ted Shiner, looking uncomfortable. 'Lil, I need a Jimmy Riddle. And the door of the lav is locked. Has been for the past ten minutes.'

'Did you give it a good push?'

'Not 'arf. But all I heard was laughing. If it's kids in there, they need turfing out.'

'I'll go and see who it is.'

Lily made her way out. In the hall she found Pedro talking to Grace Padgett from number forty. Grace was middle-aged and often called the Merry Widow, as she had lost three husbands in quick succession. One in the war, another to the flu epidemic and the last in an accident on the Mile End Road. She didn't let her troubles show, however, as she always had a smile on her face.

'Are there any seats left?' Grace frowned into the noisy front room.

'Yes, just inside.'

Carol Rivers

'Thanks for inviting me, gel. You got any good-looking blokes in there?'

Lily laughed. 'There's one standing beside you.'

Pedro gave a chuckle, twirling the ends of his black moustache.

'Happy birthday, Lily. Here's your present,' said Grace, giving her a large box of chocolates. 'They're nice ones an' all.'

'Oh, thank you, Grace.'

Pedro rocked on his heels. 'Watch they don't make you fat, Lily gel.'

'They won't hang around long enough to get fat on. How was market today?'

'Sold that set of china cups and the toasting fork.'

'I'll bet Reube was pleased.'

'Oh, didn't see much of him.'

'Where did he go?'

'Said he had to see a man about a dog.'

Lily knew that Reube would have taken his leave quickly as he could only take Pedro in small doses. Reube got irritated when Pedro, in his slow and precise manner, talked to the punters at length. It always amused Lily to hear him, but she knew it could be a bit irritating.

'By the way,' said Pedro, scratching his head. 'A bloke asked about you today.'

'Who was that?'

'Some gent in a posh coat and brown hat.'

Lily suddenly felt weak at the knees. 'Did he give his name?'

'No. I was talking to me customer at the time, telling her about the china, where it come from, you know, the old lady from Cahir Street who was—'

'Yes, I know where it came from Pedro, but what did he say?'

'Nothin' much.'

'But he asked for me?'

Pedro frowned, his long, thin face pensive. 'Must of done. 'Cos I said you wasn't there.'

'Did he say he'd come back?'

'No.'

Lily felt both elated and cheated. Today was the one day that she had taken off in years and it was the day that Charles chose to call. And Reube, who would have known Charles, hadn't been there either.

She tried again. 'Can you think of anything else he said – anything at all?'

Pedro frowned, stroking his black moustache and twirling the ends. Lily caught a whiff of the hair dressing he used on it. 'Just said you was off for the day, that's all.'

'So he didn't buy anything either?'

'Didn't see the going of him as I was on me own and this punter came up, wanting to know how much I'd sell the fork for and as there weren't no ticket on it . . .'

Lily wasn't listening as Pedro's voice droned on. Charles had actually come by to see her again! She felt suddenly as if her life had been filled with joy again. Oh, why had she taken the day off? If she had been at the market, she would have seen his handsome face once more.

'Lil?' Grace was looking at her. 'You all right?'

'Er . . . yes, just a bit hot in here, that's all.'

'You've gone a bit pale.'

'Why don't you both go and sit down whilst there's seats free?' Lily didn't want to talk, she wanted to think about what Pedro had said.

'Get yerself in there, gel,' said Pedro, pushing Grace in front of him.

When they had gone, Lily made her way to the kitchen. Why had Charles come to the market? Was it to ask her to help him again? Or, dare she hope that it was for something of a more personal nature?

On her way out to the washhouse, Lily found Ted again. He gave her an urgent look. Mrs James was reading his grandmother's palm at the table in the kitchen. Her heavy features were knitted together in concentration under her fur hat. Freda Shiner's big shoulders dwarfed the figure of Hattie's father, Len, who sat next to her. At the other side of the table, was Mrs Parks and Sylvester. Lily thought that poor Sylvester looked like death warmed up. She hoped all the noise and talking wouldn't set him off. He rarely took a step outside his own front door and she'd been surprised the Parks had brought him at all.

Freda Shiner smiled up at her grandson. 'You wanna have your fortune told, ducks,' she cried, her fat chins wobbling. 'I just got some good news. There's a tall dark stranger on me horizon. He's going to take me away from all you lot.'

'Let me know when you're off, Gran, and I'll pack yer sandwiches and a map,' Ted shouted back as he pushed his massive bulk through the chairs.

'Cheeky blighter,' his grandmother laughed.

'I'm still waiting to go,' said Ted, out of the corner of his mouth. 'I'll have find a spot in the yard, if that khazi door ain't open soon.

Lily nodded and opened the back door. The darkness was illuminated by Uncle Noah's Tilley lamp hanging in the yard. As Marie Lloyd's voice echoed from the phonograph, two young people broke out from the closet. Laughing, they rushed through the kitchen past Lily and Ted.

'Who the flipping 'eck were they?' demanded Ted.

'That's Billy Bird and Maggie Novaks,' Lily giggled. 'We all dance together at the Dockland Settlement. They're very good at the Charleston.'

'Looks like the Charleston ain't the only thing they're good at either,' Ted chuckled.

'They're only having a bit of fun.'

'I don't blame 'em, girl. I was the same at their age. But I'll be glad to see the inside of that khazi.'

Lily closed the back door and listened to the laughter. Before Pedro had told her about Charles, she had resigned herself to not seeing Charles again. Now, all her hopes had been brought back to life. Charles wanted to see her! She didn't know why, but she didn't care. It was enough to know that he had tried to reach her. Would he call round the house? What would he think of all these people if he did?

It was half an hour later when Ben arrived. 'Sorry I'm late, Funny Face.' He wore a light-coloured suit and snappy blue tie that Lily hadn't seen before. 'I've only just finished on the lorry. Here's your present.'

She smiled, taking the gift.

'Then it took me half an hour to wash and change. Want to look me best for my favourite gal. Good job me nose straightened up after that ding-dong with the Blackshirts.'

'I hope you don't go fighting again.'

Ben laughed. 'If I do, I'll be quicker to get out of the way. Now, go on, open it.'

It was easy for Lily to guess what was inside the parcel. A large, shiny record slipped into her hands.

'Surprise, surprise!' said Ben. 'Bet you didn't think you was getting that.'

'No, I didn't.' It was the popular song ''S Wonderful', from the musical *Funny Face*, which was no surprise at all, seeing as how he was always singing it to her.

Ben did a little twirl, humming the tune and giving her a Fred Astaire foot shuffle. Reube appeared behind him with Hattie on his arm.

'Happy birthday, Lil. Blimey, I didn't 'arf miss you at the stall today. Pedro talked me ear off.'

'He said you wasn't there.'

'Didn't think he'd notice the way he was rabbiting. Anyway, stick these somewhere, gel.' He gave Lily a bunch of flowers wrapped in newspaper. 'Grew them meself specially for you.'

'And I'm the Queen of Sheba,' Hattie giggled, stretching out her arms. 'Give them to me and I'll find them a home. Ben, take her in the parlour and put that record on. The girl is supposed to be dancing. It's her twenty-first.'

Ben grabbed her hand as Hattie took the flowers. He pulled Lily into the parlour. 'Here you are, Mr Kelly, can you play this?'

'What is it?'

'A tune we can dance to.'

Her uncle squinted at the label. 'Oh, the one you're always trying to sing,' he muttered. 'Go on then, boy, pull the carpet back and we'll start the knees-up.'

Lily watched Ben and Hector Flock roll back the carpet, but her thoughts were still on Charles. If only Pedro had asked him what he wanted. Or taken a message that she could reply to. It wasn't beyond her to call at his house. The thought made her weak at the knees.

'Dancing room only!' Ben shouted, as everyone squashed back against the walls. 'Come on then, Lil, let's show them how it's done.' He reached out and drew her into his arms.

How she wished it was Charles she was dancing with. If only she was dressed in a long silk dress and they were somewhere up West, in one of those posh hotels, dancing the night away. She let her imagination roam, closing her eyes as she pretended that Charles was holding her against his strong chest and guiding her around a softly lit dance floor. Lily was in another world, far away from Love Lane and the rough and tumble of everyday life. Her body was close to the man who had lit up her life with his presence. She was not gazing into Ben's soft grey eyes, but another pair, dark and mysterious. As the lovely song flowed, all she could think of was Charles.

Finally the melody came to an end. Ben swung her out at arm's length and Lily made an elegant arc of her body as she always did. Slowly he curled her back to his chest and on the final bar, he whispered, 'Happy birthday, Funny Face, you're swell!'

Lily smiled, even though these weren't the words she wanted to hear and Ben wasn't the man whose arms she craved to be in.

But the surprise came when in front of the whole room, Ben bowed his head and kissed her passionately.

A cheer went up. Lily tried to push herself away but he refused to let her go. When he finally did, he kept his arm around her waist, hugging her to him as everyone began to clap.

It was past midnight when the party ended. The Parks and the Jameses were the last to leave and Hattie, Reube and Ben remained to help with the clearing up.

When Josie and Uncle Noah had gone to bed, Hattie

helped Lily to clean the kitchen and do the washing-up. It was left to Reube and Ben to restore order in the parlour.

'It was a wonderful party, Lil,' Hattie said as she swept the last of the crumbs into a pan.

'I hope everyone had a good time.' Lily took the pan from Hattie who collapsed on to a chair.

Hattie laughed. 'Dancing with the Flocks' kids wore me out.'

Lily was still in shock after what had happened with Ben. Afterwards, he had followed her around and not left her side all evening. It was clear that he intended people to think that now they were a couple.

Hattie stretched and yawned. 'So are you pleased with all your presents?'

'They're lovely.'

'You and Ben were getting on all right tonight.'

'We always get on.'

'You know what I mean. It was nice to see you both together –' Hattie added quickly, 'in that sort of way.'

'You above all people, Hat,' Lily replied anxiously, 'should know that Ben and me are just friends. There ain't nothing romantic going on. I've told you that before.'

Hattie just shrugged. 'That kiss looked genuine to me.'

'It was only a peck.'

'A *what*?' Hattie exploded, sitting up. 'Your lips looked they were glued together!'

Lily was embarrassed. 'Listen, Hat, I don't know why Ben – well, kissed me. He's never done it before and to be honest I was annoyed that he did such a thing in front of everyone.'

'There's always a first time.'

'It's going to be the last as well,' Lily said, getting annoyed now.

Hattie sat forward, looking up at Lily with a puzzled expression. 'Look, Lil, that kiss shows just how much he thinks of you and he's proud to announce the fact to the world. He's crazy about you and by the way you kissed him back, you're nuts about him too.'

'I didn't kiss him back,' Lily protested. What was Hattie suggesting?

'Then I must have been watching another girl.'

Lily hadn't meant to let him kiss her, but how could she have stopped him? It had happened so quickly and all her thoughts had been on Charles, that she had been in a state of shock.

'What's wrong with you?' demanded Hattie, jumping to her feet. 'Why don't you just admit it?'

'There's nothing to admit,' Lily said as she faced her friend. 'I've told you time and again that me and Ben are just friends.'

'So you keep insisting. But actions speak louder than words. And what we all saw tonight, was not a handshake, Lil. Can't you see you're special to him – he worships the ground you walk on. If ever there were two people meant for each other it's you two.'

With a sinking sensation Lily realized why Hattie had been so against Charles. It wasn't because he was a stranger, but because they had all assumed it was Ben she would marry.

'Hattie, please listen to me,' Lily pleaded, desperate to make Hattie understand. 'What Ben did tonight came as a big surprise. I never encouraged him. Honest. I don't know what's happened.'

But Hattie just stared at her coldly. 'The trouble with you, Lil, is that you've got high falutin' ideas now you've met that posh bloke. But remember, it was Love Lane you were born in, not Buckingham Palace. And it's Ben and Reube and me who are your true friends, not someone like him who only wants one thing from you.'

Lily felt sick. How dare Hattie say that? 'He's got a name Hattie, it's Charles. And he's never once suggested anything improper.'

'Not yet maybe, but he will.'

'How can you say that?'

'What does any bloke like him want with a girl that ain't of his station? It's obvious, but you're just too daft to see it.'

Tears filled Lily's eyes. She couldn't believe her best friend was saying such spiteful things. 'Are you trying to make me feel guilty about liking him?'

'So you *do* like him?' Hattie gulped. 'I thought so! I told Reube you did but he said it was just a silly girl's crush and would wear off.'

'You've talked to Reube about us?'

Hattie looked defiant. 'Why shouldn't I? You're not like the old Lil. And it's *him* who's turned you against us.'

Lily tried not to show how much Hattie's remarks were hurting her. A big lump came in her throat; she felt betrayed.

'They say love blinds people and it's certainly made a fool of you, Lily Bright.'

'I . . . I didn't say it was love,' Lily stammered, close to tears. 'I haven't had chance yet to know how I really feel. I've been too busy trying not to upset me friends. But now I see that whatever I say or do won't make you happy. Not unless I stop seeing him.'

Hattie stuck out her chin. 'That's the first sensible thing I've heard you say in a long time.'

But Lily shook her head slowly. 'Given half the chance, Hattie, I'm going to see more of Charles. And if you don't like it, then I'm truly sorry.'

Hattie opened her mouth to speak then shut it. She reached for her coat on the back of the chair. As she did so, the front door banged.

Reube walked in the kitchen. His face was white. 'Ben's just gone.'

'Why didn't he say goodbye?' Lily asked.

'I would have thought that was obvious.' Reube glanced at Hattie. 'Next time you two have a ding-dong, keep your voices down.'

Hattie's eyes suddenly filled with tears. Before Lily

could speak she ran out of the room and the front door banged once more.

Reube looked at Lily, his face even paler. 'Well, that's set the cat among the pigeons, ain't it?'

'I can't help how I feel, Reube.'

'Obviously not.'

'I don't want to upset Hattie or Ben, or anyone. But I mean what I say about seeing Charles again. He came to the market today whilst you were out.'

Reube's shoulders sank. 'He did, did he?' Rubbing his hand across his jaw, he asked, 'Does he feel the same about you as you feel about him?'

'I don't know, Reube.'

'You could be taking a risk, like Hattie said.'

'I don't care. I have to find out.'

'You're refusing the love of a good bloke like me brother for someone you've only known five minutes?'

'I didn't know how Ben felt, not till recently.' Lily hoped that Reube, of all people, would understand.

'But it's been on the cards for years, you and him.'

Lily dug in her pocket for a handkerchief. 'If I knew Ben felt the way he did, I would have—'

'What would you have done, Lil?' Reube broke in sharply. 'Say you never met this Charles Grey, say that tonight Ben asked you to marry him. Would you have said yes?'

It was a question she hadn't considered, because before meeting Charles she hadn't known what love was or wanted to marry any man, other than the one in her dreams. She couldn't even imagine that Ben, being the flirt he was, would ever have asked her to marry him.

'I'll take that as a no,' Reube said before she could answer. His voice thick with emotion as he looked at her. 'Well, Lil, I'll tell you this for nothing, it would take someone blind, deaf and dumb, not to know that Ben's in love with you and has been for a long while. And I don't mean just a five minute wonder. He's got it bad. And what he overheard you say to Hattie tonight might have just about broke his heart. And that, gel, is gonna take a while in mending.'

With one last long look in her direction, he squared his shoulders, then turned and left the house.

Ben was sitting in the charabanc as dawn came up. He could see the pink sky crawling into the stars, lifting the Quarry's old roof into daytime relief. There was smoke already funnelling out of one of the chimneys. Ernie and Gladys must be up, preparing for another Sunday and he envied them.

He envied the normality of their life, the certainty of the hours ahead. It was a certainty he had shared himself once too. The belief that the universe would provide the wherewithal for life. You may be penniless, thirsty, hungry and unemployed, but there was always tomorrow. Another day on the horizon, a chance at survival. Every East Ender lived for that day and the opportunity to make good. But for some reason, he knew that his own private universe had within the last few hours, taken a violent knock. His thirst for the things he believed in, his dreams of becoming a self-made man, they were all a million miles away. And why? Because without Lily, none of them mattered. And yet he'd never known it before ... never guessed ... never given it a single thought that she might not be in his life for ever. He played at being the Romeo with other women, kidding himself as well as kidding her. And now he'd lost her.

Last night was like having a leg removed. And the rest of his body wasn't bleeding, just not sure how to walk again, because you certainly didn't function the same without a limb. You expected to always have arms and legs, they were part of your makeup. Just like Lily, she was part of his living and breathing. And now she had fallen for someone else.

He pulled hard on the cigarette, its glow dying as he opened the window and chucked it out. The birds were scooting over the roofs, dancing in the clouds above the scarlet wash. Red sky at night, shepherd's delight. Red sky in the morning, shepherd's warning.

A warning too late for him.

Mustering up what strength he had left, he jumped out of the vehicle and stretched his back. His spine was aching from the hours of sitting, trying to reason out what had gone wrong. Last night he was thinking of proposing, going down on one knee in the old-fashioned way and popping the question then asking her dad for her hand in marriage. Not for a minute had it occurred to him that she'd refuse. In his dreams he'd even had them walking over Blackheath, deciding on a house, a nice little terrace away from the Smoke. He reckoned he could afford it now. He had enough money saved and he'd work like a slave to make her happy.

But none of it meant anything now. Not without Lil.

Broad shoulders drooping under his crumpled new suit, he turned away from the Quarry and began to walk home.

Chapter Ten

On Sunday morning, it was Uncle Noah who brought her a cup of tea.

'Thought you'd like this,' he said as he shuffled into the room.

'What time is it?' Lily sat up in bed as he put the cup and saucer on the table.

'Eight o'clock.'

'Are Mum and Dad up?'

'No, they're having a lie-in after last night.'

All that had happened came back in a rush. After all the things that had been said, her birthday had been ruined and Lily had cried herself to sleep.

Her uncle sat on the end of the bed. 'There was a lot of bangs last night.'

'I'm sorry. It was the front door.'

'I heard a lot of shouting.'

The tears were very close. 'Hattie and me had a row.'

'You were going at it hammer and tongs.'

Lily sniffed. 'It was awful. I don't know if we'll make it up again.'

'Course you will.' Her uncle patted her leg.

'Do you think Mum and Dad heard?'

'Doubt it. They sleep like logs. I was still reading me Sunday paper.'

Lily was having trouble seeing through her sore eyes. 'You must have heard everything, then?'

'No,' said her uncle, 'But I 'spect it was over a bloke.'

'Yes, it was.' Lily sipped the hot liquid, grateful for its comfort. 'And you know who, don't you?'

'That Charlie boy was it, who came round here? Your mother has been on at me to warn you off him.'

'But why?' Lily couldn't believe that everyone's opinion of Charles was so poor. 'He only asked me to help him buy things, not run away with him to Gretna Green.'

'That's what they're afraid of, see?'

'What, of me running away? They know I wouldn't do that.'

Uncle Noah sighed as he wiped his pince-nez on a piece of rag and balanced them on his nose again. 'You're just an innocent in their eyes. And he's much older, ain't he?'

Lily nodded slowly. 'He said he was twenty in 1917 when he went to sea so that makes him thirty-three.'

'It ain't young, is it?'

'It's not old.' Lily put down her cup. 'But what does age matter? He's a business gentleman who has paid me more than fairly for my time. The money he gave me helped to clear all our debt. He ain't made me no indecent proposition as Hattie seemed to think he would . . .' Lily's voice broke at the memory of all her friend had said last night. She scooped away a tear.

'Listen, Lil,' said her uncle firmly, 'they're worried because it might not stop at business. Strikes me, you're not thinking of him just in the way of being employed. And, if that's the truth and things go further, your friends will be slow to accept an outsider. He's a gent and always will be.'

'But he came here, Uncle Noah, and you met him. He's not the sort to look down on anyone, no matter who they are.'

'It ain't him, gel. It's us who know our place and don't like to be reminded of it. This is the Depression, Lil, money is scarce, there's no jobs and half the island or more is out of work. Charlie boy appears, with his shiny motor, and good clobber, and arouses suspicion. It ain't so much class, as downright envy. Why should he have it all and people like us, have nothing?'

'But we have got everything!' Lily protested. 'We've got each other, we're a family. He's on his own and is lonely.'

'And the loneliness is of his own making.'

'His wife died,' Lily argued gently. 'He didn't want that to happen.'

'Look, Lil, I'm sorry for his loss, but our losses are greater. He's got his money and good standing, the world is his oyster. As for us, no bloody politician, union or Blackshirt, quack or preacher is going to relieve us of our poverty. We've got to make the best of what we have, in other words, there ain't any hope for our future to change.'

'We're happy, Uncle Noah!'

'We could be a bloody sight happier.'

Lily sighed. 'I s'pose Mum and Dad want me to end up with a man like Ben.'

'That's 'cos we trust 'im. Like attracts like, ducks. It's an unwritten rule. And your gent ain't like us.'

Lily hadn't thought about breaking rules, written or unwritten. She understood what her uncle was saying, but she couldn't change her feelings. Every time she was with Charles she was happy. Was that so wrong?

'What am I going to do, Uncle Noah?'

'Only you can decide that,' he smiled, pushing himself up from the bed. 'You're a woman now and as such, should know your own mind.'

Lily looked confused. 'I want to keep my friends. I want Mum to be happy. But I want to see Charles.'

Her uncle shook his head despairingly. 'A woman is a bag of mixed tricks.'

'I wish I knew a few more.'

'And you've just reminded me why I never got spliced,' he opened the bedroom door. 'Now I'm going to cook yer all a breakfast and hope your mother don't nag me to blazes for messin' up her kitchen when she comes down.'

Lily slipped out of bed and began to get dressed. What did she really want in her life? Was it selfish to yearn for happiness and excitement? She didn't want to hurt her friends, but she didn't want to give up Charles either. What was she going to do?

Later that morning, there was a knock on the door. Lily rushed to open it, hoping to see Charles. The look of expectancy on her face soon died when she saw who it was. 'Oh, Ben, it's you.'

'Have you a minute to spare?' He looked tired and cold as he stood with his hands in his overcoat pockets.

She quickly glanced behind her. 'I'm helping Mum to cook the dinner.'

'It's about last night.'

'Oh.' Lily was afraid of what he might say. Was he still angry and upset? How could she explain her feelings without upsetting him again?

'Who's at the door?' Josie shouted from the kitchen. She came along the hall. 'Oh, hello, son. Did you have a good time at the party?'

'Yes, thanks, Mrs Bright.'

'That was a lovely dance you two did,' Josie smiled at them both. All morning she had been hinting to Lily that after seeing Ben kiss her, she thought he was the right man for her daughter.

'Can you spare Lil for a moment?' asked Ben quickly. 'I won't keep her long.'

'You two go off and enjoy yourselves,' Josie said eagerly. 'Lily, wrap up well as those winds are still biting.'

Lily didn't want to go out. She wanted to wait in for Charles. After speaking to Uncle Noah she had decided to give Ben and Hattie a wide berth this week, hoping they would have time to forgive and forget. But now she couldn't refuse Ben.

Five minutes later they were walking towards Island Gardens. Neither of them said much until they arrived in the green space and sat down on a bench overlooking the river. It was cold, but a bright morning sun broke through. The white puffs of clouds were scudding joyfully along and there was evidence of spring everywhere. Little green shoots had appeared overnight, the birds were flying from the trees to the glistening rooftops. Across the water the oval dome of Greenwich Observatory shone like a jewel in a crown. Being Sunday, the river traffic had ceased, the tugs and barges, lined up for tomorrow. But there were children playing on them, despite the dangers of falling in, as they jumped from one to the other. Their cries rose up in the air and travelled up to where they sat.

'Me and Reube couldn't resist a challenge like that,' Ben said suddenly as he sat with his hands in his overcoat pockets. 'Before Dad was called up he tanned our hides something rotten when he found out we jumped the barges. It was our aim to jump three in a row.'

'Me and Hattie used to watch you,' Lily nodded. She couldn't recall Mr James very well, only that he looked like an older version of Reube. When he had died in the war, he had left his good friend Pedro, who was too old

190

to be called up, to take charge of the stall. But Reube had left school at fourteen, eager to help. Ben had joined him a year later. The James brothers had grown up quickly after that.

'We were only about six or seven,' Lily smiled, 'and nearly died holding our breath as we watched you.'

'They was good days, Lil.'

'I never thought they were going to end. I never thought Samson would die or we'd lose the yard or that we'd grow up.' She turned to him. 'But we did.'

He nodded and looking at her said softly, 'Lil, I know I've lost you. And I know it's me own fault.'

'Why didn't you say something before?'

'I was too busy showing off, pretending to be Rudolph Valentino.'

'I always thought you was funny.'

He sighed. 'Is that all?'

Lily blushed. 'I never really thought about it. You've been like me brother—' She went to continue but he held up his hand.

'Listen a minute, because what I've got to say is important. If I don't say it now, I might lose me courage and never say it all.' He took a deep breath. 'Last night I caused you a lot of embarrassment, and made meself look a right clown into the bargain. It was me own daft fault, waiting too long. I suppose I never grew out of being that kid jumping the barges, showing off to the girls. Now I know I should have grown up a bit faster. I managed to run a market stall all right, but inside there was this kid, still trying to impress.' His soft grey eyes looked deeply into hers. 'Anyway, that's enough about number one. What I want most, right this minute, and for always is to keep what we had once, our friendship.'

'We'll always have that, Ben.'

'Are you sure? I ain't spoiled things forever?'

'It's not your fault what happened,' Lily fumbled. 'I . . . I just met someone . . .'

'I know.' His face looked tight. 'And I don't want you to get hurt.'

Lily looked away as she remembered the words of her friend. 'That's what Hattie said to me once.'

Suddenly Ben chuckled. 'Old Hat is the fount of eternal wisdom, ain't she?'

They both laughed and Lily felt a relief from the tension.

Ben seemed on the point of saying something, but then stood up. 'Come on, let's have a gander at the water.'

They walked to the river and looked over it. On the South Bank, a picturesque dome was a dazzling, burnished gold. 'Lil, if ever you need me, I'll be there, right across the road, all right?'

She felt close to tears. 'I'm sorry if I hurt you, Ben.'

He gave her a big grin, and put a hand on her shoulder. 'Me? You couldn't hurt me. This skin is as tough as one of them wild animals with a big horn on their nose.'

Lily smiled into his gentle gaze. Had their heart to

heart now resolved their problems? As they walked home, Ben told her enthusiastically about the work he had arranged for the charabanc. She was happy that he seemed to have a bright future.

When he left her at the door, he gave a cheery wave goodbye.

But Lily was not convinced that everything was really all right again.

It was barely light when Ben heard a noise at the window the following morning. Yawning and stretching he got out of bed and drew the curtain. A figure was standing in the road. Lifting the sash, he called softly, 'Who's there?'

'It's me. Sweetsy.' The man came closer. 'Got a minute?'

'What do you want at this time of the morning?'

'Come down and I'll tell you.'

Ben closed the sash and pulled on his trousers. Careful not to disturb his brother, he crept downstairs.

'Cripes, Sweetsy, what's all this in aid of?' Ben grasped the young man's sleeve and pulled him in.

'I thought knocking would wake everyone. So I threw a stone.'

'Well, I'm up now. What do you want?'

'There's a job going.'

Ben knew Johnny Sweet to be a bit of a flyboy. But he was harmless enough and he'd always got a few quid in his pocket, ready to do a deal. Swathed in a coat, scarf and hat, the early visitor smiled. 'I always give you first refusal, my friend.'

'Is it kosher?'

'As kosher as my old mum.'

'Your mum died years ago.'

'Yeah, but she ain't forgotten.'

Ben smiled. 'Get on with it, then.'

'The goods have gotta go out today. This moment to be precise.'

Ben frowned suspiciously. 'What's all the rush?'

'I've important customers waiting.'

Ben nodded thoughtfully. 'How long's it gonna take me?'

'A week, in that old crate of yours. It's all up north.'

'Don't knock my lorry,' Ben grinned. 'It's done you a good turn in the past. How much is on the line?'

'Ten readies. Five up front, five on your return.'

It was a nice offer but Ben shook his head. 'Ten readies now and ten when I come back.'

Johnny Sweet let out a groan. 'My friend, you drive a hard bargain.'

'Seven days on the road with no prior booking comes at a price.'

'All right, you're on. Here, I've drawn you a map, and written the names and places on the back.'

Ben took the crumpled paper and laughed. 'Is this Chinese?'

'I was in a rush. Now, what did we agree on the figures?'

Ben grinned. 'Ten smackers in my palm right this minute or you're gone.'

Reluctantly the visitor reached inside his coat. He brought out a wad of notes.

Ben pushed the money in his pocket. 'What's the stuff I'm carrying?'

'Peanuts.'

'And I'm a monkey's uncle.'

'I told you, this is straight up, my son. Now go to Pointer's warehouse. Two of my men are waiting to help you load if you're there within the hour.'

They arranged a further meeting and Ben closed the front door. He washed, resisted a shave, stoked the range and prepared a plate of bread and dripping. Quietly he returned to the bedroom. Pulling on old clothes, a thick jumper, heavy trousers and boots, he made certain he was prepared for all weathers.

'Wake up, lazy bones,' he whispered in his snoring brother's ear. 'You're late for market.'

Reube yawned as he lowered his feet to the floor. 'Where are you off to in that getup?'

'I'm on a job for Sweetsy. It'll take about a week.'

Reube shrugged and began to dress. 'So where did you disappear to all day yesterday?'

'Come on downstairs and I'll tell you.'

'What's all the rush? I thought you was dying of a broken heart?' Reube grunted as they made their way to the kitchen.

'The ten nicker I've just earned has helped cure it.'

'Ten nicker?'

'And ten more to follow.'

'Blimey, that's tasty.'

The two men ate silently together until finally Reube asked, 'So what did happen yesterday, then?'

'Me and Lil walked to Island Gardens.'

'And?'

'And no surprises for guessing what happened.'

Reube scratched his head. 'Go on then, enlighten me.'

Ben rolled his eyes. 'What could I say to her? An apology was in order, I think.'

'You didn't do anything wrong, except kiss her.'

'I had a lot more than that in mind.'

Reube pasted another slice of bread with dripping. 'So what's gonna happen now?'

'Nothin' as far as I know. I'm a free man, and I'm gonna enjoy me liberty.'

'So there ain't no hard feelings?'

'None at all.'

'Well, you're a better man than me, 'cos I'd be really choked if Hattie ditched me.'

'Lil didn't ditch me. It just never got started.'

Reube sat back in his chair and shook his head. 'If you say so, bruv.' He smiled as he drank his tea. 'Well, today I don't need to inform Lil that me brother's about to jump off London Bridge then?'

Ben laughed and waved the joke aside. 'You can tell her that I went off to work with a big smile on me face.'

'I'll do just that.'

196

'You finished your rosie?'

'Yeah. I'm gonna pay me dues to the khazi.'

Ben stood up. 'Tell Mum I'll see her in a week's time.' He smiled as his brother left the kitchen. When the back door closed and Reube disappeared into the washhouse, he let out a long, relieved sigh. At least he had recovered a little pride. A week away from Love Lane was just what he needed to let the dust settle.

Ben took the two remaining slices of bread and wrapped them in newspaper; they'd make a nice bite on the journey.

Outside he was relieved to find a cold, bright Monday dawning. He liked driving through the countryside early and seeing all the villages along the way.

As he hopped over the wall of the Quarry public house where he stationed his vehicles, he looked forward to smelling the pigs and cows and country air. With his window down and his consignment safely on the back, seven days would be a doddle.

This job would give him a chance to make plans. He was going to turn his business into a real cracker. Though he might not talk with a cut glass accent he intended to show the island what he was made of.

An hour later, with the help of Sweetsy's two men, Ben was on his way, without any lifting bridges to delay him.

As he drove, he was relieved for once, to leave the city well and truly behind him.

★

All week Lily listened to the depressing news of the growing unemployment. There were riots and demonstrations throughout the East End. Though her father kept saying how lucky he was to be at the timber yard, she knew he felt guilty. Even though he came home each day with bleeding hands and an aching back from carry all the rough timber, he was envied by his old mates. They still stood on the stones all day, with no prospect of work in sight.

The newspapers said that the latest figure was one and a half million out of work, with no indication of it decreasing and most men on the island were now fighting each other for the few jobs there were.

'Since they come into power nine months ago, Labour have made a right pig's ear of the country,' Uncle Noah complained as they ate supper on Friday night.

'Between them and that Oswald Mosley promising us wealth through borrowing, they want their brains tested,' agreed Bob Bright. 'Stands to reason if you take from Peter, you gotta give it back to Paul. Those Blackshirts would get us in a worse muddle than Labour if they got in.'

'They won't, will they?' asked Lily.

'Mosley wants to form what he calls a New Party. It's sure to attract some attention.'

'Only from the cranks, surely?' said her mother.

Lily suddenly remembered that Charles had mentioned a New Party on the day he saved her from the

Blackshirt. He had threatened to expose the group to their leader. Did Charles know about all this then?

'I dunno,' said her dad worriedly. 'There's a feeling of unrest everywhere and you can't blame the blokes when they have a go.'

'I wish the fighting would stop,' said Lily, putting down her knife and fork.

Everyone looked at her. 'We're fighting for our rights,' pointed out her father. 'We have to, or we'll be trodden over.'

'But isn't that how wars start?' Lily was upset. Was it because she was growing older that she felt this way? Once, her dad's word was law. But now she was beginning to think other kinds of thoughts. Why couldn't people resolve problems through talking and not hurting each other?

'Wars are going on all the time, Lil. I heard the coppers arrested four of the blokes I used to work with,' her father continued, coughing and hitting his chest as he became angry. 'Blokes just the same as me, who would do anything for a crust, and were willing to wait in the cold and wet every day, from dawn to nightfall. Them buggers carted 'em off by the scruff of their necks, just 'cos they waved a few placards. No wonder there's anarchy and wars start.'

Lily could see her dad was upset. He was getting very angry as all the men seemed to be lately. Reube had been on edge all week, walking over to Ted and Samuel, waving the stick as though he wanted to use it again. Even the women were on the lookout for trouble, egging their men on.

'I met Flo Parks yesterday,' said Josie, turning to look at Lily. 'She asked how you were, as Hattie hadn't met up with you last Sunday.'

'I hope you told her I was well.' Lily wasn't going to say that she had fallen out with Hattie. She didn't want to add to the depressing atmosphere at the table.

'Yes, I did. Flo said that Hattie didn't say much about the party. I would have thought you two girls would have wanted to chat about it.'

Lily shrugged. 'We will when we've got time.'

'Yes, I suppose that's it. Your lives are very full.'

Lily didn't reply but stood up to collect the plates.

'Now, I've made a nice bowl of semolina,' Josie said as she smiled at the two men. 'And I've got half a teaspoon of jam for the top. That'll be nice, won't it?'

Lily knew her mother was trying to change the men's topic of conversation, but as Lily placed the pudding bowls on the draining board, she heard her father speaking angrily again. Her heart began to sink. The strikes, unemployment and riots were discussed fervently in every household lately. Trouble, unrest and bitterness was on everyone's tongue.

Lily wished that she and Hattie were speaking. Their long and enduring friendship seemed to be threatened too.

Suddenly she knew what to do. On Sunday she

would call for Hattie. Her thoughts had all been centred on Charles, and her attention had slipped from her best friend. Their small fight was turning into a war and after all she had learned from her elders, Lily was determined to put right her own world.

Late on Sunday morning Lily put on her coat and hat. She didn't know what she was going to say to Hattie, but she would think of something.

It was a dull grey day and Lily stood on the pavement uncertainly, waiting for inspiration. But then the door of Hattie's house opened. Her friend was pulling on her coat. It was the first time they had met since the party.

'Morning, Hat,' Lily said brightly.

'Oh, it's you.'

As much as Lily wanted to repair the damage she felt that Hattie had said some hurtful things. Did she still feel the same? 'Are you going out?'

'Me dad wants a paper. There's a seller by the Queen sometimes. Don't know if he's still there.'

'Can I walk with you?'

'If you like.'

Hattie was wearing a soft grey coat and gloves with a little grey scarf tied around the collar. Her hair, as usual, was shaped around her head into two kiss-curls.

'I wondered if you was coming round this afternoon?' said Lily as she pulled her old coat closer and wished that she looked as smart as Hattie did. Even with the money coming in to the house since her dad had started work, there hadn't been enough left over to buy anything from Vera Froud.

'No, I'm a bit busy.'

'What with?'

'This and that.'

Lily tried to ignore her friend's tone and the fact that Hattie was making it obvious she had not intended to see Lily.

'Well, at least we can have a chat whilst we walk.'

Hattie merely shrugged, quickening her step.

Lily kept up with her. 'Hattie, I've missed seeing you. It don't seem the same any more.'

'You don't want to see the likes of me.'

'I wish you'd stop saying that.'

'It's true, isn't it?'

'No, course not. Look, can't we forget what happened at the party? We both said things we didn't mean.'

Hattie stopped still. 'You mean what you said about Ben—'

Lily shook her head. 'No, I meant that. It was all a bit of a misunderstanding and Ben and me are friends again. We went for a walk and talked things over.'

'So you're just friends?'

Lily nodded. 'Good friends, Hat. Like you and me. He understands that now.'

Hattie stared at her, her eyes narrowing. She began to walk again. 'Well, that's Ben for you. I suppose he's not one to show his feelings.'

They walked on in silence, heads down against the

wind. When they arrived at the Queen public house on the junction of East Ferry Road and Manchester Road, they stopped. Hattie sighed. 'Me dad's out of luck. The newspaper seller's gone.'

'Why don't we walk to the foot tunnel? It's only a short way. There might be one there.'

'All right.

Lily was beginning to wonder what she could say to Hattie to break the ice. As they walked by the river, a small boat chugged by, leaving its wake on the surface. The factories and warehouses were closed, but the kids were still larking about in the mud, searching for wood and coal that had spilled from the boats. A strong, tarry essence blew off the water. A ship's hooter sounded and in reply came the bark of a dog.

Lily and Hattie both spoke at once. 'You first,' smiled Lily.

'I was only going to say I was sorry about having a go at you. It was your birthday after all.'

'And I'm sorry too.'

Hattie frowned. 'It's always been you and Ben, you see. We just took it for granted you would go on like that.'

'We'll all go on being friends I hope.'

Hattie looked thoughtful. 'Perhaps he'll find a nice girl.'

'He deserves one.'

'There was that girl who was always knocking on his door, with dark hair and a good figure. She was really keen on him. And there are plenty of girls he knows from the Dockland Settlement. They all like him. Perhaps now he'll ask one of them out.'

Lily smiled. Hattie hadn't given up trying to make her jealous. 'I don't want us to fall out again, Hat.'

'Neither do I.' Hattie shuffled her feet. 'I'm fed up with staying in on Sunday afternoons.'

They both laughed. 'Well, you'd better tell me all the news about your new love,' Hattie said after a while.

'There's nothing to tell,' Lily said quietly. 'I haven't seen him although Pedro did say he called by the stall on me birthday.'

'But he didn't show up last week?'

Lily shook her head. 'No.'

Hattie immediately linked her arm through Lily's. 'Never mind, you've got us.'

'Yes,' nodded Lily, aware of Hattie's sudden change in mood. She was all smiles now.

'I don't want to break up with you, Lil. Like I wrote in me card, you're my best friend.'

'Yes, it's all worked out for the best.' Lily felt a big ache in her chest, as she felt herself being led along by Hattie. She knew that Hattie was pleased Charles hadn't turned up. She couldn't know how it felt to have a heartache like this, as though someone was turning a knife inside you.

But at least they were on good terms again and had patched up their differences. She wasn't going to think about what Hattie had said at the party about her having high faluting ideas and that Charles only wanted one thing from her and she was too daft to see it. The home truths had hurt at the time, but bringing it all up now wouldn't serve a purpose. It was better to forgive and forget.

'I've a couple of nice patterns I brought back from work, a dress with a V-shaped neckline with a skirt made from three panels. The other is a really beautiful long dress, just right for a tea dance,' Hattie said eagerly. 'Do you want to come up to me bedroom and see?'

'That would be nice.'

'Come on then, let's go home.'

Lily listened to Hattie as they walked. She told her about the fittings that had taken place for the aristocratic young bride. And how everything was even more hush-hush than it was before as they tried to camouflage the weight she was rapidly putting on. Hattie thought it was hilarious and laughed as she was telling the story of the young girl as she was made to suffer the indignity of Madame Nerys' obvious disapproval when she had to let out the waistline even more than she'd planned. But Lily could only feel sympathy for the poor girl, even though she had wealth and status on her side.

'And I ain't told you about me ring either,' said Hattie excitedly.

'The sapphire and diamond one in the shop at Aldgate?'

'Yes. Reube's going to buy it for me.' Hattie did a little flounce, throwing back her head. 'Ben's gonna drive us up there. Why don't you come to. And then we can make a day of it.'

Lily guessed that Hattie was still trying to matchmake. She still hadn't given up hope. 'There'll be no one to mind the stall,' Lily pointed out.

'Pedro can stand in,' Hattie shrugged, a twinkle in her eye. 'I'll get Reube to ask him.'

As they walked down Love Lane Lily began to wonder if the price of Hattie's friendship was too high. Would she ever give up trying to get her and Ben together?

Chapter Eleven

At Easter, the market reflected the country's Depression and even the barrows and fruit stalls were suffering. Lily knew her father had been very lucky to get the timber job. Even the skin ships were now few and far between and the dockyards were in a state of deep gloom. Lily feared that the Blackshirts would seize the opportunity to return to places like Cox Street but that would be a mistake as the traders dislike for the peddlers of fascism was even more intense. They had all paid more attention to the news after the last visit and everyone knew that Mosley, their leader, was insisting the country go deeper into debt by borrowing from abroad. To the ordinary man's thinking this was a fanatic's theory, and would make things even worse than they were.

No one wanted that.

In her quieter moments Lily wondered what Charles would have said about all this. He seemed to have influence over that Blackshirt, his quiet words having more effect than any weapon. She felt that although he was an outsider to the island, he might have been able to help in some way. She didn't know how, of course. And now it was weeks since she had seen him last. His face was becoming a distant memory, as though she had dreamed it all.

One Saturday morning in May, Lily was alone at the stall whilst Reube went off for stock. They were getting very low on good items, whilst the junk was multiplying. Yesterday, in desperation, Reube had visited the Caledonian Market. When he'd returned with only one broken clock, a box of bed knobs, a few screws, nuts, bolts, two sets of false teeth and a large reel of bell wire, Lily had been disappointed.

'I know ironmongery ain't our line, Lil,' Reube had said when he saw her expression, 'but the bloke I bought it all from was at his wits' end. He had this placard round his neck. It said: "I know two trades and speak two languages. I have six children and haven't worked for six months. But I only ask for one job."' Reube had shaken his head as he repeated these words, his voice thick with emotion. 'So I gave him five bob for the lot.'

As Lily placed the bits and pieces out, she remembered the sad look in Reube's eyes. He was a good man at heart and had done the poor man a service. Five shillings was generous, although they would be lucky to get their money back. She was deep in thought as she was about to stand the wooden clock which had long ago lost its hands, on the top shelf. Five shillings must seem a great deal but it wouldn't go a long way to feeding six children. How would the man and his family survive when it was gone?

'Excuse me, is the clock for sale?'

Lily turned and almost dropped the clock. Her mouth fell open. Charles' tall figure was swathed in a light-coloured coat that was the height of fashion and elegance. He was hatless and his dark hair was brushed back from his face, smoothed cleanly down to his collar. He looked even more handsome than she remembered.

He gave her one of his radiant smiles. 'Lily, how wonderful it is to see you.'

She attempted to speak but her heart was beating too fast.

'Please, let me help you.' He relieved her of the clock and as he did so there were many rattles inside. He laughed. 'Despite the noises this has a very nice case. How much is it?'

Lily was trying to gather her thoughts. She felt faint and dizzy, as a wave of joy flowed through her at seeing him. 'I'm not sure as Reube hasn't priced it yet.'

'Would he take ten shillings?'

'Ten shillings!' Lily exclaimed. For a broken clock it was a wonderful offer. 'Are you sure? It won't tell the time as it has no hands.'

'No matter. I have a good watch mender.'

'Is it for your house?' She couldn't resist asking. Had

he bought any more things? Is that what he was here for today?

He smiled. 'No, Lily. I have a client who I am sure would like it.'

Lily felt dismayed to learn this as it might mean that he still didn't want her help. She reached under the stall. 'I'll wrap it in some newspaper for you.'

'No, don't bother, the car is close by. Here.' He placed ten shillings in her hand.

Lily stood silently. She wanted to say so much, but mostly that she had missed him and had counted the days since they last saw each other.

'How are you?' he asked quietly.

'Very well, thank you.'

'You weren't here the last time I called.'

'It was my birthday, March the fifteenth.' If only he knew how disappointed she had been when Pedro told her of his visit.

The smile slipped from his face. 'Your birthday?'

'Yes, I was twenty-one.'

'Oh dear. It seems I missed a special occasion.' He arched one dark eyebrow. 'I hope you enjoyed yourself?'

'Reube gave me the day off. I've never had a whole Saturday off before.'

'And of course I chose that very one to call.' He looked deeply into her eyes as he used to do and Lily felt transported with joy. It was as though they were alone in the world, just the two of them, blocking out the sights and sounds of the market.

Suddenly another voice broke the spell. A woman had picked up a doorknob. 'This'll do me hubbie, love. Does it work?'

Lily saw Charles smile.

'Yes,' said Lily. 'You can have it for tuppence.'

'You couldn't have made much profit on that sale,' Charles observed when they were alone again.

'I didn't need to,' Lily confessed. 'I sold you the clock. The knobs and screws came with it for much less than you paid me. We've already taken a five shillings profit and have the rest of the ironmongery still on display.'

'That's very honest of you to tell me,' he nodded, a twinkle in his eyes.

'It was very generous of you to buy the clock.'

'That's because I shall make a lot more profit on it than you when it's restored and sold to my client,' he grinned and they both laughed together.

'The reason I haven't returned to see you,' he said after a while, 'is because I've been travelling abroad.'

Lily felt so happy that she could jump for joy. The reason he hadn't come to see her was because he had been away. Not because he had no use for her or didn't want to see her again.

'You see, I had something important to ask you on the day I came here. Unfortunately, due to the pressure of business I was unable to call again until now.'

Lily was so excited she almost didn't feel a tap on her shoulder.

'Ere, gel, whose are these choppers?' demanded an elderly man as he examined the false teeth. 'Do they work?'

Lily shrugged. Why wouldn't everyone go away and let her talk to Charles?

'You got another pair over there. What's the bite on 'em like?'

As the man shuffled round the stall to examine them, Charles drew her to one side. 'We can't talk here, Lily. Would you come to my house? What I have to say may be of great interest to you.'

Was he going to ask her to help him buy articles again? 'When?' she asked eagerly.

'Sunday morning perhaps?'

'Yes, that will be fine.'

'I'll come to collect you.'

She didn't know what her parents would say. 'It would be better if I could meet you at the top of Westferry Road as we did before.'

He looked at her with a frown. 'As you wish, Lily. And the time?'

She intended to be out of the house early as she didn't want anyone or anything to stop her from seeing Charles.

'Is nine o'clock too early?'

'Not at all.'

Suddenly a hand appeared in front of her clutching a pair of false teeth. 'I'll take 'em!' cried the elderly man. 'They're a bit loose, but I'll boil 'em up and shrink 'em.'

Lily turned and wrapped the teeth in newspaper. When she had put the money in the tin, she looked back for Charles. But he'd gone.

All afternoon she couldn't stop thinking about him. She wouldn't tell anyone she was going to see him as she was determined that this time she wouldn't let others' opinions influence her. As Uncle Noah had told her, she was old enough now, to know her own mind.

Lily was waiting on the corner of Westferry Road bright and early the next morning. She had hardly slept a wink, waiting for this moment to come. She had left early, telling Uncle Noah, who was the only one up, she was going for a walk. She didn't want to lie, but it was only a small one. She couldn't wait to see Charles and discover what it was he was going to ask her.

At nine o'clock on the dot, the ruby red car pulled alongside the curb. Charles jumped out and came round to open the door. Lily had nothing new to wear, but she had bought a beret from Vera Froud last night, a pretty Tam o'Shanter style in a light fawn colour. On her collar she wore Hattie's rabbit foot to bring her good luck.

'I hope this isn't an inconvenience, Lily,' Charles said as he drove them along.

'No. Now the weather's better I often go for a stroll.'

'Does your friend accompany you?'

'Hattie? Sometimes in the afternoon. If her brother isn't well though, she stays in to help.'

'Ah yes. This is the young man who you told me was gassed in the war.'

Lily nodded. He had remembered so much of their conversations. She felt elated. Their meetings must have mattered to him, if only in a small way.

'Is there any hope of his recovery?' he asked after a while.

'No one knows. The fits seem to come on after the nightmares that he still has.'

Charles nodded slowly. 'I had many friends who died in action, and some of those who survived are still haunted as Hattie's brother is. The memory of the conflict is hard to bear, though I hear that medical science is discovering new treatments all the time. There are certain institutions that deal effectively with such cases like an officer friend of mine who has had some success with his health.'

Lily shook her head. 'Mr and Mrs Parks couldn't afford to send him to such a place. And anyway, I don't think Mrs Parks would let him go.'

'And that is to be commended of course. But it must be a strain on the family.'

'They're used to it now. Every island family lost someone in the war or had someone injured. Like Mr James, Ben and Reube's father who never came back from France.'

'Was he a market trader too before enlisting?'

'Yes. A family friend looked after the stall until Reube was old enough to run it.'

Charles nodded slowly. 'Your island families are remarkable indeed.'

Lily sat quietly, his interest in the island impressed her. Although he was, as Uncle Noah had pointed out, an outsider, his concern seemed genuine. Even though he couldn't understand true poverty, she was sure he didn't look down on them.

At last they came to Dewar Street and Lily's heart leapt at the sight of the terraced houses. Number four was exactly as she remembered, a tall, slim building with long windows and black railings outside. The white steps led up to a grand front door with a brass lion's head knocker. Her heart banged fiercely against her ribs. She had thought she would never see this place again!

But Lily was disappointed when they went in. The house looked even emptier and was dark and cold. On her previous visit it had seemed a little neglected, but now all the drapes were half closed and darkness filled the hall. She couldn't even see the aspidistra at the bottom of the stairs.

'I'm afraid I've had no time to light a fire,' Charles said as he escorted her into the drawing room. 'I breakfasted rather late. Please sit down, Lily.'

She chose one of the silk-covered chairs by the window. Charles drew the heavy green curtains wide apart failing to secure them with the tassels as he removed his heavy coat at the same time. He disappeared from the room one moment and was back the next. Lily looked for the young maid, but she didn't appear.

'I shall make tea,' Charles said, as he looked around him. 'Although I'm not quite certain if I can offer you milk.'

'I'm not thirsty,' Lily replied, feeling more awkward by the moment. 'Please don't trouble.'

'Lily, you must forgive this disorder,' he gestured to the table that had once had a polished surface covered in dust. Now it supported a large dirty plate with the remains of food, a knife and fork, and cup and saucer. Beyond, the fireplace held ashes which had spilled out of the grate. Gone was the decorative fan and scattered over the carpet were a large number of newspapers and periodicals.

Lily looked at the general disarray. On her previous visit, the house had at least looked clean and tidy. Now it felt abandoned. Was it because he had been away? She looked on the walls for the painting they had bought at Petticoat Lane. Could it be in another room? The statuettes and rug were also missing, but perhaps he had chosen not to put them in here?

Her heart sank. Had the purchases not been to his liking after all? Lily was dismayed and confused, she couldn't imagine what he would want to ask her?

'May I take your coat?' He was not sitting down but pacing uneasily from window to window.

'No, thank you. I . . . I can't stay very long.' She felt like an intruder.

He suddenly stopped. 'Lily, you must have wondered

why I came to the market that day and failed to return? I told you I have been travelling . . .'

She nodded as he began to pace again.

'Before I left England a problem arose. It was very upsetting and I had urgent need of – of specific help. That was why I came to see you.'

Lily was mystified. Other than helping him to buy things for the house, how could she help him?

'You see,' he went on hesitantly, 'my young assist-ant, Annie, was . . . er . . . called away, that is to say, she was . . .' He stopped, turning to look at Lily, then sud-denly he collapsed into a chair close beside her. Drawing his hand over his face, he gave out a long sigh as though he couldn't bear to continue.

'Are you feeling well?' Lily asked. She was beginning to think it was a mistake to have come here on her own. Doubts began to flood into her mind as she looked into his unhappy face.

He slowly met her gaze. 'I cannot deceive you, Lily. I must tell you the whole truth. It is still very difficult, I'm afraid, for me to talk about my late wife.'

Lily felt a sudden relief. His unhappiness was con-nected with his wife! She sat back a little, waiting, as he composed himself.

'You see, Annie was . . .' he shook his head sadly, 'was not the honest young woman we thought she was. She came to assist my wife shortly before she died of consumption. It was a sad time as you may imagine.'

Lily nodded silently. He had suffered greatly and her heart went out to him again.

'Delia was the kindest of souls and being delicate, the girl became her confidante and nurse – everything!' He lifted his hands slowly as though tormented by memories. 'After Delia's death, I began to find things disappearing. Small things at first – there were many trinkets still left from my wife's possessions – then money. I confess to leaving coins in places they should not be. But I'm lazy as you can see,' he gestured to the dirty china on the table, 'and after a good cigar and glass of port at night, or perhaps a game of cards with a friend . . .' He frowned at her. 'Do I make myself clear, Lily?'

'You mean, Annie stole from you?'

'I'm afraid so.' He sighed heavily again. 'One day I left a small brooch that I had bought from an auction house in the chiffonier in the bathroom. There is an empty drawer there and I thought perhaps I would make some use of it. When I went to retrieve it, the brooch had gone.'

'And Annie took it?'

'There was no one else in the house at that time.'

'Did you confront her?'

He nodded. 'I did. The very next day she disappeared. Her room was empty, her belongings gone. There was no note. And so I must assume the girl was guilty and fled before I pressed more questions.' He cleared his throat. 'If she had given me a good reason for the theft, I would have made allowances.'

Lily shook her head. 'I don't know if there is a good reason for stealing.'

He shrugged. 'Who knows.'

Lily looked at his handsome face and the slight growth of dark stubble on his chin and jaw. His hair, she noticed, was not in its usual style, but had fallen across his forehead. 'Why did you think I could help?' she asked uncertainly.

He sat back, his eyes intent on her. 'Lily, my profession demands a high degree of discretion. You see, I entertain many of my clients here. Our business is conducted, as many lucrative ventures are, within the comfort and security of four walls. Some of the merchandise is very valuable. My clients come to me in the strictest of confidence. Much of what I sell is transported abroad. Gems, for instance, to the United States. Paintings too, and very often gold in one form or another. So you see, it was not the value of what Annie took that distressed me, it was the fact she might have been indiscreet or even ... unaware of just how much I rely on complete honesty within my business. Now I have explained, do you have some idea of what I am about to ask you?'

Lily shook her head slowly. 'No, I don't.'

He smiled. 'Lily, I've come to know you as an honest and hard-working young woman. You have all the qualities I admire; a good head for business, excellent taste and a charming and attractive disposition. I would consider it an honour if you would come to work for me. I must fill Annie's position and there is no one I could think of more suited to it than you.'

Lily didn't say a word. Was he really asking her to work for him?

'Your duties would include managing the household,' Charles went on. 'I shall employ a scullery maid to light the fires and clean. I am away frequently and have no time to organize all this. As you know, I have often remarked this house needs a woman's influence.' He paused, smiling hopefully at her once more. 'Annie's rooms, which would be yours, command a wonderful view over London and are comfortable, with their own toilet facilities. Perhaps we could come to an arrangement by which you took leave to see your family at the weekends?'

'You mean I would be expected to live here?' Lily almost gasped.

'It would be very tiring for you to travel each day and at night. Sometimes I would ask you to act as hostess at my business meetings of an evening – some of which can end quite late.'

'But I wouldn't know how to do that,' Lily said, her imagination unable to stretch that far. She didn't have any idea of entertaining, or how things should be done in the proper way.

'I will teach you.'

'But even if . . . if I wanted to, I've got a job already.'

'Of course, and I am well aware of this. But after the conversation with your family I am also aware that you have been the breadwinner for some time. I am prepared to offer you a generous wage, Lily, of five guineas a week, with a commission on the business that you can arrange for me.'

'Five guineas,' Lily whispered. It was a fortune. Almost three times as much as she was earning with Reube.

'You will have the weekends free to see your family and friends, take your outings with Hattie. I shall be most happy to provide the transport to anywhere you should wish to go.'

Lily could only sit there. It was her dream come true. Yet, how could she agree to it?

'I couldn't let Reube down.'

'He would find someone else. This other man who helps . . .?'

'Pedro,' Lily said uncertainly.

'Quite. Or if not him, I am sure there are others. And Lily it was you yourself who told me that you had no intention to work at the market for ever. A family you said, ultimately you would like a family of your own. So would it not be in your own interest to better yourself and invest in the future? Perhaps save a little money and prepare to make your dream come true?'

Lily felt her heart flutter as he painted the picture, his dark eyes glimmering as he talked and she began to imagine herself being here in this lovely house. But could it really happen? What would her family say? She would be expected to move away from home. Her mother wouldn't like that idea, nor her father. And Hattie would probably never speak to her again.

'Lily, don't let the past hold you back,' he said quietly, but his voice was firm.

'I've only ever worked on the market.'

'Then this is a golden opportunity, is it not, to spread your wings?'

Lily was torn. Uncle Noah had advised her to know her own mind. But as much as she wanted to accept Charles' offer, she was afraid of stepping into the unknown.

'It's not that I'm not grateful . . .'

'So the answer is no?'

They looked at one another. Charles sighed heavily, shaking his head. 'Such a pity. A talent gone to waste. You would have gained a great deal of knowledge and improved your standard of life.'

Lily felt terrible. How could she tell him she wanted to accept but couldn't. She and Hattie were only just getting back together after what happened at the party. Her parents had already made their feelings clear on Charles. And Reube, who had always been a good friend, would be deeply upset if she left. As Lily gazed around at the beautiful house that she was being invited to work and live in, it seemed like a dream, an impossible dream. She knew though, her dream could never come true.

That afternoon Lily wanted to tell Hattie all about what had happened. But Hattie was full of excitement about her engagement ring. Reube had promised her that next Saturday they would go up to Aldgate and buy it.

'You will come, won't you?' Hattie said as they walked, arms linked, to the park. 'Reube said he'll get Pedro to mind the stall in the afternoon. It will be just like the old days,' Hattie promised excitedly, 'the four of us going out to have fun.'

Lily looked into Hattie's happy face and couldn't refuse. She had to tread carefully after all the upset. As they walked, Hattie's excitement bubbled over as she described her wedding plans for next year. Lily listened, wishing that she could reveal her own inner-most thoughts. Thoughts which she knew wouldn't please her friend.

That night as Lily lay in bed, the picture came to her of Charles this morning as he had offered her the miracle of making her dream come true. Why had she refused? She wanted to be with him so much. Yet she was afraid to leave her family and friends behind. What would it be like to live in that beautiful house, to care for it and furnish it as she knew she could? And what of his late wife, Delia? Would Charles ever recover from his loss? Would he find love again?

These and many other questions tumbled through her mind. But Lily knew as much as her heart longed for him, her head was saying no.

The following week the sensational news was released that Sir Oswald Mosley had stormed out of parliament.

His radical policies had been overthrown and he had defected immediately, causing his followers to become angrier than ever that their leader could not mount a challenge to Britain's leadership. On Thursday morning, as Lily arrived at the market, a small group of Blackshirts had gathered on the corner. They were not wearing their uniform, but everyone knew who they were. One of the men was waving a book in the air and the others were all cheering.

'What are they shouting about?' Lily asked as she took her place behind the stall.

Reube had got out his stick, so too had the other traders as a shadow seemed to fall over Cox Street. 'They got this book they call their bible and are trying to thrust it down everyone's throat.'

'What book is that?' Lily felt her legs begin to shake. Trouble was in the air. Where were the police when they were needed?

'It's called *Mein Kampf*. It's said that the royalties go to the Red Cross, but I don't believe that. Who wants to know about that bloke Hitler anyway?'

'Perhaps they'll leave,' said Lily hopefully.

'If they set one foot in our direction,' said Reube, swinging the stick, 'they'll regret it.'

Lily clutched his arm. 'It's only a book. Can't we ignore them this time?'

Reube looked down at her in surprise. 'What, and let them spout off at us with all their rubbish?'

'They'll get fed up and move on.'

'Meanwhile we lose custom. Look at the street, it's deserted.'

Lily tried to pull Reube back as he took a step from the stall. He was joined by Ted and Freda Shiner, Sammy and Elfie Goldblum, the two barrow boys and Vera Froud's husband, Jock. Soon, the rest of the traders left their stalls and banded together across the street. The Blackshirts stopped creating a din and turned to face them. Lily felt more afraid than ever. What could she do? There was only one thing she could think of. Somewhere there had to be a policeman on duty. If she could find one quickly, she might be able to stop the fight.

When, a little later, Lily returned with a constable, she soon realized she was too late. Her mouth fell open at the scene. The market was in chaos, with Ted's and Reube's stalls upturned and Vera Froud's clothes scattered over the cobbles amongst the fruit and veg. Lily looked at the broken china, glasses, ornaments and nuts and bolts that were scattered far and wide. As the traders sifted through the wreckage, Reube was nursing a black eye.

'What's happened 'ere?' demanded the young constable, as he studied the damage.

'Them bloody Blackshirts!' exclaimed Reube as he searched for his cap, found it under a broken pot and shook it out. Pushing it on his head, he kicked at his broken stall angrily. 'See what they done? Look at all me broken stock. And me stall! The two legs at the front are snapped in half where one of 'em fell into it.'

'You say it was the Blackshirts?' the policeman frowned.

'Course it was.'

'They were in uniform, I take it?'

'No, but we knew their faces.'

The policeman frowned. 'You're saying they were Blackshirts, yet they weren't in uniform.'

'We seen them before causing trouble,' Reube answered indignantly.

'And, of course, you informed the police – before?' The policeman's tone was sarcastic.

'No bloody good telling you buggers, is it?'

'No need for that kind of language, sir.'

'Then why don't you go after 'em,' Reube shouted, losing his temper again. 'They went that way, ran off as soon as we taught 'em a lesson.'

'Did you teach them a lesson with that?' The policeman pointed to the stick Reube was still holding in his hand.

Reube looked at Lily. 'What did you bring this daft 'apporth round for, Lil? Christ, I told you the law was no good.'

'But Reube—'

'The young lady did her duty as a good citizen,' the constable interrupted sharply. 'Now, perhaps you'd like to come down to the station, where you can make a formal complaint.'

'You must be jokin'!' Reube almost jumped back. 'I'm not going anywhere with you, chum.'

'What's up?' Ted Shiner asked as he came up, mopping his bleeding nose.

'He wants to take me down the station,' cried Reube, waving the stick in the air.

'You got nothin' better to do with yerself?' accused Ted, his face streaked with dirt and blood. 'You should be off chasing the criminals. See what they did to me stall? That's half me stock gone for a burton, and a good day's trade lost. You wanna find them buggers and make 'em pay. That's what you should be doin' not giving aggravation to innocent parties like 'im and me.'

The policeman looked at the two men then rocked back and forth on his heels, an unpleasant smile on his face. 'Well, if that's the attitude you want to take, you leave me no choice but to insist you both come with me and make your complaints to my sergeant.'

Reube laughed without humour. 'I ain't going nowhere, nor is he. It'll take us all day to mend our stuff.'

The policeman took out his whistle and waved it in their face. 'I'm within five seconds of blowing this and summoning reinforcements and you're within five seconds of getting nicked. Now, we'll start again, shall we?'

Lily felt her heart sink as both Reube and Ted, with expressions of fury on their faces, were made to follow the constable, leaving the devastation behind them.

Chapter Twelve

'Them bloody Blackshirts, now they've gone and spoiled everything,' complained Hattie as they sat in Lily's bedroom. It was Friday evening and the day after the big fight. 'Now I won't be getting me ring because Reube has to mend the stall and buy a lot of new stock.'

'You can go for the ring another day.'

'I doubt it.'

'Why do you say that? You're getting engaged. You must have a ring.'

'Now Reube's saying with all the damage, he can't afford it.'

'It might not be as bad as he thinks.'

'I dunno. He's too angry still to talk any sense.'

It wasn't only Hattie who was suffering the repercussions of Thursday, Lily thought unhappily. She, too, had been given the cold shoulder by Reube after he'd returned from the station. Ted had told her that Reube had got so angry at the sergeant, that he'd been locked in a cell. It was only when Ben had arrived and smoothed matters out, that they'd agreed to release Reube.

'A fat lot of good calling the law was,' Hattie continued, her chin sticking out. 'It only made matters worse.'

'I wanted to stop a fight before it got started.'

'Yeah, so you said,' Hattie answered in a martyred tone. 'Anyway, you must be pleased. You've got a day off tomorrow whilst the stalls are mended.'

Lily and the other market traders had salvaged what they could of the broken stock and squashed fruit. But the two stalls were damaged so badly some pieces had to be replaced. Meanwhile, business had continued out of boxes, whilst Reube had gone around like a bear with a sore head.

'As I'm not at work we could walk over to Greenwich tomorrow,' Lily suggested, trying to take her friend's mind off the ring. 'And have a coffee and cake in the park?'

Hattie nodded. 'I suppose so.'

'It'll be something to look forward to.'

Hattie yawned and got up from where she was perched on Lily's bed. 'I'm all in. See you tomorrow, then.'

Lily went with her friend to the front door and waved goodbye. It was a soft, warm May evening and the light had still not faded. A tangerine sun was setting and spinning shadows across the houses on the other side of Love Lane. The James' house was silent. There was no sign of Ben or Reube.

Lily went back indoors to the sound of her father coughing. His chest had become troublesome again. Her mother came out of the parlour, a small bottle in her hand. 'Your dad didn't go into work today as he had a bad coughing fit. I've just given him the last of his medicine.'

'Does he need more?'

'Yes, but I can't afford any till next week. I haven't got anything left in me purse and he didn't pick up his pay packet.'

'Will he be docked a day?'

'Yes, they ain't gonna pay him if he don't work, are they?'

'I've got me wages to give you,' Lily said quickly, reaching for her bag on the coat stand and pulling out her purse. 'I only got twelve and six this week because of the upset with the Blackshirts.'

'It wasn't your fault they came,' said her mother indignantly.

'No, but we lost all our business on Thursday and today it wasn't much better as everything that's left is in boxes and crates. I can't expect to be paid if nothing's coming in.'

'When will you be up and running again?' her mother asked anxiously.

'Reube ain't much good with repairs, so Ben's gone to help him out.'

'Those Blackshirts should be lynched,' remarked her mother.

'I just hope we've seen the last of them.'

Josie looked down at the money in her hand. 'I wish I didn't have to take this off you but I'll be able to buy some medicine now.' She glanced up at Lily. 'Have you got a few pennies to keep for your needs?'

'Yes, but I don't need much. Only a bob to go out with Hattie if we stop for a coffee and cake.'

Lily accompanied her mother to the kitchen, where the kettle, as usual, was boiling. She saw her mother pick up the tea caddy and peer into the bottom of it. 'I'm afraid this brew is going to be worse than cat's pee as we've run short.'

Lily knew that running short on tea was the first sign of danger. Were they behind with the rent again? And what other debts were accruing?

She sat down and watched Josie make the tea, her actions slow and deliberate as she scooped the last few leaves from the caddy. 'I don't know where it all goes, Lil. Even with you and your father working, we're only just making ends meet. I seem to be spending a lot on medicine and the doctor but they come first before anything.'

Lily nodded her agreement. 'What does the doctor say about Dad?'

Her mother shrugged as she placed out the teacups. 'That with his bad chest he shouldn't be out in all weathers. But he's lucky to have a job at all. At least the winter is over.'

Lily looked into her mother's face. Was her father

really well enough to work at the yard? Outside in the hall, she heard her father climb the stairs slowly, wheezing loudly as he did so.

'Take him his tea, love,' her mother said. 'He's going to have an early night. Tomorrow he'll be right as rain.'

Lily hoped that was true.

The next morning when her father got up for work, he said he would be at work all day Saturday to make up for the money he'd lost.

'I tried to reason with him,' Josie said after he'd gone. 'But you know your father. You can't tell him anything.'

Lily wished it was her that had been able to work all day. The money would have meant her dad didn't need to do overtime. As usual it was money or the lack of it that dominated the household. It seemed that there was never enough to pay the bills and keep them out of debt.

That morning Lily helped her mother with the chores before calling for Hattie who was eager to get out as Sylvester was in the depths of depression. His nightmares coloured his moods and he would become very tiresome and gloomy. The family put up with this because they knew he couldn't help himself.

Soon they were falling into step along Westferry Road, with the smell of spring in the air. They weren't wearing coats for the first time that year and a mild breeze blew through Lily's soft blonde waves as they bounced gently on her shoulders. She was wearing a thin summer frock that was as old as the hills, but the pale green colour was very attractive.

As they entered the foot tunnel to Greenwich, Hattie was strangely quiet. Usually their voices echoed out, bouncing from the tiled ceilings and walls along with the heavy drops of condensation. But today, it was only their footsteps that could be heard and the whistle of a faint wind as it rustled round their skirts.

'Is there something wrong?' Lily asked after a while, as she drew only monosyllables from her friend.

'I've got a feeling that Reube wants to get out of buying me that ring,' Hattie confessed.

Lily laughed. 'Don't be daft. Course he will.'

'He didn't come round this morning,' Hattie went on anxiously. 'Sometimes he calls over as I'm leaving for work.'

'He probably went off early,' Lily suggested. 'Before you was up.'

But Hattie shook her head fiercely. 'No, I saw him outside his house waiting for Ben who brought the lorry round. Reube just jumped in it without so much as a backward glance.'

Lily didn't know what to say. 'I shouldn't pay too much attention to that. They were in a rush I expect.'

Hattie sniffed. 'Once upon a time he would have knocked on the door and given me a peck.'

'You're making a big thing of it, Hat.'

'No, I'm not.'

'You're worrying too much,' Lily assured her as they walked out into the bright sunshine. 'After all, you're getting married next year.'

'I want to be engaged first, show everyone that we are a couple.'

'Everyone knows that already.'

'You don't understand, Lil. I want to be engaged so badly. It's such a disappointment not to have that ring on me finger today.'

'As a matter of fact,' Lily said quietly, 'I do understand. Disappointment is a very painful thing to bear. It hurts for a long while, as though you swallowed a sweet and it sticks in your throat and you just have to wait till it goes away.'

Hattie turned sharply to look at her. 'That's right. That's just how it feels. But what makes you say that?'

'I know what it is to want something, or rather someone, too.'

'You don't mean you're still mooning over that bloke?' Hattie gasped.

Lily turned slowly to face her friend. She couldn't hide her feelings any longer. Hattie was upset over not having a ring, but it was only a ring! What if she was threatened with losing Reube altogether? 'Mooning's not a very nice word, Hat. I try not to wear my heart on my sleeve.'

Hattie looked bewildered. 'But as you've never said anything more, I thought you'd forgotten him.'

'I wish I had. But that stuck sweet still hasn't gone away.'

'So you've seen him again?' Hattie asked, looking taken aback.

Lily nodded. 'Yes, last Sunday.' She didn't want to lie or hide anything now.

Hattie's face was shocked. 'You didn't tell me.'

'I thought it wouldn't go down well.'

'So all this time you've been keeping it a secret?'

'I've wanted to discuss Charles with you so many times, Hat. I needed to get my feelings off my chest, but this is the first opportunity that's come along with you saying what you did about your ring.'

Hattie looked as though she was seeing Lily for the first time, her frown deepening as she gazed into Lily's eyes. 'Oh dear, that paints me as a bit of a selfish moo, don't it?'

'Now you see, I have upset you,' Lily replied exasperatedly. 'I knew I would if I said the truth.'

'No you ain't.'

'I can't help feeling this way,' Lily persevered, desperate to make Hattie understand.

'No, I can see that now.'

'Don't let's argue again, Hat.'

'I don't intend to,' said Hattie taking Lily's arm. 'I've had more than my fair share of disagreements lately. You've touched on something that makes me realize what a cow I can be at times. Come on, let's go into the café, and I'll tell you all about it.'

★

They sat in the café with coffee and scones, but it was Lily who was doing the talking. She explained how Pedro had told her that Charles had called by the stall on her birthday and how she had waited, day after day, for him to return. And how, when she'd almost given up hope, he'd suddenly appeared and told her he had something important to ask her.

'So I arranged to meet him on the corner of Westferry Road,' she continued as Hattie sat listening attentively. 'I didn't want Mum and Dad to see me getting into his car as I know it would have caused trouble. It wasn't only you who disapproved of him, Hat, it's me mum and dad too.'

'So you went round to his house on your own?'

'I just knew he wouldn't do anything to upset me, as he's such a gentleman.'

Hattie smiled. 'And you was curious.'

'Of course I was.'

'Describe his house again for me, Lil,' Hattie said with enthusiasm. 'I never paid attention before but now I am.'

Grateful for the opportunity of reliving the experience, Lily began from when she first went with Ben. She explained how Charles' house had seemed a little neglected as they'd been shown round, but on her second visit, how it looked quite the worse for wear, with even dirty crockery left in the drawing room. Hattie's eyes grew wider and wider as Lily described how Annie had begun to steal after Delia's death and how Charles' business and reputation depended on the utmost discretion.

'And so,' Lily said as she took a deep breath, 'when Annie disappeared, he thought of me as a suitable replacement and came by the stall to offer me her job.'

Hattie's eyebrows shot up. 'You mean, he wants you as a maid?'

'No, more like a housekeeper,' Lily explained, deciding not to add that Charles had also asked her to perform some business duties, as this sounded rather grand.

'Is there other staff there?'

'He said he would take on a scullery maid to do the cleaning and lighting of fires.'

'I hope he didn't want you as a skivvy.'

Lily smiled. 'Well, it's beside the point now, as I said no.'

'You did?' Hattie frowned again. 'I would have thought you'd have jumped at the chance.'

'Half of me wanted to, but the other half was afraid to make any changes.'

Hattie turned her cup round thoughtfully. 'Are you sorry now that you said no?'

Lily hesitated. 'I sometimes think of how it might have been.'

'And all this time I didn't know.'

'So you see, Hat, I do understand how you're feeling. But at least you've got Reube and that's the most important thing.'

Hattie looked under her lashes. 'I don't know about that.'

'You love Reube and he loves you.'

Her friend now had a faraway look in her eyes. 'You know, Lil, you'll be surprised at this but I've never thought about marriage that much as I knew Reube and me was always going to be together. It was just a question of time. And believe it or not, I never fancied another boy anyway. No one at school or the club, had what Reube had. See, after his dad died, his future was mapped out at the market and looking after his mum and brother. I always admired Reube for getting on with it, doing what his old man would have wanted. That was the attraction, knowing Reube was my rock, reliable, dependable, and even if he counted the pennies, I could forgive that, as he was always the man I was going to be with.'

'Nothing's happened to change that,' Lily said quietly.

'I thought I knew him so well,' Hattie sighed, shaking her head as though she didn't.

'You do,' Lily laughed but Hattie's eyes narrowed.

'Well, the truth is, Lil, we've broken up.'

Lily laughed again. 'Stop kidding me.'

'I'm not.' Hattie's expression was serious. 'Reube said we wasn't going out to buy the ring and this made me mad. I couldn't keep me tongue still, could I? So we had this dirty great row that couldn't have happened at a worse time. Reube was still furious about being chucked in that cell and when I complained about the ring, I suppose it was the last straw. You know what he called me?'

'What?' Lily murmured, almost afraid to hear the answer.

'He said I was a spoilt kid. Told me I should grow up a bit before we got married.'

'But everyone says things they don't mean when they're cross.'

'He meant it all right.'

'You've had words before and got over it,' Lily was quick to point out.

'Not like this. I told him that if he felt that way, the wedding was off. Course, I expected him to come round an hour later, cap in hand, like he usually does and we'd kiss and make up. But as I told you, this morning he went off without so much as a glance over at our house. It upset me so much I couldn't concentrate on me work. I cut out a bit of pattern that I should have left in and all the way home on the bus, I kept thinking what am I gonna do without him?'

'He'll be round, just wait and see.'

'What if he isn't?'

'Can't see him staying away, Hat,' Lily said, patting her friend's hand. 'Give it a week or two, and he'll be breaking down your door with frustration.'

Hattie made an effort to smile. 'I wish it was like the old days when we were—' Hattie stopped and groaned. 'Here I go again down memory lane. But I'm supposed to be turning over a new leaf, as I want you to be happy.'

She gave a quick laugh. 'We've certainly drowned our sorrows today, ain't we?'

As they walked home, the two girls talked together about old times. Lily felt certain it was only a lover's tiff that was causing Hattie such heartache. Reube and Hattie were made for each other. But Lily was dismayed that Hattie seemed certain it was the end of the affair.

At last they turned the corner into Love Lane. They were still deep in conversation when Hattie stopped. 'There's a car outside your house, Lil.'

'It's Charles,' Lily gasped as she saw the ruby red car in the road.

Hattie squeezed her arm. 'What does he want?'

'I don't know.'

'What are you going to do?'

Lily shrugged. 'Go in, I suppose.' Her legs had gone weak and wobbly.

In the soft evening light, as the sun slowly faded, Hattie said softly, 'He still hasn't given up, Lil.'

'But I refused.'

'He obviously hasn't taken no for an answer.' Hattie give her a little push. 'Go on, this is a second chance. You'd better grab it whilst you can.'

Lily looked into Hattie's eyes. They were soft and understanding. Lily hugged her and then slowly walked on. Suddenly her world felt alive and full of happiness again. She felt like clapping her hands and jumping for joy.

Chapter Thirteen

'Oh, Lil, I'm glad you're home.' Her mother burst into tears.

'What's happened?' Lily took her in her arms.

'A lot's happened since you went out.'

'Is Charles here?'

Her mother nodded. 'Look at me, I'm shaking.'

'Come on,' Lily said gently. 'Let's go and sit down.'

To Lily's surprise the parlour was empty. Only the roaring fire crackled in the grate as Lily sat beside her mother and wondered where Charles was. What had gone on in her absence? Why was her mother so upset?

'Give me a minute to get my breath,' Josie said as she closed her eyes, then opened them, giving a deep sigh. 'After you'd left, there was a knock at the door. A young boy stood there, about nine or ten and gave me a piece of paper. He said he'd come from the timber yard.'

Lily sat upright. All the happiness and excitement

she had felt at seeing Charles' car, suddenly evaporated. 'Dad! It's Dad, ain't it?'

Josie nodded slowly, putting her hand on her heart. 'The note was from Bob's boss, Mr Drewitt, asking me to come as quickly as I could to the yard, where your dad had been taken ill.'

'Oh, Mum, not again.'

'I'm afraid so. But this time there was no one to bring him home, all the vans were out. How in heaven's name me and your uncle would have got there – and brought your dad back – if Mr Grey hadn't arrived, I don't know.'

'Charles took you to the yard?'

'He pulled up in his car as the boy was leaving. I don't mind telling you I was in a state of panic. Mr Grey asked what was wrong and I gave him the note. As calm as you like, he told me to get your uncle and he would take us straight down. I didn't even stop to thank him, or ask why he'd come, I was so upset. And when we got there, you should have seen your father. He was white as a sheet and couldn't speak properly for coughing. Mr Drewitt was very good and had done his best but I could see that a doctor was called for.'

'Oh, Mum, what did you do?' Lily felt terrible that she'd been away whilst all this had happened.

Josie dabbed at her eyes with her handkerchief. 'It was Mr Grey who came to the rescue and suggested that we get your dad into the car and bring him home straight away so he could lie down and rest. He told me he would then go round for the doctor if I told him where the surgery was.' Josie blew her nose noisily. 'Lil, I only had the money you gave me for medicine, nothing put by for the doctor to call. I didn't say anything then as I was too embarrassed, but your gentleman took it all out of me hands. After we got your dad upstairs, I tried to give Mr Grey your five bob, but he wouldn't hear of it. He took it upon himself to pay for everything, only the best medicines that I couldn't afford. And, in fact, Doctor Tapper said his bill is taken care of until your dad gets over this episode.'

Lily felt relief and yet full of shame that they had accepted Charles' money, which must have been a considerable amount. What must he think of them? And how could they impose on his goodwill?

'Where is Charles now?' Lily asked.

'He's been sitting upstairs with your dad and uncle. Although now Noah has gone out into the back yard for a smoke.'

'What did the doctor say about Dad's cough?'

Josie twisted the hanky between her fingers. 'He's got a bronchial fever because his chest is so bad. He won't be able to work for a while, but then that don't come as a surprise. Mr Drewitt was kind enough but said your dad has been under the weather a lot. He said he's a reliable worker, but not fit enough to move all that timber in the wind, rain and cold. It really is a younger man's job. If he's off again this week, I doubt whether Mr Drewitt will have him back.'

Lily knew then that he wouldn't be returning to the timber yard as she saw the look of defeat in her mother's eyes.

'I should never have let him go to work today,' Josie said hopelessly. 'Made him stay home and rest . . . that's what I should have done . . .'

What could she say to comfort her? Lily wondered. It was clear now that her father was incapable of performing any rigorous work and indeed, there seemed very little that he could do, unless he sat at an office desk, pushing a pen. But even if he was an educated man, those jobs weren't available now. He had always lived by his physical abilities and would be broken in spirit if he was told he could never go back to doing a man's job.

'Don't worry, we'll get Dad better,' Lily said, putting her arm around her mother.

'I don't know how we can.'

'We will, somehow.'

'Oh love,' sighed Josie, 'just when things seemed to be getting better, this happens. What are we going to do?'

Lily squeezed her mother's hand. 'We'll think of something. Now you put on the kettle whilst I go upstairs to see Dad.'

Lily watched her walk dejectedly out to the kitchen, her shoulders drooping, head bowed. Why had this got to happen to such hard working and honest people? But it was no use railing at fate. Determinedly Lily squared her small shoulders and made her way upstairs.

★

'Lily!' Charles stood up as she came in. He had been sitting beside the big double bed in which her father lay.

'Hello, Charles.' Her voice quivered. She went to her father who had two bright patches of red on his cheeks. The rest of his skin was porcelain white. Lily's heart felt like breaking as she saw him struggle to speak, then begin to cough.

She put her arms round him and helped him to sit up, banking the pillows behind him.

'What an old fool I am,' he whispered as he sank back, breathless and wheezing.

'You can't help being ill, Dad.'

'Mr Grey has done a lot for me.'

She turned to Charles. 'I don't know how to thank you – again.'

'No thanks are necessary, Lily.'

Lily noticed that the room smelt old and damp and she felt ashamed as she saw the threadbare cloth of her father's pyjamas, the frayed collar and little darns that her mother had made. They were from a different world to Charles, yet he had helped them out of their troubles today.

'Don't try to speak, Dad,' she said, as Bob Bright mumbled something then held a cloth to his mouth to hide the noise of his coughing. 'You need plenty of rest now and you'll soon be better.'

Very soon, his eyes closed as the fit of coughing subsided. She felt like trying to rouse him in case he never opened his eyes again, but then she managed to quell the moment of panic as Charles moved quietly beside her and whispered, 'He'll sleep now.'

'Will he get better?' she murmured, looking up at Charles as if he should know the answer.

'I'm sure he will, in time. The doctor has given him something to make him more comfortable.'

Lily knew that they wouldn't have been able to afford the treatment and the medicines had not Charles come today. She was very grateful, but also deeply ashamed of having to accept his charity.

Lily waited at the front door as Charles said goodbye to her mother and uncle. When he came out of the parlour, she said simply, 'Thank you.'

'I'm glad to have been of some help.'

'I don't know what Mum would have done if you hadn't called by.'

'It was fortuitous indeed.'

'I intend to pay you back every penny, Charles.'

'You may intend it, Lily, but I do not expect it.'

She felt humiliated by this sudden awareness of their poverty. Why did it seem like a disease that was even worse than a physical ailment? She couldn't look into his eyes. And yet even as she stood there, a tiny flicker of hope burnt in her heart. Had he come to ask her again if she would work for him? This time, if he did, she knew without question that she would accept. Five guineas a week would solve all the problems that were beginning to drown them. She could do so much for her family as

Charles' housekeeper. As for her job at the market, well, it was a small sacrifice to make. And to learn a new skill, as Charles had said, would be reason enough for making such a change in her life.

'Was there a reason you came today?' she asked, her heart beginning to beat very fast as she looked hopefully into his beautiful dark eyes.

He nodded. 'Yes, indeed. Two as a matter of fact.'

Lily felt every nerve in her body straining. Excitement and joy began to take hold of her as she gazed expectantly into his face.

'Firstly, I wanted to return this.' He reached into his pocket and held out his hand, in his palm was a small fur brooch.

'Hattie's rabbit foot!'

'I discovered it in the car.'

She took it. 'I don't even remember losing it.'

'A rabbit's foot is lucky, is it not?'

She smiled. 'Yes, it's supposed to be. Hattie bought it for me on my birthday.'

'A perfect gift indeed.'

Lily clutched the soft fur in her hand. Her heart was beating so wildly she looked up and murmured, 'And the second reason?'

He looked into her eyes, causing Lily to feel all the old feelings once more. 'I'm leaving England on business this week.' His gaze was penetrating. 'This time it is for a number of months.'

Lily felt as though she had been dealt a physical blow.

She clutched the rabbit's foot as her knuckles turned white around it.

'I wanted to say goodbye and to let you know . . . to tell you . . . should you call at Dewar Street in my absence . . . that I have filled Annie's position.'

Lily swallowed. 'You have?'

'Yes, a pleasant enough young woman who comes with references. She is – trustworthy – and reliable.' His voice seemed unsteady and she almost didn't catch the words he said next. 'But sadly, lacks all the qualities I saw in you, Lily, and I would have given the earth to see them flourish had you allowed it.' Bending slowly he lifted her hand to place a kiss there, then he turned, stepped outside into the evening and was gone.

Chapter Fourteen

July 1934

L ily gazed at the reflection in the long mirror
hanging on the fitting room wall. It was the end
of a busy Saturday morning at Madame Nerys'.
The staff had all gone home and outside the compartment, a dozen sewing machines sat idle, their covers
over them. Roll upon roll of fabric hung from the
shelves on big iron arms and on one of the tables were
spread the cutter's patterns. But Lily's attention was
not on these, but on her own reflection. It was a long
time since she'd felt this way, feminine and attractive.
The beautiful pink bridesmaid's dress that Hattie had
asked Madame Nerys' permission to work on, in co-
ordination with her wedding dress, looked to Lily like
a swirl of ice cream. This was the last fitting before
Hattie's wedding the following week and Lily could
only stare in wonder.

'You've done a lovely job, Hat.'

'You go in and come out in all the right places. It's

rewarding to make a gown for someone so slim.'

'It's a long time since I've thought about me figure,' Lily sighed. 'In the factory you get used to wearing an overall all day and the clothes underneath all end up smelling of paint so you wear the same thing week in and week out.'

'I don't know how you stick that job.'

'Because it's good pay, I do. And it's not so bad once you get used to it. Some of the women are a bit bitchy, but I've been there over three years now and they don't bother me.'

'Three years, is it?'

Lily nodded. 'I got the job just after you went back with Reube, remember?'

Hattie took a pin from the pad on her wrist and slipped it into the dart on the bodice of the dress. 'Will I ever forget! That six months we were apart felt like a lifetime. It was a horrible patch, especially as trade at the market went from bad to worse. And in the end he even had to let you go to keep the stall afloat.'

'We weren't taking any money,' Lily nodded as she looked in the mirror. 'And Reube ended up paying me out of his own pocket.'

'He hated losing you.' Hattie pulled the material a little tighter as she slid in another pin. 'Breathe in, I want to give you a nice waist.'

Lily inhaled as Hattie worked swiftly, then both girls gazed into the mirror.

'What do you think?'

They frowned critically at the soft pink satin gown overlaid with lace.

'Are you sure you don't want something towards it?'

'It didn't cost me a penny,' Hattie assured her. 'Madame Nerys said the two gowns are her wedding present. All she wants in return is a photograph of me wedding day to put in the sample book so she can show her customers. She said it was nice to see a design that wasn't still twenties.'

'It is very modern looking.'

'Let's try the headband.'

'Is it finished?'

'Yes, it's a smaller version of mine. And of course mine is white whereas yours is pink.'

Lily was going to be the only bridesmaid at Hattie's wedding. She wanted to do her friend proud. It had taken Hattie four years to get Reube up the aisle and the big day had finally been settled on; Saturday July the 28th.

Hattie returned with a dainty pink band embroidered with flowers. Securing it behind Lily's ears, she frowned into the mirror. 'What do you think?'

'It fits just right.'

'These bands are very fashionable now. A definite improvement to the mobcap Queen Elizabeth wore at her wedding.'

'Did you embroider the flowers yourself?'

'No, our embroiderer stitched them,' said Hattie lowering her voice. 'Don't let on though, as Madame

Nerys didn't give anyone else permission to work on you.'

'Oh, no, I won't say a word.'

Hattie looked at Lily's hair. 'I don't like to say it, Lil, but your hair reeks of paint.'

Lily blushed. 'I haven't had time to wash it yet.' The distemper fumes that filled the factory were so strong they clung to hair, skin and clothes alike. To get rid of it, you had to thoroughly wash anything that was contaminated.

'I'm having my hair cut short after me honeymoon. Reube likes it long, so as soon as we get back from Brighton I'm going up West for a Marcel Wave. Perhaps we could go together.'

'Has Reube booked the place you're staying at?' Lily didn't want to say that a West End Marcel Wave was beyond her means.

'Yes, a boarding house called Shalimar.'

'Is it on the front?'

'Yes, quite near.'

'Oh Hat, what a dream!'

Hattie giggled. 'It will be nice not to have to find places to go to have a cuddle.'

'You'll be Mr and Mrs then and allowed to have all the cuddles you want.'

'Yes, and they'll be free, which will please Reube no end.'

Both girls burst into laughter as they gazed in the mirror.

'Mrs Heather James,' Lily murmured, 'has certainly got a ring to it.'

'I hate Heather,' Hattie sniffed. 'But Mrs James sounds lovely.'

'Just as long as you don't start wearing fur hats.'

Once more the two girls laughed. 'I hope Reube's mum don't wear that dead animal to the wedding. Did you manage to get the Saturday morning off all right?'

'Yes, though the foreman didn't like it much.'

'What a sauce! You ain't had time off since you've been there. If you ask me I think you could do much better if you tried harder to look for another job that was more suitable.'

Lily had looked for another job but nothing was as secure or well paid as the factory. Her wage packet meant a roof over their heads and food in the larder. She didn't have to worry that the factory would close or that her overtime would dry up. Each week she collected a brown envelope from the office and gave it to her mother. And in no time at all it seemed, the contents were spent.

'What are you doing the evening before your wedding day?' Lily asked quickly.

'It's bad luck to see the groom the night before. The market traders are taking him down the pub.'

'Do you want me to help with your hair?'

'I was hoping you'd say that. Follow me, now, and I'll show you me dress.'

They went through to the main rooms where Hattie

pulled aside a curtain. Lily gasped. 'Oh, Hat, it's gorgeous!'

The long white satin gown hung on the wall. Its wide, scooped neckline was adorned with pearls, its semi-fitted bodice and long sleeves the latest statement in fashion. The silk-tulle veil with a headband of embroidered white flowers was a perfect match to Lily's.

'You'll look breathtaking, Hat.'

'I never did get that engagement ring though.'

'He bought you another one.'

'But it's not as nice.' Hattie held out her finger. 'Just a plain gold band with a tiny diamond.'

'Well, I think you're lucky.'

As they returned to the compartment where Lily's clothes still hung, Lily thought yet again how fortunate Hattie was to have everything she wanted. As she reluctantly removed the beautiful gown and put on her skirt and blouse, she was ashamed of her appearance. Drab and shabby against the perfect pink, her clothes looked worn out. Even though Hattie had waited four years to marry, now she had it all.

'Have you found a place to live yet?' Lily asked as Hattie hung the bridesmaid's dress on a hanger.

'Not yet. We're going to live with Mrs James for a short while. I told Reube it will have to be a short while an' all as I'll go crackers not having a place to meself.'

Lily knew Hattie wanted to move over to Greenwich where some of the houses had real gardens and were decorated nicely. Reube hadn't wanted to move, but

Hattie was insisting. She wanted somewhere she could start a new life, away from her parents and Sylvester.

Hattie pulled the curtain open. 'Did you know Pedro's popped the question to Mrs James?'

Lily gasped. 'No!'

Hattie nodded. 'Surprise, ain't it?'

'What did she say?'

'She's going to think about it but doesn't want to commit herself yet.'

'What do the boys think of that?'

'Reube don't mind either way. But I told Reube if Pedro moves in, it's all the more reason for us to move out.'

They walked to the lockers where they collected their bags. Hattie locked the big door of the workshop and the two girls skipped down the stone steps to the bright afternoon outside.

'Let's stop at the market on the way home. I'll buy you a coffee,' said Hattie as they walked to the bus stop.

'All right, but I mustn't be long,' Lily agreed reluctantly. She had a lot to do at home whilst her mum had a rest.

'How is your dad these days?' Hattie asked curiously.

'He don't get about much.' Lily didn't like to say that he stayed in bed a lot, refusing to get up all day sometimes. She didn't think it was good for him to be waited on hand and foot, but her mother had got into the habit. He relied greatly on the medicines, which he said stopped his cough and eased the pains in his back.

When they reached the bus stop, Hattie looked at her watch. 'We're just in time for the early one. Now, don't forget, we have a church rehearsal this evening.'

'No, I haven't forgotten.'

'We'll collect you at seven, all right?'

'Yes, I'll be ready.'

'Ben said he might take us out in the lorry to a country pub after. It's only for a quick drink. You can tell your mum you'll be back for ten.'

Lily smiled at Hattie's attempt to reassure her that the outing would be informal. If the weather was nice in the evenings the four of them sometimes went for a drive in the lorry. Everyone bought their own drinks, the cost of which Lily had to take out of the few shillings she kept from her wage. It seemed a sin to spend it on something that went down her throat and disappeared. But she didn't want to appear a bad sport to her friends and have nothing.

The sun shone as they hailed the bus coming towards them. As it arrived, Lily took a last deep breath of fresh air. Even the fumes from the traffic were better than the polluted gases of the factory.

The market was busy as Lily listened to the familiar cries of the traders. 'Apples a pound, pears!' from Ted Shiner and 'As good as new,' from Vera Froud as she held up a bright red skirt. Lily missed the market, but she would never forget the dreadful winter of her unemployment.

As they walked to Reube's stall, the traders called out

to them. 'That old man of yours gonna make an honest woman of you?' Vera Froud yelled to Hattie as she stood in her gabardine mac and boots.

'He ain't my old man yet, Vera,' Hattie returned mischievously. 'I'm still footloose and fancy free.'

'Make the most of your freedom, ducks. You'll miss it when you've got half a dozen kids in tow.'

'How are you, gel?' Ted Shiner called to Lily. 'How's that rotten job of yours?'

Lily laughed. 'It's not that bad.'

'You should come back to the market. If that ugly bugger over there don't want you, come and work for me.'

Lily laughed again as Reube gave Ted a rude sign. She knew that although Ted wasn't joking, he could never match the factory wage.

'Don't forget me wedding present,' cried Hattie. 'I don't want any of your mouldy old fruit either.'

'Fussy cow, ain't she?' Ted grinned. 'See you at the church then, gel.'

Reube finished serving a customer, dropping the pennies in the tin that still stood under the counter. 'To what do I owe the honour of these two lovely ladies calling?'

'Got anything nice?' Lily asked, turning over what looked like an assortment of junk. She had noticed now that Reube's stock was just bits and pieces.

'Nah. No one wants quality now.'

'We used to have some good stuff.'

'That was the good old days.'

Lily felt a little sad to see that Reube had allowed his stock to deplete. She knew that he had put all his savings into pleasing Hattie.

'Oh, don't worry about him,' dismissed Hattie waving her hand. 'I'll buy us a coffee.'

Lily sat by the coffee stall and gazed across to the corner where once the Blackshirts had stood, shouting their heads off. Since Oswald Mosley had fallen out of favour with Labour, he had fallen from grace. Ordinary people were worried about another war starting. Fascism was regarded as dangerous and the police had been given orders to actively curtail any demonstrations.

Suddenly Lily's heart missed a beat as her gaze fell on the figure of a tall gentleman. His broad shoulders were covered in a light-coloured jacket and on his head he wore a good quality trilby hat.

She couldn't take her eyes away and almost stopped breathing. His attention was taken by a pretty young woman standing beside him. Lily clutched her fingers together. Could he be Charles? He was the same height. If only she could see his face!

Slowly he moved away from the stall. Lily swallowed. He was coming towards her. Then as he looked up, his face became clear. Lily released a long sigh.

It was a trick of light that made him look like Charles. He was a young man of about twenty, with fair features and light coloured eyes. He passed by, smiling attentively at the young woman on his arm.

Lily watched them go. Her shoulders slowly slumped as bitter disappointment filled her. If only she had accepted Charles' offer when she'd had the chance! She might have been like that young girl, so prettily dressed and happy . . .

Did Charles ever think of her? she wondered. Did he recall the evening they had spent on the Embankment and the Sunday morning at Petticoat Lane?

Did his thoughts, even for a second, go to her, as hers did so often to him? As Lily watched the couple disappear into the crowds, she knew she would never know.

Noah Kelly sat high on the cart, beside his old friend, the coalie, Charlie Brent. He could feel the rumble of the wheels stir his bones as they passed from the East India Dock Road towards Limehouse.

Close to the river, Charlie reined in the big dray and jumped down. A chuckle of amusement escaped his black lips as he reached up to help his passenger.

'I never thought I'd see the day when Noah Kelly couldn't hop down from a cart without assistance.'

'Oh shut your gob, you cheeky bugger,' Noah growled as he gripped the extended hand. 'What do you expect for a man of my age?'

'You ain't lost your power of speech though, me old friend.'

Noah grinned, despite his rheumatics, as he dropped unsteadily to his feet. 'Thanks to the good Lord, I'm still equipped with a tongue to defend meself.'

'You should get yourself a good stick,' commented his friend lightly. 'A nice willow. Strong enough to take yer weight. Though there ain't that much of you these days.'

'I'll be on me last legs when I do that. Whilst I can put one foot in front of me, I'll use me two pins.'

'What brings you over this way so regular?' Charlie enquired curiously. 'Limehouse is a tidy step from Love Lane.'

'Mind yer own business,' Noah responded, making his companion chuckle once more. 'What time are you due back this way?'

'As usual, you want another free ride?'

'Well, I sure ain't gonna pay you.'

'Damn cheek you have, old man.'

Noah looked at his friend, a man half a dozen years younger than himself and still active. He was a lucky blighter. Noah envied him his blackened cart and the strong horse that pulled it. As the smell of the animal blew into his nose, he remembered past times. If only he was still sitting up on the cart now and driving his beast, with Lily beside him. If only he was fit and able and two decades younger, he would provide for her but life had taken away his strength and now every breath he took was an effort.

'I'll return at four,' said his friend. 'You know me rules, I ain't waiting about if you're not here.'

'I'll be on this spot, don't you worry.'

'Then, take care.' The coalie hesitated, his eyes

showing concern for the elderly man who looked as delicate as a cobweb. 'You're a daft old man, you know that? Coming over this way so often yer pushing yer luck with the Yellows. A bloke half your age don't want to be wandering round these parts even in daylight.'

'I can take care of meself.' Noah Kelly turned and, pulling down his cap and buttoning up the collar of his overcoat, walked unsteadily towards the river.

He was relieved to hear the clip clop of the horse's hooves as the cart left. For a moment there he had thought his friend would follow him. Despite the insults they traded, he had known Charlie for all of his life. The kid had been born in the Flocks' house, his mother expiring as she birthed him. His old man had run off and the boy put into a home up Essex way. It hadn't stopped him returning fifteen years later to work for a bargee, humping the great sacks of coke on his back. Noah recalled how when the boy had bought himself his first cart, they would stop to discuss the day's business, then nip smartly down to shovel up the dung. Those were good times; the best.

He made his way gingerly past the old warehouses on the waterfront and eventually turned into Stowe Street. The sun's rays illuminated the cobbles and the leaning, tumbling buildings on either side. It was a clear day and he stopped to remove his pince-nez, swat them with a rag, and rebalance them again.

The mission he had undertaken for Bob Bright four years ago had caused him to make this journey many times since. Perhaps he should never have begun it, but Bob Bright was a good man at heart. He had ailed though, and grasped desperately at any little relief.

As Noah neared the dismal shack, his heart pounded. He'd followed this path when he was young. The memories tumbled back of the woman, then a great beauty. Her hair had been as black as a raven, eyes like black almonds. His heart had missed a beat every time he'd tied Samson to the post and gone inside with all the daring and passion of youth.

But now his mission was for his brother-in-law and Noah shivered as he tried to catch his breath. No noise, just the river and its journeymen and the scent of the ebbing tide and a deeper more pungent smell, that forced his old heart even faster.

Ramshackle and decayed, the little houses leaned this way and that. Some missing altogether where the river had washed them away. He stood quietly, assessing the slum, the crossed struts of wood barring entry or exit. He walked towards it, as though it might disappear in a blink. Then raising his clenched fist he knocked three times in slow succession. He said, without being asked, 'It's me.'

Receiving no reply, he pushed and the hinges rattled. Even this noise aroused him still, a promise of what and who was inside. The door creaked open. A bent figure paused in the shadows. And all around him the stench of the den, creeping into his lungs.

'Woman, is it you?'

The bent figure halted. An oil lantern glowed on a table. He walked towards it, watching the roaches skim and scuttle. He heard the door creak behind him and turned sharply. The big Lascar had dropped the bar down.

Noah paid little attention to the Indian seaman who stood a head and shoulders above him. It was the woman who interested him.

'Want smokey, Kelly-Kelly?' she enquired. Her once black hair hung limp and grey, woven into a plait. The emerald silk of her robe shone lustrously in the light.

'Up from the bowels of the earth, are you again, Mai Chi?' he demanded, a catch in his voice.

'Mai got plenty for Kelly-Kelly.'

He nodded slowly. 'Aye, that I know.'

The small, bent figure moved sharply back into the shadows. 'Follow Mai, Kelly-Kelly.'

She beckoned and he followed. Down into the room below, taking each step with care as the rotten wood creaked and groaned beneath his weight. When he reached ground, he saw nothing. The woman touched his arm. He shuddered once more. Then followed again, to the single light of a candle.

Ben drove the lorry through Whitechapel to Shadwell, enjoying the summer's day. It was late afternoon and he had finished early, intending to pause at the Quarry for refreshment. The tavern would be closed, but Ernie would take him to the back room and join him for a smoke and swift ale. He would be home before six and still have time to wash and brush up before supper.

At seven he and Reube were off to the church and Ben smiled to himself. He didn't care much for the religious formalities, but afterwards he was taking them all for a drive. Reube and Hattie could sit in the back, on a blanket. With the canvas roof removed they could look up at the stars, enjoy a bit of romance. It would be an excuse to be alone with Lil.

Whistling happily, he turned towards Limehouse. The late traffic was noisy, held up by a slow-moving cart. Absorbed by his thoughts, he slowed the lorry. Where would he take them tonight? Perhaps up Bromley way, through a nice bit of green, to watch the dusk blow over the trees and melt softly into their path. He knew a tavern off the Manor Road, the Black Cat. It had a garden and benches where they could enjoy a drink.

The traffic moved slowly along, until the bus in front of him turned off. The cart that had slowed things down was a coal cart. It was piled high with empty sacks and at once Ben recognized the two figures that sat above the big horse. Noah Kelly and Charlie Brent. This was not the first time he'd seen them on his return from the city. For a short while, Ben followed at a distance, his eyes steady on the cart.

Slowly it began to roll off. Ben watched it turn towards the island, whilst heading the lorry to his last port of call, a tobacconist's in Poplar.

As he drew up at the shop and parked outside, Ben

considered the puzzle of Lily's uncle. Limehouse was not a salubrious place to visit by any stretch of the imagination. The Chinese ran the district, the Yellows as they were known. Ben scratched his chin thoughtfully.

Limehouse ... not a place even the island coalie would have business in. What interest could Noah Kelly have there?

Lily had sung and laughed so much as they travelled home from the Black Cat, that her sides ached. As she sat beside Ben in the cab, they could hear Reube and Hattie's voices drifting in from the back through the open windows. They were singing 'Walkin' My Baby Back Home' as they snuggled on the blanket thrown over the lorry's floor, affording them a view of the star-filled night and a beautiful silver moon.

The evening had been a great success. Lily sighed contentedly as the lorry rumbled along. She was happy for Hattie who so wanted her wedding day to be a roaring success. Reverend Smart from St Peter's had conducted a faultless rehearsal of the wedding. No one had forgotten what to do or where to stand. The elderly organist had played the Wedding March with a few missed notes, but had finally ended on a triumphal flourish. As she and Ben, who was to be best man, followed bride and groom down the aisle, a lump had come into her throat. It was going to be a perfect wedding, all that Hattie had desired.

When the practice was over, they had climbed in the lorry, laughing and happy. Ben had driven them out to the Black Cat where they had enjoyed their drinks on the benches outside.

It was midsummer and all of nature was ripe. From the nearby field Lily had heard the bark of a fox and they'd watched in awe as the bats dived low over their heads. And all around there was the smell of the country as it filled the night air.

As the headlights illuminated the large moths in the lights of the lorry, Reube and Hattie began to sing again. 'I'm Just Wild About Harry' became 'I'm just wild about Hattie', followed by a chorus from 'It's Only A Paper Moon'.

'I don't think I can sing anymore,' laughed Lily breathlessly, after a rousing verse from 'Rose Marie'. 'I've sung meself out.'

'Them two at the back have gone quiet as well.'

Lily glanced back through the small glass window. She could see the top of Reube and Hattie's heads close together.

'They're otherwise occupied,' she said softly, glad that Ben couldn't see her blush.

'Romance is in the air,' he chuckled. 'Talking of which, did you know me mum might be tying the knot again?'

Lily smiled. 'Hattie told me Pedro had popped the question.'

'I reckon Pedro is a decent enough bloke and my old man would wish Mum good luck if she chose to wed again. He'd want her to be happy.'

'She'll always love your dad, but it's the here and now that counts,' Lily nodded.

'I'll not argue with that, Lil.' They travelled on in silence until Ben said suddenly, 'I was meaning to come over and have a smoke with your dad. Ain't seen him around lately.'

Lily wanted to say how worried she was about her father. She knew she could tell Ben but what could he do? 'He doesn't go out much. In fact, he just stays indoors.'

'Would he like a ride out in the lorry?'

'I don't know, Ben.'

'I'll ask him if you like.'

'Yes, but I don't know what he'll say. The only thing that seems to mean much to him is his medicine.'

After a small silence, Ben said quietly, 'So you'll be staying on at the factory then?'

She nodded. 'Looks like it.'

Ben slowly returned his gaze to the road. 'Is your dad coming to the wedding?'

'Hope so.'

'Tell you what, I'll have a word with your dad meself. Tell him he can sit right up the front of the charabanc with me.'

'Thanks, Ben.'

She hoped that nothing would prevent her dad from attending the wedding as she wanted him to see her walk up the aisle in her pink dress. But would it be the closest to white she ever got?

Chapter Fifteen

It was the day of the wedding. Noah Kelly left his bedroom, making his way downstairs. The house was still, only the sounds of the river squeezing in through the windows. The faint whiff of coke fumes and tar caught at his throat and he coughed, attempting to clear the rattle of phlegm on his chest. He cursed the congestion and shook his head as if to clear his sight as he shuffled down the cold passage in his slippers.

When he reached the kitchen and glanced through to the larder he saw the old nosebag hanging on the peg. It was the last reminder of the old days. On a morning like today, as bright as a button, he would have made a tidy penny on the cart. Samson would have fed early and they would set out at a steady pace. The odd drip from his nose would skate down the reins and the clip of hooves on the cobbles would rouse the streets. The calm before the storm, he always thought. Before the turbans came bobbing under the sashes and the dogs ran barking at Samson's hooves. Then all hell would let loose. The filthy kids, some without socks or shoes, many freezing to the bone, all running, eager to steal the dung and pushing the muck down in rotten barrows, to flog up Poplar to the posh houses with gardens. They didn't miss a trick those kids. As cold and starving as they were, they had smiles on their faces.

He still missed them kids. Missed the snotty-nosed little devils in their patched and frayed rags who thought Lil was a little princess sitting high on the cart. She was an' all, with her long white hair flowing under the woollen cap, her eyes as round as blue saucers, watching him. She'd take those damned reins and lead the horse on like a grown man. The confidence she had! He'd taught her all he would have taught his own son and that was no word of a lie.

Noah Kelly braced himself for the day ahead. He was an old man, but he had lived long enough to want to see Lil settled. Instead, at twenty-five, she had no life of her own, was still at her family's beck and call. He tutted his annoyance as he boiled the kettle and carried the tea upstairs. Softly opening her door and treading in, he placed it on the dresser beside the bed. Drawing the long chintz curtains apart to let in the light, he smiled at the sight of his sleeping niece.

'Wakey, wakey, girl.'

She opened her eyes and when she saw him, lit up the room with her smile.

He sat on the edge of the bed. 'How do you sleep with all them curling things in yer hair?'

She eased herself up and he looked at her. Just like her

mother when she was young. As pretty as a picture, but with more spirit in her little finger, thank God, than Josie ever had.

'I've got to put waves in me hair, Uncle Noah.'

'You had plenty of waves when you was born!'

'So did you once.'

He rubbed his bald pate. 'Come on, you cheeky moo, drink yer tea.'

Her fingers were small and warm and he squeezed them gently. He couldn't help wishing it was her walking up the aisle today, leaving all this nonsense at home behind. Young Ben was the man she needed, yet she couldn't see the sense of it. He was a good lad, strong and true. If only women's minds were logical!

'Just look at me dress, Uncle Noah. It's so pretty.'

He turned to see the pink gown, all tethered up with ribbon and frills.

'Wait till you see Hattie's dress. She tried it on last night. It took me breath right away.'

'You'll put her in the shade, Lil.'

'Course I won't!' she declared, laughing. 'I'm not the bride.'

'I wish you was.' He couldn't stop himself saying it out loud. 'You could be, if you'd settled on the right man.'

Her smile faded. 'Ben ain't the one for me, Uncle Noah.'

'He's as good as any and better than most. He'd make you happy if you was to give him a chance.'

'A chance at what?' she asked him softly. 'He deserves someone who will love him back.'

'There ain't such a thing, Lil, as what you call love. It's liking and friendship that counts. And you two have got both.'

'It's not enough, Uncle Noah.'

'You've been reading too many of them magazines.'

'No, it's not them.' She looked down.

He shook his head wearily, knowing what was still in her mind. 'You're mooning over a fantasy, gel. Ain't you realized that, yet?'

'It nearly came true.'

He looked into her eyes and sighed. Then shakily he stood up and kissed her on the top of her head. 'Better go and get me togs on.'

Downstairs, he found his sister. 'Is he up?' he asked as they sat at the kitchen table together.

'No, and is not likely to be.'

'How much did he have in the night?'

'I don't know. He took the bottle.'

'In other words, you gave in.'

'What could I do, Noah? It's always more he wants. I'm frightened he'll walk out.'

'Where would he go, Josie?'

'You know very well. He'd go looking for what he needed. And where would we be then?'

'So what are you going to tell Lil?' he asked at last.

'That he's not up to the wedding. She has a father

who's sick. There's plenty like him in the neighbourhood.'

'He ain't sick, is he?' Noah said bleakly. 'Leastways,
not like she thinks.'

'Is it any different?'

He looked into his sister's eyes. 'Course it is. It's
self-imposed, a crutch he's taken on and won't let go of.
Meanwhile Lil has to work herself to death to pay for
it. We should have the decency to tell her.'

'It will break her heart, Noah.'

'You can't hide it for ever.'

'Not yet,' Josie pleaded hoarsely. 'There's nothing
anything of us can do.'

'You're wrong there, gel,' said Noah gently. 'We
could let her go back to the market, where she was
happy. And then you could make a life for yourself
outside these four walls.'

'You mean find a job?'

'What's wrong with that? It'd do you good getting
out from all this and having a new interest in life.'

Tears filled Josie's eyes. 'He's me husband, Noah. It's
my duty to look after him.'

'It's your duty to set yourself and your daughter free.
Bob must escape his own prison.'

'It was you that started him on it in the first place,'
Josie said accusingly, her eyes suddenly cold.

'Yes, and to my eternal regret,' Noah sighed. 'Well,
it's not too late to put that mistake right.'

'What do you mean?'

'I told him last night I wasn't his errand boy. That it was the last time I went to Limehouse on his behalf.'

Josie grabbed his arm. 'You didn't!'

But he pulled away his arm. 'I'm sick to death of this madness.'

Josie clutched him again, her tears spilling over. 'That's why he was in such a bad mood. You don't realize what you've done.'

'Listen, Josie, I'm not going to be responsible for his needs any more.'

'It could be worse, Noah. It's only a medicine he takes.'

Noah shook his head sadly. When would his sister admit that sooner or later – and he hoped it was sooner – Bob would be beyond their help? And the family's secret wouldn't stay a secret for much longer.

'How do I look?'

'Like a trussed chicken,' grinned Ben as he studied his brother in the dressing table mirror. 'Your dickie's choking you, for a start.'

Reube groaned, stepping closer to the mirror as he loosened his collar. 'I ain't one for dressing up, you know that.'

'Come here, let me have a go.'

Reube pulled back his shoulders and lifted his chin. 'It's them collar studs, they're too tight.'

'Keep your head still, then.' Ben attempted to resolve the problem and after a few minutes struggle, finally nodded. 'You'll do, as long as you don't breathe.'

'Charming,' Reube growled, turning to inspect himself once more. 'It's all right for you, you're only the best man.' Then closing his eyes, he groaned. 'Here, bruv, don't take any notice of me today. I just ain't never got spliced before.'

Ben laughed dismissively as he smoothed the front of his own dark grey suit. 'Once is enough in one lifetime for any man.'

'I'll second that. This wedding has cost me a few bob. But it was what Hat wanted, though I'd happily have gone for a quick do at the town hall.'

'You're a better man than me,' said Ben with a grin. 'I don't ever see meself settling down.'

'You did once,' said Reube giving him a hard look. 'Why don't you ask her?'

'Because I know the answer. Now . . .' Ben patted his pockets. 'I've got the ring and the keys to the motor. What else do I need?'

'A glass of Dutch courage,' supplied Reube dryly, 'when you make your speech.'

Ben laughed a little too enthusiastically. 'Any speech I make today will be short and sweet, I can promise you that.'

'Just make 'em laugh,' suggested Reube, taking one last look in the mirror. 'And keep the jokes clean.'

The two brothers chuckled, but Ben had to make an effort to hide his true feelings as he glanced around the bedroom. Whilst Reube and Hattie were on honeymoon, he would be moving up to the top room. He had a lot of clobber, but could dispose of much of it at market. Then when he got himself digs, he'd start afresh. Who was to know how the future would work out? Reube and Hattie might live in this room for longer than anticipated. Or maybe, they would find their little love nest and move out quick. He didn't have to worry about Mum any more as Pedro was on the scene. And anyway, he was doing well enough to rent a nice place for himself. He'd worked himself stupid seven days a week to get the business off the ground. The world and his wife seemed to be knocking on the door each day and booking the Chariot. The next thing he had in mind was that nice little cab . . .

'Hey, bruv, are we ready then?' Reube asked.

Ben nodded as he folded up two white handkerchiefs, stuck one in his breast pocket, the other in Reube's. 'Come on then, time waits for no man, as they say.'

Ben left the bedroom without a backward glance. Downstairs, Pedro was waiting, done up to the nines in a grey suit, tie and waistcoat. He had shaved his moustache and greased each end with pomade. The hair dressing reeked. Ben smiled to himself as his mother walked out from the kitchen. The stuff she usually wore on her head had now moved down to her shoulders.

'You look nice, Mum,' Reube said, slyly winking at Ben. 'Does it bite?'

'Shut up, you cheeky bugger.' Betty James stroked the fox fur fondly. 'I paid two and six for this up Cox Street.'

'No kidding?' Reube grinned. 'If you'd have told me I'd have gone up the woods and shot you one for nothing.'

Betty reached up to clip her son's ear. 'None of your lip, son!' She turned to Ben. 'Is that blooming great car of yours ready to take us to church?'

Ben nodded. 'I'm putting Mr Bright up the front, if you don't mind.'

'Me and Pedro will sit at the back, then,' said his mother. 'I want to wave at all the neighbours. Now, where's me bag?'

Ben went outside where the charabanc seemed to be taking up most of the road. He'd washed the vehicle until it shone and rolled back the hood. All Hattie's white ribbons were tied to the bonnet.

He walked jauntily across the road and knocked on Lily's open door.

'All set to climb aboard?' he called.

'Some of us are, lad,' muttered Noah Kelly dressed in his best bib and tucker. 'Josie, we're off!'

Ben frowned into the house. 'Mr Bright ready is he?'

'Afraid not, son. He ain't coming.' Before Ben could speak he added sharply, 'Don't want to spoil anyone's day, son, so let's not make too much of it.' He gave Ben a short smile and nodded. 'Now then, lead the way and me and Josie will follow.'

Lily and Hattie were upstairs in Hattie's bedroom. Getting dressed had gone according to plan, though Lily was still upset about her dad. She was trying not to be disappointed, but as she looked out of the window she saw the charabanc filled with happy faces. She had hoped to see her dad sitting up front with Ben.

'What's going on?' Hattie called from under her white veil as she gazed in the mirror.

'Ben's taking everyone to the church.'

'Is Mum and Dad and Sylvester aboard?'

Lily smiled. 'Yes.'

'Hang on, I'm coming over.'

'But isn't it bad luck to see the groom?'

Hattie giggled. 'Well, he can't see me, can he?'

Lily, careful to keep her own long gown in check, helped Hattie to lift her veil. They progressed slowly to the window and peeped out. 'Oh, look, there's Reube,' gasped Hattie. 'Don't he look handsome?'

Lily nodded. 'Very.'

Hattie gave a little shiver. 'I'm not used to seeing him all done up in a suit.'

'It's not every day you get married.'

The girls laughed. Hattie indicated the large cream hat with a feather that her mother was wearing. 'I hope that don't blow off on the ride. And look at Sylvester! His suit is as old as the hills, but it pressed up nice. I hope he doesn't leap out or do anything stupid.'

'You dad is next to him, so he'll be all right.'

Lily smiled. She was happy for Hattie that Sylvester had agreed to attend. Mrs Parks had been fussing all morning over him so in the end it was Lily who had helped Hattie with her make-up and arranged her hair under her veil.

'Your mum looks nice in her grey coat,' said Hattie peering closer to the window. 'I'm sorry your dad is ill.'

'So am I.'

'Never mind. We'll cut a big piece of cake for him at the church hall after. Blimey, what's that on Mrs James' shoulders? It looks like their cat.'

Both girls burst into laughter until they had tears in their eyes. When the charabanc moved off, Hattie grasped Lily's wrist. 'Come on, Ben will be back in no time. Let's take one last look in the mirror.'

As Hattie stood all in white, her hair drawn away from her face and her big brown eyes wide, Lily thought how lovely she looked. She was the perfect bride, just as she had always planned. Even though Hattie and Reube had had their ups and downs, Hattie had always dreamt of this moment.

'You make a lovely bride, Hat.'

'Thanks, Lil.' Hattie turned to her. 'It'll be you next. And you better let me be your bridesmaid!'

'You would be matron of honour,' Lily pointed out.

'That sounds a bit old.'

'Well, you'll be an old married lady.'

Once more the girls were laughing. But as Lily considered her own reflection, the dainty pink headdress and flowing pink gown, she couldn't help wishing that what Hattie had said would come true one day. She wanted to be married, to have a home of her own, a husband and children. But when she really thought about this, she knew there was only one man in her heart. And until his face slipped from her memory she would never find another.

A quarter of an hour later, they heard the charabanc return.

'It's Ben!' exclaimed Hattie, looking frightened.

'Here,' Lily said calmly, 'take your flowers.' She lifted the spray of white lilies and pink carnations from the bed. These and her posy and the men's buttonholes had been delivered freshly this morning from the market. She placed the flowers in Hattie's arms and gathered her own posy.

The two girls stared at each other.

'I'm gonna chuck these flowers at you,' Hattie promised. 'So you'd better get ready to catch them if you want to be a bride yourself. Now, wish me luck.'

'You and Reube deserve all the luck in the world,' Lily murmured as tears pricked her eyes. Grasping the veil, she followed Hattie slowly along the landing and very carefully down the stairs.

'In the presence of God the Father, the Son and the Holy Spirit,' the vicar said in a clear voice, 'we have assembled together to witness the marriage of Heather Ellen Parks to Reuben William James. To pray for God's blessing on them, to share in their happiness and to celebrate their love.'

Lily was only half listening as she felt quite overcome

with emotion. The congregation was still, without a single murmur. The bride and groom stood centre stage before the altar. They had eyes only for each other. 'Will this ever happen to me?' Lily asked herself silently. And even if she did fall in love and want to get married, how could she ever leave the factory? Her parents needed every penny she provided. And even with her wage, they were still struggling. No matter how much overtime she put in, they always needed more.

'Marriage is a gift of God,' continued the vicar, breaking into Lily's suddenly chaotic thoughts. 'As you grow together in love and trust, you shall be united in heart and body.'

Lily saw Reube look down on Hattie with eyes full of love. She knew that whatever problems lay ahead, they were meant for each other and would solve them together.

'Heather and Reuben, you are about to make solemn vows and exchange rings. We pray the Holy Spirit will guide and strengthen you, fulfilling God's purposes for your earthly life together.' The vicar looked at the congregation. 'If there is anyone here present who knows of a reason why these persons may not lawfully marry, they must now declare it.'

All was quiet. Lily's heart began to race as Ben stepped forward to give Reube the ring. She looked at Ben, with his clean-cut features and kind grey eyes. He had become more handsome in his maturity and Lily tried to imagine what it would be like to think of him in any other way than she did. But she couldn't. Her mind and heart was still full of a face that never seemed far from her thoughts.

When Reube slipped the gold band on Hattie's finger, Lily felt a lump fill her throat. Her friend had finally got all she ever wished for. Hattie was now married. She was Mrs James and her whole married life stretched before her.

'I now pronounce you husband and wife,' said the vicar.

Reube bent forward to kiss Hattie. As his lips touched hers, Lily remembered the night on the Embankment when she had wanted the moment with Charles to last forever. If only she had accepted his offer, she might be Mrs Charles Grey at this very moment, a matron of honour instead of a bridesmaid.

The church hall was overflowing. Friends and neighbours had all been invited and were enjoying the food set out on the long trestle tables. The Mother's Union that Mrs Parks belonged to had prepared the buffet and Reube and Hattie had shaken everyone's hands as they entered the hall. Although there was dancing and singing to the church piano, most people were intent on talking, eating and drinking. Lily had begun to help serve the steady flow of drinks at the open hatch that led through to the kitchen. She was wearing an apron to cover her dress and had removed her hair band. It was now perched on top of an empty lemonade bottle on a high shelf so that none of the kids could get hold of it. As the afternoon wore on and the supplies began to diminish, Lily took the opportunity to enjoy herself.

It was the first time in four years that she had danced with Ben. As he whirled her around the floor, she felt her legs move of their own accord to the piano music.

'You're still as good on your pins as you used to be,' Ben chuckled as he held her close and did a little twirl.

Lily laughed. 'I've only trodden on you twice.'

'Didn't feel it. You're as light as a feather.'

She gazed up into his happy face. 'It is nice to dance again.'

'You should do it more.'

Lily held her breath whilst they seemed to fly over the wooden boards. 'I'd forgotten how good it feels,' she said breathlessly.

'In that case, why don't you come out with me sometime. We could go up West for an evening.' As he saw the look cloud her face, he added quickly, 'No strings attached, Lil. Just two old friends enjoying an evening out together dancing. I must admit I'm out of practice meself.'

Lily smiled. 'I don't have much time.'

'I know that. You live at that flamin' factory.'

'Well, I can get a lot of overtime.'

'You don't work Saturday nights. What about one of them in the near future. You say when and I'll fall in. I got a tight schedule meself, but we can work it out. It will do us both good.'

'How much are the tickets?'

'Dunno. Why?'

'I'll pay me way.' She looked up at him, but he was laughing as he spun her round the floor.

'Little Miss Independence.'

'That's right.' She began to laugh too, but she wanted him to know it would be, just as he said, two old friends going out together.

'Blimey, hold me tight,' he said then as a large lady walked towards them. 'It's a ladies' excuse me, this one.'

Lily burst into laughter again as he hurried round the floor. She carried on laughing as he cracked more jokes and by the end of the dance she felt wonderful. He squeezed her hand as they walked off the floor and gave her a wink.

As Lily sat talking to their friends and neighbours, she thought how happy she felt for Hattie. Her friend was radiant and in love. Reube would be a good husband. As she looked across the crowded room, she saw the two brothers talking and laughing together. As she gazed at them, Ben turned slightly and met her eyes. There was something in them she responded to and almost unwillingly she returned his smile. Then realizing he was still looking at her, she turned back quickly to the woman who was speaking. Why did her cheeks feel glowing? And would she really accept his invitation to go dancing?

She wanted to.

But would it start all the old trouble again?

★

It was late afternoon and Lily walked out to the church garden. A pale pink sun was spreading wings across the sky. Hattie's wedding day had been a success; everything had gone well, down to the last slice that had been cut from the two-tiered cake. Lily breathed the soft air into her lungs, enjoying a moment of solitude.

She thought of her father. It had been a big disappointment not to have him there. He was almost a hermit since the timber yard. If only he would try to come out.

As Lily walked past the church hedge, two figures left the church. Both tall and well dressed, the men stopped still and their voices reached her. In a moment of sudden panic, she held her breath. Was she dreaming again? One of the figures turned, his features all at once familiar.

Lily closed her eyes and opened them.

Charles was walking towards her.

Chapter Sixteen

C harles was still as handsome but his face was gaunt. Lily looked into his dark eyes and felt all the old feelings flood back.

'How wonderful it is to see you again,' he said, his eyes going over her pink dress and flushed cheeks. 'May I ask what the occasion is?'

'It's Hattie and Reube's wedding day. They were married here at St Peter's.' She couldn't believe she was replying in a calm voice. 'Their wedding breakfast was in the church hall.'

'Then congratulations to the happy couple. I wish them all the success in the world. Are your parents with you?'

'Mum and Uncle Noah came. Me dad isn't very well.'

'I'm sorry to hear that.'

'He still has his cough.'

'I see.' Charles shook his head as if unable to believe it was her. 'I can't express in words how delighted I am to see you, Lily.'

'And I'm pleased to see you, too.' She wanted to throw her arms around him but she knew she couldn't let him guess her feelings.

'I often wondered about you.'

At this her heart leapt even more. 'Do you still live at Dewar Street?' she asked uncertainly.

'Yes,' he nodded. 'Much is the same. And you?'

She looked down. 'I left the market four years ago.'

He gave an audible gasp. 'I cannot believe that!'

'In the Depression, trade fell off, and Reube had to trim down.'

'Oh, Lily, I'm sorry.' He paused as he frowned. 'And your circumstances now – how have they changed?'

'Well, I still live at home, if that's what you mean. But now I'm working in a factory.'

He was silent for a moment then said, 'Are you happy, Lily?'

There was something about the way he said her name that made her shiver. But before she could answer, a voice called out and he turned round, raising his hand in answer.

When he looked back, he said regretfully, 'I must go as my colleague is waiting. He has links with this parish and came to see the vicar today on some matter. It was quite by chance that I accompanied him.'

Lily felt her heart sink to the depths of her soul. She wanted to hold on to his sleeve, never to let him go again. How cruel was life that he should be taken away again?

'I . . . I thought I saw you once,' she blurted, a feeling of panic overwhelming her, 'at the market. But it was someone else.'

'I am sad to say I've had no more time to spend on looking for furnishings for the house. I've been abroad a great deal.'

'Did you hear any more of Annie?' Lily asked, hoping it wasn't too personal a question.

'No, and perhaps it was all for the best. The poor girl must have had her reasons.' As he gazed at her a strange look came into his eyes. He put his hand to his chin and began to speak then stopped again. After a few seconds, he said haltingly, 'Lily, I do hope I can still address you as a friend?' She nodded, but he swept all further words from her lips, as he added quickly, 'I wonder if you would consider taking a walk with me again one day? Your time, I appreciate, must be limited. But I would deem it a great favour if you could spare just an hour? I have been very busy of late and your company would be the perfect antidote to the pressures I have been under.'

Lily stared at him, wondering if she had heard him speak the words that her dreams were made of? After all this time, was he flesh and blood, not an apparition or someone that resembled him?

'I'd like that too,' she whispered.

He smiled that wonderful smile. 'One Sunday morning perhaps?'

'Yes,' she agreed without hesitation.

'Are you free next weekend?' He touched her arm

gently. 'I shall call for you with pleasure, but perhaps you would rather meet me?'

She nodded. 'Next Sunday at the same place.'

The smile was still lingering on his lips when he said softly, 'Yes, at the same place.' Then with one last long look, he turned and strode quickly across to the older man who was waiting by the church.

Lily watched them leave, her gaze intent on the tall, straight figure, in his dark jacket and flannels. She wanted to remember every moment and when the two men were out of sight, she stood very still, savouring the space he had occupied. Her life seemed to have transformed in the last few minutes. All the feelings she had forced down inside her had come alive again. She was shivering with anticipation and happiness.

Going over every word he had said in her mind, she turned slowly towards the church hall. Her thoughts were all on Charles when suddenly she saw Ben. Digging his hands into his pockets, he turned and walked away.

Lily knew that he had been watching them. He had seen everything.

The time came for Reube and Hattie to leave. Ben was driving them in the lorry as the charabanc was too big for just the two of them. Lily hadn't told Hattie what had happened. This was Hattie's wedding day, she had her honeymoon ahead and was only thinking of love and romance.

Lily hugged her secret to herself. She refused to let

anyone or anything spoil her joy today. Lady Luck had sent Charles her way and this time, she was not going to refuse it. Charles had asked to see her! He *wanted* to see her, to walk with her and, he said, to enjoy her company! He hadn't asked her to help him buy anything for the house. So it was not in a business sense he had spoken. His words meant he must have some feelings for her. Hadn't she always hoped that was true? Deep in her heart, she had known she meant something to him. And today was the proof.

Lily was walking on air as the guests assembled outside the hall to say goodbye to the happy couple.

'It was a wonderful day.' Lily had to contain her excitement as she kissed Reube on the cheek and hugged Hattie tight.

'You'll be able to shorten that dress and use it again,' Hattie said as she held her bouquet in one arm, against her lovely going away outfit, a cream two-piece suit. Lily saw tears in her eyes.

'I know. I'll treasure it always.'

Ben drove up in the lorry and everyone cheered. As confetti was thrown over their heads, Reube helped Hattie inside it.

'Wait a minute, I want to chuck me bouquet,' Hattie cried. Stretching out of the window, she threw them to Lily.

Lily pressed them close. As the lorry rumbled off she blew Hattie a kiss. It had been such a thrilling day!

The kids all ran after the lorry trying to catch the old

boot and tins tied to the bumper. Ben waved a last goodbye.

Lily gave a sigh of contentment as she returned his salute. Even though Hattie was going to spend a week in Brighton, Lily wasn't envious. Not now. For today, she had seen her true love again.

Lily, her mother and uncle walked home from the hall, enjoying the summer evening. Josie carried a bag of left-overs whilst Lily had changed her clothes and now wore a skirt and blouse. Her arms were full of flowers and her pink dress.

'These titbits will do us for a week, you know,' Josie said happily to Lily. 'There's ham and cheese and two big slices of pie, plus our wedding cake. Mrs Parks did us proud.'

'Looks like we won't need feeding tonight,' said Lily. She was thinking about her appointment in seven days' time. What would she wear? Where would Charles take her?

'I'll have the pie tonight,' said her uncle, puffing on a cigarette. 'I fancy a bit of that.'

'I was going to save it for tomorrow,' declared his sister.

'I didn't have any at the do,' he replied, to which Josie gave him a frown.

'Don't 'spect you did as you had a glass to your mouth for most of the time.'

Lily smiled, unaffected for once by their bickering.

294

The secret she had was warming her inside. Nothing could prevent her from feeling happy. The evening was beautiful, and the streets were still full of kids. Lily looked at the young couples who strolled lazily along to the public houses. She didn't envy them either, for she had a love of her own now. She possessed an inner glow of happiness. In one week's time she would see Charles. If someone had told her that yesterday, she wouldn't have believed it. But today, when she looked into his eyes, she felt that fate had played its part in her destiny.

There was a spring in her step all the way home. It must have shown because her mother said suddenly, 'You look happy, love.'

'I am,' Lily smiled.

'You and Ben were like your old selves today.'

'We had a few dances, yes.'

'That boy had eyes only for you.'

Lily felt her spirits deflate. 'Mum, don't start that again, please.'

'Why don't you admit it, Lily? He thinks a lot of you.'

'Because Ben and me are friends it don't mean to say there's a big romance.'

Her uncle chuckled. 'You won't have any luck on that subject, Josie. I've tried already.'

Josie lifted her chin. 'You're a man, Noah, you don't understand the workings of a woman's mind.'

Lily felt as though they were talking as if she wasn't there. 'Mum, there's no romance going on.'

'You're twenty-five, love,' said her mother as they neared the house. 'Most girls are settled by then.'

Lily stopped and looked at her mother. 'And just where is it that I'm supposed to be settled?'

'You would live with us.' Her mother shrugged as she stood there. 'Why should you live anywhere else?'

'Mum, there's four at home.'

'You and Ben could have the top room. Lots of couples do it.'

A flush of scarlet flowed into Lily's cheeks. 'When will you accept that Ben and me aren't going to be together?'

Her uncle shuffled forward. 'You two ain't gonna row on the street, are you?'

'Keep out of this, Noah,' said Josie angrily.

'Mum, let's go in.' Lily walked to the house. She wasn't going to allow herself to be upset. She drew up the key and entered the house.

Her mother went to the parlour. 'I was hoping your father would make up the fire,' she said as she sank down on the couch. 'There's still a chill in the evenings. It would have been nice to come home to a flame in the grate. Never mind, I'll just rest me legs a moment. Then I'll go up to see him.' She held out the bag to Lily. 'Put this in the larder, would you, ducks? And don't let your uncle near it.'

'Don't really want none anyway,' muttered Noah Kelly as he joined his niece in the kitchen. He took off his coat and draped it over the back of the chair, then undid his collar. The two sides sprang out and he breathed a sigh, collapsing in a chair. Opening his tobacco tin, he rolled a cigarette.

Lily put on the kettle. She sat down, her mind far away. She had one week to decide what she was going to wear. She wanted to make an impression this time. She had to look her best for Charles.

'So what did he say?'

Lily came out of her trance. 'Who?'

'Your gent,' said her uncle.

'How did you know?' she gasped.

'I saw you and him at the church. I walked out to have a fag, and these two blokes came out by me.'

'Did you know it was Charles?'

'Not until I saw the look on me girl's face. She looked a different person. She was happy for once.'

Lily looked down. 'I can't forget him, Uncle Noah.'

'So what's he have to say for himself?'

'He's been travelling a lot and hasn't bought much for his house.'

'Are yer seeing him again?'

She nodded. 'In a week's time. He asked me to go for a walk. And just because he says he likes my company.'

'Well, you're old enough now to know right from wrong. Just keep your wits about you.' He shifted his pince-nez up and down the ridge of his nose. 'You know that boy was watching yer too?'

Lily nodded. 'Yes, I saw Ben.'

'What did he have to say about it?'

'Nothing,' replied Lily indignantly. 'Why should he? Charles has nothing to do with him.'

'I was only asking, that's all.'

'I never wanted to hurt Ben – ever.'

'I know you didn't, girl.'

'I hope he finds a nice woman to marry.'

He inclined his head to the next room. 'You gonna tell your mother about the gent?'

'I don't know. She keeps on about Ben all the time. I would have thought by now, she understood.'

'Well, I wouldn't blame you for one, if you looked to pastures new.'

Once more she stared at her uncle in surprise. 'What makes you say that?'

'You ain't got no kids to tie you down.'

'I haven't thought ahead that far.'

Her uncle crushed out his cigarette in a saucer. It took a long time to grind it down. As he did so, he sighed. Then he looked into Lily's puzzled gaze. 'Lil, there's something you gotta know. By rights, it ain't up to me to tell you. But I—'

'Noah! Lily!' The scream went through the house. Lily jumped to her feet and ran into the hall.

Her mother stood there. 'Oh my God, Lil!' Her face was drained of colour.

'Mum, what's the matter?'

Josie clenched her hands. 'Your dad's gone!'

Lily laughed. 'He can't have gone. He don't go out anywhere.'

'Well, he's gone now. The bedroom's empty.'

Lily looked up the stairs. 'He could be up in the top room.'

'No, I've looked.'

'Then he must have got fed up by himself. That's good news not bad, Mum.'

'No . . . no . . . that's not it at all.'

Lily didn't understand what was happening. Why was her mother so anxious? 'Come and sit down.' She led her into the parlour.

'This is all your fault Noah Kelly!' Josie suddenly exclaimed as she pointed to her brother.

Lily looked from one to the other. 'What do you mean, it's Uncle's fault? What's going on?'

'I knew this would happen if—' Josie covered her face with her hands.

Lily felt fear flood into her heart. What was this all about?

Bob Bright was desperate. There had been nothing left in the bottle and the stomach cramps had begun. What was a man supposed to do? He was in pain and the cough had seized up his lungs. Now he could hardly walk. His feet seemed like lead weights as he stumbled along, the left half of his body seeming to slow him down. The chest pain that had wracked him had sent him tumbling out of the house. He had to find relief. And with the old man so stubbornly refusing, he had no choice but to go there himself.

It was a long time since he had been out in the fresh air. A longer time still since he had followed this path. In the days after his dismissal from the timber yard, he'd come once or twice with Noah, then when his brother-in-law had refused to accompany him, he'd come under the cover of darkness, until Josie had discovered it wasn't the tavern he visited, but Limehouse. At her insistence, he'd tried to abstain and for a while he had managed. But then the dark feelings returned. It was as if a hole had swallowed him up. Trapped in it, he was powerless, confronted by inadequacy and guilt. What good was a man who couldn't look after his family? What purpose did he serve in this life? The torment wouldn't stop until he succumbed to his habit.

Bob shambled painfully into the broken streets of Limehouse. His darting eyes were narrowed and furtive. The assault on his belly grew more acute with each step.

At last he came on the door. He hammered the boards, his need murderous. Where was the Lascar? Where was Mai Chi? Sweat beaded his brow as he stepped back, swaying and cursing.

He shouted, careless now of who heard. If she was gone, then let them take him, imprison him, do away with him. His existence meant nothing without the draught.

He fell to his knees, his palms heavy on the filth. A gasp rose from his chest. 'A curse on you, old woman,' he sobbed and unable to right himself, Bob Bright sunk with the curse on his lips to the earth.

Lily was staring at the two people she thought she knew everything about. Now they seemed like strangers. Her mother's eyes were red with weeping. Her uncle looked crestfallen.

'Why didn't you tell me?' Lily couldn't believe they had kept her in ignorance.

'Because I hoped he would get better,' said Josie with another deep sob. 'And no one would ever have to know.'

'Your mother tried her best, girl. But the habit grew too strong.'

Lily caught her breath. She couldn't cry, she was too angry. 'All this time you've lied to me.'

'It wasn't lying,' Josie protested. 'I just thought of it as medicine.'

'But it didn't come from the doctor.'

'Course not,' said her uncle, fidgeting uncomfortably. 'They won't give the strong stuff out unless you've got a good reason, like being in the war and ending up disabled.'

'But Dad has a cough medicine,' Lily said, standing up and walking to and fro. 'He used to take that.'

'It wasn't strong enough,' said her uncle. 'Your dad got depressed after being laid off. He was at the end of his tether.'

'So you took him to this place you say is in

Limehouse. Is it one of them dens you read about?'

Her uncle looked away.

Lily sat in front of him. 'Why did you go there?'

'It's the only place you can get it cheap. I used to pass the old woman's cottage on me rounds, years ago. Got to know her a bit, knew what she was selling. I didn't think a little help would go amiss for your dad. It was only a drop at first, gel,' said her uncle, his voice rough with emotion. 'A few spoonfuls of paregoric.'

'A tincture,' said Josie quickly, glancing at her brother. 'It cleared up the loose tummy that came with his cough. I would say to meself, I'll tell Lily where the money's going just as soon as he don't have to take it any more. Each day I tried to get him to go out, to act as normal, but he wanted more each day.'

Lily felt a shiver of cold down her spine. 'What happened then?'

'The old Chinese gave him something else.' Noah Kelly sank back on the couch. 'Something stronger.'

'What's that?'

Her uncle sighed. 'It was laudanum.'

Lily blinked. 'But that's what the doctor gives Sylvester.'

'Yes, gel, I know.'

'It stops his bad dreams and calms him.'

'Well then,' said her mother, her eyes suddenly wide as she sat on the edge of her chair, 'it can't be so bad, can it, that your dad takes it once in a while for relief.'

'But it's not once in a while, is it, Mum?' Lily jumped

to her feet. 'I wondered why we weren't managing. We're always short. We've run up more on the slate again. With all the overtime I do, we should be all right.'

'I know, Lily, and I'm sorry.'

'Do you know where Dad's gone?'

Josie wrung her hands together. 'To buy it himself I should think.'

'Did he have any money?'

'He took all I had in me apron pocket.'

Lily sniffed back her tears. 'We'll have to find him.'

'Not at night we can't,' objected her uncle. 'Not up there. After dark you'd take your life in your hands. It's risky enough in daytime when I get a lift up with the coalie.'

Lily tried to think what to do. She loved the good and gentle man who had provided a roof over their heads when she was a child. He had always been there for her and now she must help him. She had to make him see that the drug he relied on was slowly killing him.

'We'll leave it till morning,' she said at last.

'It's me that will go,' protested her uncle. 'Those places ain't no place for a woman.'

'He's me dad, Uncle Noah,' Lily replied. 'We'll go together.'

'But what state will he be in?' protested Josie, clenching her hands once more. 'And how will you bring him back? The coalie don't work on Sundays.'

Lily looked at her mother and shrugged. 'We'll find a way. And when he comes home, we'll call in the doctor.'

'I don't want him told,' said her mother, looking alarmed.

Lily knew that her mother was worried what the doctor would say. People who lived in poverty were the first to be ashamed of their circumstances. If the fact could be hidden or disguised, women would go out of their way to do so. But worrying what other people might think is what had begun the trouble in the first place. She had grown up with the shame of poverty instilled into her. Now nothing mattered more than bringing her dad home and making him well again.

Ben stretched and heard a loud creak. Flexing his arms and rolling his neck, he realized his head had been at an angle overnight. He'd slept so soundly that it would take more than a Sunday dinner and trot down the pub to cure his stiffness. A stride out, that was what he needed. Or maybe he'd give the charabanc a good wash?

He eased himself up and glanced at the empty bed beside him. He hoped the lucky bugger who'd slept beside him for the past thirty years was enjoying himself. A smile touched his mouth as he thought of the boarding house he'd delivered the pair of lovers to. There was a bit of an old dragon inside, who had barked out orders as they'd heaved up the two suitcases to the third floor. But the room had been large and the bedclothes looked clean. And from the look in Hattie's eye anyway, it wasn't those sort of details she was interested in.

Ben pulled on his trousers, thinking of what he would

do after a wash and shave. First he'd begin to clear his clothes out of the wardrobe and take them upstairs to the top room. There wasn't a great deal of stuff as he'd trimmed down over the last few weeks. It wasn't going to be long before he, too, was off. Mum still hadn't agreed to wed Pedro, but she had Hattie and Reube to look after her.

Rubbing the stubble on his chin, he made his way downstairs. It was a bit quiet, with just him and Mum at home. But when Hattie and Reube were back, they'd soon cheer it up. He glanced through the lace at the lorry outside. He'd been too damned tired at three o'clock this morning to park at the Quarry. Next week he'd start looking round for that four-seater, an Austin or Hillman perhaps. Whistling his way to the kitchen, he put on the kettle.

He was ruminating on the day ahead, when he heard the knocker go. Glancing at the mantel clock, he saw it was eight on the dot. Early for Pedro. But then the poor bloke was probably eager, without half of the family around.

But when he opened the door, he found Lily there. 'Blimey,' he said hesitantly. 'Lil! What are you doing up and about this early on a Sunday?'

'Can I come in?'

'Course you can.' He stepped back, self conscious of his appearance. He hadn't washed or shaved or even brushed his teeth.

'I got to talk to you, Ben.'

He led her into the parlour. 'Sit down, take the weight off your feet.'

She perched on the edge of a chair, her blue eyes staring up at him anxiously. For a moment he wondered if this had something to do with what he'd seen at the church. He'd been a fraction away from thinking they could pick up the broken pieces of their friendship in a more intimate way, when that fella had appeared. What was his name? Grey ... Charles Grey! He'd seen the way she looked at him and knew that it still wasn't over between them. Yet, it wasn't the look of love in her eyes right this moment. It was more like fear.

'I saw your lorry,' she said, her face parchment white.

'Yeah. Got back late from Brighton,' he nodded. 'Was too tired to park it up. So I left it outside. Now how can I help?'

'I need a favour.'

He shrugged. 'Anything, Lil. Just name it.'

'It's me dad ...'

He frowned, shaking his head. 'Is it his cough? Shall I come over?'

'No, it's not his cough. When we was at the wedding, he went off somewhere and he's still not back.'

Ben waited, a troubled feeling growing inside him. 'You mean he's been gone all night?'

'Yes.' Her eyes were full of sadness. 'Me dad's sick, Ben. But not with his cough. He needs something else to help him ... not regular medicine ... something not easy to stop.'

For a moment he drew in his breath. In his mind's eye he saw Noah Kelly in the cart, riding beside the coalie. The cart had always turned out from Limehouse.

'You'd better tell me what's going on,' he said.

Slowly, as she spoke, the puzzle all fell into place.

'You stay with your mum,' he told her as he quickly pulled on his jacket. 'Your uncle and me will find the place.'

'Me dad might need me,' she said and he shrugged.

He wanted to take her in his arms and protect her. What had Mrs Bright been thinking of? Her daughter working all hours that God sent. An old man, running the gauntlet to Limehouse. Proper barmy that was. No wonder the Brights were always hard-up. The poppy didn't come cheap. No wonder Bob Bright was half the man he used to be.

Ben growled softly to himself as he took Lily's arm and led her out to the lorry. He should have guessed. The times he had spotted Noah on the cart and the strange decline in Bob Bright. He should have seen signs! There were men he'd known who'd taken to drink, but this habit took a toll of a man's brain as swift as it emptied his pocket.

'I'll fetch your uncle,' Ben said as she sat in the cab.

At the back of the lorry he reached under the canvas. Sliding the wrench under his belt, he went quickly across the road.

The door of number thirty-four opened. Noah Kelly

frowned up at him. He looked older than Methuselah, Ben thought in dismay.

'She told you, then?'

'She did, Mr Kelly.'

'It was all me fault.'

'It don't matter whose fault it was. We'll bring him home, don't worry.'

Noah Kelly nodded slowly. 'Thank you, son.'

Five minutes later they were driving up Westferry Road. The lorry rattled and shook but this was the only noise. His two passengers sat silently beside him.

The best form of defence was attack, he could remember his old man saying. He wished his dad was here now to lend a hand.

But uppermost in Ben's mind was one question. Bob Bright was a grown man. If they found him here, would he willingly return home?

Chapter Seventeen

B en turned the lorry into Limehouse and Lily felt a shiver go through her. The roads had been deserted, but one or two figures now emerged amongst the dilapidated buildings.

'It's Chinese round here,' said Ben as he pulled on to the waste ground.

'Merchant seamen from the East,' nodded her uncle as a tall man and oriental woman came their way. 'Lascars. They settle on the banks, don't go far from the river.'

'Where is me dad?' Lily gazed in dismay at the half houses and roofless cottages.

'The place we want is over there,' Noah pointed to a tumbled dwelling that seemed deserted to Lily. There were boards across the windows and weeds grew tall outside. She could hear the chatter of the couple passing by, a foreign language, with glances thrown slyly towards the lorry.

Ben sighed as he turned off the engine. 'Well, Mr Kelly, it ain't the most salubrious place in town.'

The old man heaved a sigh. 'You're right there, boy.

I would cut off me arm if I could turn back the clock and change things but then I thought I was doing him a turn, temporary like, to give the poor bloke a bit of relief.'

'Is there anyone else inside, except the woman you've told us about?' Ben enquired.

'One fella,' nodded Lily's uncle. 'And he's twice the size of you, boy. If they've got Bob in there, he's not likely to be above ground, but below stairs.'

'You mean there's a cellar?'

'As black as Hades it is too.'

'That's comforting,' said Ben as he opened the door slowly.

'Say it was me that sent you. Let her think you're a customer,' warned the old man beside him. 'Watch every move she makes, lad. She looks like a harmless old girl, but she's as hard as nails, a real pro.'

'I'll bear that in mind,' Ben nodded as he slung his legs out of the cab and jumped down. He looked quickly back. 'You stay right where you are an' all, Lil. You and your uncle don't move, right?'

Lily nodded although it was hard for her to just wait. She felt the tension tightening in her stomach. Her heart jumped into her mouth as she saw him bang his fist on the door. Was he in danger? And if her father was inside that hovel, how would Ben get him out again?

Ben's heart was hammering as he stepped inside and heard the door close behind him. It was dark as he took a breath and felt his head swim with foul and pungent air. Coughing, he put his hand to his mouth, then managed to breathe again.

A figure moved in front of him. Bent and tiny, she flitted across his vision to stand by a lamp. Her green gown glowed and above it, he could see an ancient face with almond eyes.

'What you want, nice-boy?' Her voice was as inquisitive as a child's.

'What have you got to offer?' Ben glanced quickly round. He couldn't see the guard but to turn and look behind him would show fear.

She gave a birdlike twitch. 'How you know Mai Chi?'

'A friend sent me. Noah Kelly.'

'Ah ...' She closed her small hands together. 'Kelly-Kelly ol' friend of Mai Chi.'

'So I understand.'

'Kelly-Kelly sent you have good time with Mai?'

Ben nodded abruptly. 'He did that.' Was Lily's dad here? he wondered. What if, instead, Bob Bright had taken a drink to ease his troubles? Had old Mr Kelly put the wind up them all for nothing?

Ben frowned into the darkness. He could see nothing in this pig sty that resembled a man.

'You want smokey-smokey?'

Ben nodded once more. The woman gave a gentle chuckle and crooked a finger. A man appeared from the shadows. Ben caught his breath at the sight of the tall figure. The Lascar's black face glistened in the lamplight, his muscles bulged as he folded his arms.

'Nice boy follow Mai.'

Ben felt his blood quicken as she led him down the rickety stairs. Grasping the rotting walls, his fingers slid helplessly against damp and filth ingrained in them.

'This way, velly nice boy.'

Ben blinked, trying hard to adjust his eyes. He felt swallowed up by the thick, dope-filled air. A candle flickered from a corner and she turned

'You lay here, Mai make you happy.' She pointed to a mattress on the floor.

Ben felt his stomach heave as he sat gingerly down. A mist curled before his eyes like a thin curtain and the stench became putrid. In the darkness he was left alone.

Slowly, his vision became clearer. He saw another mattress and on it lay a figure. Ben rose stealthily and went over. Shaking the limp shoulder, he took a sharp breath as a pair of watery eyes gazed up at him.

'Mr Bright!' he exclaimed.

'Who . . . who is it?'

'Ben James, sir.'

A hand clutched him tight. 'Get me out of here, lad.'

'Can you walk?'

'I dunno. I can't feel me legs.'

'Sling yer arm round me shoulder and we'll try for those stairs.'

Ben lifted the fragile weight, shocked at the change in the man. If only they could get up those stairs . . .

'Where you going with old man, nice boy?'

Ben froze. The woman appeared out of nowhere. In her hand she held a pipe, long and smoking. The smell that exuded from it made his stomach revolt.

'I ain't staying, and nor is he,' Ben said, unable to hide his disgust.

'You try smokey-smokey,' she whispered, pushing the pipe towards him. 'You come, sit with Mai. You forget all troubles.'

'The only trouble I got, is getting up them stairs,' replied Ben as he shambled himself and his burden forward. 'Now let me pass.'

Quickly she laid down the pipe and sprang on him. 'You not go till you give Mai money!'

'You'll be lucky, you evil crone. After what you've done to me mate, you're lucky I ain't calling the coppers.'

Her almond eyes were like fire. 'You threaten Mai Chi?'

'Get out of me way.' He was on the stairs now and his grip on Bob was tight. But there was the Lascar to deal with at the top.

'Nice boy ain't so nice,' came the cold words and with them the glint of a blade.

Ben gasped as it flashed to his chin. He had five pounds in his pocket, but he'd be damned if he was going to give it up.

'You pay Mai,' she demanded, her voice thick with menace. 'No coppers round here. This Mai's place. You pay money or else.' She levelled the knife at his throat.

He had never hit a woman in his life before but it was her or them. He felt the knife prick his skin. 'All right,' he nodded, and she smiled.

Ben curled his fist and struck out. She staggered and fell and seizing his chance, he hauled his friend up the stairs.

As they stumbled into the lantern glow, the Lascar barred their way. 'Let me pass,' Ben warned as the guard came towards them, arms outstretched. As they struggled, the lantern fell and a slick of oil leapt into fire. It spun across the rotten boards and nipped at the Lascar's feet.

Taking advantage of the distraction Ben hurled himself and Bob Bright at the door. It gave with a snap and they stumbled through the splintered wood. Grasping the older man's arm he dragged him forward towards the lorry, hauling the pure air deep into his lungs.

Josie was waiting anxiously in the parlour. Getting up from the chair she went to the window and carefully moved aside the curtain. Would they bring her husband home? Would she be able to hold her head up high again? Word would soon get round after this. Tears of self pity filled her eyes.

'How could you do this to me, Bob?' she asked the empty street. 'How could you bring shame on our family?'

She had managed to keep his secret hidden until now.

Who had seen her husband leave the house whilst they were at the wedding? People thought he was house-bound, that it was his chest that made him unable to walk very far. But now they would know different.

What was she going to do? She sank down on the couch again and trembled with a sudden shudder. How unfair life was! If Bob had been injured in the war he would have been thought of as a hero, like Sylvester. As a young man, her husband had been strong and healthy. That was before the conflict and the Depression. Now he was old before his time. She still loved him but he wasn't the man she married.

Josie pushed her hands over her face. Her pale blue eyes were full of tears. She had tried to do her best and keep her daughter from the worry of knowing what her father had become. Instead, Lily had blamed her. Life was unjust!

It was all Noah's fault. Taking Bob to that place – how could he? Josie felt a sob rise in her throat as she plucked at the loose thread of her cardigan sleeve. She looked down at the holes in her clothes. Once, she was a young girl with a good figure and nice hair, just like Lily's. Now her hair had turned grey and lines of worry had carved themselves into her skin.

She felt like running away. But she had nowhere to go.

An hour later the lorry rumbled into Love Lane. Lily glanced at her father who sat in between her and her uncle. It was a bit squashed in the cab, but Ben had said he could drive well enough. Her father looked ravaged and very old. Every now and then his head dropped on his chest. He muttered some strange words in his confused state and he smelt rather badly. Lily knew that whatever had happened to him in that place, he simply hadn't known what was going on. Now he was beginning to shake and hold himself tightly. Was this what the drug had done?

When the engine stopped, she took his hand. 'We're home now, Dad.'

He raised his head wearily and nodded. He must have understood her, she thought with relief.

Ben helped her uncle down first, then taking her father's weight, took him inside.

'Oh, Bob, why did you go off like that?' gasped her mother as she rushed towards them. 'Look at the state of you!' She turned to Lily. 'Did anyone see you get out of the lorry?'

Lily took her arm. 'Put the kettle on, Mum, and I'll get Dad upstairs.'

'Come along, Josie,' said her uncle, 'let's make ourselves useful and leave the young 'uns to it.'

Lily helped Ben to get her father upstairs. 'I'll take his clothes off and give him a wash and shave if you like,' Ben offered, lowering him onto the bed.

Lily nodded. 'I'll get his things.' Going downstairs she hung her coat on the stand and stood still for a moment trying to calm herself. She was shaking.

'I'll take up Dad's shaving soap and razor and a bowl of hot water,' she told her mum in the kitchen.

'Did your dad say why he ran off like that?' Josie asked as she collected the items together and gave them to Lily.

'No, and it don't matter why, Mum. We've got him back and that's what counts.'

Half an hour later, her dad was washed, shaved and lying in bed. 'You'll be all right now, Mr Bright,' Ben said as he gave Lily the dirty clothing.

Lily saw her dad's lips move before he closed his eyes again.

'He'll have a bit of kip now,' said Ben as they stood out on the landing. 'Meanwhile I'm off for the doc.'

'Mum won't like that.'

'Why?'

'She's worried about everyone knowing.'

Ben shrugged. 'She'll soon see it's for the best.'

Lily had one question. 'When we drove away from that place I saw smoke coming out.'

He nodded. 'The lamp went over and caught fire. I couldn't do nothing, Lil. It was your dad I was looking out for.'

The tears pricked Lily's eyes. She didn't wish harm on anyone. But what if someone was hurt?

Ben reached into his pocket. 'Look, I want you to take this. It's only a few quid, but it will help.'

'You've already done enough for us.'

He pushed the notes in her hand, then hurrying down

the stairs he slipped quietly out of the house. Deep in thought, Lily went to the kitchen.

'I've made the tea,' her mother said. 'Is Ben coming down?'

'No, he's gone for the doctor,' Lily replied.

Her mother almost dropped the cup she was holding. She sat down with a sob and the tears gushed forth, trickling down her already tear-stained cheeks.

Lily walked to the factory early the next morning. She had spent most of the night sitting at her father's bedside, watching him slip in and out of delirium. The medicine Dr Tapper had prescribed soothed his racking cough but did very little else. As she had sat in the darkness her thoughts had turned to Charles. Selfishly, she was afraid that she wouldn't be able to go out with him. Sunday was going to be a wonderful day. Now she could see her happiness slipping slowly away. What would he think if she didn't turn up? Would he go away again?

Lily tried to put these thoughts from her mind as she hurried up the long flight of stairs to the foreman's office. She hoped he would let her have a week's leave. But when she told him her father was sick, he laughed.

'If I gave everyone a week off for sickness in the family, the factory would close,' he stormed. 'If you ain't at your place in five minutes, I'll fill it within the hour.'

'What about me pay?' Lily protested.

'You had it on Friday. And don't expect more as it's you that's let me down.'

She looked into the foreman's hard face. What of all the overtime she had put in? But she knew arguing would get her nowhere. At least she had Ben's five pounds, enough for several weeks. Would her dad be better by then?

Josie was up in the bedroom when she arrived home. 'He's got a fever,' she sighed. 'What happened at the factory?'

Lily took the wet rag from her. 'I won't be going back.'

'Why not?' Josie asked, alarmed.

'The foreman sacked me.'

Her mother let out a wail. 'What will we do now? We counted on your money.'

Lily rinsed out the rag in the bowl beside the bed. Gently she soothed her father's forehead. 'We'll think of something. Now go and have forty winks as you look all in.'

'I couldn't sleep last night. So perhaps I will.'

Later that day, Lily gave two pounds to her mother. 'Ben gave us this. Go to the market and buy some vegetables and meat. We'll make a broth for Dad and make it last all week.'

'The rent's due today.'

'I've got enough for that.'

Josie put on her coat. 'I don't feel like going out.'

Lily gave her the basket. 'Course you do.' She knew her mother didn't want to talk to the neighbours.

'If anyone asks me about your father I'm going to say it's a mystery illness!'

This brought a smile to Lily's lips. As she watched her mother walk hurriedly down the road, she decided that although losing her job was a setback, losing her father would have been much worse. With time and patience, he would recover. And Lily was determined to see that he did. No matter what.

The days passed and Lily spent long hours at her father's bedside. Slowly the fever receded, and gradually he began to eat the broth that Lily and Josie had made for him. In moments he seemed to know what they were doing for him was for the best. At others, he would argue, push away the dish and try to get up. But he was too weak to go far. One night, when Lily had fallen deeply asleep on the couch downstairs, he tried to escape again. But Lily had locked the front door, putting the key safely in her pocket. She had finally persuaded him back to bed, where he had fallen into a deep sleep.

On Friday, Lily woke up in the chair. She had slept there all night. Her heart gave a violent jerk when she saw the empty bed. Hurrying to her bedroom, she found Josie asleep, as was her uncle next door.

She went downstairs to the parlour. It was deserted. Where was her father? He couldn't have gone out the front door. The key was in her pocket.

Lily went to the kitchen. What if he had escaped over the fence? Then through the window, she saw movement. Peering out, she saw the closet door open. A frail figure emerged. Her father stood in his pyjamas, looking round uncertainly.

Lily rushed out. 'Oh, Dad, you're here!' She put her arms round him. 'I thought you'd gone off again.'

'Why should I do that?'

She stepped back in surprise. Had his memory come back?

'I went to the lav. I ain't gonna use that bloody pail in the bedroom again.'

'You've been in bed for a while.'

'Well, I'm up now.' He frowned as she took his arm. 'Where are me clothes?'

'We put them away.'

'Why's that? They're always over the chair for work. There's a new boat coming in an' all.'

Lily's heart sank. He had forgotten the last four years and still thought he was on the boats. 'You must have been dreaming,' she told him.

'It weren't no dream.'

'You've been sick,' she explained gently. 'This is the first time you've got up for days.'

He stopped as they entered the kitchen. It was as though he'd never seen the room before. His brow wrinkled under his shock of pure white hair. 'I'm a bit muddled, ducks. What's been wrong with me?'

'You've had a fever.' She wasn't going to say any

more as the doctor said it would take time before his memory came fully back.

'Me mind is a bit of a blank. What day is it?'

'Friday.'

'Is it really? What month?'

'It's August. Now, come inside and I'll make you a cup of tea.'

'I could do with one.'

Lily felt her spirits rise. Even though he was finding it hard to remember, he didn't seem upset. 'Sit down at the table.'

He nodded and sat, putting his arms around himself as he started to shiver and shake. 'Now you come to mention it, I don't feel so good, gel. And me stomach has a touch of the gripes.'

'Yes, but you'll get over it.' She put on the kettle. When would he remember what terrible things had happened to him? As she turned to look at him, his lined face was full of confusion, his eyes set deep in dark hollows. She knew that as the days wore on, events would come back to him that perhaps he would prefer not to remember.

It was late on Saturday night and Noah Kelly was making his niece some supper. The sandwich comprised two hefty slices of bread and a layer of dripping. She was getting thin. He would have to keep an eye on her. She had spent long hours nursing, determined to effect a recovery. Noah wasn't so sure that in Bob's case, there would ever be a full one. The crisis might be over, but he was still sick. Although he had dressed, he stayed in the bedroom, smoking and shaking. Even reading the newspaper was beyond him. Noah knew that his belly was aching for the laudanum. It would take many weeks before his stomach and bowels were right again.

'This is for you, gel,' he said as he entered the parlour. Lily was sitting by the window sewing a patch on her dad's trousers. 'You ain't eaten much all day.'

She put down her work and laughed. 'I can't eat all that.'

'Yes, you can.'

She took a small bite. 'Have you looked in on Dad?'

'Yes and he's asleep, just as you should be.'

She nodded. 'I'll finish this first, then get me blankets out.'

'You can't sleep here on the couch for ever, gel.'

'Mum needs a bed more than me.'

'This house has got to get back to normal.'

She laughed again. 'Oh, things ain't so bad.'

'I've been thinking.'

She looked up at him warily. 'About what?'

'How we're going to manage,' he said, indicating the hardly touched sandwich. 'That money Ben gave you ain't gonna last forever.'

'I know. But we'll manage.'

'How?' he said gently, wishing that he didn't have to upset her, but he knew that what he was about to suggest would do just that.

'I'll get meself a job, of course.'

'You can't do everything. Besides which, you'll need references, won't you? Is the factory gonna give you them? That foreman was a cussed old blighter. He might not make it easy.'

'I'll cross the bridge when we come to it, Uncle Noah.'

'We could go to the Welfare.'

'What! Mum would never have that!'

'She don't have much choice. Your dad is ill. They'll give us something, even if it's only a pittance.'

Lily was shaking her head. 'They'd give us a means test and we'll have to sell every stick before they give us anything.'

'It's the only way, Lil. The Relieving Officer would let us keep the beds and a table. I know that 'cos I saw it often enough on me rounds. But the piano and Talking Machine will have to go, along with all the records.'

Her eyes suddenly were moist. 'There must be another way.'

'No, love, it's the only way.'

Lily wiped her eyes. 'Mum would never get over the shame.'

'Bugger the shame,' he said fiercely. 'It's food in the stomach that counts. We've never had to call on the Welfare before and what they give us will be barely enough to keep a cat alive. But at least we'll have something.'

Lily stared down at the trousers in her lap. A tear

dropped on to the cloth and Noah's heart bled for his niece.

'Now come on, Lil, your dad is going to get better and ain't that a blessing? We've come through the worst.'

She looked up. 'Have we?'

Noah knew that it was only words he was saying. They both knew that worse was on its way when they were means tested. The Relieving Officer selling all the household effects and poking his nose into every corner. It was the lowest you could sink. And even if they were given any money, it would be a frugal amount. But, Noah thought, it was their only choice now.

'Listen,' he said, taking her hand. 'We've decided on our course of action and can pull together through this.'

'But what about Mum?'

'Leave her to me. Josie's strong underneath. It's you I'm worried about.'

'I'm all right.'

'It's Sunday tomorrow. Young Ben is calling by. He can sit with your father whilst you go out for some air.'

'I don't know . . .'

'Well, I do. I want to see a bit of colour in them cheeks.'

She nodded slowly. 'I suppose I could.'

'That's settled then.'

He watched his niece carefully. The suggestion had been a good one. At last he had brought a light to her eyes. He must see to it that she got out more often. And as for the Welfare, he would not put Lily through the embarrassment of going up to the offices. He would take it on his own shoulders and go to the town hall next week to set things in motion.

Chapter Eighteen

Lily hurried along Westferry Road towards the Marsh Wall that bordered West India Docks. It was a balmy August morning, with a sun that was already shining brightly. She breathed in the early morning air and wondered if Charles would really meet her there. Her mind was full of worry at leaving Uncle Noah and her mother in charge of the escapee. Would Ben visit in her absence, as her uncle had said?

Lily quickened her steps. How long would she wait for Charles to arrive? She couldn't be away too long. What would she tell him? The truth? What would he think of them if he knew that her father had frequented an opium den? Lily walked faster, the doubts and worries going round in her mind. This was supposed to be her special day.

Lily found herself breathing hard. She stopped to take a breath. Her thoughts went back to Charles. Was it better to turn round and go home? How could she see him like this?

She looked down at her thin summer's dress. It was

old and unfashionable; the heels on her shoes needed repairing. And she hadn't had any time to wash her hair. It probably still smelt of paint. She knew she looked unattractive. Suddenly she thought of how he had last seen her, in her pink dress. So much had happened since Hattie and Reube had been married. Tonight the newlyweds returned. When would she see the new Mrs James next?

Lily didn't see the large blue car coming towards her. She was deep in thought and jumped when the horn blew. The vehicle pulled in and a tall figure jumped out.

'Oh, it's you, Charles!' was all she could find to say. 'I was looking out for a red car.'

'I changed it last year for this one.'

She saw this was even bigger and shinier, with two large lamps on the front. As always the sight of his handsome face, thick, dark hair and magnetic eyes made her heart race. This man had the effect of making all her problems seem distant. With his smile, he made her feel that life was full of excitement.

He glanced at his watch. 'I waited at the crossroads, but thought something may have happened.'

'I didn't realize I was late.'

He smiled gently. 'What matters is that I've found you.'

She felt suddenly elated when she heard those words. Did he mean them?

'Is there something wrong?' he asked gently.

'No . . . it's just that—'

'You were having second thoughts about our meeting?' he interrupted.

Her cheeks flushed guiltily. There was so much she couldn't explain.

'Lily, you are upset!'

She looked down and once again caught sight of the hem of her frock. The stitches had come out and it was dangling over her knee. Her shoes were rough and worn. She hadn't had time to polish them. Tears sprang to her eyes as she stood there, trying to hide her emotion.

'I . . . I don't know where to begin.'

'Then I have a suggestion. Instead of walking let me take you back to Dewar Street. We shall sit in the quiet and talk about old times. I think that would do very well for a start, don't you?'

She nodded and he smiled, taking her arm and leading her towards the car.

She sank gratefully onto the leather seat. As he walked around to the driver's side, a lump formed in her throat as she tried to swallow. She should be delighted that once again she was in his company.

But now all she could feel was confusion.

Lily sat in the very same watered pink silk chair that she had sat in on her first visit. Beside her was the small polished table that had been somewhat dusty. On it now stood a white china teapot, cup and saucer placed on a silver tray. The drawing room was unchanged, with the

Indian rug spread luxuriously at her feet and the long thick curtains held back by their tassels. Number four Dewar Street was just as it was in her memory, its faded elegance seeming even more beautiful in reality.

Charles, who was dressed in a white shirt and dark flannels, sat on the other chair. He had told her that over the years he had travelled to different countries bringing back exotic items from all over the world for his wealthy customers. He had even been on a big game hunt in Africa and brought home the skin of a large man-eating tiger. Lily had listened with eagerness to his description of the Velte and the stunning African countryside and its people. In return she had told him about the last days at the market and how it had not been possible for Reube to keep her on. She described her job at the paint factory and Hattie and Reube's brief separation four years ago.

'Then true love found a way in the end,' he smiled as he sat there, his dark eyes penetrating and alert.

Lily smiled and sipped her tea. 'Being married was always what Hattie wanted.'

'I'm very pleased that she did,' he said quietly, 'but for selfish reasons, I'm ashamed to say. The occasion gave me another chance to meet a long-missed friend.'

Lily realized he was talking about her! She felt her heart thump erratically inside her chest.

'And what of your family?' he asked then.

Lily averted her eyes.

But he nodded and sat back before she could reply, a

knowing expression on his face. 'So here we come to the root of the problem?'

Lily gazed into his beautiful eyes. What would he say if she told him the truth?

'Lily, do you regard me as your friend?' he asked after a long pause.

She smiled then and nodded.

'A friend you could discuss any problem with?'

She replied without hesitation. 'Yes, Charles, I do.'

'In which case, as a friend, please tell me what is so disturbing you?'

If only she could! It would be such a relief. But would their friendship survive the truth that might reflect so badly on her family?

'It's Dad,' she told him uncertainly. 'As you know he was ill and couldn't come to the wedding.'

'Yes, indeed.'

'When we got home he wasn't in his bedroom. He'd just disappeared.'

Charles nodded encouragingly. 'So where did he go?'

'He went to ... Limehouse,' she stammered, 'to the Chinese quarter.' She paused, waiting for understanding to come into his eyes.

He lifted his hand to his chin. 'Go on.'

'When Dad lost his job at the timber yard four years ago, he just seemed to give up. He was too sick to find other work and nothing the doctor gave him seemed to help. So Uncle Noah gave him paregoric.'

'Paregoric?' He lifted one dark eyebrow. 'An opiate? But used wisely, this can be beneficial.'

'Yes, but he needed more,' Lily tried to explain. 'So he took laudanum.'

'Laudanum,' Charles breathed as he looked at her keenly. 'Well, in many cases of sickness, this too can be of great value.'

Lily looked away.

'Am I to gather that this was not the case as far as your father is concerned?'

'Dad couldn't stop.'

'So it became a habit?'

'Uncle Noah went up to Limehouse on the coalie's cart to fetch it for him.'

'Forgive me, Lily, but did you bear the cost?'

'I must have been a bit daft not to know.'

'You mean it was kept from you?'

'Mum was afraid everyone would find out.'

'What would you have done if you'd known, Lily?' he asked after a while.

'I would have done what I did this week. Stayed home to make sure he didn't take any more.'

'And are they holding your job at the factory for you?'

'No, I lost it.'

He nodded slowly as he sat back in his chair. 'You are a very resourceful and caring young woman. But how do you propose to live whilst you are about all this?'

'I don't know. But I'll find a way.'

His eyes shone with admiration as he gazed at her. 'Lily, I have never met a woman like you.'

Lily felt the colour sweep into her cheeks. 'He's me dad, Charles. What else would I do?'

'Many would cast judgement and blame.'

'What for? He just made a mistake.'

'How simple you make that seem.'

'It's family that counts.'

'How I wish that I was able to say the same myself.'

Lily looked into his suddenly bleak eyes. Was he referring to Delia and the life they could have had together?

'And so, Lily, what is to be done now?' He frowned, resting his elbows on the chair and bringing his hands together, placed them in a point.

'About me dad, you mean?'

'Yes, and indeed your own future.'

Lily dropped her head. 'I don't know. I want him to get well and until he does, I'll look after him.'

'Are you certain he will recover?'

Lily nodded fiercely. 'Yes.'

He smiled. 'Very good, then.' He leaned forward. 'Lily, I have a proposition for you. Annie's successor left after only a few weeks. She was quite unsuitable for the post. Since then I have managed on my own, and had decided to continue in the same vein as my trips abroad take up the best part of my time. However, fate has brought us back together again. And, as old friends, I believe we could both help each other greatly.

I understand that you would not be able to start immediately, but I am happy to wait until you are ready.'

Lily could hardly believe she was being given another
chance. This was an answer to her prayers. As she sat
silently, with the excitement building inside her so that
she could hardly speak, he went on.

'I should require you to live here during the week,
but you will be at liberty to return home at the weekends. The duties are those I explained before. Looking
after the household and helping me to entertain my
guests whenever the occasion should arise. I will engage
someone for the heavy work and would expect you
to complete only light household duties. As I'm away
a lot, you would need to cater for yourself, but when
I'm home and have a dinner function, I would engage
a cook for the evening. Of course this would be subject
to your father's health.' He added cautiously, 'If your
mother has kept your secret until this point, I see no
reason why she should not maintain it.'

Lily understood what he was saying. He couldn't risk
being involved with a scandal of any kind.

'I understand,' she said quietly.

'In that case, perhaps you would like time to
consider?'

She knew that she had already made up her mind. 'I
would like to accept, Charles.'

His smile reached into his eyes. 'Wonderful, Lily.' He
stood up. 'Now, may I show you the rest of the house
and your quarters.'

Lily's heart was beating fast as she was escorted out of the room and upstairs. What he showed her were two large rooms at the top of the house that were comfortable and spacious. They needed some attention but she would soon make it home.

Lily could barely speak as again he took her round the rest of the house, pointing out the things that he liked to be kept clean and tidy. She was overjoyed to discover the aspidistra was still alive, though moved to a window on an upstairs landing.

'You recall this little gem?' he asked.

'Yes,' she nodded, her fingers going to the soft green leaves. 'But it needs a good dust.'

Charles burst out with laughter. 'A plant to be dusted! I never thought of that.'

Taking her arm he escorted her down the wide staircase. Lily was rewarded with the sight of the painting they had bought at Petticoat Lane that now hung on the wall.

'It always reminds me of that wonderful day,' he said quietly.

As they reached the ground floor and stood in the dark hall, Lily gazed about her. She could do so much to bring life into this place. It only needed a woman's touch.

As she stood there, her eyes going from wall to wall and her imagination already running riot, Charles turned to her. 'Well, Lily, is the answer still the same?'

She nodded. 'Yes. But I don't know when I can start.'

'I've told you I'm happy to wait. But I should like

to discuss the disbursement of your wage as some years ago I offered you the sum of five guineas a week, with possible commission. However, I will now increase it by a guinea, bringing it to six guineas a week.'

Lily's jaw dropped and he smiled at her expression.

'My dear, you have the responsibility of the whole household and my business events in your hands. This would not suit everyone!' He took her into the light of the open doorway. Standing with his hands behind his back, he said with a smile, 'I would also suggest that I advance you half of your first month's pay – which will help you over this difficult period with your father. You will only then receive the other half when you begin. However, your food and keep and travelling expenses will be paid, making it only a small imposition to begin with.'

Lily stared up at him. She couldn't believe it. He was giving her a way to solve all her problems. She could look after her father until he was well and provide for her family in a very good way. They would be out of debt and life could begin again. For her own part, she could be near Charles. After all this time, her heart's desire had really come true.

'If you are willing, Lily, let us go into the drawing room and drink another cup of tea to celebrate our good fortune at finding one another again.'

Lily could hardly contain her excitement as he offered her his arm.

★

Ben dug the tobacco tin out from his pocket. 'Here's a couple of ounces of the best, Mr Bright.'

'Thank you, son.'

'Do you want me to roll you one?'

'Yes, if you don't mind.'

Ben occupied himself with the task of making the thin cigarette. He was trying not to let his shock show. Bob Bright looked a shadow of the man he used to be. Now that he was up and sitting in his chair, the difference was noticeable. Even in the week he'd been home, he looked thinner and his skin was a funny yellow colour. But saying all that, he wasn't beating down the door to get out, something he'd tried once or twice since he'd come home, so old Mr Kelly had told him. It must have been a rotten week for the Brights. Reube wouldn't believe what he had to tell him when he saw him tonight.

'How are you going on then?' Ben enquired gently as they both took a puff on their cigarettes.

'All right, thanks.'

'You got everything you need?'

'Lily sees to it all.'

Ben sat back and enjoyed the smoke. 'Gone out, has she?'

'For an hour or two,' said Bob, coughing and clearing his throat.

'You got a bit of jollop for that tickle?' asked Ben lightly.

'Don't do any good though.'

'Better than nothing, though, eh?'

'That's what Lily and the wife tells me, son.'

A silence descended, broken by the older man's coughing. Ben's thoughts turned to Lily. He missed her a great deal when she wasn't around. After what had happened, he wanted to see how she was. That flaming foreman up the factory had been no help. Noah Kelly had told him she'd lost the job. He'd like to give her a couple of bob more to tide her over as he'd been thinking about how she'd manage. Of course knowing Lil, she'd get on her high horse and refuse, but unless the Brights applied for Welfare, Ben was at a loss to think of where the money would come from. He was sure that friends and neighbours wouldn't see them go short. The market traders, if they knew the situation, would have a whip round. All the blokes at the Quarry too. The trouble being Mrs Bright wanted the whole thing kept stumm. Not that his own mum wouldn't do the same if put in the same position. But people would help if given half the chance.

As Ben was considering the situation, his companion broke into a heavy fit of coughing. Ben leaned forward in concern. A light film of sweat beaded his friend's forehead and his eyes looked glassy as he gasped for breath. Ben took the cigarette from his hand and put it out.

'That didn't do you much good, did it?' He waited till the cough subsided. 'Fancy a breath of air, Mr Bright?'

'Aye, son. Aye.'

'Let's give you a hand, then.' He went to the frail

man and lifted him, feeling the sharp jut of his bones under his grasp. Carefully supporting him, they made their way to the kitchen.

'Bob, what is it?' Josie Bright put down the saucepan she was holding. Drawing her hands down her apron, her pale eyes looked apprehensive.

'He just needs a breather,' said Ben, giving her a wink.

Outside in the yard he walked with his companion, slow as snails, his heart going out to the ailing man.

'I'll make a visit here, son. I've still got the trots.'

Ben opened the latch of the closet. Ten minutes later, Bob Bright shuffled out.

'You fancy a lie down?' Ben said cheerfully, taking his arm.

'After the shame I brought on me family, I'd say yes to a permanent one.'

'Now then, I didn't turn out last Sunday to hear you say that,' laughed Ben, trying to make light of it.

Bob stiffened and glanced up at him. He shook his head and as the sun shone over the top of the houses he said, 'I never did thank you properly for what you did for me. Snatches of it keep flashing before me eyes, and I know I'd be a gonner without you. Trouble is, I can't remember what happened half the bloody time.'

'Good job too,' grinned Ben. 'Now, you ain't feeling up to a jaunt down the Quarry just yet, but I'm willing to lay you a tanner, that in a couple of weeks, you'll be supping an ale along with me and the rest of the lads.'

Bob Bright gave a wan smile. 'You're a good man,

Ben James. But if I had a tanner I'd not be down the pub. I'd be putting it where I should have years ago, in Josie's apron pocket. Not taking it out.'

The intimacy embarrassed Ben. 'We've all done a trick or two in our time,' he dismissed as the door of the kitchen opened.

'Come in you two,' said Josie as she wiped her work-worn hands on the bottom of her apron. 'Before next door sees you and start asking questions.'

Ben gave the older man a conspiratorial smile and together they went inside.

'You just leaving, young man?' Noah Kelly came down the stairs, relieved to see a friendly face. He had been upstairs in his room, turning out his records. The ugly mug of the Receiving Officer had appeared like a ghost to haunt him as he'd sat on his bed thinking of any way possible to cheat the RO. He'd put the pile of His Master's Voice classical records that he loved so much beside the Talking Machine. After polishing the big horn and making it shine like a new sixpence, he'd not had enough energy to go to the piano. That could be done tomorrow, because he'd be damned if he was going to let the RO take them. His mate, the coalie, would put it on the cart and take it to his yard, where they could be kept and sold on the QT. At least he'd have the satisfaction of cheating the buggers – they wouldn't find much to interest them under the roof of number thirty-four Love Lane when he was done.

'I've left Mr Bright in the parlour,' said Ben as he stood at the door. 'Don't seem too bad, does he?'

Noah looked into the boy's eyes. 'He's bearing up, but it ain't easy. Now, whilst we're alone, I have something to tell you.'

Ben moved closer, as the old man took his arm. 'Me mate Charlie, the coalie, took a gander up Limehouse.'

'Blimey, did he see anything?'

'Not the ruin we expected.'

'You mean, the fire didn't spread?'

'Charlie asked around and was told the man and woman was got out. Those bloody Chinese have got nine lives.'

Ben let out a long sigh. 'Thank Gawd for that.'

'Being that the place is illegal, the upset was kept quiet. Charlie says she upped sticks and moved on.'

'So if Bob ever returned there . . .?'

Noah shook his head slowly. 'He ain't gonna do that, son. You seen what he looks like? Can hardly put one foot in front of the other now he's weaned off it.'

'A bit of time and he'll shine up.'

'We're all banking on that.'

Ben smiled as he laid a hand on his shoulder. 'Give us a call if you need me.'

'When are the happy couple back?'

'T'night.'

'What you gonna tell them?'

'Reube can be trusted, Mr Kelly.'

'I hate to ask yer to lie, if anyone quizzes you, son, but it's Josie. You know how she is.'

'I'll tell any nosy parker to sling their hook,' grinned Ben. 'The secret's safe with me.' He went to open the door then stopped. 'The only other one to know is the doc.'

'I've had a word in his ear.'

Ben nodded. ''Spect Lil will tell Hat, though. They're best mates.'

At this Noah smiled. 'They're gonna have a lot to chat about, ain't they? But Lil will make sure Hat keeps stumm.'

'All right, then, I'll be off. Oh, er ... tell Lil I said hello, won't you?'

'I will indeed.' Noah saw the young man out. Was there still hope for him in the romance department? Bob's troubles may have brought them closer ... in which case, thought Noah, the Brights could have no finer man take the hand of their daughter in marriage than Ben James.

Lily had so much to tell Hattie, but she wasn't sure when she'd be able to speak to her privately. She knew that Hattie would be settling into her new home this week. Lily had come home from Dewar Street, but hadn't told anyone about Charles. She would keep her plans to herself until her father was a little better. On Monday, Lily gave her mother the last few shillings from Ben's money.

'I'll give it to the landlord,' said Josie. 'But he won't wait for ever for the rest.'

'Something will turn up.' Charles had advanced her half her wage, but she couldn't explain about this until she told them the whole story. And she wasn't ready to do that just yet. She wanted to have everything ready in her mind.

'I hope so, as we haven't got much in the larder.'

'I've enough in me purse for a few things.'

'We can't go on like this.'

'Stop worrying, Mum.'

'It's all right for you to say, but how?'

The two women had just finished the washing and were hanging it on the line to dry. Lily glanced over the fence at the long line of yards. Monday was wash day and most had washing billowing on the lines.

'I wonder if Hattie has seen her mum yet?' Lily mused as she pegged out the last sheet.

'Could have called by last night when they came back.'

'She wouldn't have had much time before she went to work this morning.'

Josie looked up at the sky. 'Looks like rain.'

'We'll keep an eye on the weather.' Lily picked up the laundry basket. 'Is Dad up and dressed yet?'

'No, he's sitting in his pyjamas. Won't come down.'

Lily pulled back her shoulders. 'We'll see about that.'

'Don't upset him.'

Lily turned to her mother. 'He's got to get back to

343

normal. At least make an effort to cheer himself up.'

'Yes, but we don't want him running away again.' Josie glanced over her shoulder as though she was being overheard. 'It was a miracle no one saw him go off that day.'

Lily knew her mum was still worried about the neighbours seeing or hearing something untoward. 'Well, no one appeared to.'

'What are you going to tell Hattie?'

Lily shrugged. 'The truth, of course.'

Her mother looked like a frightened mouse. 'She might tell her mother or someone else.'

'She won't if I ask her not to.'

'What about Ben?'

'He's doing the same with Reube.'

'So Betty James and the Parks won't know?'

'No, Mum. You can stop worrying.'

'That's a relief,' Josie looked round furtively again, then hurried indoors.

Lily smiled to herself. It was not only her mum who wanted the secret kept now, it was her too. Charles depended on her to be discreet, and she had every intention of being so.

When a knock came on the door that night, it was Hattie. Lily flung her arms around her old friend. 'Oh, Hat, I've missed you.'

'I couldn't come over before, I had me wifely duties to attend to.'

'Come in and tell me all about it.' Lily stepped back, but Hattie shook her head.

'I can't Lil. I told Mrs James I'd cook the supper tonight.'

'What, on your first day back?'

'I thought I'd try to get off to a good start. And anyway, I want to flaunt me culinary expertise to me husband.'

'In that case, good luck. Have you seen your mum and dad and Sylvester?'

'Yes, briefly, when we came home. But only to say hello.'

'Being married you don't half get busy.'

Hattie giggled. 'It's fair wearing me out. Now have you any good gossip?'

Lily couldn't help blushing. 'A bit, but don't you know some already from Ben?'

'What do you mean?'

Lily could tell from her expression that she didn't. But before Lily could reply, Hattie gasped, 'I know what's different. You don't stink of paint!'

Lily nodded. 'That's right.'

'You ain't at the factory?' Hattie spluttered.

'No, but it's a long story. I'll tell you another day.'

Hattie rolled her big brown eyes. 'I ain't gonna sleep tonight now.'

'Yes you will, in a pair of strong arms.'

'Cripes, I'd forgot that for a moment!'

Both girls burst into laughter again. Lily gazed at her

dewy-eyed friend. 'Married life seems to suit you.'

'Something certainly does,' said Hattie, causing them to fall about once more.

'Let's meet next Saturday,' Hattie finally suggested. 'Go over to Greenwich to the café.'

'All right. But me dad . . . well, he ain't been well.'

'What's been wrong?'

'That, too, is a long story. But if he's all right, I'll call for you.'

Hattie hugged her again. In the pale light of the August evening, she ran across the road. Lily felt grateful to Ben that he hadn't said anything, although she was certain he must have told Reube.

Chapter Nineteen

As the days passed, Lily watched her father carefully. He lacked an appetite and his cough was troublesome, but he seemed slowly to accept reality. He preferred to stay in bed, but it was her uncle who persuaded him to wash and shave himself. Lily knew that the two men were becoming close. Her uncle still felt responsible for what had happened and was doing everything in his power to put the mistake right.

Lily couldn't wait for Saturday and prayed the weather would be fine for her outing with Hattie. When eventually the day came, it was sunshine and showers. Lily left Josie with strict instructions to lock the front door behind her.

'What are you going to tell Hattie?' her mother asked anxiously, as she was about to leave.

'Nothing you need worry about, Mum.'

'I saw Mrs Parks at the corner shop. She asked how your dad was. I said his cough was bad.'

'What about the mystery illness?' Lily asked flippantly.

'I thought I might have to explain it. So I kept to the cough.'

Lily smiled. 'Don't worry, this will all blow over.'

'But I am worried as your dad spends a long time in bed.'

'That's nature taking its course.'

'I hope so.'

Lily crossed the road to the James' house where Hattie opened the door immediately. 'It's cloudy. Do you think it will rain?'

'It might. Why?'

'Because I want to show off me new present.'

Lily was not surprised to discover this was an umbrella.

'Reube bought it on Brighton sea front,' said Hattie as she put it up on the way to the foot tunnel, despite it still being dry. A label hung from the spine saying one and six. 'The dark blue pattern is supposed to be the sea,' Hattie explained, 'but Reube said it would remind me all winter of the honeymoon, 'cos it rains nearly every bloody day in England.'

'What else did he give you?'

'A pair of French knickers.'

'What! He bought them himself?'

'No, you daft thing. He gave me the money to buy them. Reube wouldn't be seen dead near a woman's shop.' Hattie giggled. 'But I let him have a good feel afterwards.'

As Hattie continued to describe the boarding house, the old dragon who watched their every movement as if they were illicit lovers and some of the more intimate moments of the honeymoon, Lily listened with rapt attention. Hattie left her in no doubt at all that the romantic side had surpassed all expectations.

'Where else did you visit?' Lily asked, smiling, 'that is, when you weren't canoodling?'

'Oh, just the Pavilion and the gardens and along to the shops. We didn't go out much, it was too nice in bed,' she laughed, returning to her favourite subject. 'It was a lovely big double, something we'd always wanted as pushing two singles together ain't very comfortable.'

'I wouldn't know about that,' Lily giggled.

'No, but I do.' Hattie nudged Lily. 'We've done it a couple of times as you know.'

Lily blushed. 'Well, you seem to have enjoyed yourselves.'

'Yes, and it was nice being waited on at breakfast.'

'So you got up for that, then?'

'Only because Reube don't start breathing till his stomach is filled. If it was me I'd have messed around all day under the sheets.'

Lily gasped. 'Hattie!'

'Well, a bloke's dick is already up when he wakes. It's very tempting. Just waiting there for you to get hold of.'

They exploded into laughter once more, until wiping the tears from her eyes, Hattie continued. 'I'll give the old dragon her due. The bacon was crispy and there was bags of toast. But the wooden chairs in the dining room were a bit hard.'

'What about your evening meal?'

'There was this little eating house by the Pavilion. It was only small, but it had dim lights and was ever so romantic. Then we'd stroll home by the sea, look at the moonlight on the water. You know, Lil, I'd like to live on the coast. The air there is different to the river.'

'Would you live there then if you had the chance?' said Lily in surprise.

Hattie shrugged. 'It's only a dream.'

'You and Reube could open a boarding house.'

'Too much like hard work for me. I don't want to turn into an old dragon.'

Laughing again they entered the park and went to the café. Lily got out her purse. 'It's my treat today, Hat.'

'You can't afford this.'

'Yes, I can.'

'What do you mean?' Hattie stared at her. 'You're not at work.'

'Wait till we sit down.'

'I'm all ears.'

After the tea and scones arrived, Lily began her story. Hattie's jaw dropped as she listened to what had happened to the Bright family after the young newlyweds had gone on honeymoon.

★

Hattie for once, was speechless.

'I can't believe all that happened in a week. How is your dad now?'

'Not as bad as he was.'

'Has he still got the cough?'

Lily nodded. 'Yes, but it was the laudanum that changed him. The reason why he'd never go out or see people.'

'Did he smoke from one of them pipes when he was down that place?'

'I don't know. Ben didn't say.'

'Didn't you ask him?'

'I didn't want to know. And anyway, it wouldn't make any difference. Doctor Tapper said he will improve if he can get over the next few weeks.'

Hattie gave a deep sigh. 'I know what it's like when Sylvester ain't well. Mum and Dad are always worried he's going to fit. I don't suppose he'll ever leave home. A wife wouldn't put up with it.'

'Me mum's put up with a lot.'

'It must have been a great worry for her.'

'I wish she'd told me.'

'I can see why she didn't, so as to keep the peace.'

Lily nodded. 'She was afraid if there was an upset, the word would get out. She blames Uncle Noah for getting him started on it in the first place. But he only tried to help me dad.'

Hattie screwed up her eyes. 'You just don't think things like this happen to your neighbour or your friend.'

351

Lily thought of her father and the deep, dark pit he must have been in in his mind. He'd lost his ability to make a living, to provide for his family. As the days went by, the hopelessness got worse instead of better. She didn't blame him for trying to find some relief. But now, that part of his life was all over. Who would have thought that it was through Charles the answer to their problems had come?

As if Hattie had caught her train of thought, she said, 'Now tell me all about Charles again.'

Lily proceeded to repeat all she had said. By the time they had finished their scones, she came breathlessly to the end.

Hattie was silent, her big brown eyes thoughtful. 'Lil, I'm going to miss you something awful if you go away.'

'I'll be home at weekends.'

'I hope so.'

'Anyway, you have a husband to look after now. And Mrs James. That is, until you move.'

Hattie nodded. 'I want a place of our own.'

'Do you know when Mrs James and Pedro are tying the knot?'

'Nothing's been said. I think Mrs James is waiting to see if her daughter-in-law will be a better investment than a husband.'

Both girls looked at one another.

Hattie sighed. 'Our lives are changing, ain't they?'

Lily smiled. 'Yes, but it's nice we've got each other to confide in.'

Hattie grinned mischievously. 'Do you realize you'll be rich on six guineas a week.'

'Not rich, but I can pay our debts and the rent each week. I'll try to put a bit by for a rainy day.'

'You've had a lot of rainy days already. I reckon the sun has to shine on you now.'

Lily smiled at her friend. 'Hattie, all I've told you is in confidence.'

'Course it is. But I'll clip me old man's ear for not telling me as Ben must have told him.'

Lily smiled. 'They're thick as thieves those two.'

'When are you thinking of letting your mum and dad know about your new job?'

'As soon as Dad is better.'

'He don't try to escape any more, then?'

'No, but I want to make sure he don't get tempted again.'

Hattie sighed heavily. 'There is someone else who's going to miss you, you know.'

Lily looked into her friend's gaze. 'You mean Ben.'

'Yes. After all you two have been through. It's not every girl who has a bloke go into an opium den on her behalf, and save her father.'

'I know.' Lily's heart felt heavy. 'The first thing I'll do when I get me full wage is return him the five pounds he gave me.'

'He won't want it back.'

'I'll make him take it.'

'Don't you have any feeling for him at all?' Hattie

353

leaned forward, a puzzled expression on her brow. 'He's good looking and kind and always got a joke. He was a flirt but he ain't any more.'

Lily smiled wistfully. 'Hattie, something happened to me the day I met Charles. It was like having a blindfold taken off. I saw everything so vivid; all the colours of life became brighter. I felt everything keener; I heard things with different ears, as if I was a kid and everything was new. That's what Charles did to me. And even though a long time has gone by without him, those sights and sounds remained in me heart, as alive as ever. Just sleeping. When I saw him again at the church, they sprang into life, just like before. So when you ask me about my feelings for Ben, I can only repeat that he means a great deal to me as a friend.'

Hattie took her hand across the table. 'I wish you every good thing in your new life with Charles, Lil, as much as you wish for me and Reube.'

'Thanks, Hat. That means the world to me.'

The two girls looked at each other with tears in their eyes. Then Lily looked down at the white china plate, where a fragment of scone remained. 'We ain't gonna waste that, are we?'

Hattie laughed. 'Bags the bit with the currant in.'

Lily felt happy as they laughed again. But she couldn't ignore the feeling inside that it would be a while before they sat here again.

*

Noah Kelly was taking the Talking Machine downstairs from it's spot in his bedroom. He was puffing and panting with the exertion. The box was heavier than he thought, the large horn being cumbersome more than weighty.

He was also trying to do it very quietly, as he didn't want the balloon to go up. His sister would create blue murder when she knew the RO was coming round. He'd been up to the offices this week and had a long grilling under the powers that be. Most of the questions they'd asked him had been aimed at finding out if they had any money hidden away. They hadn't actually accused him of lying, but they had shot questions at him from every angle. He'd been ready for them though. And he'd told them if they wanted to tear up the planks from the floor they were welcome, just so long as they nailed them back.

The RO was coming round next week. It would be a lengthy appointment they'd warned him. All the family had to be present. The rent book and list of debts must be produced. That would be the tricky one. Somehow he'd have to persuade Josie to admit to what was on the slate. How much they'd pawned and what was owing to the landlord. She'd sat tight on that information, like a constipated hen for the last four years. Noah suspected his sister had been borrowing from Peter, Paul and the rest of the disciples as well.

Just as he was creeping into the parlour with the

box in his hands, Josie appeared from the kitchen.

He stood still, looking around the glistening horn.

'Where are you going with that?'

'Into the parlour.'

'Why? We ain't having a knees-up.'

'We could do with one.'

'Be serious, Noah.'

'I thought I'd give it a clean up.'

Josie came forward, running her fingers over the shining metal. 'I can see me face in it.'

Noah tried to push past but she stayed him. 'Noah, what's going on?'

'Nothing. Let me pass or I'll drop the lot.' He didn't want to tell her till nearer the time. She would make a great fuss about it and he couldn't stand more drama after the last few weeks.

Charlie Brent and his lad was calling round with the cart tonight. As a favour, he was taking the piano and the box and all the records down his yard. There he would store them until such time as it was safe to bring them out again. Whenever that would be, Noah wasn't sure as the RO and his spies would be dropping in without notice whilst they were in receipt of the pittance they deigned to give them.

'What are you up to, Noah?'

'I told you, woman. Nothing.'

'I know you of old, brother. There's nothing that passes me by.'

'And a bloody shame it is too, Josie. You was always

worried about others poking their noses in your business, but that didn't stop you from doing it first.'

Her mouth began to tremble. Noah at once felt bad. Why had he gone and said that? He was nervous, and felt guilty, but he was only trying to get the family out of a jam.

Josie clutched the edge of her apron as though expecting tears. 'There's no need to speak to me like that.'

'I'm sorry.' He sank into the chair, exhausted by his efforts.

Josie sat too. 'Are you going to tell me what you are doing?'

He nodded. 'Yes, but you won't like it.'

'Then you better get it over with.' She sat stiffly, her eyes pinned on him.

'I'm putting the box, all me records and the piano with Charlie Brent. He's gonna keep them for us.'

'Why should he do that?' His sister looked indignant. 'I don't want me piano to go. It's the one good bit our mother left us.'

'Precisely.'

'Noah, what have you done?'

'I've been up to see the RO.'

Josie gasped, her hand going to her neck as though she felt strangled. Her face went as red as the cushion behind her. 'The Receiving Office!' she shrieked, jumping up. 'No, you can't! You can't!'

'Calm down, Josie.'

'How can you say that? The RO coming! Oh God!'

'It ain't the end of the world.'

'It might as well be.'

'Look, it won't be for long. Just till Bob's well again, then Lil can find another job.'

'But I'd rather die than have me house invaded!'

'You might not have a house to invade, if you can't pay the landlord.'

'And what would people think if they saw the RO coming round?'

'Josie, sit down, you're going red.' He tried to calm her but she was out of control. The tears and the screams all poured out as if he'd taken the top off a lemonade bottle. He took hold of her hands but she pushed him back, her cries of distress going right to his heart.

'For the love of God, Josie ...' He stopped as she stood still, gasping and choking and her eyes suddenly turned up to their whites. Then with a little sigh, she sank down in a heap on the carpet.

Lily said goodbye to Hattie, breathing in the last of the summer's evening as she did so. It was far too good to be indoors. Perhaps she could put chairs in the yard and they could sit for a while before dark.

She slipped her key in the lock, entered the house and as she locked the door once again she heard voices coming from the parlour. They were muffled but when she opened the parlour door, she drew in a sharp breath.

'Thank Gawd you're home, Lil,' spluttered her uncle

as he knelt beside the prone figure of her mother on the floor.

'Mum! What's happened to her?' Lily ran over and fell to her knees.

'I heard all this screaming and came down,' said her father who stood looking bewildered.

'She had a bit of a turn,' said her uncle shakily, looking at Lily from behind his pince-nez. 'And just fainted away.'

Taking her mother's hand, Lily patted it. 'Mum, mum, wake up.'

'She's out for the count.'

'Where are the smelling salts?'

'I'll get 'em.' Noah Kelly rose unsteadily to his feet.

'Josie, Josie,' mumbled her father.

'Are you all right, Dad?'

'Is it my fault?'

'No, of course not.'

Her uncle returned with the smelling salts. Lily put them under her mother's nose. At once Josie coughed and spluttered. Lily helped her to sit up.

'What happened?' she asked in a daze.

'You fainted.'

'I told her about the RO coming next week,' said her uncle in a small voice.

Lily looked up at him. 'The RO?'

He nodded. 'I got it all arranged.'

'He was getting rid of me piano,' cried Josie suddenly. 'I was only going to hide the piano and me Talking

Machine,' said her uncle. 'Charlie's taking them up the coal yard. Away from prying eyes till it's all over.'

At this Josie began to cry. Lily put her hand under her mother's arm and helped her to a chair. Lily sat beside her. 'Did you bang your head when you fell?'

'No,' Josie sobbed. 'It's not me head that's broken. It's me heart. How could you do such a thing, Noah? Me own brother, calling in the RO of all people.'

'That's what you do when you're skint.'

'You weren't even going to tell me.'

'I would have.'

'When it was too late I expect.'

Lily held her mother's hand. 'You can stop crying now, Mum. Here take this hanky.'

'Think of the shame it will bring!'

'I was thinking of our bellies,' replied Lily's uncle, beginning to lose his patience. 'And putting something in them.'

'How could you even—'

'Stop it you two.' Lily held up her hands. 'Uncle Noah, sit down please.'

'I can never do anything right.'

'You were trying to help, I know.'

'What else can we do?' he demanded as he sat on the chair.

'There is something else as it happens.'

Her mother stopped crying. 'What?'

'If you'll both give me a chance, I'll tell you. Now, where's Dad gone?'

They looked around. 'Did you lock the door behind you?' asked her uncle.

'Yes.'

'Then he must have gone back upstairs.'

'I want him to hear what I've got to say.'

'He don't know what's going on half the time,' said her mother in a rush. 'You'd best leave him out of it.'

A sudden rattle came from the hall and the door swung open. Bob Bright stood with a mug of tea. His hands were shaking so much it was spilling over the sides.

'Dad!' Lily went to him.

'It's for your mum.'

'Bob, what are you doing with that?' Josie cried as she blinked her wet eyes.

'He's made the tea, that's what!' Lily exclaimed happily as she took the mug and gave it to her mother. 'Dad, this is wonderful. We thought you'd gone back upstairs.'

'I made a bit of pig's ear of the brew, I'm afraid.'

Lily put her arms round him. 'It's early days. You're only just back on your feet. It's so nice to see you up and about.'

'It was the shouting that brought me down.'

'Well, everything's going to be all right now. Go and sit beside Mum. I've some good news to tell you all.'

Lily took a deep breath. She hadn't intended to reveal her plans just yet. But the prospect of a visit from the Welfare had given her the perfect opportunity.

'You can put your Talking Machine back upstairs, Uncle Noah. You won't need to hide it,' she began. 'And the piano is safe where it is.'

She gazed at the three confused people staring up at her. It was time to put a smile back on their faces.

'You mean my little girl is leaving home?' Bob Bright was the first to speak.

'I'll be home at weekends.'

'I don't want you to go.'

'I won't until you're better.'

'But this Charles Grey,' said her mother, as though she had just understood, 'what does he want with you after all this time?'

'He offered me a job once before, now I've accepted, as it's a job I can do and is still available.'

'But we don't know who he is. Can he be trusted?'

'We've been through all this before. He's perfectly respectable and has a house and business to run. He's away a lot, so I shall be left to me own devices. The pay is six guineas a week.'

'But that's a fortune!' cried Josie.

'Yes, it is.'

'Are you sure?' asked her uncle, his big eye in the pince-nez more magnified than ever.

'Yes, quite sure, Uncle Noah. I'll be able to give Mum half of it and clear up our outstanding debts.'

'Then if you are happy, Lil, this is a small miracle.' He

looked at his sister. 'It will mean I can tell those buggers at the town hall to get stuffed.'

'You mean we don't have to go on the Welfare?' Josie gasped.

'No, as Charles has given me an advance to keep us until Dad is recovered.'

'It's all too much to take in, Lily,' said her mother, looking confused. 'All I can say is, although this will solve our problems, the house won't be the same without you.'

'Of course it will. On Saturdays and Sundays I'll be back to make a nuisance of meself again.' Lily laughed softly. 'Just think, you can go up the market and to the corner shop and spend what you want without having to put it on the slate.'

Josie smiled. 'That will be a new experience.'

'And Dad and Uncle Noah can buy a few cigarettes instead of tobacco.'

Josie nodded, her face brightening. 'Are you sure you want to do this for us, Lily?'

'I'm sure, Mum.'

There was silence until Bob Bright coughed and hit his chest with his fist. As he patted his cardigan pockets, he mumbled, 'I could do with a fag now.'

They all laughed. 'Oh, Dad, it's nice to have you back with us again.'

'I didn't like to see your mother on the floor.'

'Well, it got you down here, didn't it?'

'I suppose so.'

Josie looked at her husband sitting beside her. 'You do look much better, love. Thank you for the tea, it was a very nice thought even though half of it went on the floor.'

Everyone laughed again. Suddenly Lily felt the floodgates of relief open inside her. The nightmare they had been living in was receding and there were better times ahead.

On a fine Sunday morning in September, when the first autumn mist crawled over the island, Lily said goodbye to friends and family. She joined Charles in the large blue car that waited outside her house and waving to her family and the Parks and Jameses who had congregated outside her house, she could hardly believe she was leaving home. But, as Charles gave a toot on the horn, her heart leapt at the wonderful smile he gave her.

As she sat beside him, watching Love Lane disappear in the mist, she gave a little tremble. She was both excited and apprehensive. She had no real idea what her duties would include, nor whether she'd be able to perform them well enough, and that, in addition to sleeping in a strange bed for the first time in her life, was enough to make her stomach churn with anxiety.

How quickly the last five weeks had passed! All the time her father had improved and, best of all, had shown no signs of wanting to escape or resume his old habit. Occasionally he would go upstairs and detach himself from life, but most of the time he was content to sit by the fire with Uncle Noah or have a short walk around the block. Her mother was still cautious and kept an eagle eye on him. But he was not the strong man he once was. Even walking to the end of the road was a challenge, although Lily knew that with time he would grow a bit stronger.

Josie was happy again. She had already grown accustomed to a renewed income, provided by Charles. She enjoyed the luxury provided by three pounds, three shillings every week.

As Charles drove steadily towards Dewar Street, half of Lily was enthralled at his presence and the prospect of being in his life, living in the beautiful home that she knew awaited her was a dream come true. But her other half was naturally missing the people left behind. Hattie had promised to write and Ben had told her that if ever Charles couldn't drive her back to Love Lane on Saturday mornings, he would come for her in his new car.

'I was most pleased to see your father up and about,' Charles said, suddenly breaking into her thoughts.

Lily nodded, smiling as she thought of her father's brave smile as he hugged her goodbye.

'Do yer best love, and don't worry about us,' he had comforted her, just as the old dad would have said.

'He's much better now,' Lily replied. She wanted Charles to know that he need not be concerned her father would relapse into his old habits. That part of his life was finished now. He'd had a big shock seeing her mother on the floor and thought he was responsible. Lily had noticed that since that day he was deliberately making small steps into taking his place in the home again.

'And your friend Hattie?' asked Charles, his perfectly formed hands grasping the steering wheel. 'How is married life suiting her?'

Lily glanced down at the rabbit's foot on her collar. She had bought herself a new coat for today and as she fingered the fur, she smiled. 'Hattie's very happy. And business is picking up at market.'

'I'm glad to hear it.'

'And what of your friend Ben? Do you have his blessing on your new life?'

Lily glanced quickly at her companion. 'He's very happy for me.'

'I'm glad to hear that.'

'He's just bought a new car.' Lily was proud of Ben as he was determined to make a success of the expansion of his business.

'How very interesting. What is he going to use the car for?'

'City work, I think.'

'A very enterprising young man.' Lily nodded, reflecting on how last night Ben, Hattie and Reube had come in to wish her good luck. They had made it a happy occasion and she had been grateful for that. It was only Hattie who, as she left, shed a tear.

As they passed the Queens Theatre, Lily reflected on all that had happened since she first met Charles four years ago. Would she have ever guessed then that she would be sitting beside him in a beautiful car, on her way to live at Dewar Street? She smiled. No, not in a million years.

But as she stole a glance at his handsome profile, in her heart she felt that her destiny was to be with him. That is what she believed. And Lily felt certain that one day, her life would change yet again. In her most private moments, she saw herself wearing not the pink bridesmaid's dress, but a long, flowing white one with a veil. And beside her, looking down on her with love filling his deep, dark eyes, was the man who had never left her thoughts in all the time they had spent apart.

Chapter Twenty

October 1936

Lily stood in the well-lit hall of number four Dewar Street. As always, at the end of the week, she cast her eye over the polished wood floors and long flight of stairs. Everything was spick and span. For two years now, Mrs Brewer had been a blessing. Not only could she rely on the older woman to turn up each day, but her work was faultless. Small and rotund, Mrs Brewer cared for the house as if it was her own. The fires were always lit before nine, the washing attended to on Mondays. The other four mornings were divided equally between upstairs and downstairs. Her trustworthiness made it quite unnecessary for Lily to check her work.

Now it was Friday evening and Lily was eagerly awaiting Hattie. Charles was away on one of his trips and Lily had suggested that Hattie come straight from work and spend the night at Dewar Street. The offer was eagerly accepted and Mrs Brewer had prepared the guest bedroom in readiness.

'Is there anything else you want, Miss?'

'No, thank you, Mrs Brewer. My friend will be here soon.'

'I hope she finds the room to her liking.'

'I'm sure she will.'

'Are you sure you won't want me to come back after I've fed me old man, and save you the bother of cooking?'

'No, that's all right. I've prepared the trolley. We'll just eat lightly tonight.'

'Well, if you're sure? I've set the table in the back parlour and there's a nice fire going in the drawing room. The bed is all made up for your friend and clean towels left in her room.'

'Thank you. Are you doing anything nice this weekend?'

Mrs Brewer gave a frown of concern. Her plump face under her black felt hat gave her a homely appearance, but now she looked anxious. 'We was going up to Tower Hill to see our daughter and her hubbie. They've got two rooms above a shop, nice and comfy it is. But the rumours are rife there's going to be a meeting.'

'What sort of meeting?' Lily asked politely. She was only half listening as her mind was elsewhere. Charles had seemed distracted when he'd left at the beginning of the week. His absences had grown more frequent in the past few months and his mood had not always been easy on his return. Over the past two years she had learned to recognize the signs. Sometimes he would say very little and yet at others he would ask for her company at supper. The stories he told her were all very amusing of the upper class circles in which he moved.

'Ain't you read the *Daily Herald*? It's those bloody Blackshirts again.'

Lily came quickly back to the present. 'What about them?'

'My Tom says Mosley plans to march on the East End. I tell you Miss, if he tries there will be a riot. The commies and fascists will be at it like mad dogs, with the dockers in between.'

'I thought all that was over,' said Lily, 'when Mosley left government.'

'Don't you believe it. Since thirty-four they've been digging in down this way, trying to recruit as many as they can. Tom works for a Jewish concern. Don't usually employ the gentiles, but without him they'd be lost. As you know he keeps all them weavers' machines running like clockwork. A real magician he is and they know it. Anyway, he tells me some of the Jewish blokes and their families have had a bad time of it with the Blackshirts. Beaten up, some of them are, by these thugs. Now, I'm no sympathizer to any religion and I ain't no Socialist either, but me and Tom believe in British justice and fair play. The Jews, the Poles, the Frenchies, whoever they might be – seeing women beaten up of any creed or colour don't sit well with us.'

'They beat up women?' Lily said in surprise.

'That's what's happened, yes.'

Lily suddenly remembered the man who had accosted her at market. He'd had a mad look in his eye and she was only saved by Charles. Were the Blackshirts still as threatening?

'But what do they want with the East End?'

'They want power, that's what. Think they'll get it through dockers' votes. Mosley intends to get a foot back in government whilst he hobnobs with the aristocrats on the quiet. My old man gets all the information first hand. But as me daughter lives up Tower Hill, I take exception to not being able to visit her, just because of some hooligans.'

Lily thought of the days when there was trouble at the market. They seemed a long way off now. She would ask Hattie if there was any recurrence at Cox Street.

'Anyway, better be off.'

After the older woman had gone, Lily walked through the newly decorated hall into the drawing room, admiring the work which she had arranged to be done. The aspidistra stood in a new pot, its broad leaves shining under the electric light that had been installed in the house. What would Hattie think of the pastel colours of the walls that had replaced the heavy green and red flock wallpapers that left the house so dark? The new cream muslin curtains were modern and the stylized birds and foliage patterns she had found in the upstairs rooms were long gone. Lily had created simplicity, combining the pale greens and yellows of the walls to contrast with darker shades of carpeting. Charles had applauded everything she had done. He had spared no expense to accommodate her wishes.

Lily looked out of the drawing room window. Through the now sparkling panes of glass the street was quietly fading into dusk. She drew the curtains as the warmth from the big open fire that burned in the grate gave a cosy glow to the room. The two pink chairs that she had retained were drawn up either side of it. Lily looked around her with satisfaction. She couldn't wait to see the expression on Hattie's face when she showed her upstairs.

Half an hour later the two girls stood in Lily's private quarters. Over her large bed was spread a deep blue cover, the same shade as her long linen curtains that fell from a gleaming brass rod. The thick Turkish rug that covered the pine floorboards was of different shades of blue and sunflower yellow and Hattie gazed around in wonder.

'Fancy this being yours, Lil.'

'I think how lucky I am when I wake up each morning.'

Hattie sighed wistfully. 'I wouldn't mind something like this meself.'

'When you get your new house, I'll help you to paint it.'

Hattie looked glum. 'I don't know when that will be.'

'It will be worth the wait.'

'I hope so.'

'Come and sit down on me new couch.'

The two girls went into the next room. A walnut coffee table was placed next to a beige couch that Lily had filled with cushions.

'This is nice too,' said Hattie, sitting down. 'Were these expensive?'

'I bought them in Oxford Street.'

Hattie nodded to the walnut bookcase. 'Have you read all them?'

Lily nodded as she sat by her friend. 'I sit here at night after I've finished downstairs.'

'What time is that?'

'After dinner, about nine o'clock.'

'That's a long day.'

'Yes, but I get the weekends off.'

'I like that.' Hattie pointed to the statue of a young woman dressed like a nymph. It was made entirely of pink frosted glass.

'Charles gave it to me.'

'I wish Reube would give me an expensive present.'

Lily laughed. 'I don't know if it's valuable. But it looks nice.'

Hattie stood up and went to gaze in the large black-edged mirror above the bookcase. She wet her middle finger on her tongue and drew the tip over her eyebrows. 'You and me should go into business,' she said as she studied her reflection. 'We both like quality, the better things in life.'

'What sort of business?' Lily asked, amused.

'If we had our own shop we could divide it up. Fashion and home decoration.' Hattie's eyes sparkled.

'How would we get customers?'

'I'd poach all Madame Nerys' clients.'

'You wouldn't!' Lily gasped.

'What's wrong with that? She's got more than enough rich women buying from her.' Hattie turned round, her face animated. 'I've got me own designs that I want to create. And you could do all their furnishings. Just think what we could achieve between us.'

Lily laughed. 'We could take over the world.'

'I mean it,' said Hattie, pouting. 'But I don't suppose you want to leave Charles.'

'I don't know what the future will bring.'

'Neither of us do.'

'I thought you wanted to move to Brighton.'

Hattie giggled. 'That's right, I did. Me head is always full of plans.'

'Come on, I'll show you your very own room.'

Hattie gasped again as they entered the guest room. 'It's like a posh hotel.'

From the window they could see lights twinkling from the houses and streets below. Hattie bounced lightly on the big double bed that Mrs Brewer had furnished with a cream silk cover and pillows to match. 'Now, all I want is a bloke in it, waiting for me.'

Lily chuckled. 'You've got one already. Don't be greedy.'

Hattie opened the door of the bird's eye maple wardrobe that was part of the luxurious set of three pieces. 'I could get used to all this luxury very quickly.'

'I'm glad you like it.'

'The last time I came here you had the decorators in. I couldn't see much. It was all so dark and gloomy before.' Hattie turned suddenly. 'Does Charles know I'm staying?'

'Of course he does.'

'How long is he away for?'

'It could be another week.'

'Don't you know when he's coming back?'

Lily shook her head. 'That's part of me job. I have to be prepared for anything. It's all part of his business, you see.'

Hattie looked around her again. 'Do you know how old this house is?'

'Yes, I've studied its history. It was built in 1840, in a Georgian style, but the Victorian influence was what made it so dark and overpowering. When Charles and Delia took it over, they began to improve it, but then Delia got ill.'

'How sad. What else has Charles told you about her?'

'He doesn't talk about her much. He never has a lot of time to discuss personal things as he's such a busy man.'

'So all the organizing is left to you.'

'Luckily I've got Mrs Brewer to help me. She worked in service to an aristocratic family when she was young and has given me a lot of tips. And she is a wonderful cook and can knock something up at a moment's notice. She knows all the best butchers and greengrocers in Poplar and gets them to deliver here.'

Hattie rubbed her rumbling tummy. 'Talking of which, Lil, I'm famished. I didn't stop at twelve for something to eat as Madame Nerys kept me on my toes today. I had to oversee a new customer, who is so bloody fussy I felt like stitching up her mouth.'

Laughing together, the two girls left the bedroom and went downstairs. The thick red carpeting was still spread over them, but Lily had bought a fine, Georgian styled desk to enhance the hall and an exotic Turkish rug to make a stunning entrance. In the back parlour which was now used as a dining room, Mrs Brewer had set the big oval mahogany table with the best silver and china.

Hattie gasped. 'Is this all in aid of us?'

Lily smiled. 'I thought you deserved a treat. Now sit down, whilst I bring in the trolley.'

As Lily served the food she had prepared, Hattie looked round her. 'Lil, this is kept like a palace.'

'Thanks to Mrs Brewer.'

'Do you eat your meals in here?' Hattie asked.

'No, I eat with Mrs Brewer in the kitchen. We keep this for the guests.'

'Listen to the "we"!' Hattie exclaimed as she made quick work of the meal set before her.

Lily blushed as she sat on the carver chair, one of eight placed round the table. 'I mean Charles, of course, as this room is where he entertains his guests.'

'Who are they, do you know?'

Lily shook her head. 'Some of them are foreign. Charles travels abroad, you see.'

'So you can't understand what they say?'

'I don't have time to listen what with taking their hats and coats and serving up the food.'

'Are they all men?' Hattie asked, intrigued.

Lily hesitated. 'There is one lady, a Mrs Covas.'

'Is she foreign too?'

'Don't know. She don't say much. But Charles once told me she's a widow. He said she has a house in the country that he has furnished for her.'

'Is she young and attractive?' Hattie was swift to ask.

Lily frowned. 'In her thirties I would say. She has black hair and flashing black eyes.'

Lily didn't add that she didn't much like Mrs Covas who always looked round critically, her dark eyes ignoring Lily. Although Lily had studied the illustrated magazines and read lots of books on housekeeping, she felt that Mrs Covas disapproved of what she had done to the house.

'Would you like some afters?' Lily asked quickly.

'Yes, please.'

Lily returned from the kitchen with a large round fruit cake.

'I could eat all of that,' laughed Hattie, as Lily slipped

a slice onto her plate. Hattie rolled her eyes as she sampled it. 'Oh, Lil, I ain't tasted anything like this before.'

'Mrs Brewer is a very good cook, as I told you.'

As she ate, Hattie began to tell Lily her news. 'At home, Sylvester's no better, but at least I don't have to worry about him now that I've got worries of me own.'

'What worries are they?'

'Reube has decided he doesn't want to leave home. Now Ben has gone he says the house is big enough to take us all. His mum and Pedro seem to have forgotten all about getting married and Reube says whilst we don't have kids, we can save up for somewhere better than an ordinary two up, two down.'

'That's a sensible idea.'

'Don't you start. Me master plan was to leave Love Lane and have me own place. But Reube simply won't get off his arse. Ben's done it, so why can't we?'

'Is Ben happy in his new home?'

'You should see it. A nice little terrace in Stepney.'

'I'm sure you'll get your house.'

'Only if I get pregnant.' Hattie looked miserable.

'You must be patient as you've only been married two years.'

'Yes, but we did it before, didn't we?' Hattie went pink.

Lily smiled. 'Yes, you've had a bit of practice.'

Hattie stifled a giggle. 'And we're still at it like rabbits.

All in all that's the best bit of marriage. The other stuff like housework and shopping is a bit of a drudge.'

'Hattie!'

'Well, it's true, Lil. Who wants to spend their life sweating over a hot stove and cleaning floors?'

'You will when you have kids.'

'If you ask me, that's not so easy. Me and Reube always took a chance on him – well, you know . . .'

Lily shook her head. 'No, I don't.'

'A bloke can keep a woman from getting pregnant,' Hattie said, lowering her voice. 'He just doesn't go the whole way. He withdraws before he comes inside her.'

Lily blushed too. Hattie had never told her that before.

'But I have to admit,' went on Hattie, 'that we took a few chances when Reube had had a couple of beers. Nothing ever happened though and I always got me monthly, even though it was late.'

Lily frowned. 'So it's not that easy to get pregnant then?'

'Not for me it ain't. And there's another girl at work called Irene, who's been trying for a baby for nearly ten years.'

'That's a long time.'

'I ain't going to live with Mrs James for that long!' exclaimed Hattie indignantly. She leaned forward, her eyes twinkling. 'Are you enjoying yourself with Charles?' Hattie put her chin in her hands. 'Come on, you can tell me.'

'Not in the way you mean.'

'So you're still a virgin?'

Lily looked embarrassed. 'Trust you to come straight out with it.'

'I thought by all the questions you was asking, you'd done it.'

Lily looked down in her lap. Hattie never minced words. She would have liked to have told her friend something different, but she couldn't.

'Hasn't he tried it on?'

'No, he's always very gentlemanly.'

'But you wouldn't mind if he did?'

Lily looked up. Both girls giggled.

'Even a gentleman gets his urges,' said Hattie, spluttering. 'He's free and single and so are you. He can't be so busy that he don't have time for a bit of romance. You do still like him, don't you?'

'You know I do.'

Lily knew that if Charles was ever to take her in his arms, she would give herself to him. But that had never happened. Although she loved everything about her life at Dewar Street, she longed to be close to him. He had done so much for her. She had been given a chance to learn about the finer things in life, she had even refined her own accent as she met more and more well-spoken people. Added to which she had supported her family and her father had recovered from the terrible ordeal he had suffered. The only thing lacking in Lily's life was time with Charles. His absences from the house were long and frequent. But even this only made her heart grow fonder of him. At night in bed she would long to see him again and welcome him home. She still dreamed about how it would feel to be his wife. In her heart, she believed they were meant to be together forever.

Hattie cupped her chin in her hands thoughtfully and said nothing. As Lily could find nothing else to relate on the subject of a budding romance, she stood up. 'Let's sit in the drawing room by the fire.' It sounded very grand.

'What about the dirty dishes?' Hattie asked.

Lily grinned. 'We can leave them on the trolley.'

'Who washes them up?'

'Mrs Brewer usually.'

'You ain't half lucky. I wish I had a servant.'

'You can train all your kids to wait on you,' said Lily before she could stop herself. But at the mention of children again, Hattie's face fell.

All evening they sat laughing and talking. Curled up in the pink watered silk chairs, the fire filled the room with a glow. Lily heard how Mrs Parks and Josie now went shopping together. Last week, Ben and Reube had taken Bob Bright to the Quarry for an ale.

'A definite improvement,' Lily nodded, 'to know me dad is getting out and about again.'

'I often see him and your uncle walking round the houses.'

Lily nodded. 'Last Sunday we walked up to Island

Gardens. It's something we've not done since I was a kid. The only thing that worries me is his cough.'

'The fags he smokes don't help.'

'Tobacco is his only indulgence. Now did you get that pay rise you were expecting?'

Hattie shook her head. 'No, and we've got all these new clients that I have to take responsibility for.'

'Why don't you ask her for one then?'

'Because I was hoping I'd get pregnant and leave.'

Lily smiled. 'So that's your master plan?'

'Me dream is to live in Brighton.'

'You had a lovely honeymoon there.'

'It probably wouldn't seem the same now I'm married. I wonder if that old dragon still runs the boarding house?'

'You and Reube should go on holiday there.'

'That's an idea. We could stay in bed all the time!'

The two girls burst into laughter, until finally Hattie sighed and murmured wistfully, 'I just wish I could conceive, Lil, then all my big problems would be solved.'

'You'd have a lot of little ones instead.'

Hattie chuckled. 'I'd like that, though.'

'You'll make a good mum.'

'I'd like to think so, but like you, I'm twenty-seven,' said Hattie as she frowned lightly. 'And I want to have a family before I'm thirty. I don't want to be too old to enjoy me kids. I imagine meself playing with them and taking them up to Lyons for tea when they get old enough.'

Lily, too, had imagined children of her own. Her son

would have black hair and earth brown eyes, just like Charles. He would grow tall and strong, followed by a blonde-haired, blue-eyed little sister, whom Lily could dress in pretty, feminine clothing. Lily had even thought about the day when she could design her own nursery and playroom. Now, as Hattie's comments brought all these dreams to life before her eyes, it seemed as though a future with Charles was almost possible.

Hattie yawned and stretched her arms. 'Lil, as much as I'd like to sit here all night gassing, I'm all in.'

'Come on then, let's go up to the bathroom.'

'You mean I can have bath?'

'I'll run the hot water.'

As they went up the stairs, Lily felt so proud of her lovely house. Quickly she rephrased her thought – of Charles' lovely house. But she had put all of herself into it. She knew every nook and cranny and had spent hours debating with herself on what was best for it. Surely in time Charles would show his true feelings for her. She loved him because he was a gentleman in every sense of the word, but sometimes she wished he wasn't. That he would forget she was his employee and allow his feelings to show.

'Here are some of Mrs Brewer's freshly washed towels,' she told Hattie a few minutes later as the steam began to fill the room.

'Lil, you're spoiling me. I won't want to go home,' Hattie said as she pressed the fluffiness against her cheek.

Lily's sentiments were entirely the same and had been

for some while. Home for her now would always be Dewar Street. She couldn't imagine living anywhere else.

Ben parked outside number four Dewar Street and honked his horn. He had just dropped off his last fare in the city and had made his way to Aldgate through the Saturday morning traffic in time to collect Hattie and Lil at midday.

The two girls soon came out of the house, as always, with their heads together, gossiping. Ben climbed out to greet them, taking their bags. How beautiful Lily looked these days! She was not the pale, thin girl who had worked at the paint factory but was now an elegant and fashionable young woman. Her short, wavy hair was freshly washed and bouncy. Her slim figure was attired in the latest fashion, a pale blue suit with the padded shoulders that gave women the film-star look. Ben smiled to himself. He couldn't for the life of him see how they walked on those shoes, but with the legs Lily had, she looked a million dollars in them. He knew from Hattie that Lily shopped up West now. Not that she didn't take a stroll down to the market on Saturdays. She never forgot her roots and her friends. But the past two years had changed her into an elegant, self-confident young woman of her time. His only regret was that he couldn't have instigated the change that another man had. Charles Grey had given Lily everything she could want. Ben was under no illusions about that, as her happiness clearly reflected in her eyes.

Smiling at their girlish chatter, he helped the two girls into the car. He was happy enough to drive Lil in her employer's absence, though he would like to have seen a bit more of her. But now that he had moved to Stepney and lived in his own little house, he had his own affairs to deal with.

As he glanced at the two girls sitting in the back seat of his cab, laughing and chatting, Ben wondered what the future held for his old friend.

Were there to be wedding bells, a lavish and no-expense-spared wedding ceremony that was a reflection of her new status with Charles Grey?

At this thought, Ben felt a heaviness inside him. But as Lily sat forward to eagerly include him in their topic of conversation, he quickly put the thought aside.

'Well, well, let me look at you.' Noah Kelly held his niece away from him. In her high heels she towered above him. Her smart clothes always took him aback. 'You look a real bobby dazzler, our Lil. I don't recognize you.'

'You say that every week,' she laughed.

'I know. But each week you've got something different on.'

Josie pushed past him. 'Come and give your mother a hug. I've got lots I want to ask you.'

'I'll put the kettle on,' Noah said, but his sister caught his arm.

'No, I'll do that Noah, or we'll be waiting all day. Take Lily in to see her father.'

In the parlour Bob Bright looked up from his newspaper. 'Lily girl! You're a sight for sore eyes.'

'Hello, Dad. I've got lots of nice things for you.' Lily opened her bag and brought out tea and coffee, cake and chocolate.

'Your mum will be pleased with those.'

'Yes, but you better hide this.' She passed him a tin of tobacco which he quickly put away. 'And one for you, Uncle Noah.'

He gave her a wink as he did the same. 'Thanks, gel. Josie has us out in the yard now, to smoke.'

'Well, with two of you at it, no wonder!'

He laughed with her and listened as she told them about the evening she had spent with Hattie.

'I expect you two stayed up all night gossiping.'

'We gossiped, but not all night. You look better, Dad.'

'Not bad, considering.'

'Are you getting out?'

'Yes, your mother makes sure I do.' He coughed and hit his chest with his fist. 'Just this bloody cough still.'

'It ain't the coughing that carries you off,' said Noah with a grin, 'it's the coffin.'

They all laughed at the joke now many times told.

Noah listened as his niece and brother-in-law spoke. It was just like old times, but nothing would make up for the lack of her presence in the house. From a little girl, he'd watched her grow, but he'd never seen her look like she did now. Shining, with a kind of inner glow. Was this down to her gent? What was the situation there? Was the bugger going to make an honest woman of her?

'Did the boy drop you off?' her father was asking.

'Yes, Charles is away.'

'Goes away a lot, don't he?'

'That's his job, Dad.'

'Do you ever get lonely, Lil?' Noah asked. 'That's a big house you've got there and with only you in it.'

'No, I'm always busy. And anyway, I've got Mrs Brewer.'

'Young Ben has his own place now,' said his brother-in-law. 'Up Stepney.'

'Yes, I know.'

'He's cabbying in the West End with his new motor. Managed to buy himself a licence and is doing very nicely now.'

Noah saw the look on her face. Bob was on a losing wicket there. She wasn't interested. There was only one man in that girl's head.

'Now tell us about yer news, love,' said Bob, settling back to listen.

As she began to speak, Noah wondered if what he'd heard from Charlie Brent was true. And what connection Charles Grey had with the disturbing rumours that were circulating the docks.

Chapter Twenty-One

It was half past eleven on Sunday morning when Ben drove Lily back to Dewar Street.

As she got out, Lil opened her purse.

'Put it away,' Ben told her as he carried her bag up the steps.

'You won't ever let me pay,' she complained as she followed him. 'I'll always be in your debt.'

'Nothing of the kind.' Ben placed her bag at her feet. He never went in the house. It reminded him of all those years ago when he had first brought Lil in the lorry. He hadn't known then that the love of his life was about to meet her Prince Charming.

'I still owe you five pounds, remember?'

'It wasn't a loan, it was a gift.'

She smiled up at him. 'You've got an answer for everything.'

'I'm a cockney, ain't I?'

She laughed and Ben felt that same old sensation inside as he looked into her beautiful face. He resisted the urge to put his arms around her and hold her tight.

Instead, as usual, he leaned forward and pecked her cheek. 'Well, I'm off now.'

'What are you going to do with yourself?'

'I'll motor on up West this morning for a few fares.'

'Well, see you next weekend?'

Ben seized his chance. 'How about we all go out to the Black Cat next week when you come home? Hattie and Reube and you and me. Just for a run in the country and a quick drink.'

Her face clouded. 'I'd have to see, Ben.'

'It would be nice before the weather turns.' He shrugged and pulled on his driving gloves. 'Well, cheerio, Lil.'

'Bye and thanks for the lift.'

That was a daft thing to do, he berated himself as he drove away. The girl wasn't interested. 'When will it sink into that thick skull of yours?' he muttered aloud as he pounded the steering wheel with his palm. 'Get yourself a nice bit of stuff to knock around with, just make the effort.' He knew Lily wasn't bothered about a trip out. She was in a different league now.

After driving for a while, he suddenly put on his brakes. Two cars sped past him, forcing him over to one side. He was about to move off again when another vehicle hurtled past. It was a lorry full of men. Some were shaking their fists, others pieces of wood and pick axes. They looked like dockers and he began to wonder if the rumours he'd heard were true. Were Mosley and his supporters really marching on the East End?

Shaking his head in confusion, he began to continue his journey, but no sooner than he had gone a mile up the road, the same thing happened again.

Winding down his window, he shouted to a group of men. These, too, were dockers, with their flat caps, working jackets and heavy boots secured by string. 'What's going on?' he frowned as one of them came over.

'Don't you know? Mosley and his Blackshirts are meeting at Tower Hill.'

'It's true then?'

'The buggers are planning to come down to the docks. But we're gonna see they don't.' He held up a smooth wooden laundry bat and shook it. 'They won't find a welcome here no more.'

'Ain't that a bit risky, chum? Shouldn't you leave it to the law?'

The man leaned down, resting the wooden stick on the window ledge. His face became red and angry. 'The law? You're having a laugh, ain't you? When have they stopped Mosley and his ilk before? I tell you, son, we're set for another war with all the agitators in this country. Old Blighty has got to stand up for what she believes in and it ain't what the bloody commies or fascists expound.'

Before either of them could speak again, another band of men marched past. Some were carrying placards, others homemade weapons. 'We're heading for Cable Street just up the road,' called one of them. 'That's where we plan to stop 'em.'

The docker nodded. 'You'd better turn round if you don't want to join us,' he told Ben.

Ben wound up the window. He tried to reverse the car, but another mob formed behind him. He realized he was cut off and neither way was open to him. Then he saw a turning opposite and drove into it. But at the end someone had rolled a line of barrows across the lane. Ben felt the sweat trickle under his collar. This was a riot and he was in the middle of it.

At the sound of raised voices, Lily hurried from the kitchen to the drawing room.

From the window, she saw a procession of men. They walked together, shoulders hunched against the October breeze. 'The dockers are coming!' they shouted angrily.

At this time on a Sunday the street was usually deserted. Most families were eating or resting. As she stood there, more men followed. She wondered where they were going. Then she thought of Mrs Brewer. What had she said about the meeting of the Blackshirts at Tower Hill? Lily had meant to ask Hattie about this, but had forgotten.

As more men followed, some clasped wooden sticks and others raised their fists angrily. A few women joined them. They looked as militant as the men.

When at last all was quiet again, Lily went back to the kitchen. Dockers were normally hard-working men and sat with their families on Sundays and enjoyed their one day of rest. What was their intention today?

Did Oswald Mosley and his Blackshirts plan to visit the East End?

Lily sighed as she thought of the last time there had been riots. Ten years ago the general strike had caused ordinary men to take up arms and protest. She hated to think the same thing could happen again. And if it did, she prayed that no one would be hurt.

Ben hoped his motor would be safe. He'd paid an old man ten bob to hide it in his backyard. When he'd left it, there were chickens clucking on its bonnet. He'd have a lot of mess to clean off no doubt, but it was better than the street. The mood of the crowd was frightening. As he walked along he was joined by others.

'The dockers are coming, you commies!' some shouted.

'We'll get you, BUF boys!' yelled others.

Everyone seemed to want a fight. Ben pulled up his collar and took his driving cap from his pocket. He flattened it down over his forehead and kept alert.

The crowd was like a great sea. There was no hope of fighting against the tide. He'd just have to do his best and try to keep out of trouble.

But he found it wasn't so easy. The thrust of the mob forced him onwards, some men urging him to rise up and fight. Others were shouting slogans against the Blackshirts. Many were wielding their weapons and even prising up the cobbles on the roads. Some had broken windows and others were building barricades.

There were loud bangs from fireworks and just beyond Blackchurch Lane he saw an overturned lorry. It made him think of his own lorry safely parked up at the Quarry. He hoped the riots weren't about to spread.

The men around him pushed him forward. Ben ducked a large missile thrown from a roof. It hit the man next to him who fell to the ground.

'Are you all right, mate?' Ben bent down to help. The man's face was streaming with blood.

'It was a bloody Blackshirt!' cried the dazed man as Ben helped him to his feet. 'Look what they done to me.'

Ben frowned. 'You don't know who it was, chum. It came from out of nowhere.'

'And whose side are you on?' the man shouted back angrily as he wiped the blood with his fingers.

'There seem to be a lot of different sides,' said Ben unwisely.

The man clutched him by the lapels. 'You're a fascist, ain't you? Or are you one of them commies?' he demanded as more stones and bricks rained down on them.

Ben pushed his assailant off as he heard a warlike cry in his ear. 'Here are the coppers, let's get 'em!'

The man lost interest in hitting him. He had seen the group of mounted policemen approaching. The horses were nervous and shied away from the militants. But soon police reinforcement appeared using their truncheons to beat back the crowd.

Ben saw many injuries. He was so shocked that he almost missed the sight of the large car that suddenly appeared from a side road. Some men began to rock it and the driver quickly reversed the way he had come.

As the fighting grew more violent, Ben squeezed himself into the open doorway of a shop. The man behind the glass window looked out with frightened eyes. Ben flinched as a large brick hit his shoulder and bounced on the window.

Suddenly the door gave way. 'Come in quickly or you'll get my window smashed!' The shopkeeper quickly locked the door again.

Ben took off his cap and brushed the dirt from his shoulders. 'Thanks, that was a close one.'

'They're turning into animals out there.'

'They seem to have forgotten what they're fighting for. Some blokes are even having a go at each other.'

'I'll draw the blinds so they can't see in. They might want to steal my stock.'

Ben could smell paraffin and oils. The hardware store was full of saucepans, brooms, brushes and pails.

'How did you get mixed up with them?' the shop-keeper asked as he drew the blinds.

'I couldn't get through to the city with me cab.'

'You're a cabbie?'

'Yes, I hid it in someone's yard.'

'I hope it is safe. Have you seen what they did to that lorry?'

Ben nodded. He felt sick as he thought of the angry

crowd and how quickly they had destroyed the vehicle. His motor was his livelihood, he couldn't imagine what state it might be in when he returned to it.

'What is the world coming to?' the shopkeeper asked, 'when men as meek as lambs become demented lions?'

Ben nodded anxiously. He was thinking about Lily. What if the trouble spread down to Poplar? It wasn't the Blackshirts he was worried about. It was, as the shopkeeper had said, ordinary men who were taking up arms to fight for what seemed like the sheer hell of it.

Lily heard a commotion outside. Turning down the light, she went to the window. All she could see at first were lanterns swinging in the dusky light. Then, as her eyes accustomed to the dark, she saw the grey shapes of men pushing and shoving a broken barrow. One of its wheels seemed to have come off. The procession passed by with a few loud shouts, but gradually the men made their way along Dewar Street and disappeared into the night.

Lily closed the curtains and turned on the light again, wondering what had happened in the city and whether the Blackshirts had been stopped at Tower Hill. She hadn't been able to hear what the men were shouting.

Suddenly a knock came at the front door. She went into the hall and waited. The knock came again. 'Who is it?' she called out.

'It's me, Ben.'

Relief flowed through her as she unlocked the door.

'Lil, are you all right?'

'Yes, I'm glad it's you. Some men have just gone by pushing a broken barrow. I thought it might be one of them.'

He looked inside. 'Are you on your own?'

'Yes, come in.'

He took off his cap. 'Only for a minute.'

Lily noted his ruffled appearance. 'Mrs Brewer told me there might be trouble at Tower Hill where Oswald Mosley and his Blackshirts were holding a meeting. Then after you left, some men marched past. I guessed it was true.'

Ben nodded. 'I was caught up in the crowds in Cable Street so I took refuge in a shop and sweated it out. Everyone outside was fighting. Didn't seem to matter who they fought just as long as they had a good scrap. The coppers did their share of bashing people on the heads. But in the end everyone just seemed to give up. Even the bluebottles just walked away with their helmets in their hands. When the coast was clear I went back to me car. I'd hidden it in someone's yard. Luckily it was safe but I was worried trouble might come down here.'

'No, the dockers only passed by. Were many hurt?'

'I did see a few casualties.'

'I felt sorry for those men. They were only like me dad, but something had got into them.'

Ben put on his cap again. 'I think they're stirred up to cause trouble.'

'What happened to the Blackshirts?'

'Dunno. I hope they've learned their lesson. Anyway, must go. Couldn't drive home without checking, could I?'

'Thanks, Ben.'

'Lock up after me, Lil.'

A little later she went upstairs. The warmth of the fire engulfed her as she sat on the couch and thought about all that had happened. Turning on the radio, she heard a serious voice.

'Today, one hundred thousand people gathered in the streets of London. Their intention to prevent Sir Oswald Mosley's Blackshirts from an organized march from Tower Hill, achieved a successful result. But police were called out to stop rioting, the worst of which was in Cable Street. Under a storm of protests, the Metropolitan Police heroically brought calm to the streets. But many were injured in the process and damage was incurred to buildings and vehicles alike . . .'

Lily sat up, her heart beating fast. She was certain that tomorrow, Mrs Brewer would tell her all the gruesome details that her husband was certain to have found out about.

Lily woke in the middle of the night, something had disturbed her. Was the rioting starting again? As she climbed out of bed and pulled on her robe, she listened for sounds. Pushing her feet into her slippers she went to the door and opened it.

There was a light on downstairs. A strange noise made her heart beat faster. It couldn't be Charles, not at this time of night. Could someone have got in? Or had she left the light on by mistake?

Fear travelled through her body. She was often alone in the house but had never been afraid as Charles and Mrs Brewer were the only ones to have keys.

Lily went out on the landing. She couldn't hear anything. Creeping slowly down the three flights of stairs, she paused at the bottom and listened again. Would an intruder put on the light? No, she must have left it on herself. Slowly she went down the passage to the kitchen.

For a moment, she felt frightened. Taking a deep breath, Lily went to the kitchen door and pushed it open. A man stood at the sink.

Lily gasped as Charles turned round.

'Oh, Charles!' She gave a sigh of relief.

'Did I wake you, Lily?'

'I thought it might be some of the rioters coming back. They passed the house shouting and dragging a cart.'

'The city has been quite disrupted.'

He came towards her and she saw a stain on his forehead. 'Are you hurt?' she asked in concern.

'It's just a small wound.' He put his fingers to his head. 'I broke down in the car having taken a diversion to avoid the riots. In my haste, I ran the fender into a lamppost. The car isn't damaged as I drove it back all right, but the windscreen shattered. I think a piece of the glass flew in and cut my head.'

'In that case, you were lucky it wasn't your eye.'

He said no more as he sat down and Lily carefully parted his thick, dark hair. Gently she began to clean the injury. 'The bleeding has stopped now, but tomorrow you must see a doctor,' she told him as she gently applied a small square of lint.

'I'm sure that won't be necessary.'

After she had done what she could, he looked into her eyes and smiled. 'You've been very kind, Lily. I'm sorry to have given you such a fright.'

'I was relieved it was you,' she admitted.

'Go back to bed and sleep. We must both get some rest.'

Lily returned to her quarters but was still awake at dawn. Why had Charles, who was a good driver, gone into a lamppost? Had it been more of an accident than he had told her about?

And would she find out more in the morning?

There was a banging on the door as Lily came downstairs the next morning. Two men stood on the steps dressed in raincoats. Neither of them bothered to remove their hats as they addressed her.

'There's a large blue car parked round the back,' one of them announced. 'The windscreen is smashed. Does it belong to someone in this house?'

'Who are you?' she asked, straightening her back, not liking the look of them one bit.

'We're police officers investigating the riots.'

'Why do you want to know about the car?'

The policeman put his foot in the door. 'We're asking the questions. Now, let us in.'

Before Lily could stop them they had entered the hall. Charles walked down the stairs. He was fully dressed and had removed the dressing from his head. Combing his dark hair over to one side, he had disguised his wound.

'May I help you?' he asked in a calm voice.

'Does that car with the broken windscreen belong to you?'

'Yes, why?'

'What were your movements yesterday, Sunday the eleventh of October?'

Charles glanced swiftly at her. 'I was at home all day.'

Lily wondered if she had heard him correctly. But as he glanced at her again, she saw a message in his eyes.

'Can anyone else in the household vouch for this?' demanded the other policeman aggressively.

Charles nodded and turned slowly to gaze at her. His dark eyes were penetrating as they spoke silently to her.

'Well?' demanded the policeman impatiently.

'My assistant Miss Lily Bright was with me all day. I'm sure she will be pleased to confirm it.'

Lily felt her head spin. Was she to lie on his behalf? Why hadn't he told them the truth?

'Well?' the policeman barked at her.

Lily nodded. She couldn't betray Charles.

'Is that a yes?' said the second policeman.

401

'Yes, Mr Grey was here.'

'All day?'

She looked at Charles who was still regarding her intently. 'Yes, Mr Grey was here all day,' she confirmed as she looked away.

'Then how do you account for the condition of your car?' the first policeman asked Charles.

Lily felt a chill go down her spine. Now Charles would have to tell them something quite different to what he had told her.

'I have no idea, officer. I can only assume that it was done in the night.'

'So you're telling me that you wasn't in it when it was done?'

Charles nodded. 'That is correct.'

'And you didn't see or hear anything?'

'Nothing, nothing at all in the night. I can only assume that some of the roughnecks who passed this way yesterday evening must have returned and attacked it. As Miss Bright will tell you, we heard a disruption that we put down to the rioting of the dockers.'

Lily was speechless. She couldn't believe Charles was saying this, and so sincerely that if she hadn't known better, she would almost have believed him.

'So how do you account for the fact there ain't no glass on the road?' said the taller policeman with a glint of satisfaction in his eye. 'If it was done out there, you'd see the damage.'

'That's easy to explain,' said Charles with a shrug.

'I'm in the habit of taking an early morning walk and cleared the damage myself.'

Both men stared at him. Lily felt sick with disbelief. The lies seemed to be growing. Why was Charles doing this? Her heart was banging so fast under her ribs she wondered if the policemen could hear it.

'Well, if that's all?' said Charles, moving to the door and holding it open.

Reluctantly the two men followed him.

Lily's heart gave another jump as Charles said brazenly, 'Incidentally, I would appreciate it if you would report my mishap to your station. Perhaps the culprit will be found during the course of your investigations.'

The larger policeman turned, his face growing red under his hat. 'We've more important things to do,' he grumbled, 'like catching the troublemakers behind the riots and putting them where they belong, behind bars. If you want to report the incident you'll have to go to your local station.'

'Then I wish you good luck and a satisfactory outcome,' said Charles politely. He watched them tread heavily down the steps then closed the door.

When he turned to face her, there was sweat on his brow and his face was suddenly bloodless.

Mrs Brewer came bustling in. 'Is Mr Grey at home this morning? I saw the car. What happened to it? Was it the riots?'

Lily was still in a state of shock. No one liked the

police banging on the door at the crack of dawn and certainly those two had been rude and discourteous. But why hadn't Charles told the truth?

'Yes,' Lily nodded. 'Mr Grey's home.' She didn't know what to say to Mrs Brewer. She couldn't tell her about the accident as Charles might tell her something else. Lily looked up the stairs. Why had he rushed up there after the policemen had gone? All he had whispered was that he would explain everything later.

'I'll bet it was one of them daft dockers,' said Mrs Brewer, not waiting for Lily to answer. 'They came through Poplar on their way back. Stepney got a few bashed windows and all. But it was Cable Street that got it worst, so everyone is saying.'

Lily nodded. 'Did you see your daughter?'

'No, more's the pity. Tom went to work this morning wondering if there was going to be any damage. The big workshops are in Leman Street. He'll get the truth from the Jews, but the government won't let on how serious it is.'

'Why is that?' asked Lily, confused.

'Looks bad for them, don't it? They can't control the dockers and tailors, a small minority who defeated the fascists and the whole of the Metropolitan Police put together.'

'Is that true?'

'Don't know, ducks. We'll have to see. Tom'll come home with all the news, though the papers are bound to be full of it. Not that you can trust them either, as they give us a lot of soft soap. Has Mr Grey had his breakfast yet?'

Lily shook her head. 'No.'

'I expect he'll be upset about his car?'

'Yes, he is.'

'Anyway, I'll get the fires going. It's a cold wind outside. Then I'll cook him a good bit of bacon to cheer him up.'

But Mrs Brewer was never to cook the meal. Ten minutes later, Charles hurried down, pulling on his coat, informing them that he didn't want breakfast and was going out to see to the car repairs.

Lily left Mrs Brewer to do the laundry. She didn't want to answer any questions. She had enough of her own. Like why hadn't Charles given her an explanation for his strange behaviour? What was wrong? She had an unsettled feeling inside her, brought about not just by Charles' lies, but also at the thought that the police might return and she'd have to lie again.

Chapter Twenty-Two

It was late in the day when Charles returned. Lily was banking the fire as Mrs Brewer had left strict instructions to put on more coke at teatime. Lily had just replaced the tongs when she heard a key in the door.

She rose to her feet expectantly. In the hall she found Charles. 'Let me take your coat.'

He nodded silently and after hanging it up, Lily followed him in to the drawing room. He stood, gazing into the scarlet flames, one elbow propped on the mantelpiece. Lily could see that he hadn't shaved this morning, as a dark growth spread over his chin and his black hair fell in an unruly fashion down to his collar.

'How are you feeling today?' she asked. Even though she was upset at what he had expected her to do this morning, she couldn't be angry with him for long. He looked tired and weary.

'I'm well enough, Lily.'

'And your wound?'

He nodded. 'That is the least of my worries.'

Lily clasped her hands together. She felt that he was on the brink of saying something. After a few moments she spoke. 'I'll go and set the table.'

But he looked up and shook his head. 'I'm not hungry, thank you.'

'But you must eat.'

'I've no appetite yet. Perhaps later.'

Lily stood uncertainly. 'I'll put on the lights.'

'No, leave them. The fire is sufficient.'

She looked around. 'Is there anything I can get you?'

At first he shook his head, but then, sighing, he nodded. 'A little brandy, Lily, to revive the spirits.'

She had never known him to drink before eating. Occasionally he would enjoy a glass of port after a meal, but that was only in the company of his guests.

She obeyed, going to the back parlour where a large cabinet was stocked with a variety of alcohol. She found the brandy and placed a large balloon glass on a silver tray. As she had never poured this spirit before, she used the measuring cup. It smelt strong, but the amber colour looked warm and inviting. Perhaps it really did lift people's spirits.

When she returned to the drawing room, he was sitting in one of the pink chairs, gazing into the fire. She sensed he had withdrawn into himself and didn't want to talk. Curbing her own need to discuss what had happened, she placed the silver tray on the small table beside him. Then, saying nothing, she was about to leave when he looked up.

'Lily, you deserve an explanation.'

She kept silent, looking into his haunted eyes.

'Without you this morning I would have been in trouble.'

Alarm filled her. 'What do you mean?'

'Come and sit down.'

She moved slowly across the floor to the couch.

'No, not over there. Here in this chair beside me.'

Feeling her cheeks warm, she did as he told her. The fire crackled and spat, but this was the only noise in the darkened room.

Lily waited patiently. She had a feeling that what she was about to hear would turn her world upside down. And the first words he said, confirmed that.

'Lily, I don't wish to burden you with my problems, but in giving you a satisfactory explanation, you must be made aware of my situation.'

Lily sat quietly, but her mind was in turmoil. She couldn't imagine Charles in trouble, it was quite out of character. But then, before this morning, she would never have expected him to lie, much less ask her to lie on his behalf.

Noah Kelly was restless. He wanted to get to his Monday meeting, but he'd been choked off by Josie last week after expounding on his beliefs. He wasn't listened to at home any more. And yet it wasn't just him that felt this way. There were others, old men perhaps, but they remembered the conflict, sensed the same vibrations floating over from Europe. It didn't take a great brain to understand the turmoil. Much less to know that no country was safe whilst Germany was re-arming.

Noah pulled on his coat and opened the front door.

'Where are you off to, Noah?' His sister came down the hall.

'Going out for a breather.'

'At this time of night?'

'It's only half six.'

'Well, it's cold out there. Not like a summer's evening. What if there's still rioters out? I read in the papers that eighty people were injured on Sunday and the Blackshirts threw a poor Jewish man and his son through a window.'

Noah laughed as he pulled up his collar. 'Well, they ain't going to throw me through one.'

'I don't want you caught up in trouble.'

'It ain't the rioters you've got to worry about it's them bloody politicians who are doing nothing to stop a far bigger crisis.'

'Oh, you ain't going on about them again, are you?'

'What if I am?'

'You are a crazy old man! The war is over. There ain't going to be another one.'

'That's what you think.'

Josie walked slowly up to him. She smelt of cooking, of the thick meat pie they'd just enjoyed, with mash and brussels sprouts. She represented the calm and orderly, and he envied her blind faith. 'Noah

Kelly, don't you think you're a bit too old to start a revolution?'

'It's no revolution. It's fact. Europe's on the move.'

He stood uncertainly. He wanted to get his feelings off his chest, but Josie wouldn't understand. She'd already accused him of being too old to think straight. Old he may be, but his memory wasn't gone. And there was the rub, Noah thought to himself angrily. The country had come through one conflict this century, and refused to admit another. Seventeen years on and all Baldwin could do was sit in his ivory tower and twiddle his fingers. Yet right under his nose the insurgents were gathering force. They'd been stopped at Tower Hill, but it wouldn't rest there. Laugh in his face, some might, when he foretold of another catastrophe but bloody Mussolini was gathering strength along with that fascist madman Franco. And Hitler, as bold as brass, had outright defied the treaty of Versailles and goose-stepped his way across the Rhineland. What use was the flaming League of Nations now? And here were the British government begging the French to give full consideration to the German High Command's actions! It was unbelievable!

'Noah, you're not going up to the Mission Hall again?'

'Yes, I am.'

'They're a lot of silly, cross old men.'

'So you keep telling me. But we know what we know.'

'You'll sit there and catch your death.'

'I'll sit there and talk to me mates. Nothing wrong in that, is there?'

Josie put her arm out. 'I wish Lily was here. She'd talk some sense into your head.'

He wanted to tell her it was Lily he was concerned about. Her most of all, but Josie wasn't the person to tell. No, even Bob was past it now. Since he'd come off the jollup, he was content with his fags and the occasional ale. He didn't want to remember the war, he had enough skeletons in his closet, he said, to sink a ship. There was Ben, of course, but the poor lad wasn't to be involved. He'd done enough for the Brights in the past and had his own life to lead.

Noah smiled gently at his sister. She was a good woman, but a blind one. 'I won't be late. Charlie's giving me a lift on his cart. I'm meeting him at the end of the road.'

'Well, have it your own way. You always do.'

Noah let himself out and into the chill of the October evening. Digging his hands in his pockets, he stumbled along Love Lane towards the cart that was slowly drawing up on the cobbles.

Lily looked at the man she cared for so deeply. She knew she could forgive him anything. This morning had come as a shock, but it was obvious he was troubled. She wanted to help if she could, and she knew she had to wait until he was ready to explain.

'Lily, when we first met, I told you I bought and sold works of art, curios, furniture . . .' He paused, then looked at her. 'That was true at the time, but it wasn't all of the truth. You see, I have a greater interest. One that is a passion and yet I have never been able to indulge myself fully in it's precarious nature. That interest has grown considerably over the past two years.'

Lily frowned. She had no idea what he was talking about.

'Indeed, it's not to my business in Shoreditch that I travel to each day, it's into the city.'

'The city?' Lily repeated, frowning.

'I have an office in Westminster as I need to be central to my real work. You may have guessed by now that I am involved in politics. This is the reason why I am away so frequently.'

'But I thought you were travelling abroad to buy different things.'

'I'm afraid I encouraged that assumption. Many of my visits to other countries are to – shall we say – secure funds for my political interests.'

'But when we first met—'

'When we first met,' he interrupted gently, neither of us knew each other very well . . . and it was only after a period of time that we became close friends. Is that not right?'

She nodded slowly. 'Did you really want my help to buy things for the house?'

'Of course. That was entirely genuine. I missed

413

Delia's influence as I told you. And although I would have liked to take you into my confidence, I'd had a difficult experience with Annie; I was wary. As a new political group, our image must be untarnished.'

'What is your party called?' Lily asked.

'We have no name as such yet. But we like to call ourselves new thinkers.'

Lily was still confused. 'I don't know much about politics.'

'All you need to know is that one day we intend to make a great difference to this country. Do away with oppression and provide work for men like your father who have been treated so unfairly.'

Lily was filled with admiration. She might not understand much about politics but she understood the problems of the poor and needy. His voice was filled with passion as he went on. 'The men who come here to speak with me are of the same mind. We have great plans for the future. For this reason we meet in private in order to pursue our goal.'

'And you want it all kept secret?' she asked, frowning.

'Simply because, as a new party, others would try to discredit us. As I warned you once, discretion is an absolute necessity, especially at the more sensitive times, like now.'

Lily sat quietly, absorbing all he had said. His eyes were filled with energy, his face alive with a burning enthusiasm. She had never seen him like this before.

'This morning,' he went on, 'I left my office in the company of a prominent man, who is sympathetic to our cause. As we drove towards Tower Hill, we came upon the rioters who broke our windscreen. I simply had to drive on, knowing that if the newspapers got hold of the incident, they would distort the facts. My colleague holds a high rank and any connection with the riots – however innocent – would endanger his career. Therefore I was obliged to lie on his behalf to the police. I had to scotch any rumour. Unfortunately Lily . . .' he reached across and took her hand, 'I put you in an awkward position. All I can say is, I owe you a great debt, my dear friend.'

Lily felt his strong hand tighten around hers. It was the first time he had ever touched her in this way.

'I beg your forgiveness,' he said huskily as he gazed into her eyes.

Lily knew that she had forgiven him even before his explanation. But she wished he had told her some of this before. Even last night when he came home would have been better than now.

'There's nothing to forgive.'

'And you understand my reasons?'

She nodded slowly, her senses beginning to reel as he took hold of both her hands. He pressed them tightly to his chest.

'Oh, Lily, my beautiful girl.' His eyes glimmered brightly in the firelight as he pulled her closer. 'You mean so much to me, Lily. As a dear friend, yes, but our connection is much more, don't you think? We share something quite wonderful.'

Lily swallowed. What was he telling her? Could she dare to hope that he returned her feelings?

'We have a bond that begun the moment I saw you that day at the market,' he told her eagerly. 'A bond that has deepened over the years. When I saw you at the church, I couldn't let you slip out of my life again.'

Suddenly he swept her into his arms. He held her tenderly, then passionately. Drawing his hands over her face he looked into her eyes. 'Oh, Lily, my sweet girl.'

Lily thought she was about to expire with joy. So this was what it felt like to be in his arms, to be so close to him that she could feel his heart pounding. Her body trembled as he kissed her forehead. Slowly he drew her chin up and tenderly placed his lips over hers. Lily wondered if her heart would stop. Desire gripped her like an exquisite physical pain. She had never felt like this before. She knew she was in love and that whatever he asked of her, she would do.

'Oh, Lily, Lily,' he whispered, kissing her again. Then in the firelight, he began to unfasten the buttons of her dress.

The meeting at the Mission Hall had followed its usual pattern. Someone had a complaint, then another trumped in. Noah Kelly was beginning to think his sister had been right. He was cold right through and he'd only joined Charlie in order to get out of the house for a few hours. But these were old men, past the age of action. The Prime Minister, Stanley Baldwin, was usually the first to be slated. But tonight it was the Jarrow marchers. The poor buggers were struggling all the way down from the north and intended to present Baldwin with their petition.

'Let's join 'em when they arrive,' several old boys up the front shouted. 'They've got the same troubles as us, with their shipbuilding and steel works in the grip of depression. They've got mouths to feed and want jobs as bad as we do. Let the East End dockers meet up with 'em at Hyde Park and put our four penneth in.'

'Like we did at Cable Street?' cried another contemptuously.

'Our blokes was infiltrated there,' someone replied, 'by the commies and fascists. Cable Street was a fiasco and everyone knows it.'

Noah knew that all this talk was ineffective hot air. The men filling this smoke-filled hall could hardly wield their walking sticks, let alone muscle at Hyde Park. He couldn't distinguish one grey head from another, except for the odd balding pate like his own.

A bent figure in the next row finally spoke some sense. 'Oh sit down and shut up. How is a lot of old codgers going to help them poor sods from Jarrow? Our time is over.'

'They should go to the horse's mouth, Baldwin himself,' was the vehement reply.

'Baldwin will snub 'em!'

'Labour won't let him!'

'Labour won't do nothing except sit on the fence!'

'The King might. He's off to Wales to see the jobless.'

Noah sighed to himself as the voices grew louder. He'd heard it all before, in other words, with different faces, but now every bone in his body ached. He wanted to go home where there was a hot cup of tea and nice fire and time to nap.

Then a voice made him sit up and take note. 'I heard the commie's have a welcome in store for the Northerners! Me son-in-law works in city town hall. He's heard they plan to accompany the lads from Jarrow when they march on Downing Street.'

At this, the small, smoke-filled room was filled with a new and energetic exchange. Charlie next to him, nodded fiercely.

'I told yer, Noah.'

'You think they're going for another Cable Street?'

'Why not? Baldwin fears a civil uprising and that's what the subversives are after.'

'I haven't forgot what you told me.'

'Your girl don't want to be involved in any of that.'

Noah shook his head firmly. 'It's how to tell her that's the problem.'

'Just keep your ear to the ground for now.'

Noah glanced at his friend and decided to keep his seat a while longer. He wanted to hear what more was going to be said on the theme of anarchy. He had a vested interest in its outcome. So, stamping his feet on the flagstone floor, he took out his tobacco and carefully rolled a thin smoke, turning his better ear to the next speaker.

Lily lay next to the man with whom she had fallen in love on the first day she had seen him, six years ago. Now she had surrendered her body. Charles' love-making had been the most thrilling thing that had had ever happened to her. She was a woman now and it was Charles who had taken her to this place of self-discovery. He had seemed shocked as she had cried in pain the moment he entered her.

'Lily, I'm your first!' he'd whispered huskily. 'I had no idea.'

Lily hadn't known what to say. She was frightened and excited all at once. She loved him and wanted to make him happy, but she didn't know how. Then as he swept her away on a wave of emotion, all her worries had disappeared. She had never felt a man's naked body beside her and Charles was the most beautiful of men. His lean, muscled frame, long limbs and strong hands were like a work of art. He had aroused her until she had cried out again, but this time with a wanton desire. The need inside her became all consuming and she couldn't deny it.

Now she lay listening to his rhythmic breathing. He had brought her here, to her own bed, to make love to her. This was the only regret she had. Was Delia's memory never to be forgotten? She had felt his wife's ghostly shadow for just a few moments, but as he had made love to her, that had soon passed.

How wonderful had been that moment in front of the fire! He had been a gentle lover at first as he removed her clothes. His dark eyes had been filled with hunger as he'd gazed at her nakedness. She had felt self-conscious and tried to hide her fear, but sensing her embarrassment, he had taken her hands and shown them where to explore.

She had been so nervous that he'd held her to him again. As she had relaxed, and his manhood had become apparent, Lily had thought she was going to faint at the desire that she knew she had caused. The man whom she had never seen other than fully dressed, was naked in the firelight. Their clothes had been scattered at their feet. Suddenly she hadn't cared, as the flames of the fire glowed on their bodies like one of the old pictures painted by a Master.

Suddenly Charles stirred, bringing her back to the moment. She felt afraid all over again. Would he still want her? Was this night going to end with a brusque goodbye? Her heart was already beginning to ache as he turned and drew her against him. Lily gasped at his arousal.

'My darling, do I frighten you?'

'Oh no, no,' was all she could say as his lips found hers. This time their lovemaking was even more wonderful. Lily felt ashamed that Charles had to teach her so much. It seemed that he brought life into her soul, as though she was tasting heaven.

Lily knew she would never forget this night. Even if it was the only night she was to spend with Charles. She had never felt so complete.

As he continued to kiss her, she gave herself completely. He was an experienced lover, older and wiser and the passion that he lavished on her made her hungry for more. She didn't know she could ever feel such abandon.

When at last he lay asleep, Lily thought of the things they had done together. Had her own parents done it too? And Mrs Parks and Mr Parks? And Hattie and Reube?

She listened again to his breathing. Would he still want her tomorrow? Her desire for him had increased but was it the same for Charles?

Chapter Twenty-Three

Ben crossed the road and knocked on the door of number thirty-four.

'Oh, Ben, come in a minute. I was just making me Christmas pudding. It's only November, but I like to have everything ready.' Josie wiped her hands on her apron.

'Smells lovely. Won't keep you a minute.'

'Would you like a cuppa?'

Ben stepped inside. 'No thanks, Mrs B. Got to get up to the city for the Christmas fares. Don't run the lorry or the Chariot much now.'

'Oh, why's that?'

'I'm making a good enough living with me cab.'

'You're going up in the world, dear. But you deserve it, you work all hours God sends.'

Ben glanced down the hall to the kitchen from which a delicious aroma came. 'Have you had word from Lil?'

'Yes, and I'm afraid you'll be disappointed again. Like I told you last week and the week before, she ain't coming home.'

'But I thought she was?'

'No, ducks. She sent me a note saying she's been asked to work again. It's Christmas soon and Mr Grey has a lot of entertaining to do around the festive season.'

'Will she be home for Christmas?'

'I hope so. It would be nice to be all together and we could have a few carols round the piano. Your mum and Hattie and Reube are coming over on Boxing Day. And I hope you'll come too?'

'Yes, that'd be nice.'

'After all, you don't want to be alone in your little house. Do you like living up at Stepney?'

'Yes, it ain't bad.'

'Do you know any of the neighbours yet?'

'Not really. I'm out at work a lot. But what I've seen of them they're a good natured lot.' Ben turned his cap in his hands. He wanted to ask more about Lily but felt he couldn't. 'Well, I suppose I'd better let you get on with your cake. I was only making sure that Lil was all right for a lift.'

Josie smiled. 'Between you and Mr Grey she does very well for transport.'

That didn't help much, thought Ben silently as he tried to smile. He wanted Lil to be happy, course he did, but he realized he was losing her. He'd been content to feed off the crumbs, collecting and delivering her when her lord and master was away, but now even that was being taken from him.

'Are you sure you wouldn't like a cuppa, dear?'

'No, I must be off.'

'Is that you, young man?' Noah Kelly appeared, pulling on his coat.

'Mornin' Mr Kelly, where are you off to?'

'Up the shops for me tobacco.'

'Want a lift?'

'That'd be just the job.'

'Noah, you're not going out in this freezing weather,' said Lily's mum and Ben smiled.

'Josie, it ain't freezing.'

'Well, you're a—'

'A daft old man, yes I know. Now, is there anything you want up the shops?'

'No, thank you. Now I see you have your cap, but don't forget your gloves.' She handed them to him from the stand, arching an eyebrow.

The two men left the house and climbed into Ben's vehicle. 'How's Mr Bright these days?' Ben enquired as he drove.

'Same as always, under the thumb. Don't put no energy into resisting it.'

The two men smiled knowingly at one another. 'Sorry to hear Lily's not coming home,' said Ben.

'Me too, son.'

'The job must be going all right, then?'

'Looks that way.' Noah pushed his pince-nez along the ridge of his nose. 'Did you hear the news this morning? The Prime Minister has refused to see the poor sods from Jarrow. Said he fears a civil uprising.'

'Sounds as though he's worried after what happened at Cable Street,' Ben nodded. 'There were a lot of injuries and the law took a fair trouncing too.'

'I wish I was ten years younger. I'd have been right up the front meself.'

'Only ten?'

'Well, twenty or thirty then. Fifty'd be nice.'

They both laughed. Ben drew up at the row of shops in Manchester Road. 'This all right for you?'

'Thanks, son.'

Ben jumped out and opened the door. The wind cut across him as he helped the old man out. 'You know, it is a bit parky, Mr Kelly. Do you want me to wait for you?'

'No, you get off.' But before Ben could leave, the older man gripped his arm. 'Son, I don't want to put the wind up you, but I don't like me girl not coming home. We ain't seen her in a month.'

'I'm sure she's all right.'

'Yes, but you hear some funny things going round these days.'

'Now you're worrying me,' Ben frowned.

'Oh, take no notice,' his companion shrugged. 'Josie says I'm a daft old man and she's probably right.'

'You're far from that. Look, I intend to knock off early tonight, do you fancy an ale down the Quarry. Mr Bright too, if he's up for it.'

'Now you're talking, lad.'

'See you about seven then?'

'Thanks, son.'

'Don't mention it.'

Ben jumped back in the car and drove away. The more he thought about what Noah Kelly had said the more he was puzzled. What had he heard that was connected to Lily that had put the wind up him? Well, whatever it was he'd find out tonight when they had a good old chinwag.

Lily gazed at the tall Christmas tree standing in the hall. It was now the first of December. She was going to put up the decorations before the guests arrived. Most evenings now, Charles was busy with entertaining. There had been many new faces at the house and Charles had impressed it on her that it was important she told no one about the meetings. These men were very important to his career and they came from all over the world to see him. She was flattered he had taken her into his confidence. Even though she couldn't converse with their visitors, she imagined herself as the lady of the house. Then, as they sat behind closed doors until late into the night, Lily would go upstairs and wait for Charles.

When the tap came on her door, she fell into his arms. Every time he made love to her, it was more wonderful than the last. As the weeks passed, she wished she could talk about the love of her life. But Hattie was the only one she could tell.

Lily was decorating the tree when Mrs Brewer appeared. 'The beef and the vegetables are all prepared,' she said as she took off her apron. 'Enough for your six guests tonight.' Lily knew Mrs Brewer would like to have known who they were. But Charles had told Lily she must never mention any names. 'Are you sure you don't want me to come back and help?'

'No, that won't be necessary. I can serve it up easily.' Charles now only wanted Lily to be present.

'That looks pretty, dear,' Mrs Brewer went on, casting an eagle eye over the tree.

'Yes, it makes the house festive.'

'Which reminds me,' Mrs Brewer said as she reached for her hat and coat on the stand. 'Mr Grey has given me two weeks off. And you'll be going home for Christmas no doubt. So how will he manage?'

Instead of going home, Lily intended to be with Charles at Christmas, though of course she couldn't tell Mrs Brewer that. The house would be their own with no one to disturb them. It would be like being a real married couple. 'I'll make sure he's catered for,' she assured the daily help.

Lily knew Mrs Brewer still had something to say as she hovered by the Christmas tree. 'You'll be pleased to see your family, won't you, ducks? I reckon you've got yourself a nice young man tucked away somewhere!'

Lily tried to hide her blush as she thought of Charles.

Mrs Brewer dug her playfully in the ribs. 'I thought so. But just you be careful, my dear. I expect you know all about the birds and the bees, but take my advice and keep him at arm's length till you're married. You are a very sensitive young woman. You ain't experienced like some women are today, like that Mrs Simpson for instance, trying to steal our king.'

Lily stopped what she was doing. The royal affair was something she felt deeply about. She didn't understand why there was such a fuss about two people who obviously adored one another. She had studied the photographs of Mrs Simpson, an American divorcee who was elegant and beautiful and stood up for her man. Everyone knew that to marry her, the king would have to relinquish the throne. But if two people were meant to be together, even a crown couldn't come between them.

'I think it's sad,' replied Lily fervently, 'that they aren't allowed to do what they want. After all, it's not a crime to fall in love!'

Mrs Brewer looked shocked. 'But he's our king, love, and she's just a commoner and an American at that!'

'What difference does that make?' Lily was becoming cross at the older woman's bigoted outlook. 'I believe love conquers all.'

Mrs Brewer patted her arm as though she was a child. 'Just you be glad you're not in their position and have got a nice ordinary young man to stand by you.'

Lily wanted to say that when two people were really and truly in love they could overcome anything, just like she had with Charles.

When Mrs Brewer finally left, Lily sat down on

the stool, feeling upset. How could someone be so narrow-minded? It was love after all! What would Mrs Brewer say when she knew the truth about her and Charles?

Lily gazed up at the beautiful tree. It wasn't important what other people thought. She was happy. She had a beautiful house to live in and the man she loved. It was only a matter of time before he made her his wife. She allowed her mind to wander, picturing the moment when he proposed. He would go down on one knee and her eyes would fill with tears. She would fling her arms around him and cry, 'Yes, I will be your wife.'

Lily was still lost in her dreams when the big clock in the back parlour struck five. She jumped up. Hurriedly tying the rest of the decorations on the tree, she dragged her mind back to the arrival of the guests.

It was December the eleventh and Lily was listening to the radio. With a heavy heart she heard the king's words. 'At long last, I am able to say a few words of my own . . . a few hours ago I discharged my last duty as king and emperor. You all know the reasons which have impelled me to renounce the throne . . .'

Lily felt sad for the man who had been forced to come to such an agonizing decision. She understood how much in love he was with Mrs Simpson. But at least now the decision was taken, they wouldn't have to live a lie. Lily knew that when she could tell everyone that she and Charles were together she would be the happiest woman in the world. Even happier than Mrs Simpson!

That night Lily lay in bed, waiting for Charles. Although he didn't always come to her bed, every lonely minute was forgotten when he did. She had begun to realize that there were many different ways of love-making. When his ardour overcame him and he was rough, he was always remorseful. Lily knew that she was only just learning how to please him.

She jumped as she heard a noise. Was it Charles? She got up and pulled on her robe. Going out to the landing, she saw a light below. Peering down into the well of the hall she saw the top of Charles' head by the Christmas tree. Beside him was another figure. With a shock, Lily recognized Mrs Covas' elegant coiffeur.

An hour later, Lily was lying in bed with her eyes wide open. Mrs Covas had gone into the drawing room. What could they be talking about? Why had she called so late?

Lily waited and waited for Charles to come to her. But in the morning, she woke alone.

Charles was already up when Lily went downstairs. 'Oh, there you are, my dear.'

She wanted to ask about Mrs Covas, but was worried Charles would think she had been spying on them.

He kissed her cheek. 'You look a little pale this morning.'

It was true, Lily didn't feel quite herself. But she thought she knew the reason why.

'You must look after yourself whilst I'm away.'

She looked up at him. 'You're going away?'

He took her arm and steered her gently to the chair. 'Sit down, Lily, I must talk to you. This is all rather unexpected.'

Was he going to tell her about Mrs Covas? What had happened in the night?

'Some friends have asked me to spend Christmas with them,' he began to explain. 'I know you'll understand when I tell you that complying with their wishes is very important.'

Lily's heart sank. Was he going to Mrs Covas' house in the country?

'When will you be back?' she asked anxiously.

'Sometime after Christmas. But you mustn't worry yourself about that. I want you to have a wonderful Christmas with your family. So, here is a special present. You've worked hard on my behalf this year and most certainly deserve it!'

Lily looked at the thick envelope in her hands. 'You don't have to give me this. I don't want it.' She wanted to tell him that she didn't want to go home. This was her home! All she had dreamed of was being in this house and looking after him.

'It's my pleasure, Lily. You can buy some nice things for your family.'

'But I—'

'And when I return,' he interrupted firmly, 'we shall have our own celebration. I was looking forward to spending time with you, my dear, but this visit is critical to me. I must speak to people who are very important to my cause. And you, above all people, know that I must put my duty before my personal life.'

He was gently reminding her of the importance of his career. For a while she had forgotten this as she became overwhelmed by her own desires. Suddenly she felt very contrite. When she was Mrs Grey, there would plenty of time to spend with her beloved husband, but even with this thought Lily found it hard to hide her disappointment.

'My darling, don't be upset.' He took her in his arms. 'We'll be together soon, I promise.'

Her heart beat faster at these words. Did he mean really together, as man and wife?

'I suggest at the end of next week, you go home to your family. I've left Mrs Brewer's wages on my desk and if you will just see that the house is closed up?'

She nodded. 'Yes, of course.'

He kissed her tenderly. 'I'm so fortunate that I can leave everything to you. Now, although I have everything I need for my trip, a few well-ironed shirts would be most useful.'

In the kitchen Lily took down the shirts from the pulley. She held them against her cheek, smelling

Charles. Then she looked at the envelope he had given her. What had she done to deserve the money? It made her feel cheap, as though she was a prostitute.

Later she took the shirts to his room. When Charles opened the door, he held a book in his hand, but closed it quickly.

'Thank you, Lily.'

She wanted to throw her arms round him and beg him to stay. But she knew she couldn't interfere. She must accustom herself to their separations as he was such an important and busy man.

Once more on her own, Lily let the tears fall. Charles had promised to return to her in the New Year. She should be satisfied, but she wasn't. She wanted to be with him, to help him in his work, to show that as his wife, she could support and encourage his career. Perhaps one day she too would go to Mrs Covas' house, as the new Mrs Grey.

Lily didn't light the fires that day. There was no one to light them for. The Christmas tree in the hall was a reminder of the Christmas with Charles that she now wouldn't have.

'Noah, don't stay out there for too long; it's freezing. And mind that latch, it sticks worse than ever.'

'I know. I know.'

'I want to set the table tonight, ready for dinner tomorrow. You can help me lay up.'

Noah looked round the warm kitchen, that was piled

with dirty pots and pans. He didn't fancy washing up tonight; it was Christmas Eve after all. But Josie would have him standing at the sink no doubt, wanting to put everything just so. Now Lil was home for Christmas, she was determined to have everything her own way. Women!

But as he went out into the cold backyard, Noah could understand how she felt. His sister was as happy as he was that their girl was home. She looked a bit peaky to him. No doubt she missed her gent. But as much as he felt for her, he had to have a word too. Now, how was he going to put it? He opened the closet door and was met with a strong whiff of disinfectant. Josie was nervous of the mice and rats and a trap was set in the corner. He hung the Tilley lamp on the hook and closed the door. The latch fell down.

'Bugger,' he groaned as he pulled down his trousers. 'That bloody latch. Why don't someone fix it?' He remembered the last time it had been seen to, many years ago. The lad from across the road had attended to it. Noah smiled in reflection as he sat there. The boy had been sweet on Lil even then. What a pity his feelings had never been returned. Ben James was salt of the earth. At least he had been able to tell the lad of his recent concerns. But there was no proof, only rumour. And as Ben had said, they couldn't go upsetting Lil on a tall story, could they?

No, it was better to keep quiet for the present. The boy was going to keep an eye on her. And for that Noah was grateful. The youngsters had all gone down the Quarry tonight. Well, it was Christmas Eve after all. Maybe Ben would get a bit more out of her than he could. Lily had been home all week, but as much as he'd tried to engage her in conversation about her gent, she'd kept tight-lipped. Well, perhaps there really was nothing to be alarmed about. However, he'd like to see her without that wistful expression. Put on a bit of weight. And run to a laugh once in a while, like she used to.

By the time he had pulled up his pants, he was feeling the cold and his head swam a little. His whole body seemed stiff and aching, and his chest felt bruised and heavy.

He tried to lift the latch. Bloody thing. It was still stuck. Mustering all his strength he tried again. Pushing and pulling, the iron was caught fast. Rusted it was, in need of an oil.

He banged on the door. Softly at first, as he knew Josie would give him hell when she let him out. She'd warned him enough times not to use the latch. But it wasn't his fault. The thing had dropped down even before he'd had time to go.

He banged harder this time, again and again. His heart raced as he kicked the boards. The lamp wavered and flickered. Suddenly there was darkness.

Noah yelled out. 'Josie! The bloody lamp's gone out and I'm freezing to death!'

There was no reply. She was probably banging and crashing with those flaming dishes. Why didn't Bob get up off his arse and help her? Noah felt a hammer on his chest. Then a pain down his arm.

Luckily he dropped on the lavatory. For a moment he sat there, waiting for the panic to pass. But then, as he tried to get up, something squeezed his ribs. He felt like his chest was caving in. Gasping, he reached out again. But it was no use. His strength had gone and he fell back, inhaling a sickly dose of Josie's disinfectant.

Hattie and Lil were sitting on the hard benches of the Quarry. Lil glanced at Ben who was standing with his brother at the bar. It was a long time since they had all been out together, but Lily couldn't refuse. She wanted to speak to Hattie anyway.

'Your mum and dad and uncle are really pleased to have you home for Christmas,' Hattie said, breaking into her thoughts. 'They thought you might not come.'

Lily had been home a week and despite missing Charles had enjoyed herself. 'Yes, it's been nice being with everyone and going up the market with you yesterday.'

'What do you think of the king and Mrs Simpson?'

'I hope they'll be very happy.'

'I thought you'd say that.'

'Did you? Why?'

'Because you're a hopeless romantic.'

'There's nothing wrong with romance.' All week Lily had wanted to tell Hattie of her own romance with Charles. But she hadn't found the right time. She glanced quickly at the bar again where Ben and Reube were still talking. Should she say now?

'Hattie, I've got something to tell you.'

Hattie's brown eyes narrowed. 'Is it about your long lost love?'

'It's not lost any more.'

Hattie sat forward, studying Lily's glowing expression. 'Are you going to tell me you've slept with Charles?'

Lily nodded.

'How many times?'

'I don't know. I haven't counted.'

Hattie gasped, then smothered her surprise. 'Why didn't you tell me before?'

'Someone's always been around.'

Hattie sat quietly. Lily expected a lot of questions, but none were forthcoming. Would Hattie be shocked if she told her the things she had done with Charles. Or was it normal for every woman to do them? But before she could speak, Hattie shook her head slowly.

'Lil, I hope you've been careful. You don't want to get pregnant.'

'I'd like to give Charles a son and heir.'

Hattie looked frozen. 'Blimey. Lil, what are you saying?'

'I mean it.'

'But does he know about this?'

'No, not in so many words.'

'Well, you'd better tell him before you start getting any notions.'

'I'm in love with him, Hat. Not like I was years ago. That was just a crush in comparison to the way I feel now.'

'But does he love you?'

'He must do.' Lily blushed deeply. 'I feel like his wife in bed.'

'But Lil, that could just be sex for him.'

Lily flushed again. How could Hattie say that? 'He wouldn't do the things he does if he didn't love me,' Lily said, hurt.

Hattie took her hand. 'Listen, Lil, I don't want to upset you, but a man doesn't always love a woman because she lets him do what he wants under the sheets. Sometimes it's just a bit of slap and tickle for him, without the commitment. You have to remember that becoming his mistress is one thing and marriage is another.'

Tears sprang to Lily's eyes and she pulled away her hand. 'Hattie, how can you say such a thing?'

'I'm sorry, but it's true.'

'Charles loves me.'

'All right then, if you say so.'

'I thought I could tell you everything,' said Lily tearfully.

'You can, but I'm worried you're so inexperienced.'

Reube walked over, holding the drinks. 'Here you are girls, get this down you. A nice port and lemon.'

Ben joined them. 'Come on you two, cheer up.'

Lily and Hattie tried to smile.

'Happy Christmas!' Reube and Ben said as they picked up their ales.

Lily looked at the glass of port. The sight of the rich dark liquid made her feel queasy. Perhaps she should have eaten more before she came out tonight?

She wanted to be able to talk to Hattie again. She needed to ask about the period she had missed. Even though she had told Hattie she would like to be pregnant, did she mean it?

Chapter Twenty-Four

'Oh my God, oh no!' Josie pushed the closet door. 'Noah, are you all right?' It was so dark she couldn't see a thing. She put her shoulder to the door. 'Noah, speak to me.'

Josie ran back inside. 'Bob! Noah's in the lav and there's no reply.'

Bob Bright put down his newspaper. 'Did you tap on the door?'

'Course I did. I can't get in. I warned him not to drop the latch.'

They both ran outside into the cold night. Josie watched her husband push at the door. 'He's stuck in there, Josie.'

'He's not answering! Oh God, what's happened?'

'He must have fallen or something.'

Just then the back door opened and Lily appeared. 'I wondered where everyone was.'

'Oh, Lily, thank God you're home. Your uncle's in the lav and we can't get him out.'

'Have you pushed the door?'

'It won't move. And Noah won't answer us.' Josie thought she was going to have a heart attack. She felt faint as Lily tried without any result.

'I'll go over for Ben,' Lily cried and disappeared.

Bob took his wife's shoulders. 'Come inside whilst we wait. We mustn't panic. Everything's going to be all right.'

But Josie had a dreadful feeling it wouldn't be.

The long hospital passage was decorated with a few balloons but it still looked very depressing. Lily stared along the cold, shining tiles and felt her tummy revolt at the antiseptic smell. In one hour it was Christmas Day. How could all this have happened in an evening? If she hadn't gone out with her friends, she might have found Uncle Noah sooner. The images of Ben and Reube breaking down the closet door were fresh in her mind. The terrible crack of splintered wood still resounded in her ears. Her mother's cries seemed to fill her head. And the sight of them carrying her uncle out to Ben's car was almost more than she could bear.

She looked at her mother sitting beside her. 'It was the latch,' she kept repeating over and over.

'Shh, don't upset yourself,' said her father, but he looked bewildered too.

Lily watched Ben and Reube pace up and down the corridor. How long had her uncle been trapped in the closet? She had felt his hands as they had carried him out, and they were stone cold. He was semi-conscious but he hadn't recognized her.

Lily lost track of time as she sat there. Why didn't someone tell them how he was?

When the door opened and the doctor came out, Lily knew it was bad news. He walked to her mother and shook his head.

'Mrs Bright, I'm sorry to have to tell you that there was nothing more we could do.'

Lily froze. She couldn't believe what she was hearing. It was Christmas. Things like this didn't happen to people at Christmas.

Her mother cried out like a wounded animal. 'Oh, no, no!'

The doctor waited as she sobbed. Lily couldn't shed any tears. It was too unbelievable.

They listened in disbelief as the doctor explained that her uncle had died of natural causes and that his heart had just worn out. He said his passing had nothing to do with the latch or the cold, though he may have lasted longer in the warm.

Lily stared at him as Ben put his arm around her shoulders. She just couldn't believe that Uncle Noah was gone.

'Would you like to see him?' the doctor asked.

One by one they all trouped into the small room to say their goodbyes.

★

It was Christmas day and Ben was listening to the gulls. They were swooping early on the mud flats of the river for a feed. He needed to get a few hours kip. At least he had done all he could for the old man, but it hadn't been enough.

Ben shut the front door behind him and went into his darkened front room. He had made a feeble effort to transform it into home, but it wasn't like Love Lane. His plans for the New Year had been to find a lodger. Rent out a room and have a bit of company. A working bloke like himself would have done. Someone he could have a chat and a fag with. Now it didn't seem that important. Life was full of hustle and bustle, everyone striving to pay the bills and make a living. And then as bold as brass, the Grim Reaper swings his scythe and hey presto: there you were, waiting to see if you had wings on your back or a red-hot poker up your jacksey.

Noah Kelly had been a good man in his time. He'd made a few mistakes, but didn't everyone? In the last year or so, he'd got close to the old fellow. They had a lot in common, he'd discovered, as he'd listened with interest to his tales of totting. They'd both run businesses and though Noah had driven a horse and cart, not a four-wheeled vehicle, they'd both been bachelors with a double dose of ambition. The old man had loved his girl, his Lily. She'd been his companion as he'd totted the streets when she was small and he'd often talked about those happy days. Well, now he was with Samson and was driving his cart again in the clouds. That's how Ben liked to think of him anyway.

It wasn't for Noah he was grieving. He'd had his four score years and ten. It was for Lily he felt. The girl had taken a big blow. And he didn't much like the way she was looking. All pale and skinny, when once she was a real good eyeful, with a bit of meat on her. What, he wondered not for the first time, was happening in her life?

Was she happy? That was the question that needed answering. Had Noah got confused when he'd shared his thoughts recently about her safety? It was an old man's ramblings perhaps. On the surface, there seemed nothing amiss. And she certainly didn't want for a penny. But that look in her eye, all distant and sad . . .

Ben frowned thoughtfully as he sat in the darkness. What a Christmas this would be for the Brights.

'Well, Mr Kelly, I'll tell you this for nothing,' he said aloud, 'that girl to me, is what she was to you and until I know she's in good hands, I'll not rest.'

The moon suddenly shone a little brighter through the window, as if it were an answer. It was as though if you believed hard enough, you weren't disappointed. He'd never thought much about an after-life, only when his dad had gone, but he'd only been a kid then at that age and you think life goes on for ever. That one day you'll be walking round the corner and then you'll meet up again, all smiles and hellos and slapping of backs.

Ben smiled as the light streamed through the cheap

lace. It was so bright, that he could have read by it. He had the uncanny feeling that he wasn't alone, that someone up there had heard every word he'd said.

Lily sat in the back of the charabanc with Hattie. Her mum and dad were in front with Mrs James, Pedro and Reube and the Parks behind them. Charlie Brent, all done up in his best suit, was sitting mid way beside Ernie Roper who had left Gladys in charge of the Quarry. Grace Padgett and Mollie and Hector Flock had attended too; it had been a good turn out at St Peter's. The vicar, who had last seen them all at Hattie and Reube's wedding, had managed to hint from the pulpit that his Sunday back benches remained empty, but on the whole, his tribute to her uncle had been appropriate. Lily thought of how Uncle Noah, had he been there, would probably have disagreed with most that was said. But it was a good send-off despite that. The coffin, overflowing with flowers had been taken to the East London cemetery, and laid to rest amongst the broken angels and overgrown graves.

Lily knew her uncle had expressed a wish to be buried close to the island. His forebears and Josie's, were over at Greenwich. No one ever went over there. He would expect a visit or two, being within close proximity, although he would have preferred to be remembered for what he did in his life: his totting days and Samson, and the yard that had once overflowed with junk.

'You all right, Lil?'

'Yes, thanks.'

Hattie squeezed her hand. They were both wearing black gloves, hats and black coats, as were most of the women sitting in the charabanc. Ben had put over the roof, but it was still freezing. The New Year had brought with it snow, high winds and a fog, all within weeks of each other.

'Your Uncle Noah would have liked the service but I dunno about up there at the cemetery.' Hattie shuddered. 'It was a bit of a jungle.'

'I'm going to take flowers up once in a while.'

'He'd like that.'

Lily shook her head slowly. 'I still can't believe it all happened. I wake up thinking he's still here and getting in me mum's way and having a smoke with Dad in the yard.'

'It's early days yet,' Hattie said sympathetically. 'Soon you'll be going back to Dewar Street. Does Charles know what's happened?'

'I wrote to him and said Uncle Noah had died at Christmas and we couldn't arrange the funeral till the New Year. I said I'd be back at work as soon as I could leave Mum.'

Hattie sighed as the charabanc trundled along. 'It's a bit sad to think this is the last time we'll ever sit in the charabanc.'

Lily turned to look at Hattie. 'Why's that?'

'Ben's selling it. Those new coaches are more comfortable and cheaper to run.'

Lily fiddled with the end of her glove. 'I don't know what I would have done without Ben and Reube that night. They bashed the lav door down and got us to hospital. I just wish we'd come home sooner and found Uncle Noah. I keep thinking of him out there in the cold.'

'You must stop that,' Hattie replied sternly. 'The doctor said it would have happened anyway. Your uncle had a good life and was active right up to the end.'

Lily wiped away a tear.

Hattie patted her arm. 'A good stiff drink is what you need.'

But at the mention of this, Lily's stomach revolted. A stiff drink was the last thing she fancied.

Ben pulled the car up outside number thirty-four and glanced at his watch. Ten minutes to eight. It would take him a good half-hour to get to Dewar Street. Lil had told him she wanted to be there for eight thirty, so they were on time.

He jumped out and knocked on the door. Lily opened it. 'Come in, Ben.'

He looked at her white face. She didn't look well to him. Was she still grieving?

He stepped inside in time to see Mrs Bright hug her daughter goodbye. 'I wish you wasn't going, Lily.'

'The girl's got her job to do, Josie.' Mr Bright smiled. 'Thanks Ben, for running her back.'

'It's no trouble at all.' Ben wished the old boy was

here; he missed him a lot. The place didn't feel like it used to 'All right, Lil?' He took her bag.

She only nodded.

'Best be going.'

He didn't want to see her leave either. With all that had happened he hadn't had a chance to talk to her. It had been a rotten Christmas for everyone and he hadn't wanted to make it any worse. After all, Mr Kelly might have been wrong. He'd said so himself. Perhaps it was all a storm in a teacup as his mum would say. Them old boys down the Mission Hall had tales to tell as tall as Nelson's Column.

It was a sad farewell. Ben wished there was something he could say to cheer her up as he drove along. He wasn't very good at small talk. And what he wanted to say might not come out right.

As it was, the Monday morning traffic took up his attention. He kept his curses of other road users to a minimum and by half past eight, he pulled up outside number four Dewar Street. Now he could tell she was all on edge, her hand on the door.

'Well, here we are,' he said, glancing at the house.

'Thanks, Ben.'

'Come on, I'll see you safely in.'

He hopped out with her bag and opened her door. She looked very smart all done up in a hat with a feather and high heels that clattered as she let herself be led across the road. He could tell she'd had a good cry, but who wouldn't shed a tear after what had happened?

She got out her key. This time he went in with her and what shocked him the most, was the smell. It was musty and dark inside. He had to blink as he followed Lily, his eyes unaccustomed to the darkness. Lily turned on the electric light.

'There don't seem to be no one home,' he said, looking round. The big Christmas tree stood with its decorations.

He watched her walk into the drawing room and open the curtains. Light filled the big room, though the musty smell still pervaded.

'Mrs Brewer's supposed to be here. I'll look in the kitchen,' she told him.

Ben wandered round the hall, wondering what sort of a bloke could pay for all this and not live in it? It was a smart gaff all right, thanks to Lil. But it seemed to him that no matter what had been done to it, the heart and soul was absent. Just like the first day when they'd delivered that bloody aspidistra. He saw its green leaves now, poking out from behind the stairs. He drew his finger and thumb over them. If Mrs Brewer was here, she'd missed the dusting.

Ben strolled into the drawing room. It was cold and lonely with the curtains drawn to. He shuddered. He didn't want to leave Lily here. What intentions did this Charles Grey have towards her? He was a gent and a wealthy one at that, but was he all that he made himself out to be?

Lily appeared, looking like she'd seen a ghost. 'What's up, Lil?'

'Mrs Brewer has been and gone. She left me a note. Charles won't be home till next month.'

'What! February?'

Lily nodded. 'She didn't say why.'

'In that case,' he shrugged. 'I'll take you back home again.'

'No, I've got plenty to do.'

Ben walked towards her. 'Lil, this is a big place to be in all on your own. If he ain't living in it, what's the point of you being here?'

'It's my job.'

'You've had a bereavement,' he argued gently. 'You ain't got over it yet. Come home till he's back.'

She pulled away from him. 'No, I ain't a kid, Ben.'

'You're far from that, Lil. But it's like a tomb in here.'

She walked to the door. 'I'll be all right.'

He sighed, knowing he wasn't wanted. But for all its swank, he didn't like the place. Or perhaps, Ben thought as he reached the doorstep, he didn't like the bugger who owned it.

'Thank you for everything,' she said and kissed his cheek. 'Don't worry about me. I've got lots to keep me busy.'

He turned his cap in his hand. 'When will we see you next?'

'I'll write to Mum and say.'

451

'Lil?' He wanted to tell her that any time she needed him, he would be there. But she was holding herself apart and he knew it would probably do more harm than good to express his feelings. He gave her a big smile. 'Look after yourself, Funny Face.'

It was a long time since he'd called her that. The years rolled away. There was just her and him, like it used to be. He wanted to take her in his arms and protect her, but he couldn't. Instead he went down the steps and across the road. Jumping in the car, he made a last breezy salute.

Soon he was driving towards the city. But his mind was still on Lily. Something was wrong. And he hadn't been able to find out what.

Lily walked through the empty, neglected house. It was cold and lonely. From her pocket she took the two letters that Mrs Brewer had left on the table. One was open and addressed to Mrs Brewer. It was a dismissal note. Lily was shocked. Charles had told Mrs Brewer that her services were no longer needed as he wouldn't return to England until February. The other letter was sealed. It was to her.

Dated Friday, first of January 1937, there were only a few lines.

Dear Lily, I am sorry to tell you that I am overseas and won't return home until February. I would be pleased if you would take care of the house during this time. I have notified Mrs Brewer of my change in plans and have dispensed with her services. My best wishes for the New Year and I look forward to seeing you in due course. Yours, Charles.

Lily read it again and again, trying to find a personal sentiment in the words. But there was none. Why had he written such a cold letter? It was impersonal, little better than Mrs Brewer's. Why hadn't he sent his love or asked if she'd had a good Christmas? Why hadn't he told her that he missed her?

Her own letter informing him of her uncle's death was left unopened on the hall desk. Mrs Brewer had placed it there with several others when she had come to work after Christmas. It must have been a bitter disappointment to find she was dismissed.

If only Charles was here. He would tell her how much he loved her and everything would be all right again.

She sat in the drawing room, her thoughts in turmoil. Then, picking up her letter once more, she re-read it. Suddenly a thought came to her. Perhaps Charles had written this for Mrs Brewer's benefit! The two letters were almost identical. Perhaps he was concerned she would open it. Yes, that must be it!

She had forgotten how cautious Charles was. It was to be expected that he was discreet when writing. Lily sprang to her feet and hurried upstairs. She would light the fires, clean and cook, filling the house with mouth-watering aromas. There was the Christmas tree to dispose of and she would stock the larder with good, wholesome food.

When Charles arrived home they would sit by the fire and talk again. Lily shivered in anticipation. As she looked at her bed, she thought of the many nights they had spent there. It wouldn't be long before they were in each other's arms once more.

Chapter Twenty-Five

It was a clear, cold Friday in February. Lily was feeling unwell. She had told Hattie that she wouldn't mind having a baby. Now she was frightened. Was she expecting?

Should she see a doctor? But there was only Dr Tapper and she didn't want him to tell her mother.

Lily put on her best hat and coat and, taking the short walk to Poplar, caught the bus for Aldgate. As the shops and streets passed by she hoped Hattie wouldn't mind her calling at her work. But she had to talk to someone.

Lily alighted from the bus and hurried through the busy streets. Madame Nerys' was on the first floor of the big, smoke-blackened building where Lily had last visited three years ago.

Hurrying up the stairs, Lily knocked on the door above the nameplate.

'Come in,' someone called.

'I'd like to speak to Mrs James,' Lily said to the typist who sat behind a cluttered desk. Above her there were shelves of pattern books and thick, well-thumbed ledgers. She could hear the rattle of machines in the background. Lily was glad she had put on her best coat and feathered hat as the girl looked her up and down.

'Our manageress is very busy.'

'I won't keep her long. I'm a friend.'

'Well, I'll see.' A few moments later, the girl returned. 'She'll be out in a minute.'

Lily sat on one of the hard wooden chairs. Hattie would have a shock when she saw her. She sat nervously waiting, aware of the curious looks the typist gave her.

A door opened and Hattie appeared. She wore a buff-coloured dressmaker's coat and looked very harassed as she slipped off the pincushion on her wrist. 'Lil! It's you! Is something wrong?'

'I'm sorry to bother you.'

'It's no bother. Lil, you don't look at all well.'

'Can we go outside for a minute?'

Hattie turned to the typist. 'Peggy, I'm just stepping out for a second. If Madame Nerys calls, give me a shout will you?'

When they were alone on the landing, Hattie frowned. 'What's all this about, Lil?'

'I wanted to speak to you. You're the only one I can ask.'

'Why haven't you been home? You haven't been home since your uncle's funeral. We could have gone over to Greenwich together.'

'I know. But I don't want to see Mum.'

'Why ever not?'

'Hat, I think I'm going to have a baby.'

Hattie gripped her arm. 'You're not!'

'I don't know for sure. I wanted to ask you all about it. Me skirts are tight and I'm always feeling sick.'

'Have you had your periods?'

The door opened sharply. 'Madame Nerys wants you, Mrs James.'

'Tell her I'm coming, Peggy.'

When the door shut again, Lily stepped away. 'I'm sorry, I shouldn't have come here. I know how busy you get.'

'Lil, I can't stop now, but me dinner hour is at half past twelve. Sometimes I go to this café round the corner. Can you meet me there?'

'Yes, but I don't want to be a nuisance.'

'Don't be daft. You could always sit in the office with Peggy till I'm free?'

'No, thanks. I'll walk round the shops.'

'See you soon, then. You can't miss the café. Turn left outside. It's the only one in the street.' Reluctantly Hattie left her.

Lily ran down the stone steps and into the cold, wintery day. She pulled up her collar and as she walked she began to think about Charles and when he would be home. Would he ask her if she'd seen a doctor when she told him about her condition? Perhaps Hattie knew of one who would tell her whether she was having a baby or not.

★

Lily was glad to get into the warmth of the small café; it was cosy and filled with office workers. She sat at a table in the corner and ordered a pot of tea. Although she didn't really feel like drinking it, she went through the motions. When, at half past twelve, Hattie hurried through the door making the bell tinkle out, Lily hugged her fiercely. Her friend looked smart in a coat with a fur collar and her brown hair was curled neatly into a bob.

'Sorry I'm a bit late,' Hattie gasped as she returned Lily's embrace.

'You aren't. I've just been sitting here waiting.'

The waitress came over and Hattie looked at the menu. 'What do you want to eat, Lil?'

'Nothing, thanks.'

Hattie ordered two slices of sponge cake and a fresh pot of tea. 'If you can't eat it, I can,' she grinned as she took off her gloves and dropped them in her handbag. 'You look as though you could do with a square meal, Lil.'

'There's plenty to eat, I just don't feel like it.'

'Is Charles back?' Hattie placed her arms on the table. 'Ben said he'd gone away.'

'No, he's still abroad.'

Hattie glanced around discreetly and lowered her voice. 'When was your last period?'

'November.'

'So you could be nearly three months?'

Lily felt weak at the knees as she nodded. 'Yes. So you think I am?'

Hattie rolled her eyes. 'Oh, Lil, you are such an innocent.'

'I thought it might be Uncle Noah and all the upset causing me to stop.'

'I think that's highly unlikely. If your skirts are tight and you're sick and you've had no periods for three months I would say you are expecting.'

Lily swallowed. 'I thought I would be happy about it.'

'I did ask you if you'd discussed it with Charles,' Hattie said reprovingly.

'I haven't had chance.'

'What do you think he'll say when you tell him?'

'I'm not sure.' Like the proposal she had imagined, Lily had pictured him taking her into his arms and telling her that he couldn't be happier. Then in the next moment, all her dreams had evaporated as he was no longer around to tell her what she wanted to hear.

'Lil, have you considered . . .' Hattie's pencilled eyebrows arched as the waitress arrived with the order. They waited for her to leave before speaking again.

'Considered what?' Lily asked.

'Well, he might not want a child.'

'Why wouldn't he?' Lily gazed into Hattie's eyes. 'When he makes love to me, he tells me how much he cares for me.'

'Yes, but has he told you he'll stand by you if you get pregnant?'

'Not in so many words,' Lily was too embarrassed to say that Charles had not yet told her he loved her.

'We get too carried away to say much.' Lily blushed.

Hattie sat gazing into her face. 'Lil, he might not want it. Or ask you to get rid of it.'

Lily gasped. 'He would never do that.'

'Maybe not.' Hattie poured the tea and stuck the fork in her hand. 'Come on, I want to see you eat that.'

'I'm not hungry.'

'It's only a small slice.'

Lily tasted a little. Her stomach heaved.

'Do you feel ill?' Hattie's expression was now worried.

Lily nodded.

'I don't think there's much doubt you're expecting.'

Tears shone in Lily's eyes. She brushed them quickly away. For a while they sat there and then Hattie said gently, 'Lil, why don't you come home, just for a few days? It would do you good. Your mum would look after you. And we could talk this over again.'

'I don't want Mum to know.'

'But why?'

'Because she'd be ashamed of me.'

Hattie filled up her cup again. 'No, she wouldn't.'

'It would kill her.'

'Don't be so dramatic.'

'You know Mum.'

'She's got over all that happened to your dad.'

'This is different.'

Hattie sighed loudly. 'You're her daughter, she loves you.'

But Lily shook her head. 'How would she explain me having a baby to all her friends?'

'Well, it's happened before and will happen again. Just because you're not married, don't mean to say it's a crime.'

'But I want to be married!' Lily exclaimed. 'I want to be Charles' wife. I know I could make him happy.'

Hattie was silent again. When a tear trickled down Lily's cheek, she said quickly, 'Lil, remember that aristocratic girl that we made the wedding dress for?'

Lily nodded.

'Well, they had money, like your gent. Her family sent her off to have the baby and no one ever knew any different. Perhaps you could go off with Charles. He goes away a lot, don't he? And if he marries you, as you say he will, then there's no reason for anyone else to know, is there?'

Lily looked into her friend's face. It was a wonderful idea. Of course, that's what Charles would suggest, as he had more than enough money to solve the problem.

'That girl was married to her fiancé in our wedding dress,' said Hattie with a smile. 'Don't you remember how we said that wealth and position changed everything?'

Lily smiled too. 'Oh, yes. I'd forgotten.'

'So you see, it's not all doom and gloom.'

Lily clutched Hattie's hand. 'I was in a panic because Charles isn't home.'

'All the same, I think you should see the doctor.'

'Dr Tapper might tell me mum.'

'You'll have to sooner or later.'

'I know.'

'If you ask him, he won't say nothing I'm sure.'

Lily nodded. 'Perhaps you're right.'

'Now, eat the rest of that cake.' Hattie's eyes twinkled. 'Or I'll shoot you.'

Lily did as she was told. She even drank her tea. She was happy again. Charles would take care of everything. Why had she doubted him? She loved him so much. And she knew he loved her.

As they said goodbye, Hattie told Lily to keep in touch. 'If you can't come home, then send me a letter.'

'Yes, I will.'

'I wonder what you'll look like fat?'

Both girls broke into laughter. The cold February wind blew across them as they stood outside. Talking to Hattie had made her see things more clearly.

'You won't tell Reube, will you?'

'Not if you don't want me to.'

'Thanks.'

'And, Lil, make sure you eat properly. You're eating for two now.'

Lily felt better as she caught the bus to Poplar. But should she stop at the doctor's now? Could Dr Tapper be trusted to keep her secret?

There was only one way to find out.

★

Lily sat staring at the many coloured bottles in Dr Tapper's consultation room. She had seen them many times over the years. Red, purple, green and yellow. Linctus of all kinds. One of them especially she was familiar with. It was what Dr Tapper gave to her father for his cough. It cost sixpence a bottle and didn't do much good. But in the end, as they had all discovered, it was better than a drug.

Dr Tapper finished writing on the paper. His grey head came up slowly and his bushy grey eyebrows seemed to cover his eyes. Lily's heart was racing. After his gentle examination and writing down the dates of her last period, he had told her to take a seat. There had been a long and painful silence. Lily was desperate to know his verdict.

'By my reckoning, Lily, you are three months gone.'

Lily felt relief on the one hand and terror on the other. 'So I'm having a baby?'

'Yes, my dear, you are.'

Lily's mind was whirling. Now she knew for sure she would be able to tell Charles. They would decide what to do together.

'I would like to see you again next month.' He paused. 'Will the father stand by you?'

Lily clenched her hands together. 'I haven't told him yet.'

'Have you any plans for the future? Your mother, I take it, doesn't know?'

Lily sat upright. 'You won't tell her, will you?'

'Lily, you are a grown woman now. Your business is entirely your own. But of course . . . these things cannot be hidden for ever.'

Lily relaxed again. 'I'll have to think about it all. Will the sickness go?'

'Yes, it should very soon. My advice to you is to take things easy when you can. Now, how are you feeling in yourself?'

Lily smiled. 'Very well.'

'That's good. After losing your uncle at Christmas, I'm glad to hear you are recovering. And, as the months pass, I would like to see you regularly. Closer to your confinement date in August, we will arrange for you to see the midwife.'

Lily knew that could never happen. Everyone on the island knew the midwife, Mrs Hartley, who cycled on her bike through the streets, passing the time of day with all whom she met. She had delivered hundreds of babies, as had Dr Tapper. But Lily had already talked with Hattie about having the baby elsewhere. Charles would marry her and then see to it that they went away together.

'If there is anything else you want to speak to me about . . .?' He left his sentence unfinished.

Lily shook her head. 'Thank you.'

After the traumatic meeting was over, Lily hurried to the bus stop. She didn't want to be seen by any of her mother's neighbours or friends. The bus ride and short walk to Dewar Street gave her time to compose herself.

Their child would be a summer baby. Where would Charles take her to give birth?

There were so many questions she had to ask him. If only he would come home soon. Now she knew that she was having their baby, she needed him more than ever.

That night, Lily sat beside the fire deep in thought about the baby. Her condition wouldn't show for a few months yet. If, as Dr Tapper had said, she would soon feel better, she could go home and her mother wouldn't guess. By then she would have talked to Charles and made plans.

Lily was thinking about the nursery and the shade of blue she would have it painted when she heard the front door open.

'Lily! It's me!'

Lily felt a thrill go through her. She jumped up, every inch of her skin quivering and ran to the hall. A tall, unshaven figure stood there wearing a hat and long, crumpled coat.

'Oh, Charles, you're home!'

She was about to throw herself into his arms as she'd always imagined herself doing, when he swiftly bolted the door. 'Has anyone called?' he asked in a gruff, rasping tone.

'No. I was out for a few hours today—'

'But not tonight?'

'No.' Lily stared at him, at his untidy hair as he swept off the hat that he'd pulled down over his eyes. She had never seen him with a beard before. Above it his eyes looked wild and glittering.

She wanted to hold him but something stopped her. 'Charles, what's wrong?'

'Quickly, come into the drawing room.' He clutched her arm and hurried her out of the hall.

'Let me take your coat,' she said as he went to the windows and peered out into the darkness, before quickly closing them.

'Just fetch me a brandy,' he replied as he sank down on a chair by the fire. 'Please be quick. I haven't much time.'

What did he mean, not much time? she wondered as she went to back parlour. This wasn't the home-coming she had expected. Was he ill? His appearance had changed so much.

Lily poured a measure of brandy into the balloon glass and returned to the drawing room.

'Charles, there is something wrong, isn't there?'

He threw the drink to the back of his throat. 'Yes, I have something to ask of you.' He held out the glass. 'But first, another.'

Lily was confused. He didn't seem to be the same Charles that she knew; the elegant and sophisticated man who always seemed so in command of himself. What had happened in the time he had been away? She poured another drink and returned, her eyes going over the dirty coat that he still wore that looked as though it hadn't been clean in days.

'Lily, please sit down.'

She did as he told her, but even the fire couldn't warm the cold sensation that was creeping down the back of her neck.

'Lily, there will be men calling here soon. Not friends, but enemies who are determined to meddle with my career. I want you to tell them I'm not here. That you haven't seen me since before Christmas.'

'Are they policemen?'

'They are people who oppose my cause.'

As Lily didn't really know what his cause was, she lapsed into silence.

'They have followed me across the continent and tried to stop me as I set sail for Britain. It was fortunate that I was able to manage to lose them. But they know of this house and are certain to call here.'

'Would they hurt you?' she asked anxiously.

'They would go to any lengths to stop me.' He shook his head as though lost in some terrible thought. 'You see, I have been in Spain, where there is deep unrest.'

'Spain?' Lily repeated.

'Yes, I and many other intellectuals from all over the world. We are forming a party of resistance to the Communists.'

'But why do you have to go to Spain to form a party?' she asked in confusion. 'Couldn't you do it here?'

'We have been making preparations for many months,' Charles nodded. 'My friend, Mrs Covas, and I are passionate about freeing Spain. Her husband, a

Spaniard, was murdered by Franco's Nationalists.'

'Is that where you've been since Christmas?' Lily asked. 'With Mrs Covas?'

'Yes, she is a very brave woman.'

'But I thought you just furnished her house.'

'Forgive me for having misled you, Lily. We are on the edge of great change and I am privileged to be part of it. Now I can accomplish what I couldn't as a British naval officer in the war. Beginning with Madrid we can help to free the world of injustice and corruption, and do away with Communism forever.'

Lily was bemused. Spain was a long way away. She didn't understand its politics. Why did Charles want to be involved? What did Mrs Covas mean to him?

'Lily, there is so much that I want to tell you. But not now. Mrs Covas has gone to friends. I also will go to friends sympathetic to our cause. However, I must ask just one more favour of you. If you will say that you haven't seen me since last year, they will assume I am still abroad and that will give us time.'

Lily felt as though she was in some sort of play or drama. Charles was a different person. 'Charles, I'm frightened.'

He looked at her, as though suddenly seeing her. 'You mustn't be, my dear.' He stepped forward and kissed the top of her head. She trembled at his touch. All she wanted was to be safely in his arms.

'Oh, Charles, I've missed you so much.'

'And I, you.'

When he told her this, nothing mattered. Not his beloved politics or Mrs Covas. He had missed her and these were the only words she wanted to hear.

'Lily, I want you to be brave, now.'

She held on to him. 'Are you going?'

'We'll be together again soon, I promise.'

'There's so much I've got to tell you.'

'And I you, my dear girl. The world is changing. These are monumental times.'

She didn't understand what he meant. His eyes looked even more wild and filled with an expression that frightened her.

'Do you understand how important to me you are? Lily, it's only you I can trust. My dearest friend and ally.'

She looked into his passionate face. She wanted him to tell her he loved her.

'You will come back?' She clung to him and he held her close.

'Of course.' He kissed her passionately.

'Goodbye for now, my dear. Please lock the gate in the courtyard when I'm gone.'

She watched him take up his hat and push it down over his forehead. Then hurrying through into the kitchen and through the scullery, he opened the rear door. Outside the small courtyard was dark. Lily could just about see the high vine-covered wall at the end, with its small wooden gate. She heard it open and close.

Lily did as she was told and hurried to lock it. When she returned to the house, the silence deepened around her. She was very frightened as she waited. When would these men arrive?

They came very soon, pounding on the door. Lily's legs went weak. What was she to do? Charles had asked her to lie, but it wasn't really a lie as he wasn't here. It was only the part about not having seen him that was a real untruth. She waited, but the pounding grew louder.

With shaking fingers she opened the door. Four men burst in, pushing her back roughly. One of them looked foreign, with a mop of curly black hair. His dark eyes, like Charles', blazed with a fierce expression.

'Wh . . . what do you want?'

'This is the house of Señor Grey!' said the man in a heavy accent.

Lily nodded.

'Where is he?'

Lily backed away as he came towards her. She suddenly thought of the Blackshirt all those years ago, but Charles wasn't here now to save her.

'He's not here. I haven't seen him since December.' She said the words very quickly.

The man's bushy black eyebrows drew together. Her back was against the wall. 'Where is he?'

'I don't know,' she kept repeating. What was he going to do to her? He grasped her wrist.

'You see him!'

'No . . . no,' she cried out, in agony as he twisted her arm.

He began to shout in a foreign language. Why had Charles left her in the hands of these violent men?

Signalling to his friends, he directed them upstairs. She couldn't understand what was said, but she knew they were searching the house. What would they do? She heard banging and crashing from the rooms above.

Then one of the men ran down the stairs waving a book in his hand. This seemed to make them more angry. Lily thought they were going to kill her as she was thrown roughly to the floor. Her last thought was of Charles before the darkness engulfed her.

Chapter Twenty-Six

Hattie got off the bus in Stepney. Reube was working until late tonight so there was no need for her to rush home.

As Hattie walked down the road towards Ben's house, an older man came towards her. He wore a placard on his chest and on one side it advertised a meeting at the Mission Hall. 'Why are our young men fighting and dying abroad? Have your say in the Spanish Civil War!'

Hattie thought at once of Mr Kelly. He had gone to those meetings, she remembered. He'd been a bit of a rebel in his totting days, so Lily had told her. The man walked by and she smiled at him, but her mind was on Lil.

First her dad going off the rails and then her uncle dying on Christmas Eve. What would happen if she was pregnant? Hattie had her doubts as to whether Charles would support her. Lily was lovestruck and Hattie feared for her friend.

She had thought about Lily all afternoon. What could she do to help? She wanted to talk to Reube, but had been sworn to secrecy. Now Hattie found herself making her way to Ben's house. She had an idea, but she wasn't going to go back on her word to Lil. Just make a detour around it.

The terraced houses in Stepney were much smaller than those in Love Lane. She had been here once before with Reube, at the end of last summer. It was an ordinary smoke-blackened two-up, two-down, with a small back yard. Then she had been a bit sniffy about it. But now she wouldn't mind one like it herself. Her sights had been set on something bigger with a garden. But if the opportunity came to move out of Love Lane, she'd jump at it. After all, she and Reube could afford it.

A loud toot made her jump. She recognized Ben as he waved from the window of his cab and pulled into the curb.

'Hat, what are you doing round here?' Ben called as he jumped out.

She reached up to kiss his cheek. 'I got off early from work and was passing this way. You going to invite me in?'

Ben gestured towards the small terraced house with a dirty front step that needed a good clean. 'Course I am. But I ain't done much since you was last here.'

'I can see that.'

He chuckled as he pulled up the key. 'Mind yourself as you go in. There's a few bits and pieces in the hall.'

Hattie narrowed her gaze at the boxes, piles of books and clothes that littered the narrow hallway.

'A bit of a mess, I'm afraid.'

'Don't you ever clean up?'

'I would have if I knew you was coming.'

Hattie giggled. 'Oh well, I 'spect you're out working all the time.'

Ben pushed things aside with his foot and led the way to the tiny scullery. 'I'll put the kettle on.'

Hattie glanced at the draining board. It was full of dirty plates, cups and mugs. 'Blimey, I'm not drinking out of one of them!'

Ben grinned as he lit the gas. 'I got a few clean ones somewhere.'

'Your mum would have a fit if she saw this.'

'That's why I moved out, Hat. So I could please meself.'

Hattie moved a large brown paper bag and its smelly contents from a wooden chair and sat down gingerly. 'I wish I could. No offence to your mum, but I'm dying for a place of me own. I might as well still be looking after me own parents and Sylvester like I was before. Only now I've got them as well. I think you did the right thing, moving out.'

Ben took off his coat and made the tea. 'This ain't a palace, I know, but I'll get round to doing it up one day. Do you want to go in the other room?'

Hattie looked at him suspiciously. 'Not if it's full up with stuff.'

Ben laughed and set the cups before them. 'Tell you what, I'll leave the gas on, warm us up a bit.'

Hattie peered into her cup. 'Is the milk fresh?'

'No, it's condensed.'

'Oh, well, I'm thirsty so I'll drink it.' She cautiously sipped the tea.

'So what is it you want that's brought you to me doorstep tonight?' Ben said after a while.

Hattie shrugged lightly. 'I just thought I'd say hello.'

There was a teasing glint in his eye. 'You've done that so what is it really?'

Hattie sighed as she put down her cup. 'I'm just a bit worried about Lil.'

'Lil?' The smile slipped from Ben's lips. 'What about her? What's wrong?'

Hattie flapped her hand. 'Nothing, nothing. It was just she called round to see me at work today.'

'She did?' Ben frowned as he stared at her. 'What did she want?'

Hattie knew she had to be careful. 'I think she might be a bit lonely. You see, she's all on her own still.'

'You mean he ain't come back yet?'

'No, apparently not.'

'I didn't like leaving her there in the first place. Should have taken her home, but you know Lil.'

Hattie nodded. 'Yes, I do. But it occurred to me you could call by if you've got time. It wouldn't seem out of place, as you go there so often. You could just say you was passing by.'

Ben nodded thoughtfully. 'I was going to knock on the door as a matter of fact. See if she'd like a lift home sometime.'

'I'm sure she'd be pleased to see a friendly face.' Hattie sat forward and lowered her voice. 'But don't say I told you anything, all right?'

'Why's that?'

'She'd think we was both feeling sorry for her. And you know how stroppy she gets over her gent.'

Ben nodded slowly. 'You ain't wrong there, Hat.'

'Well, as much as I'd like to sit here gassing I'd better get back before Reube gets home from the Quarry.'

'I'd join him there for a quick one, only I'm gonna call round for Mr Next Door to drive him down the Mission Hall. There's a meeting on tonight for all the old boys.'

'Yes, I know,' Hattie said as she stood up. 'Personally I don't understand the politics much. Though Reube says Spain is all the talk down the pubs. It seems to have taken over where the Blackshirts left off. Some of the young blokes have boasted they were going off to join the International Brigade. Reube says they're only doing it as there ain't nothing else to do in the docks. They don't really understand the ins and outs, but think they'll get all the glory.'

'They won't find much of that in Spain,' agreed Ben. 'There's all sorts out there, knocking each other about for the hell of it. I hear these intellectuals in the back of me cab, all pretending to know what they're talking about. But I tell you what, whether it's commies, lefties, fascists, nationalists or idealists – even for a dimwit like me, I can hear the same old story. They all want the power. And the colour of power is blood red.'

Hattie looked at him carefully. 'You mean it will be a bloodbath, like the papers say?'

'Aren't all wars?'

'Yes, but it was different for us, the British. We was fighting the Kaiser for a good cause.'

Ben shrugged. 'I don't know about that.'

'But your dad gave his life for his country. And me brother was gassed for it. We've got to believe it was for something.'

'That's what they'd have us believe.'

'Who?'

'The blokes with the power. The manipulators.'

'Blimey Ben, you sound as though you should be down that meeting yourself,' Hattie shivered. 'Anyway, time to go.' She made her way cautiously to the front door, avoiding the hurdles.

Hattie sat in the back of the cab listening to Ben and his neighbour as they drove to the Mission Hall. It made her shudder again, all this talk of war. Even at work, one of the machinists had been boasting that her son was in full-time employment now. He had moved to Birkenhead docks and had helped to build a ship that cost over three million pounds to construct. It was called the *Ark Royal*.

★

Ben was up bright and early. Being Saturday he liked to get into the city as Saturday's tips were always a lot more generous. The female shoppers in the West End had plenty to spare and didn't stint when he gave them a bit of the old blarney. He enjoyed the frivolous side to his job; it was good to share a joke and at weekends it was easier, as the punters had time to enjoy themselves.

This morning, though, he drove to Dewar Street. He wouldn't stop long, just long enough to pass the time of day with Lil. He'd ask her if she wanted a lift home, but he'd throw it casually into the conversation. If her gent wasn't back then she might accept. Strange that Hattie had called by. He couldn't quite fathom that one out. But he could understand her concern as he'd shared it himself when he dropped Lily back there last time.

Pulling up outside number four, Ben glanced along the road. His lordship's car wasn't there. The more he thought about Charles Grey, the more Ben couldn't take to the fellow. But then again, Lily could obviously see a lot more in the man than he could.

Ben strolled casually across the road. Not a soul in sight. Taking the white steps in a couple of hops, he used the brass knocker. When no one appeared he knocked again, a little harder this time. Was she out? He was just about to leave when he heard a noise. 'Lil, is that you?'

The door opened. His stomach almost came up as she swayed, reached out and by a fraction, he caught her. Sliding his arm beneath her, he lifted her gently in.

Booting the door closed behind him, he stood with her in his arms, his mind in a panic as a cold, clammy sweat crept down the back of his neck.

Ben sat looking into space. He couldn't believe he was here again. Thank God it wasn't where they'd taken Mr Kelly, not to that same small room where it had already been too late to help. But to a ward, somewhere at the end of a maze of passages that looked all alike to him. They'd brought her up here, then told him to go away and return later. Of course, he hadn't done that. He'd just walked around, his heart beating like a drum as he'd thought back to what he'd found in that place. Who had been there? and what had they done to her? Ben didn't know where to put his anger. It was building up in him like a volcano. He wanted to get hold of someone and . . .

He closed his eyes, trying to block out the mental image of the bruise on her face and the bright red blood that had congealed there. He'd tried to think of what to do first, but instinct had governed his actions and he'd carried her out to the cab and driven like a bloody lunatic to the hospital. Then they'd asked him all sorts of daft questions. How could he tell them anything? He didn't know.

He got up and walked to the window. It was raining outside, the kind of cold heartless rain that went with a day like this.

A voice came from behind him. A small woman

dressed in a dark blue uniform and white cap. She addressed him. 'Mr James? The doctor would like to see you.'

'Is she all right?'

'She's comfortable, yes.'

'Can I see her?'

'All in good time. Come this way, please.'

Ben followed, his mind going round in circles. Comfortable. What did that mean? Why couldn't he speak to her?

The doctor was walking towards them and smiled as he looked Ben up and down. 'You're Mr James?'

Ben nodded. 'Can I see Lil?'

'Yes, in a moment. I understand you brought Miss Bright here today?'

'Yes, in me cab.'

'But you know her personally?'

'Yes, she's a close friend.'

'Well, Mr James, we have treated her wrist and head injuries. But she is still suffering the after effects of being unconscious. She doesn't remember anything after her fall, unfortunately. So we have no information between this time and when she said you found her.'

'Lil said she had a fall?'

'Yes, that's correct. Why? Did you think otherwise?'

Ben quickly shook his head. He didn't want to dispute Lil's story and perhaps that was what happened. But had she said anything about the house being wrecked?

'So you know nothing about what happened?'

'No.'

'Was Miss Bright in any trouble?'

'What do you mean?'

'In any suspicious cases, it's our duty to inform the police.'

Ben didn't like the way the doctor was sounding. 'I don't see there's any reason for that,' he answered. 'If Lil says she's had a fall, that's all there is to it.'

Ben stared into the doctor's unflinching gaze. He didn't know what had happened to Lily. He needed to talk to her before he said anything more.

'She also tells us that she has no family to inform.'

Ben felt a jolt of shock. Why had she said that? Now he knew that it was no accident. Lily was lying. And he had an unpleasant feeling he knew why.

'No ... no family as I know of,' he colluded. Lily didn't want anyone to know what had happened. Had Charles Grey assaulted her? A surge of anger threatened to overwhelm him, before he managed to compose himself as he decided that whatever was causing Lily to lie, he would have to go along with it for now.

What did Hattie know, that she hadn't told him? Had Lil been in trouble when she visited Hattie yesterday? Now he thought about it, Hattie wasn't likely to have turned up at his house without good reason. There must be something more to all this. Did it have anything to do with what Noah Kelly had told him about Charles Grey?

As Ben tried to think, the doctor spoke again. 'Miss

Bright has asked to see you, but I suggest you keep this visit short. She will need time to recover both physically ... and indeed, in other respects. Meanwhile we've given her something to help her rest.'

Ben felt the insides of his stomach curl as the doctor gestured for him to follow. What did he mean, 'other respects'?

Lily blinked through the pain. She kept slipping in and out of consciousness. What had happened to her since those men had come to the house? One of her arms seemed to be in a splint. Had that man broken it?

Suddenly she felt her good hand grasped. 'Lil, it's me, Ben. How are you feeling?'

She couldn't say how bad her head, back and arm felt. Or that she felt bruised inside. She tried to smile instead.

'It's all right, Lil. I'm here.'

But she wished it was Charles. Where was he? Why hadn't he come for her?

'Lil, what happened?'

The doctor had kept asking her that. She didn't want him to know what happened. She didn't want anyone to know what happened. She had to protect Charles.

'The doctor said you told him you'd fallen down the stairs?'

She nodded.

'That ain't true, is it?'

'I want to go home, Ben.'

'You can't, Lil. All the furniture is broken.'

She sobbed, trying to turn her head so he wouldn't see. 'Don't tell them about that – please!'

'I haven't.'

'And don't tell Mum and Dad.'

'Why, Lil? What's going on?'

'I don't want them upset.' She knew that if Ben told her parents they would come here. She didn't want anyone to know what had happened at the house. She wanted to see Charles, only Charles, who would make everything all right.

Another tear slipped out, followed by another.

He squeezed her hand gently. 'Look, I ain't gonna upset you now. Whatever's happened, you've got me and that's a promise. I'll let you rest now and be back tomorrow. All right?'

'You won't tell no one?'

'Course not.'

She nodded, wishing she could leave and go home. Where was home? Where was Charles? What about her baby? Then closing her eyes, she felt her fingers slip away from Ben's as she fell into another deep sleep.

That evening, Ben stood in the gloomy hallway of number four Dewar Street. He'd only had a few minutes to glance round this morning as his priority had been getting Lil to hospital. Now she was in safe hands, he could at least try to discover what had happened. He'd had the presence of mind to slip the front door key into his pocket and the house appeared to be as they left it.

The desk was broken and battered and still lying on its side. The aspidistra was crushed. In the dining room they'd smashed the ornaments, pulled down the drapes and scattered the ashes of the fire over the rug. He went to the kitchen where the dresser was pulled on its side over the broken china.

Upstairs in one of the bedrooms he found mens' clothing, which must be Charles Grey's by the look of it. Dozens of expensive suits, trousers, coats and shirts were ripped to shreds and scattered over the bed and floor. Now, that was vindictiveness of another sort, Ben thought as he frowned at the damage! If it was a burglary, they had omitted to take the imposing paintings on the wall. The mantel clock and figures were broken, not stolen. What burglar would miss out on taking the swag with him?

Ben went out onto the landing. Slowly he made his way up the last flight of stairs. Lily had told him her rooms were on the top floor.

Here, little seemed to have been touched. It was as though someone had thrown a few things about; the books and cushions and an expensive-looking coffee table was on its side. But the light coloured couch was all in one piece as was a modern, black-framed mirror still intact on the wall. Beneath it stood a pink glass statue, depicting a reclining woman. Ben picked it up, drawing his fingers over its delicate curves. His anger subsided somewhat. Whoever had come in here had taken no real interest in gaining revenge on a woman.

Lily's bedroom had also escaped the intruders' attention. It was clearly a feminine room. The frills and fancies were definitely Lil, he could smell her everywhere. On top of the dressing table were her bits and pieces and a pair of pink slippers poked out from beneath the wardrobe.

Ben breathed in Lily's essence. For a moment he forgot his mission as he gazed around him, picturing Lily here, seeing her sitting at the window and gazing out over the rooftops of London. Had she been happy here? What was her true relationship with Charles Grey? Had they ever shared this bed?

Ben shook his head as if to clear his thoughts. Then, seeing Lily's bag on a chair, the bag he had carried many times to the car, he took it to the wardrobe. Pulling out her clothes he folded them into the bag. On top of these, he added the contents of the chest, her purse and personal effects. When he had everything, he hurried back downstairs again. By the upturned desk, he saw something he had missed before; pages torn from a book.

He examined them, frowning as he read the text. Then pushing these too into the bag, he cast his eyes round for the last time. Taking a final look at number four Dewar Street, he let himself out. With Lily's bag safely beside him, he drove the cab quickly towards Stepney and home.

Chapter Twenty-Seven

The following day, Lily was moved to another ward. There were six beds on either side and a young girl was in the bed next to her.

'What's wrong with you?' she asked as Lily was fussed over by the nurses.

'I fell down the stairs.'

'Did you break anything?'

'Yes, me wrist.'

'Come on now, you two,' a nurse interrupted as she drew the curtains round Lily's bed. 'You can get to know each other later. But now it's a bed wash for you, Miss Bright.'

It was the first of many, Lily was to discover, as with her arm in a sling, she couldn't do much herself.

The day seemed very long and no doctor came round.

'It's Sunday,' said the girl whose name was Violet. 'Unless one of us is very bad, they don't bother. Are you having any visitors this afternoon?'

Lily shrugged. She just wanted to close her eyes and

make it all go away. She didn't have any personal effects. They were all at the house. The nurse had put her in a hospital nightgown and given her a toothbrush and flannel. She felt bruised and battered and was desperate to ask about her baby. Was there still life inside her?

Lily nibbled at the meal they brought round. She wasn't hungry. Her wrist ached a lot, although the nurse had given her a pill to relieve the pain. The stitches in her head had crusted over and she had no comb to use on her hair. They had given her one to use, but it was her left hand that wasn't affected and she couldn't find the energy to do a parting.

She was fast asleep when she felt a touch. 'Lil?'

She opened her eyes slowly. 'Oh, Ben, it's you. I was wondering if you'd come.' She looked round the ward. It was full of visitors.

'Course I was coming. Here.' He held up a bunch of flowers.

'Oh, thanks.'

'And here's some other things.' He put her bag on the chair.

Lily pushed herself up. 'Me bag! How did you get that?'

'I went back last night.'

Lily sat forward abruptly and felt dizzy. Ben gently pushed her against the pillow. She looked up at him. 'Was Charles there?'

'No. No one was.' He sat down on the chair, glancing round the busy ward. 'Lil, how are you feeling?'

'I'm all right.'

'You've had a big bang on your head and that wrist looks painful.' He frowned. 'Do you remember how you did it?'

'No.' She didn't want to say anything in case it implicated Charles.

'You told the doctor you fell down the stairs. But you also told him you didn't have no family. Now, Lil, I don't know what's going on, but look at it from my point of view. I call on the hop and find you looking like death warmed up. I can't help but think if I wasn't there, what would have happened?'

'Charles would have found me.'

'He ain't found you yet, has he?'

Tears sprang into Lily's eyes. She didn't want to cry, but a little of the truth hurt.

He squeezed her good hand. 'Maybe I shouldn't have said that. But I'm worried for you. It don't look to me like you fell down the stairs.'

'I don't want to talk about it for now.'

He nodded. 'If that's what you want.'

'So there was no one at the house?'

'Not a soul.'

'Did they . . .' she caught herself in time. 'Were me rooms all smashed up?'

'No, most of it was in order. I brought all your things in the bag as I didn't know what you would want.'

'All I want is to go home. Charles said he would come back soon.'

He nodded patiently. 'Well, until that happy day, you'll have to make do with me as your visitor.'

Lily knew she was being unkind to the one person who had helped her in all this. But she couldn't help herself. She was confused and hurt and she was taking it out on Ben.

'You look tired, Lil. I'll love and leave you for now.' He stood up and put the flowers on the cupboard. 'I'll call by again tomorrow.'

'You don't have to.'

'No, I don't, that's true. But I will.' He stood awkwardly in his best suit, shirt and tie with his hair smoothed back like he always liked to do it for best.

Lily felt her bottom lip tremble. Why was she being so unpleasant? She felt so alone and unhappy. All she could think about now, though, was whether her baby was still alive. Even more than Charles. What if she had lost it?

'Keep your chin up, gel.'

She managed a smile. But after he had gone, she turned her face to the pillow. She was glad the girl next to her had lots of visitors. She didn't want to talk to anyone. She just wanted to be at home with Charles.

The next day Ben called at the hospital after work. He took some chocolates and an illustrated magazine.

'That's nice, thank you.' Lily was sitting up, her bruised face was healing and there was only a slight shadow there. But Ben cringed as he looked at it. To think of her being hurt upset him so much. All the more, if he let his imagination wander.

'How is the arm?' he asked as he sat down.

'I saw the doctor this morning. He said it will be in plaster for a few weeks.'

'Can you come out before then?'

'Yes. They want to take the stitches out first. And get me back on me feet. I walked around a bit today.'

'Is there anything you want?'

'No, you brought it all. Have you gone round the house again?'

'No. There was no reason.'

'Have you still got a key?'

'Yes, I kept it in case.'

'Would you go tomorrow and see if Charles is there?'

Ben felt his stomach churn. He didn't want to meet up with Charles Grey just yet. As he didn't know the ins and outs of what had gone on, it wasn't for him to judge. But Lil had been hurt and it was under Grey's roof that it had happened. Lil was keeping stumm but couldn't she see that the bloke was not exactly rushing to her bedside in concern?

'I know I shouldn't ask you,' she said in a whisper. 'You've done more than enough for me already.'

'If you want me to, I will.'

He looked at her in the hospital bed, the sling on her arm, her bruised face and cut head. Her tiny body under all them hospital covers, she was like a little girl. Her lovely hair needed a bit of a comb. He would ask her if he could do it, but he didn't have the nerve. He tried to think of a joke to crack, but he was too choked up. The more he looked at her the more he was certain there hadn't been a fall down the stairs. The more he thought and thought, the more he wanted to get hold of the bugger who had made all this happen. He wasn't certain whether it was Charles Grey or someone else, but one day he'd find out. And then woe betide the person responsible, as his anger would know no bounds.

Lily looked at the chocolates that Ben had brought her. Together with the flowers that the nurse had put in vase, they made her little space feel more homely. All day she had been thinking about what the doctor had told her this morning. Her baby was still alive. He had survived. When the doctor told her, she had felt a great, overwhelming relief. It had been a shock to think that she had felt so deeply about her child. The little life had come by accident, but with great love. She and Charles had made a person between them. Now she knew he was still inside her, she was happy. Charles would put the house in order and they could return to a peaceful life.

Whoever those men were, Charles would not let them come again. Soon they would be a family. They would make him as happy as Delia had.

Lily closed her eyes as she lay there. She saw Charles, his dark eyes and beautiful smile. Oh, Charles, come to me soon. I miss you.

*

It was Friday again when Hattie knocked on Ben's door. She hadn't heard from him or from Lil, either. She had waited all week, thinking Reube might have seen his brother. But he hadn't. Hattie didn't like the silence.

Ben opened the door. 'Oh, it's you, Hat.'

'Yes, it's me.'

'You'd better come in.'

'I see you've cleared up,' she tried to joke as she entered. The hall was still full of things as she stepped over them. But as she neared the kitchen Hattie stopped. Her eyes widened at the sight of the dark brown bag. 'That's Lil's!' she exclaimed, her gaze travelling to Ben.

He pushed back his hair and nodded.

'Is she here?'

'No, but I've seen her.' He beckoned her into the kitchen. 'Sit down, I'll put the kettle on.'

Hattie sat down at the kitchen table, careful not to let her sleeves touch the surface of the table cluttered with dishes. Her heart was racing as she watched Ben's slow movements. What was he about to tell her?

'Reube going up the Quarry tonight, is he?' he asked as he put the tea in front of her.

Hattie nodded. 'Yes, he thought you might be up there as well.'

'No, I'm going to Poplar Road Hospital.'

Hattie froze. 'Why?'

'To visit Lil.'

Hattie put her hand to her mouth. 'Oh my Gawd! What's wrong? Is it the baby?'

493

'What do you mean, baby?'

Hattie put her hands up to her face. She had let Lil's secret out. She drew her hands slowly down. 'I shouldn't have said that.'

'Are you telling me that Lil is expecting?'

Hattie watched the colour drain from his face. He sat there staring at her. He opened his mouth, then gave a little choke.

'She might be. She was going to see the doctor.'

'Christ, Hat.' Ben leaned on the table as though he'd been winded. 'That makes it all the worse.'

'Makes what worse?'

'I found her wandering about all dazed on Saturday morning. She said she'd fallen down the stairs and hurt her arm. I took her straight to the hospital.'

'And you never told me?'

Ben looked at her keenly. 'She asked me not to tell anyone and I, like you, Hat, kept quiet.'

Hattie felt her cheeks go red.

'Come to think of it, the doctor said she needs time to recover physically and in other respects. Is he talking about the baby?'

Hattie shrugged. 'I don't know.'

'Someone had been to the house and given the gaff a good going over.'

'Oh my God, Ben!' Hattie felt sick. 'Was it burglars?'

'If it was, they didn't take nothing.'

'Where was Charles Grey in all this?'

'She don't know. Just keeps saying he'll be back.'

'Poor Lil. Can I go to see her?'

'She don't want anyone to know what happened.'

'But I'm her friend.'

'I know.' He shook his head slowly. 'All she wants is to go back to Dewar Street. She believes he'll come back for her. But now you've told me about the baby, I suppose I can understand why.'

Hattie began to get angry. 'She's waiting for a sod who don't care nothing for her, or else he would never have let something like this happen to her.'

Ben nodded. 'I can't believe she fell down the stairs, Hat. I don't know who done it, she won't say, but what kind of bloke leaves a woman – *his* woman – to face what she had to?'

Hattie sat in silence. What was going on in Lil's life? Much more than she had disclosed, that was obvious. 'I want to know if she's still . . . if she's still got the baby.'

Ben frowned. 'Does he know about her condition?'

'Lil was going to see the doctor first.'

'You know,' said Ben slowly, 'after what Noah Kelly told me, I think he's in with some dubious types.'

'What did Mr Kelly tell you?'

'There's the name of Charles Grey being bandied about down the Mission Hall. He was sympathetic to Mosley in his time, until Mosley fell from favour. This Charles Grey has fascist leanings, does a good bit of travelling abroad to drum up funds for the movement.'

Hattie gasped. 'Do you suppose it could be the same Charles Grey?'

'It would be a big coincidence if there was two.'

'Did Mr Kelly tell Lil this?'

'He was going to, but asked me to find out what I could first.'

'And did you find out anything?'

'Not until Saturday night when I returned to Dewar Street to get Lil's things. And then I found these . . .' He stood up and went out to the hall to fetch the bag. Opening it, he took out some pieces of paper.

'What are they?'

'Pages from a book.'

Hattie read the large black print on one of the torn pages. 'This is that book the Blackshirts were always waving about.'

Ben nodded. '*Mein Kampf*.'

'Why is it all torn up?'

'Someone didn't go along with his reading.'

'Do you think it was the people who hurt Lily and broke the furniture?' Hattie asked after a pause.

'Looks like it.'

'So she didn't fall down the stairs?'

'Not unless she was pushed.'

Hattie dropped the pieces on the table. She couldn't believe that this was happening to Lil.

'Ben, Lil don't know any of this, else I'm sure she would have told me.'

He brought his hand down hard on the table, making her jump. 'Do you know, Hat, I don't give a toss for any man's politics or his intention to practise them as this is a free country to choose as you want. But when a life is endangered because of them, a loving and innocent life, then I can find no sympathy in my heart for the coward who hides those beliefs behind a woman's skirts.'

Hattie felt a cold shiver go down her spine as Ben's soft grey eyes filled with icy cold anger.

Lily sat in the small waiting room next to Sister's office. It was a week since she had been admitted to hospital. She wanted to go home. Many times she had asked the Sister if she could leave.

'We'll have to see what the doctor says,' had been the stock reply.

Lily knew that they were keeping her under observation as they were concerned about the baby. But if she was at home, she would be happy. The girl in the next bed kept asking her about her life, and she didn't want to be rude but it was getting awkward.

Where was Charles? Ben had been back several times but he hadn't returned.

The Sister came out of her office. 'The doctor says we need to keep you a few more days, Lily.'

'But I'm well now.'

'Lily, it's nearly visiting time. Why don't you go back to bed and wait for your young man?'

Lily knew they all thought Ben was the father of her child as he came every day to visit her. She allowed them to think it, as Charles hadn't appeared. Sitting on her bed, Lily watched the visitors arrive. The girl in the next bed was soon surrounded. Ben was late today. Where was he? Had he found Charles? Would Charles come instead? Her heart began to beat fast with anticipation. She couldn't throw herself into his arms because of the sling, but it didn't matter. He would hold her gently and tell her he would never allow this to happen again.

Ben came through the doors and as usual, he wore his best suit and carried a small gift. He had brought her something every night. Lily looked for Charles, but he wasn't there.

She flopped back against the pillow.

'Hello, Funny Face.' Ben pushed the bag of red apples into her good hand. 'Get your mincers round these.'

'Did you find Charles?'

Ben shook his head.

'What about the letter I wrote to him?'

'It's still where you told me to leave it, on the kitchen table. Now, what did the doctor say about you coming out?'

'I've got to stay a bit longer.'

'Well, that's sensible.'

Lily couldn't contain her impatience. 'You don't understand. I've got to see Charles.'

But Ben just sat there. He didn't bother to answer her any more when she talked about Charles. He didn't even look as though he was interested.

Lily was relieved when he left. She wanted to be on her own to think of how she could get away from this place. If only Charles would come for her. In her letter she had written the details of where she was and begged him to come and get her. 'Charles,' she whispered into her pillow, 'where are you?'

Chapter Twenty-Eight

It came as a surprise when the doctor finally pronounced her well enough to leave and Lily was astonished as he drew the curtains back round her bed and handed Sister his notes.

'We've given you a date to come back and have the plaster removed,' he said, smiling. 'And now we have an assurance that you can be looked after—'

'You mean Charles has come?' Lily blurted.

The doctor frowned. 'Mr James.'

Lily sank back down. The doctor must have spoken to Ben, but it was Charles on whom she had pinned her hopes.

'Now, don't look so downhearted,' the doctor said kindly. 'If you would like to come to the office we can arrange the final details. Doctor Tapper, whose name you gave us to write to, has been very concerned about you.'

Lily sat in the office, listening to the doctor read out the information in his letter from Dr Tapper. The words of advice about her pregnancy, what she should eat and how she should rest, went in one ear and out of the other.

'Mr James has assured us that he will take care of you,' the doctor smiled knowingly. 'I'm sure you and the baby will be in good hands whilst you and Mr James make arrangements for the future.'

Lily looked up. He thought Ben was the father of her baby! She gazed at the doctor, who seemed to be waiting for her to speak. But she knew if she told him the truth, she might not get out of hospital, leaving this place was all that mattered. The moment she set foot outside the building, somehow she would return to Dewar Street.

Ben brought her bag later that day and Lily managed to dress with the help of a nurse but she still felt very weak and clumsy. The Sister and nurses were very kind to her as she left but her heart was pounding as Ben wheeled her down the corridor in a wheelchair. What had he told them about the baby? Or had they just assumed it was Ben's.

'We'll soon be home,' he said as he took her bag and stowed it in the boot, then jumped in the cab beside her. 'I'm going to take good care of you at my house for a while. After I've fed you up and got you on your feet then you can think about what you want to do.'

'I know what I want,' Lily said stubbornly. 'I want to go to home to Dewar Street.' It was all she could think of.

Ben sighed, rubbing his forehead with his hand. 'Lil, there ain't nothing there for you, trust me.'

'Charles will come back, I know it.'

'Look, Lil, there's no way I'm leaving you alone in a big, rambling house to fend for yourself. I gave the doctor me word I'd look after you and that's what I intend to do.'

Lily turned to him angrily. 'So you do know about the baby?'

Ben felt his face go scarlet. 'I know it's none of me business.'

'No, it isn't.'

'But you wanted to get out of that hospital, didn't you? When I was asked if I could guarantee you rest and care, naturally, I said yes. They must have took it for granted that you and I were ...'

'Well, we ain't.'

'I know that.'

Lily heard Ben take a deep breath, trying to disguise his hurt. She knew that all he was doing was trying to look after her but there was nothing more important to her in the world than getting home to Charles.

'Arguing is daft, Lil,' he said in exasperation after a while. 'Look, there's things you've got to face up to. I know you're not well enough to discuss them, but—'

'Please, Ben,' Lily interrupted, her eyes beseeching him to do as she asked. 'I know you mean well and what you said to the doctor was for my benefit, but I've got to see Charles and tell him about the baby.'

'I grant you he needs to be told,' nodded Ben, 'but I ain't letting you stay in that place on your own, not after what happened.'

'Then stay with me? There's plenty of room. You could even ask Mrs Brewer to come in again during the day. She could help me dress and do the house and then you could go to work and wouldn't be worried about me.'

'You drive a hard bargain, Lil.'

'Oh, please, Ben?' Lily was desperate. She knew that if Charles wasn't there, then Ben was right, she would be afraid those men might come back again. But her love for Charles was greater than her fear and if Mrs Brewer and Ben were with her, she would be protected.

'I must need me head examining,' Ben growled as he turned on the engine.

Lily closed her eyes and breathed a long sigh of relief as she realized she had finally got her way.

Ben couldn't believe he was doing this as he'd made all the arrangements for Lil at home. He'd had a big tidy up and cleaned through. Yesterday he'd bought new sheets and a cover, a blue one, for the bed in the spare room. His private hope was that after a few weeks of recuperation at his house, she would have had time to think through her future.

Now he was driving her back to Dewar Street. The girl was adamant and there was nothing he could do to change her mind. But this time, he was going to make sure that he kept an eye on her. The next few days he'd take off work – he could afford it. There was all the broken stuff to ditch, though Mrs Brewer could come in and do the chores, but if his lordship returned, then he wanted to be there when he did. Ben's face hardened as he came to the decision that he wasn't going to leave Lil without some guarantee of her safety. He had those pages of *Mein Kampf* in his breast pocket and he'd show them to Charles Grey, tell him that Lil had to be in full possession of the details before Ben left her there. Then, if it was Lily's choice to be with the man, so be it. If they had a kid between them and it was given a legitimate start in life, then Ben could swallow the man's politics. As long as he loved Lil and would take care of her and the infant, that's what mattered. Until then, he was going to sit on her shoulder like the proverbial parrot. If anyone even looked at her the wrong way, he'd floor them.

It was a grey morning, but the rain held off as Ben turned the cab into Poplar. The streets were busy with mid-week shoppers, and there was a nice bit of trade going on. He took a glance at Lily as they passed the Queen's and turned the corner, where his heart missed a few beats. He couldn't park outside number four as there was a van blocking the way.

'The door's open!' gasped Lily, clutching his arm as she sat forward. 'Someone's in the house. It must be Charles!'

Ben stopped the car on the other side of the road. His

first reflex was to clench his fists as an animal desire for revenge swept over him. Then seeing the look of joy on her face, he put his feelings aside.

'Oh, I knew he'd be back.'

'Wait there, whilst I see.' He jumped out and walked across to the van. Furniture was piled high inside. 'Robson's Removals and Storage,' was painted in bold black letters above the running boards.

Ben ascended the white stone steps. Two men pushed past him carrying a couch. Another man followed bearing a chair draped with a blue cover.

A man in a bowler hat, holding a sheaf of papers, came out of the house. 'Good morning, young sir, and how can I 'elp?' he said as he looked Ben up and down.

'What's happening here?' Ben asked, trying to get a look inside.

'Are you a buyer?'

'Of what?'

'The house, chum.' The man slid a pencil from behind his ear and made a mark on the paper. 'Now we'll take the last bed,' he shouted at two men who walked past them. 'Make sure you got all the boxes from upstairs, too.'

'I didn't even know it was for sale,' said Ben. 'I'm looking for Mr Grey, the owner.'

'You won't find him here, not any more.'

They stood aside as a large iron bedstead was brought out. With a sinking feeling Ben recognized it as Lil's.

'That's me bed!' cried Lily as she stumbled towards them.

Ben took her arm. 'You should have stayed in the cab, Lil.'

'What are they doing? That's all me stuff!'

'Well, it ain't no longer, love,' said the man, waving his papers. 'Me name's Robson and I bought everything in the house, lock, stock and barrel right down to the last ornament. Mind you, there's a lot we had to chuck away as it was all broken. Might be able to make something of the rest though.'

'Where's Mr Grey?' Lily asked in a faint voice.

'Met him here yesterday, didn't I? Seemed in a bit of a rush to get shot of this lot as he said he'd been burgled and was putting the gaff up for sale. When I offered him a price, he did the deal there and then and told me he didn't want nothing left, as the staff that used to live here had all moved out.'

'But I live here,' Lily said, tears in her eyes. 'I hadn't moved out. I was only in hospital. I left him a letter to say where I was.'

'Look, love, I don't know about that, I'm only a bloke who's trying to make a fair living. I didn't find no clothes or anything personal in the house, otherwise you could have had it. Now, we're almost finished, so I'll bid you good day.' Mr Robson walked back to the van.

'Lil, come away.' Ben tried to lead her back, but she rushed up the steps and into the house.

Ben went to go after her, but Mr Robson shook his

head. 'I should let her have a good look round, chum, to see for herself that there ain't nothing in there now. Nasty affair it must have been, that burglary. Very upsetting. Was she one of the maids?'

Ben shook his head sadly. His heart almost broke in two as he waited, looking up at the empty shell of a house that Lily had loved so much.

Lily sat on the bed in the small bedroom of Ben's house in Stepney. The room was about as large as one of the broom cupboards at Dewar Street. It was just able to fit a bed and small wardrobe. There was a jam jar on the window sill filled with fresh flowers.

She still couldn't believe what she had seen with her own eyes at Dewar Street. Everything had been sold to a furniture dealer called Mr Robson. Walking round the empty rooms, she hadn't recognized it. Hers and Charles' beloved home, desolate and empty. She'd watched powerlessly as the last of the furniture had been piled on the van.

'Lil? Can I come in?' Ben appeared and put down her bag. 'It was a good job I got all your things.'

Lily nodded.

'Is everything all right? I know this room is small compared to what you're used to.'

Lily wanted to be grateful, but her home was gone. Where was Charles? Why had he sold it and all their lovely furniture without telling her?

'Why don't you lay down and rest for a while?'

Lily shook her head. 'I don't know why you bother with me.'

'What are friends for? You've been through a lot.'

'Why didn't Charles tell me about the house?'

'He must have had his reasons.'

'He told Mr Robson it had been burgled and the staff had all moved out.' Lily looked down at her stomach. 'Is that what he thought, that I was staff?' The tears pricked her eyes. 'It wasn't a burglary, it was nothing to do with pinching things. It was these foreign men that Charles said were his enemies.'

'It was them that hurt you?'

'One of them did. He wanted to know where Charles was and got angry that I wouldn't tell him.'

'Did you know where he was?'

'No, he went out the back gate and told me he'd be back when they'd gone.'

'So he left a woman to do his dirty work?'

It was then Lily burst into tears. 'It wasn't like that.'

Ben took her in his arms. 'Oh, Lil, Lil.'

She felt as though she would never stop crying for Charles, or what could have been. Her lovely home was gone. She had watched it all loaded on to a van and taken away. Why had Charles lied about the burglary? And did he really think she was no more than a paid servant?

Ben gave her his handkerchief. 'I wish I'd been there, I would have given those buggers something to think about.'

'Charles wouldn't have left me if he'd known about the baby.'

'He shouldn't have left you anyway, Lil. It just ain't right, leaving a woman in danger. Look what they did to you, broke your wrist and left you unconscious.'

'He was only shaking me and I hit me head when I fell on the floor. I wasn't worried about meself, but I was for the baby.'

'Thank God, you was both all right.'

'Maybe it would have been a good thing if I had lost it.'

'Now, come on, that's a daft thing to say.'

'How can I find Charles to tell him?'

He took the handkerchief and wiped under her eyes. 'Before you think about all that, I'm going to make sure you get well. This house is yours for as long as you want it. Not that it's much, but there's a roof over your head and I'll make sure that food is in the larder for you and a nice fire to sit by.'

'What will your neighbours think?'

'I don't care what anyone thinks. Anyway, there's only Mr Next Door, an old boy who calls round every now and then. I give him a lift when he needs it and just pass the time of day. He's a good sort and ain't nosy.'

Lily felt so tired she couldn't think straight. Her wrist was aching and her heart was aching even more, but there was no cure for that now.

'Come on, let's put your feet up and you can rest.' He

lifted her legs on the bed and pulled the cover over. 'Now, close your eyes and take forty winks.'

Lily didn't need telling. Her eyes were already closing.

As the days passed, Lil tried to stop thinking about Charles, the house, and even the baby. She tried to remember she had Ben as her guardian angel. What would she have done without him? Each day he left her warm and comfortable, providing her with all she needed. When he came home from work he always brought her something from the market, even grapes, which were an expensive luxury.

At the end of the week there was a knock on the door. When Lily went to answer it, expecting to see Ben's neighbour, she found Hattie.

'Lil! Lil!' Hattie threw her arms around her. 'Oh, Lil, I've been dying to see you.'

Lily returned the hug. 'I can't give you a squeeze, because of me sling.'

Hattie stared it. 'Is it broken?'

'It's getting better.'

'You poor thing. I've been worried all week. I thought you were in hospital.'

'I'm out now.' Lily stepped back. 'Come in. We can't talk on the doorstep.'

'Blimey, this is a bit tidier than before. The last time I came it was Aladdin's Cave.'

'Ben gave it a good tidy up.'

In the kitchen Lil lit the gas with a taper that was kept by the fire.

'That's a good idea,' said Hattie, hurriedly taking off her coat and finding the teapot.

'It saves striking matches which I'm not too good at.'

'When are you having the plaster off?'

'Not long now. In March.'

'Are you managing to dress yourself?'

Lily put out the cups with her good hand and Hattie spooned tea into the pot. 'I only wear things with buttons I can undo. Me knickers are easy. I've had this bra on since the nurse helped me put it on at the hospital.'

'I'll help you with a clean one if you like?'

'Thanks.'

When the tea was made, the two girls sat down in the front room by the roaring fire.

'This is nice and cosy.' Hattie looked at Lily closely. 'Now, I want to know all that's happened as I only know a bit from Ben. He said not to come and visit you as you were a bit upset.'

'Yes, I was. He's letting me stay in his spare room. He's been very good.'

'You're not going back to Dewar Street, then?' Hattie asked before Lily could speak again.

'I can't as it's being sold.'

'What!'

'All me furniture's gone. Everything. It was all sold to a man named Robson.'

'Lil, before you say any more I've got to ask you a question,' Hattie said softly. 'What about the baby?'

Lily nodded slowly. 'I saw Doctor Tapper and he confirmed it.'

'Does Charles know?'

'I never got the chance to tell him.' Lily began to recount all that happened. Hattie listened in shocked silence, her mouth slowly falling open. When Lily came to the part about the way she was grabbed by the foreign man and pushed to the floor, Hattie gasped angrily.

'Lil, how could Charles leave you to face them? Did he know you were in hospital because of it?'

'I left him a letter. Perhaps he didn't see it. Perhaps he found the house empty and all me clothes gone and really thought I'd moved out.'

'Well then, why didn't he call at your mum's or even go to see Reube at the market?' Hattie exploded. 'If you ask me it's because he's mixed up with some rum types.'

'Do you think so?'

'He's done a bunk, ain't he?'

Lily looked into the fire. 'I don't know. I was just happy to think he wanted me as part of his life, even if it was only seeing to his guests. I thought I was so clever and sophisticated. I used to go through that house thinking it was mine and I would be Mrs Grey one day. I even had the nursery planned out. Now I realize there must have been a lot more to Charles' life than I understood.'

'Lil,' Hattie said quietly, 'about the baby. I'm afraid I let it slip to Ben.'

'I thought it was the doctor at the hospital. But it doesn't matter.'

'I don't like to see you like this. No man can be worth this heartache.'

Lily turned to her. 'I feel all mixed up.'

'Just remember anyone who loved you wouldn't allow you to lie for him, or to be bullied and battered. Now you are homeless and if it wasn't for Ben, you could be wandering round the streets.'

'I know. But Charles is still in me heart.'

Hattie sat silently. After a while she said gently, 'Are you going to see your mum and dad soon?'

'When I've had me plaster off.'

'Lil, I've got a bit of money if you'd like it? I always put by for a rainy day.'

Lily smiled. 'Thanks, Hat, but I managed to save quite a bit.'

'Don't be too unhappy. The rainy days always pass.'

'What about the baby?'

'You'll love him, that's what you'll do.'

But Lily didn't know now if she could.

By the time she had her plaster removed, Lily had got used to using only one hand but it was a relief to have two again. Ben took her to the hospital where they cut it off and examined her wrist. It felt limp and thin, but she was relieved she didn't bump into the doctor she knew as she didn't have to answer any more questions.

The following Sunday, Ben drove her home. She had been dreading her mum asking a question she couldn't answer, but to her surprise, when she walked in, an older man was sitting in the kitchen in her uncle's chair.

'This is Walter, Lily,' her mum introduced at once. 'He's Hector Flock's dad and has just moved to the island and wants to be near his son and family, so he's going to lodge with us for a bit.'

'Hello, Walter.'

'Pleased to meet you, Lily.'

Lily thought it might be hard to see someone else occupy her uncle's place but she immediately liked the quiet man who was, like her father, puffing away on a thin cigarette.

'Molly told me at the funeral that her father-in-law wanted to rent a room close by to them,' her mother hurried on. 'So I said he could have your uncle's and see how we all get on.'

'It's good to have company again,' nodded her father. 'We can both get in your mother's way, until she turns us out into the yard.' The two men laughed.

'As soon as the weather is warmer,' threatened Josie, 'that's exactly what I'll be doing. Now, let's set out the tea, Lily, and Walter can tell you a bit about his life. You'll be surprised to know that he was a baker and has promised to bake us some really nice cakes.'

'So we'll have a decent pudding at last, Lil,' teased her dad, winking behind her mother's back.

Lily could see the three of them were going to get along well. As they ate tea, she missed her uncle being there, but Walter seemed to have filled the gap.

'Are you stopping over, ducks?' her mother asked after tea as they cleared away the dishes and the men went into the parlour.

'Not tonight, Mum.' Lily took out her purse. 'Here's something to put to the rent.'

'No, love,' said her mother, smiling. 'Walter is well off and is paying us a nice rent. And next week I'm starting a job at the school, thanks to Grace Padgett who does a few hours cleaning there. She gave me the tip one of the other cleaners is leaving and I grabbed it.'

'But, Mum, do you really want to do that at your age?'

'I ain't that old!'

'I didn't mean that.'

Josie smiled. 'Now Walter has come along and is good company for your dad, I intend to get out of the house. I learned me lesson from your uncle who would have liked to go on longer with the rag and bone yard. He was frustrated being cooped up here all the time and got a bit miserable towards the end. I've decided that's what I'll be too if I don't take me chance now. And being with other women will be nice. Grace says they have a bit of a knees-up once in a while.'

'Well, if you're sure.'

Her mother looked at her curiously. 'Are you all right, love? You look a bit peaky to me.'

Lily nodded. 'Course I am.'

Lily was glad when Ben tapped at the door. 'There's me lift, Mum.'

Josie patted her arm. 'Take good care of yourself, then.'

In the car going home, Ben frowned at her. 'Everything go all right?'

'I didn't have to say anything about meself as Mum and Dad have a lodger; he's Molly Flock's father-in-law, Walter. So we just had tea and a bit of a chat. Mum said she's getting a job at the school, cleaning. She wouldn't take any money.' Lily sighed softly. 'I'm happy for everyone but it just felt a bit strange with all the changes.'

'Change is what life is all about, gel,' Ben replied with a smile. 'I reckon Hattie and Reube will be moving on too.'

'That's always what Hattie's wanted.'

'Reube's got his eye on a two-up, two down in Walthamstow.'

'Hattie would like that.'

'Would it be all right if I asked them both round?'

'That'd be nice. Anyway, you don't have to ask me, it's your house.'

As Ben drove steadily through the streets, Lily's mind began to wander again. She felt her thin wrist under the sleeve of her coat. Would it always remind her of the night that Charles had left her to face those violent men? Why hadn't Charles ever sought her out? Even if he didn't know about the hospital, he could have gone to the market. Reube would have told him where she was.

Had he ever loved her? Was there still a chance he would marry her if he knew about their baby?

Chapter Twenty-Nine

As March turned into April, Lily was content to cook and clean in Ben's little house, as with every week that passed she regained her strength. She was no longer sick and her wrist was less painful. One Sunday evening Ben drove her and Reube and Hattie out to the Black Cat. Lil was pleased to see Reube again. He told her all the news from the market as they sat outside on the benches. Ted Shiner had just had another nipper and wetted the baby's head at the Quarry. Vera Froud had bought herself a van to carry all her second-hand clothes in but she couldn't drive it properly. Once or twice there had been a near miss in the market vicinity. Any pedestrian vanished quickly if they saw her coming. He also told her that his mum and Pedro hadn't given up the idea of getting wed. And when he and Hattie moved out of the house, Reube thought that then they might marry.

In the soft April evening, Lily listened to the easy talk that once she had been a part of. When the two men went into the pub to replenish their drinks, Lily asked Hattie about Walthamstow.

Hattie looked as though she was about to burst. 'Did Ben tell you, then?'

Lily nodded. 'Is it true?'

'Yes, 'cos we had some good news. I'm in the family way.'

Lily clutched her hand. 'Oh, Hat, that's wonderful!'

'I haven't told anyone except you and Ben.'

'Have you seen the doctor?'

'Yes, but I've got to go again next month to confirm it. Lil, we'll both be having babies together.'

'Yes, but you're married.' Lily looked away.

Hattie shook her arm. 'It's the baby that's important.'

Lily didn't reply. Her thoughts turned to Charles and what could have happened to him. Why hadn't he tried to find her? She couldn't put her fear into words, but each day, the dark shadows engulfed her.

'Lil, there's always a silver lining to every cloud,' Hattie said as Ben and Reube came out of the pub with their glasses of lemonade. Lily made a big effort to smile. Everyone was trying to cheer her up and with Hattie's happy news she couldn't let them see how desperate she was feeling inside.

The following week, Lily decided to go shopping. There was a row of shops at the bottom of the road and though she didn't often venture out now she was putting on weight, the shops weren't too far away. It was the end of April and very warm, with a blue sky and soft fluffy clouds, but Lily put on her coat as it disguised her growing proportions.

Gathering her bag and locking the front door behind her, she was relieved to see the road was empty. Ben had been right. Unlike Love Lane, the neighbours seemed to keep themselves to themselves. She had met Mr Next Door only once when he had come round with some newspapers for Ben. Lily had passed the time of day but gone upstairs quickly. She didn't want Ben to be embarrassed about having a female living in his house. The old man had left soon after, but Ben had only chucked the papers in the bin.

Now as Lily bought neck of lamb for a stew she was making, an ounce of pearl barley and vegetables that were fresh from the market, sold on a barrow, she forgot for a while about Charles. She enjoyed cooking their meals at night. Ben was always hungry when he came home. He would tell her about his day, the punters and their funny quirks and the places he had been. He made her laugh and if he didn't go out in the cab again, they would sit and listen to the radio. But Lily knew she would have to find a place to live. The baby would show soon. She couldn't expect Ben to keep her for much longer. But who would take a pregnant woman as a lodger? She had already begun to think about what she would say to a landlord. Could the father be away at sea? Would this be believable? At least she had money to pay rent well in advance. But then, as more questions tumbled through her mind about raising her child, Lily felt the fear creep into her heart again. Was she capable of bringing up a child on her own? How would she do it? Her money wouldn't last forever.

As Lily was walking back to the house, she saw a woman coming towards her. Quickly she crossed to the other side and kept her head down. Would she always be hiding from people? What about her child? How could she tell him about Charles and how he had abandoned her? Even until now, she had hoped he would turn up. That one day, she would open the door and he would be standing there.

Lily hurried all the way back. She was sliding the key in the lock, when a voice stopped her.

''Scuse me, missy.'

Lily turned to find Mr Next Door beside her.

'Got this fer young Ben.' He pushed a newspaper in her hand. 'Thought the young 'un would like a gander. It's from the Mission Hall and a week old, but one bit is well worth a read. About this bloke we've been keeping tabs on, who we always thought was a wolf in sheep's clothing. Anyway, I can see you're busy, so I won't keep you.' He smiled. 'Lovely day, ain't it?'

Lily nodded, keeping her head down.

'Take care of yerself, gel.'

Lily let herself in and hurriedly closed the door. Did he think she was living in sin with Ben? He hadn't asked any questions, but she felt uncomfortable. Lily remembered the years of anxiety her mother had suffered, worrying about what people might think.

Taking the paper into the parlour, she sat down. If only she was wealthy, like that aristocratic girl Hattie had told her about, who had been put in the family way. Her relatives had managed to get her married and then sent her abroad. She had had her baby discreetly and no one had known any difference. But could an ordinary person do that? Would it be possible to find Charles if she really searched? He had said he had offices in Westminster. Could she find them?

The newspaper slowly slipped to the couch as her thoughts went round and round in her head. Westminster was a big place. How many offices were there? Would Ben drive her up to the city?

Lily's eyes fell on the newspaper. It had fallen open on a page with a circle drawn around a headline. 'British Fascist Sympathizer Charles Grey Flees to Rome'.

She picked up the paper, unable to believe what she was reading.

This news comes as no surprise to those of us who believe the rumours that have scotched Mr Grey's attempts to enter British politics. This wealthy supporter of fascism and his new Spanish-born wife Signóra Maria Covas, were met by representatives of the fascist dictator Benito Mussolini on their arrival in the great Latin city. Our sources inform us that Mr Grey's interest in fascism began when serving with the British Navy. Disillusioned by his wartime experiences, his political path in Britain recently took a turn for the worse when he and many idealists from all over the world made their way to Madrid to take sides in the civil war. When Grey and his compatriots fell foul of General Franco's Carlist forces, he and Covas sought refuge under the Italian dictator's wing. They are said to have sold their estates in England, making their home in the sunnier climes of north-east Italy.

Lily's heart felt as though it was about to burst out of her chest. This couldn't be *her* Charles – her baby's father! She drew her hand over her eyes to clear her sight. She read the article again and again.

Finally, she let the paper fall. All the strength seemed to seep out of her body as she stared blindly into the fire.

The bright lights of the West End were behind him as Ben dropped off his last fare. He was whistling and feeling pleasantly at peace with himself and the world.

The pocketful of heavy coins and notes, some of which were tips that his customers had given him, had provided a plump bird to cook on Sunday along with all the trimmings. Sausages, bacon, stuffing – the goods were all tucked safely away in the boot and sitting behind the wheel, he listened to the slow, rhythmic beat of the engine as he followed the traffic and allowed himself a sigh of satisfaction. He was going home to Lily.

Now, wasn't he a lucky man? All right, so she thought no more of him than a friend, but a man could live in hope. He opened the window of the cab and rested his elbow on the ledge. He'd made a good return this week, thanks to them ladies outside Fortnum and Masons, all elbowing each other for a ride. And truth was, he'd had a bit of a laugh with some of them as they'd sat in the back with their posh hair-dos and expensive purchases. A bit of the old verbal and a wink or two – it was all in the line of duty. But now he was looking forward to getting home and looking into Lily's lovely blue eyes, the only ones that mattered to him.

He couldn't wait to see the expression on her face when she saw what he had for Sunday's dinner. Not a bad day's work when the country was down in the dumps and this talk of war going on. With the Spanish unrest, many said it would only be a matter of time before conflict returned to England's shores. If there was another war, would he put his hand up to fight it?

Ben's thoughts were disturbed as he turned into Aldgate and a fine mist crept down like a ghost. At first it didn't look bad as it only obscured the tops of the smoke-blackened buildings. But then it slid down their exteriors and crawled off the pavements and into the streets.

'Sod it,' he cursed. 'Now I'm going to be late home.'

Sighing resignedly he brought the car to a halt. There he was, bumper to bumper with the Saturday traffic. Still, nothing he could do about that.

Ben sat back and thought of Lily and his little house.

In spite of the weather conditions, he couldn't help smiling.

It was gone eight when he arrived home. The mist was thicker in Stepney but it didn't matter, he'd soon be inside and having a hot cuppa and he'd be telling Lil all about them fares in the city, giving her a good laugh. It brought back the sparkle to her eyes when she laughed. And if it was only humour he could give her, then it was something.

Ben let himself in and whistled. She always came down the hall, her trim little figure just showing the babe. Sometimes she disguised the fullness with an apron, blushing as he gazed at her. If only he could tell her that he loved to see her like that. In his opinion she'd never looked so beautiful as she was now.

Ben peered down the dark hall. His stomach lurched. It was too quiet. He shot in the parlour, glanced round the kitchen, scullery and yard and then flew upstairs. But he knew even before he hammered on Lil's door that she was gone.

Lily had lost her way. She thought she knew where she was, but her bag was heavy and the fog was so dense that she'd even stepped in the road, missing the passing vehicles by inches, drawing loud toots and cries of annoyance. Although she had caught a bus on the Commercial Road, the cold and damp soon seeped into her as she left its cosy interior. If she found the Queen's, she'd be safe as Dewar Street was only a few turns away. She'd walked it often enough, but now she was confused, having turned off into a lane that looked like Dewar Street. Taking another few steps, she began to cough. For a moment, she felt the baby move. It was the first time. Her hands went to her stomach as she leaned, panting, against the railings. Coughing again, she let her bag drop. She was frightened and alone. Had Charles really married Mrs Covas and moved to Italy? She couldn't understand much of what the newspaper had said. Was it true that Charles was a fascist? It was an ugly word, but what did it mean? Charles had told her he had enemies. Was that why he had left the country?

The thought of her baby spurred her on. Her steps were slower now, as a pain went across her stomach. She felt sick and stumbled weakly along.

Ben sat in the parlour reading the newspaper article. Mr Next Door had circled it in pencil.

'Oh, Lil,' he whispered hoarsely. 'Why did you have to find out like this?'

He cast the paper aside and pushed his hands over his face. Where could she have gone? In this fog an' all. What had got into her head to go out in weather like this? Would she have gone to her mum's? Ben shook his head impatiently. No, that was the last place she'd go; she'd move mountains to keep her secret from Josie.

Hattie and Reube's, then? No, she wouldn't want to be seen in Love Lane.

Ben racked his brains, trying to think of an answer. He paced up and down, going over in his mind all the possibilities. But there were none he could believe – and then he froze. There was one place!

Jumping back in the cab, he resisted the urge to accelerate. 'Steady,' he ordered himself as he peered through the sheets of greeny grey mist sliding over the bonnet. When he got to Poplar, he found a brief clearing. Beyond the Queen's, he turned into the narrow roads behind. Edging the car round into Dewar Street, he stopped outside number four. The house gave off a faint glow.

Who was there? Was it the new people? Or was it Charles Grey back from Italy?

His heart beat fast as he leapt from the car and ran up the steps. He banged angrily on the knocker. Would it be Grey, turning up like the proverbial bad penny, who answered? If it was, what would he do?

The door opened. His gaze fell on the figure of a plump, homely looking woman. The pleasant smell of cooking oozed out of the house.

'Yes?'

Ben found himself mute for a moment. As the baby in her arms whimpered, he took off his cap. 'I'm sorry to disturb you. I'm looking for a friend, a Miss Lily Bright. She used to work here.'

He was surprised when she said, 'You'd better step in, young man.'

Ben wiped his boots on the mat.

'We're new to the house,' she told him, closing the door. 'But we had another visitor a short while ago.'

'You mean you've seen Lil – Miss Bright?'

'She didn't give her name. She just wanted to know if a Charles was here.'

'That's who she worked for,' Ben nodded urgently.

A boy and a girl came running down the stairs, yelling and shouting.

'Quiet, you two, we've got another caller.'

The three of them looked up at him.

'What happened then?' Ben asked.

'I told her I didn't know who lived here before, as my husband had dealt with the purchase of the house.'

'Did she look all right?'

'No, as a matter of fact, she didn't. I asked her to come in and take shelter from the fog but she refused.' The baby began to cry and the woman held it over her shoulder, patting its back. 'Then she just seemed to drift away.'

Ben felt the panic rise in him. What had Lily been thinking when she'd come to Dewar Street? She must have thought like him, there was a chance Grey had returned. How had she felt when she found the new family here?

'Thanks,' he nodded and rushed out. He drove the length of Dewar Street once more, up to the laundry and back, his eyes alert for any movement. Suddenly he saw something on the ground. It was Lily's bag!

Stopping the car, he picked it up. It must have been too heavy for her to carry. He looked around him. 'Lil, Lil, it's me, Ben,' he cried, but only an echo returned.

After a while he drove on again. In Poplar High Street he looked this way and that. Should he get out to search? She couldn't have gone far. Was it likely she had returned to the island? By the time he drove into Westferry Road, he had broken out in a sweat. The docks were treacherous in these conditions; one false move and you were in the drink. With the fog obscuring the wharves, their slippery edges and sharp declines, a person could be lost, never to be found again.

Ben pounded the wheel in frustration! Where was she? He passed Cuba Street and Manilla Street and was at the beginning of Tiller Road when he jammed his foot on the brake. A figure appeared. It seemed to hesitate in his path, not knowing whether to advance or retreat.

'Christ almighty!' His heart almost jumped out of his chest.

Had he hit it?

He leapt out and caught the shivering bundle in his arms. It was Lily who clung tightly to him.

Lily looked into Dr Tapper's face. He was sitting on the chair beside her bed in Ben's house and his kindly eyes under his bushy grey eyebrows were regarding her steadily.

'You gave us all a scare,' he told her sternly. 'In

particular the young man waiting downstairs in the parlour. He thought he might have run you over.'

'I couldn't see in the fog.'

'Lily, do you realize that you have put yourself and your baby at risk?'

She sat up. 'Is it all right?'

'The stress and shock you've been through caused you to lose some blood. But I think we've avoided by a whisker the miscarriage you would have had, had you not been found in time.' The elderly man put away his things in his Gladstone bag and stood up. 'Now, I have left instructions that you are on no account to exert yourself over the next few days.'

Lily nodded silently.

'I'll come to see you again soon. Then we'll decide on whether or not you can move around a little.'

'Doctor Tapper?'

'Yes?' He paused at the door.

'Does me mum know?'

'Have you told her?'

'Not yet.'

'Then if you haven't, she is obviously unaware.' He smiled. 'Now, goodbye and make sure you do as I say.'

Lily heard him go down the stairs. A tear slipped slowly down her cheek. Why had she gone off like that? The pain in her stomach had been the baby in distress. She couldn't bear to think of what might have happened if she'd lost it. She knew she wanted this little life more than anything now. More than Charles even.

Suddenly there was a tap on the door and Ben came in. 'Now then, cheer up.'

'I'm sorry.'

'What for?'

'Everything.'

'Well, I'm sorry that you felt the need to run away.'

'I read that newspaper article that Mr Next Door sent in. It was about Charles and Mrs Covas. I couldn't believe it at first, and I thought he might still be there, at Dewar Street.'

'So you went off in a pea-souper, when you was only just getting stronger after the hospital? Well, Lily Bright, this can't keep happening, you know. I enjoy you falling into me arms, but I want you fit and well when you do it.'

Lily looked down at her hands on the sheet. 'Is it true what the newspaper says, about him and her?'

He nodded. 'I'm sorry you had to find out that way.'

'You knew all the time, didn't you?' She searched his gaze.

'I had me suspicions all along there was something amiss, but I kept telling meself it was just a bit of the green-eye over you. Then just before your uncle popped his clogs, he asked me to find out about these rumours ... your gent's name had been bandied about by the old blokes down the Mission Hall. It was said he'd been over to Germany a few times, Italy and Spain too, to hobnob with the likes of Hitler and Mussolini.'

'I thought he was going to buy furniture.'

'Yes, but you wasn't to know the truth.'

'I wouldn't have cared what he did or was, anyway. I was always imagining meself as lady of the house, that it was me who would make him forget Delia and that I'd help in his career.' Her voice trembled. 'He always talked so passionately about it, but I should have known it wasn't right when he asked me to lie.'

Ben gave her a long look. 'Lil, no one knew for sure what he was up to.'

'I thought he loved me.'

'Well, who's to say he didn't?'

Lily swallowed on the hard lump in her throat. 'If he did he wouldn't have married someone else, it would be me in that house now, not a new family.' She brushed away another tear. 'I saw her standing there with a baby in her arms and I thought, that should be me.'

'We can't always have the things we think we want.'

'Charles used to talk as if we'd be together. I believed him, but I was just useful for appearances' sake. Like Annie.' She sobbed. 'I suppose even that was a lie, that she didn't pinch anything and he made her think he loved her too?'

'Lil, you won't ever know.' He leaned forward, his elbows on his knees. 'Look, he was just another charmer. A man who got himself in a muddle and couldn't get out of it. There's been dozens of them in history and will be a few more. He fooled a lot of people – people in high places – not just you. It took the civil war in Spain to make him show his true colours.'

She nodded. 'I suppose so.'

'The one lesson we should all learn from this is that every moment of peace counts. To live our lives and be happy together.'

Lily looked into his earnest grey eyes. 'I thought I was going to be happy.'

'You can be,' Ben smiled. 'Happiness is just a thought away.'

'But what about me baby?'

He took her hand. 'You've always been me girl, Lil. I want to look after that little life inside you. Count him as me own.'

Lily shook her head. 'But it's Charles' child.'

'Listen, Lil, as far as I'm concerned, when that kid opens its eyes, he's gonna see me. And like the proverbial duck, he's gonna waddle after the first ugly mug he sees and I'd like that mug to be mine.' He wiped a tear on her cheek with his thumb. 'So what's the answer?'

'You mean you'd marry me, knowing that I—'

'I'll marry you, Lil,' he whispered. 'Just say the word.'

Lily gazed into his loving grey eyes and remembered Charles' dark ones. Would she ever forget them? Was it right for her to take everything Ben offered when she had so little to give back?

Could she learn to love again?

The baby moved inside her as if in answer. As Ben leaned forward to kiss her, she closed her eyes. His touch was soft and familiar and though it wasn't the grand passion she had dreamed of, it was something deeper and wiser.

She knew then that happiness really was only a thought away.

Noteworthy Extracts from the *Mission Hall Quarterly* 1937

28th September
The fascist conqueror Benito Mussolini and Adolf Hitler staged a massive floodlit demonstration of solidarity in Berlin tonight. The German leader once again referred to the text of his book *Mein Kampf*; 'Without colonies, Germany's space is too small to guarantee our people can be fed safely and continuously . . .'

10th October
Sir Oswald Mosley was hit on the head today and rendered unconscious as he prepared to address a crowd of 8,000 in Liverpool. It was only four days ago that he led his Blackshirts through South London but was stopped by Costers' barrows, barbed wire and over-turned vehicles.

16th November
The British government have drawn up plans for the evacuation of London, if necessary, in the event of war, though MP's voted today for thousands of air raid

shelters to be erected throughout the country's towns and cities . . .

24th December

A postscript from the editor of the *Mission Hall Quarterly*, Charlie Brent, retired coal merchant.

On a lighter note to end the year, I would like to make a short report of the delightful occasion to which the Mission Hall members were invited. Bonny four-month-old Josephine Heather Bright was baptized this afternoon at three o'clock at St Peter's! I'm happy to record that the church was full to the gunnels, hours before the midnight service! The christening was held on this date to commemorate the memory of the baby's great uncle, Noah Kelly, who passed away one year ago to the day. His niece, Lily James and husband Ben, the proudest of parents, put on a wonderful knees-up for us all afterwards at Noah's old abode, number thirty-four Love Lane. The house is still occupied by his sister Josie after whom the child was named and her husband Bob. A happy Christmas was wished to one and all, as we thoroughly wetted the baby's head, making the very most of the peace that still reigns – if not in Europe, then in every East Enders heart.

All the best for the New Year, everyone, Charlie.